BLAST

BLAST

CLAIRE DEYA

Translated from the French
by Adriana Hunter

Other Press
New York

Originally published in French as *Un monde à refaire* in 2024
by Éditions de l'Observatoire, Paris
Copyright © 2024 Claire Deya
Translation copyright © 2025 Other Press

Production editor: Yvonne E. Cárdenas
Text designer: Patrice Sheridan
This book was set in Arno Pro and Pompeii Capitals by
Alpha Design & Composition of Pittsfield, NH
Title page photo copyright © Elliott Erwitt / Magnum Photos
Image Reference ERE1952XXXW00057/27 (PAR38067)

1 3 5 7 9 10 8 6 4 2

Library of Congress Cataloging-in-Publication Data
Names: Deya, Claire, author. | Hunter, Adriana, translator.
Title: Blast : a novel / Claire Deya ; translated from the French by Adriana Hunter.
Other titles: Monde à refaire. English
Description: New York : Other Press, 2025. | "Originally published in French as Un
monde à refaire in 2024 by Éditions de l'Observatoire, Paris"—Copyright page.
Identifiers: LCCN 2024038771 (print) | LCCN 2024038772 (ebook) |
ISBN 9781635425192 (paperback) | ISBN 9781635425208 (ebook)
Subjects: LCSH: World War, 1939-1945—Bomb reconnaissance—Fiction. |
Explosive ordnance disposal—France—Fiction. | Reconstruction
(1939-1951)—France—Fiction. | Riviera (France)—Fiction. |
Hyères (France)—Fiction. | LCGFT: Historical fiction. | Novels.
Classification: LCC PQ2704.E976 M6613 2025 (print) |
LCC PQ2704.E976 (ebook) | DDC 843/.92--dc23/eng/20240826
LC record available at https://lccn.loc.gov/2024038771
LC ebook record available at https://lccn.loc.gov/2024038772

Publisher's Note: This is a work of fiction. Names, characters, places, and incidents
either are the product of the author's imagination or are used fictitiously, and
any resemblance to actual persons, living or dead, events, or locales is entirely
coincidental.

To Aurélie and Guillaume,

To you, singular,

without whom nothing would have been possible,

To you, plural,

my constellation.

IF HE EVER DID FIND ARIANE, VINCENT WOULDN'T dare caress her skin. His hands had reached proportions he no longer recognized. Hard, the fingers swollen, their outer surface thick, rough, and dry; they'd undergone a metamorphosis. The callused skin over them was so arid that, even when he washed them carefully and at length, they didn't soften. There was still a constellation of black fissures burrowing deep into the bark-like covering on his palms and fingers. The soil had tattooed them with its indelible imprint by infiltrating the cracks and crevasses carved out by two winters in Germany.

Before the war, his hands used to dance when he talked. Ariane had laughed about it and imitated him. He could see her now, here, on this Riviera beach in front of him. The first time they'd come here to swim, the sun was barely up. They were still giddy from spending their first night together, and Ariane needed to get home early so no one would notice her absence. They'd walked past the beach and had been gripped by an irresistible impulse to extend their night together in the sea. Across the water, the sun bounced off the Îles d'Or, the "Golden Islands."

He remembered the swimsuit she'd improvised by knotting a scarf around her breasts with the grace of a fearless dancer.

Her squeals as she went into the sea, the way she arched her body against his, electrified by the chill water and the rising sun... That salty body, desire sharpened by the sea air, the wet silk clinging to her skin. He would give anything to return to that carefree existence and dive back into the love they'd shared.

He pulled the scarf, the one he'd stolen from her, more tightly around his neck.

He'd escaped so that he could track down Ariane. She'd vanished and no one had had word of her for two years, but he was looking everywhere for her. He couldn't believe she was dead. Impossible; she'd never do that to him. And while he'd been a prisoner, he'd received those enigmatic letters...

Now that the south had been liberated from the Germans, everything would be easier. They hadn't surrendered yet, but everyone was saying they were screwed.

He had an idea about how to find Ariane. And he played up this tenuous idea to bolster his hopes. But truth be told he was just clutching at a vague intuition to save himself from going under. He was alone, and helpless, and no, the revolver he hid in his clothes like a talisman wouldn't change anything.

While the rest of town was preparing for its first big celebration since the beginning of the war, the beach he looked down over was ravaged. Trenches and barbed-wire coils blocked access to the sea. Signs forbade entry, warned of danger. Danger of death: All along the French Riviera the beaches were mined.

Vincent could hear an amateur band rehearsing in the distance, attempting a few incursions into breezy jazz numbers. It was a beautiful day. People around him were smiling, their heads full of the promise of summer. It was almost the end of the war, and for him, most likely, the beginning of a solitary hell.

BEYOND THE BALUSTRADE WHERE VINCENT stood, a dozen men were spread out across the beach, advancing in a line, slowly, silently. Armed with just a bayonet, they inspected the sand with the tips of their metal pikes to detect mines buried by the Germans. Fabien took careful, focused steps, and all the men walking in the line alongside him matched their stride to his.

Fabien was not yet thirty but had naturally emerged as the group's leader. His brotherly brand of authority, his engineering training, his commitment, from the maquis to the Resistance... Having blown up so many trains, he was considered the uncontested explosives specialist. The officer at the mine-clearing unit had immediately singled out this recruit to his supervisor, the Resistance fighter Raymond Aubrac.

Mine clearing was the unavoidable prerequisite to rebuilding France, but her soldiers—on the Ardennes front and then in Germany—had been relieved of this task by the interim government. Who could do the work? Demining wasn't a profession. It was an unprecedented challenge. No one had the experience. There were so few volunteers... Fabien could just as easily have set off three fireworks on the deck of a ship, he would still have been elevated to the ranks of a godsend.

Rumor had it the deminers were all lost souls, godless and lawless men who'd emerged from the bowels of prisons to redeem themselves or secure an early release. Worse still, it was whispered that collaborators were trying to whitewash their dark past by melting into their ranks. Whenever Raymond Aubrac felt that anyone—at the ministry or elsewhere—was being contemptuous or patronizing about his men, he would cite Fabien as a fine example: He was the incarnation of excellence.

So much so in fact that no one could understand why he'd signed up to clear minefields. Fabien knew what people were saying about him: Having sabotaged trains, he was now sabotaging himself. The authorities put it down to some form of despair, his team thought he was hiding something, but everyone admired his courage. And you did need courage, as well as self-sacrifice, to keep risking your life rather than making the most of it.

The Ministry of Reconstruction offered assignments in blocks of three months. It looked set to take a long time: The army estimated that there was a minimum of thirteen million mines over the whole country. Thirteen million...So, despite war-weariness and exhaustion, men were encouraged to start a new assignment as soon as the previous one ended.

Since 1942, the Mediterranean Wall had been constantly reinforced by the occupiers. German mines had been intended to stop Allied landings and Allied mines to slow the German retreat. Net result: The French were trapped. First and foremost, their children.

The beaches at Hyères, Saint-Tropez, and Ramatuelle, at Pampelonne and Cavalaire: They were all mined. No dolce vita along the Riviera now. No one could venture onto the sand anymore. The port at Saint-Tropez had been dynamited along with all the buildings on the seafront, the transporter bridge in Marseille's Old Port, and the Saint-Jean neighborhood, razed to the ground. Inland, roads and railway tracks, factories and administrative buildings were all booby-trapped with the murderous devices. With every footstep you could be blown up. Scorched-earth policy honed to savage perfection.

To avoid succumbing to the dizzying numbers and despondency, Fabien stayed focused on his objective. Acting calmly and not cursing the lack of volunteers and training, the inadequacy of their equipment and, crucially, the cruel absence of land-mine maps; they were advancing blindfolded.

All at once, Manu, a wiry and ferally beautiful young man working just a few meters from Fabien, stopped and raised his arm: *Mine!* His bayonet had just come into contact with a suspect solid surface. All the men instinctively backed away, teeth clenched. They would never get used to it. With a jerk of his head, Fabien gave them permission to retreat beyond the regulation twenty-five meters. He glanced at Manu, encouraging him to continue: He had to lie on his stomach and gently probe the ground, freeing the object that had resisted the metal spike. Stroking away sand with his hands, Manu revealed a large black metal cylinder: an LPZ mine. Thirty centimeters in diameter. Twelve centimeters high. Two and a half kilos of TNT. An all-out instrument of death, capable of pulverizing a several-ton tank and any living creature unwise enough to weigh more than seven kilos.

A more seasoned deminer needed to take over and disarm the device or blow it up. Other mines were buried nearby; safer to neutralize it... even though that was more difficult because mines were designed to explode, not to be tamed. You had to tackle them with your bare hands. Fabien took responsibility for it. He knew how to—although nothing was ever guaranteed, there were so many different models—and it helped him keep his team's respect. If he was absolutely honest, if he agreed to sound out his very depths, there was another reason he put himself in danger every day despite the fact that he loved life passionately and knew his sacrifice would be forgotten as quickly as all the men he'd seen fall around him. But he wasn't ready to delve that deep, at least not today; he needed to concentrate on the mine. One slip, even a tiny one, and you ended up blasted to pieces.

Breathe. Don't shake. No parasitic thoughts. Or sudden movements. Don't concede anything to fear. The mine. Think about nothing else... How many times had he reiterated all this to his men, even though it was completely illusory?

To neutralize an LPZ you first had to deal with its percussion ignition system: Remove the cap on the pressure plate by freeing it with a bayonet, then put the stopper in the safe position. Next, take the mine out of the ground, keeping it horizontal, and sit it on its side, definitely not lying flat. Unscrew the five nuts and five detonator shafts and remove them. Without shaking.

How to stay calm? Every part of his body strained to turn and run. How to breathe, whether to breathe at all? And concentrate despite the endless assault of questions, feelings of remorse, regrets?

Impossible: Reverberating in the distance were the chords of the last song he'd danced to with Odette, his wife, and those chords were breaking his heart.

Fabien stopped what he was doing to listen properly. Maybe he'd misheard? No, that was it. "Mademoiselle Swing." The song he'd once poked fun at. Odette used to say it brought good luck. And it was so light and playful, surely it had defied all that Nazi ponderousness? Since Odette had gone, he'd stopped poking fun: The simple melody felt devastatingly intense.

It's said that before dying you see your whole life flash by. All he saw was Odette, Odette dancing, happy, free, smiling, Odette and her brown curls, her lithe big-cat body and her feline, couldn't-care-less individuality. Odette before she was arrested by the Germans.

He was hypnotized, motionless. And his team had noticed. Fabien could feel their eyes on him. He pulled himself together: If he wasn't seeing his whole life flash past but just Odette dancing, that meant he wasn't about to die.

After the neutralizing came the deactivation. Lying the mine down flat, but the wrong way up. Unscrewing all the nuts from the casing on the underside. Unwinding the duct tape that held the two covers together, sliding them apart. Taking the main charge out of the upper casing. Unscrewing the collar around the detonator. Removing the detonator.

"Mademoiselle Swing" was spilling out its final notes and Fabien had managed to master the mine. Odette was right: The song had brought him good luck. Or perhaps it was Odette herself, from beyond the grave, wherever she was. Looking out to sea, to the Golden Islands, from this beach he so loved, he acknowledged that he'd already had the best of his life. A woman loved in an atmosphere of danger can't be replaced. Odette would be forever irreplaceable.

THEIR BREAKS WERE ALWAYS A RELIEF. WITH THE amateur band rehearsing in the distance, the only thing the team could talk about was the celebrations that were to take place a week later. The whole group would go to the dance to forget the bitter challenges of their task, to strut and dazzle and mingle with the optimistic, the enthusiastic, people eager for the new world. The deminers wanted to be like them for the space of an evening, no longer behaving like solemn convicts playing Russian roulette with their lives in the minefields, but circulating like happily chatting partygoers, firmly believing in a new life, a new age.

Fabien wouldn't go. Impossible to dance with anyone but Odette. Sure, he dreamed of a new life, but it wouldn't come about thanks to a new love. He thought about her at length during every break, lingering in daydreams in which he summoned her as she had been on the first day they'd met—a troublemaker. Or at night, when he'd put his hands around her waist to lift her on top of him and gaze at her supple naked body. It was one of the misconceptions about Fabien: Everyone thought of him as a man of action when all he wanted was to wander off a sunlit path to lie down and dream.

The day wasn't over, and Fabien considered it his duty to galvanize his team. He never stopped telling his men that it was an honor to be ridding France of these deadly devices left by the Nazis. Mine clearing was still a form of resistance.

He gave the work meaning. By freeing the land of these lethal traps, the deminers were saving themselves, making amends, absolving themselves of guilt. Because everyone felt guilty: for betraying, lying, stealing, abandoning, not measuring up, not joining the Resistance—or joining only at the last minute—for killing a man, or several, for surviving when so many friends had fallen. Each man carried within him his share of this guilt, which had grown huge in these troubled times, and in order to move forward, they each needed, if not to exorcise it, at least to come to terms with it. Fabien knew how to suggest to his men that mine clearing could offer them the redemption that, although they wouldn't admit it to themselves, they no longer hoped they could secure. His men nodded, touched by what he said. And few of them were pretending: His words allowed them not to regret the risks they took—they were all so young—and to accept their fate.

Fabien noticed that the man with the scarf who'd been watching them for more than an hour from up behind the balustrade was now coming over to him.

"Hello. I wanted to ask, are you hiring?"

Fabien appraised him briefly. In the maquis, he'd acquired an intuition that rarely let him down. He knew when a man had something weighty to hide.

"I guess you don't know how to clear mines," he said.

"I heard you train people on the job."

"The only thing we ask is that you weren't a collaborator."

"Oh, no danger of that."

Despite Vincent's forthright eye contact, Fabien's first impression was confirmed by the man's short sentences: He clearly wanted to say as little as possible.

Vincent gestured toward the prisoners, framed by two guards, who were standing a little way away from the team.

"Doesn't it bother you working alongside the Boche?"

"We take them from prison camps, they do what they have to do, then go back to their camps. No special treatment. We'll use them until the whole place is cleaned up."

As he talked, Fabien watched the Germans. They made up more than half of his team. The recruiters struggled to find volunteers, and it had been the army that had recommended using prisoners. Fabien knew everything about the lives of his French teammates, but when it came to the Boche, he wouldn't allow himself to talk to them. He loathed them so much it was frightening. And he didn't want to be distracted from his goal. Even so...he would never have guessed that circumstances would force him to work hand in hand with the country's age-old enemies. Worse: When they came across a mine, they all depended on each other for their survival. The ultimate danger. What grim irony.

～

FOR LUKAS, WHO WAS DISCREETLY TRYING TO prolong their break by smoking a cigarette, it was a long time since anything had made any sense. He'd found his country's descent into madness unbearable; even his family had put its trust in the dictator who had tricked their democracy. And he himself, who was so besotted with France, who knew the works of Baudelaire and the surrealists by heart, was treated like a monster by the French, as if all Germans had sold their souls to Hitler. In the bookshop where he'd worked before the war, he'd constantly warned that National Socialism was a slippery slope, and now he'd spent nine months moldering in a prison-camp bunkhouse, a place that was glacial in winter and stifling in summer, with no blanket, no shoes worthy of the name, and no idea of when he would be released. His family still resented him—most likely for demonstrating the perspicacity they'd lacked—and even before the last few months when all mail had stopped, they'd never sent him clothes or a kind word to remind him that he wasn't alone. If he ever returned to his country, he couldn't be sure his parents would welcome him. What did it matter. Germany was about to surrender—that's what people were saying—but that didn't necessarily mean its prisoners would be freed.

Lukas had overheard Vincent and Fabien's conversation. No one suspected he could speak French. In uniform, he was feared; as a prisoner, he was invisible. He would have liked to discuss things with them like rational human beings. But who was rational anymore? Could he have told them—and would they have been prepared to listen—that he simply didn't understand how France, the land of human rights, presumptuously moralized to the whole world when it was violating the Geneva Convention by using prisoners of war? Countries weren't allowed to use prisoners for dangerous and degrading work. Of course, there were gray areas. Prisoners weren't being forced to *demine* but to *detect*. As if an exploding mine would differentiate, targeting the deminer and sparing the others...

The French also argued that demining wasn't explicitly mentioned in the convention as a dangerous activity. It was a paradox but back in 1929 when the agreement was drafted, who could have predicted the key role land mines would go on to play in war?

It was the Germans who, secretly and illegally, had decided to manufacture them by the millions, catching out the Allies, who weren't prepared for them. And this project of mass destruction wasn't the worst of it, because everyone was starting to understand what this war had really been. Unspeakable. Inconceivable. Irreparable.

Lukas found himself thinking that if the French ever suggested he have a smoke with them and chat about who was responsible for what, he would have said they were right, without challenging them. He was among the defeated and the cursed, and couldn't have borne being among the victors.

He'd been captured in the south by Resistance fighters in the French Forces of the Interior, a few days before the Provence landings in August '44. It was now April '45, nine months later. Nine months in captivity drove you mad. Mine clearance allowed him to get out of the camp, forget the barbed wire restricting his horizon, the suffering of the dying, the sickness, the injuries, and the hunger, the terrible hunger which became an obsession. It wasn't much, but deminers were given slightly more substantial rations. So they could work without collapsing.

The Allies were capturing hundreds of thousands of soldiers in Germany. They then transferred them, whole convoys of them, to the French or the Russians. In the last few weeks Lukas had seen an influx of every variety, fanatical defenders of the Third Reich, men who'd lost all hope, invalids, and soldiers like him who'd been forcibly enlisted into a war they didn't want to fight.

What he hadn't expected was to see children coming to the camp. They were dwarfed by giant pea jackets, terrorized by this war that had been going on forever, by the adults around them and the lies, by what they were told about the French who wanted them dead and were capable of grisly crimes, by all the soldiers everywhere, the transfers from one camp to another, and the train journeys in appalling conditions. They'd been enlisted in the last few months on Hitler's orders. They were eighteen, sixteen. Some had just turned fourteen.

Were the French ready to hear that some Germans also hated the Nazis?

The war had taken nearly six years of his life. Defeat would very likely rob him of the rest. To motivate the prisoners, they were fed stories of release if they showed courage clearing mines. Lukas had absolutely no illusions.

The French deminers thought they were free, and Lukas didn't envy them: They were all lying to themselves. They were taken in by their own words, fooling themselves. *For the good of France, the final battle against German barbarity. Mine clearing is an honor for a Frenchman and a punishment for a German.* These deminers were convinced they were different from the prisoners when they were really all the same: French and Germans alike, they were enslaved, trapped, ready to die for other people's pleasure, the people who were already champing at the bit because the shoreline would be out of bounds all through this imminent summer, but by the following summer they would be reinventing their lives and their loves on this beach, swimming, making the most of the sun and the sea, and very quickly forgetting the sacrifices made on this scorching sand.

Who would love a German prisoner of war? Who would love a deminer, even a French one? After all these years of war, no one felt like keeping company with death anymore. Lukas's great love, which was still so alive in his mind, might be his last if he didn't succeed in escaping. But these guys, these madmen who'd signed up voluntarily, they couldn't see that they were viewed at worst condescendingly, at best pityingly. And you can't build a relationship on pity.

The deminers could show off at the dance or wherever they chose, they could protest loud and clear that they weren't frightened, and they could believe in their lucky stars and their own heroism. No one saw them as heroes. They'd forgotten a principle as old as humankind itself: The free will always want slaves.

LEANING AGAINST THE WALL OPPOSITE THE RE-cruiting office, Vincent was hesitating. He didn't know what he was waiting for, a sign, a miracle, a meeting that would change everything. It was still just as warm, like the day before, and the next day. A young woman walked past. Maybe twenty years old. She smiled at him. On her ears, daisy-shaped earrings. Her slender body was a little swamped by a dress in very pale yellow cotton, almost white, but it was the earrings that caught Vincent's eye.

The dress was sleeveless and her tanned arms swung by her sides. Ready to set off for the ends of the earth, she strode blithely over the cobbles in open-toe sandals made of fine rope. A tiny cross-body bag bounced at her waist, and she held a book by Albert Camus in one hand; Vincent could have found her attractive, could have followed her, he decided to go into the office.

He didn't have to wait. The recruiting officer gestured for Vincent to sit down, and put on his little performance. According to him, recruitment was the most important part of demining so he would be looking into Vincent's past, his motives, and his psychological aptitude.

Just as Fabien had warned, if it turned out that Vincent had been in contact with the enemy, he would immediately be ruled out. Vincent pulled a sheepish face.

"Contact with the enemy, well, you could say I had plenty of that."

The recruiter stiffened, affronted.

"I was a prisoner in Germany. So, obviously, I lived alongside Germans. A bit more than I could stand," Vincent added with a smile.

The recruiter, clearly relieved, relaxed. He rather liked that, the complicity of it. And to point out that he'd picked up on Vincent's flash of humor, he winked at him.

Having rattled through a description of the risks involved—which was compulsory—he asked Vincent what his motives were. One of the wonders of administrative sadism, using a harmless question to dress up the harshest of realities: This painstaking, thankless work is exceptionally dangerous, absolutely no one would want to be in your shoes, but we'd like you to tell us just how keen you are to be in this hell. Vincent played along.

"My motives are simple: We cannot allow one more child to die because of a mine left by the Germans. Otherwise, they *will* have won."

Spoken out loud, his answer sounded too pompous to his ears. But not to the recruiter.

It only remained to tackle the third part of the interview.

"Now you're going to ask me what the 'psychological aptitudes' are for demining."

Vincent wasn't going to ask him anything at all, but he listened attentively.

"Believe it or not, we've been given no instructions, no forms to fill out, nothing! Luckily, I've put together my own questionnaire. You'll see."

Another wink. Not satisfied with handing him his document amid a flurry of preamble as if it were an exceptionally cogent masterwork, he made a point of giving a commentary for each question. You never knew, Vincent might not have understood.

"'How do you react when you hear a sudden noise?' Do you jump? Do you stay calm? Because if you're not levelheaded, it'll be tricky working in mine clearance."

The recruiter seemed to have forgotten that Vincent had fought in the war. He kept him there, only too happy to have an audience as he enumerated the excellent qualities of his judicious questions. And yet he surely couldn't be unaware that selection was virtually automatic: Hardly anyone came forward.

He lingered over the financial terms which were meant to be an unhoped-for boon in these straitened times—*Twice the salary of a laborer!*—along with the various bonuses, the meals, the risks, which he trumpeted as if they were unheard-of and woefully underestimated privileges—*You're a lucky man!*—and the tremendous advantages of guaranteed employment. Vincent felt the interview needed to come to an end; a feeling of revulsion was rising in his throat. Perhaps he should thank the man for this opportunity? He pulled on his jacket.

"Wait," the recruiter said to keep him there. "I don't have your ID and your signature."

"I'll bring my ID tomorrow. As for my signature, that's easy to fix."

The recruiter handed him the contract to sign. And there, it was done. Vincent was hired for mine clearance. He should have been shaking as he signed but he'd written his name with an assured flourish. He'd been training. The recruiter didn't suspect a thing and Vincent left the building satisfied. He'd signed a deal with the devil, but he'd signed under a false name.

THE SOONER VINCENT FOUND ARIANE, THE sooner he could get back to his old life. He would do what he'd done for his escape: make a plan and apply it methodically and unfalteringly. He knew how. He'd been through it. His first escape had failed because of a betrayal. But the second time around he'd undertaken it alone. And that was the lesson he'd learned—do everything alone.

Once back in France, he'd been caught out by a nosebleed. A very minor nosebleed, but one that never stopped. Overnight all his strength had left him, as if flowing out with that thin trickle of blood. He'd had to hide out at a friend's house, bedridden, anemic, unable to move. He'd been subjected to the prison camp's subhuman conditions for too long and his body had given out. As soon as they were able to, his friends had arranged for him to be hospitalized at Val-de-Grâce.

His recovery had been somewhat miraculous, but all he could do was regret wasting so much time without seeing Ariane.

He stopped his bicycle in the town square and asked in the grocery store whether there were any rooms to rent. They said there was better than that: a fisherman's cottage on the seafront.

Mathilde, a fifty-year-old woman with a statuesque face, was repainting her shutters blue-gray. The small house had once been a studio for her husband, who'd been killed right at the start of the conflict. Vincent asked no questions; Mathilde didn't give him the opportunity. She wasn't the sort of woman to open her heart to all comers.

Whitewashed walls, little round rope rugs typical of Provence, as seen in the bathrooms that Bonnard liked to paint. When he looked around the studio, Vincent decided that Mathilde's husband must also have enjoyed painting her naked in the copper tub next to the round carpet. She was the sort of woman about whom people say she must once have been beautiful, when in fact she still was.

The studio was timeless as all modest homes are if their unadorned simplicity is respected. A cat had come in through the window and was idling under the table. Vincent stroked it. And saw it as a sign. Ariane had always been drawn to cats. This house would bring her back.

Vincent was instantly taken with the bare walls, the scant, raw-timber furniture, and the floor tiles giving the only touch of coppery color; they were probably cool and smooth underfoot. The house was on two levels and wasn't large, but the white of the walls and the blue of the sky portioned out between the windows amplified the space. Behind a screen, he was moved to find a piano covered with a sheet.

He opened the lid, played the beginnings of a piece. Bach came to him spontaneously. The emotion was too strong. He stopped.

"If you like, I can ask my cousin to come over. He's a tuner."

He cursed his ruined fingers that were now so clumsy. Would they still be able to glide over the keys?

"It's a long time since I've played...but, if possible, I'd really like that."

"I'm sure we can do business, then. I trust people who like pianos and cats."

Mathilde smiled at him, relieved that she need look no further for a tenant. She obviously had other things to do.

"I live opposite. Leave the window open when you play. I'll enjoy it."

Once alone, Vincent ensured that the door was properly closed, then went upstairs and unpacked his things. Mostly books that he'd gone to collect from a friend. Some of them leatherbound. He had almost nothing else: a comb, a razor, a shirt, two white tanks—well, dirty white—and a change of pants. He put his clothes in the dresser, a book on the table, and everything else on a set of shelves, but where could he hide his pistol?

He glanced around the whole room; it was as bare as a monastic cell. After a moment's thought, he alighted on the idea of leaving the revolver wrapped in one of his tanks and wedging it behind an internal shutter. He wouldn't be closing them, he no longer liked sleeping in total darkness. At least no one would think of looking for it there. Well, so he thought.

Then he undertook a more intricate task. He sat at the small table in the corner of the room; it was no bigger than a school desk. He opened his book and inside was his ID card. It pained him to look at the photo. The carefree attitude, the zest for life, and the smile had all gone now. The expression in his eyes was radically different. He'd changed, it was plain to see, and the metamorphosis seemed irreversible. Only Ariane could turn back time and remind him who he was: Hadrien Darcourt, the man who wanted nothing but her love. He was himself only when she looked at him.

Hidden in the book's binding was another ID card. On the overexposed photo, a rather puny young man with blond hair, very pale eyes, and diaphanous skin. A face almost predestined to be erased. Hadrien took his razor blade and set about detaching the photo from the gold-colored metal eyelets without damaging it, and then replacing it with his own...

Since his escape, Hadrien had been going by the name on this card: Vincent Devailly. In Hyères, Ramatuelle, and Saint-Tropez, wherever there was mine clearance to be done, it would be easy—he knew no one. But it was still strange to be called Vincent Devailly: Hadrien hated the man, he'd betrayed him in the prison camp when he made his first escape attempt.

And so Hadrien liked to think it was only fair that, thanks to Vincent, he had found virtually total freedom to do what he wanted. Just how far he would go to track down Ariane, get the truth out of those who wanted to stay silent, take revenge on anyone who might have hurt her, he didn't know, but he didn't want to deny himself anything. From now on, Vincent Devailly, the despised traitor, would have to shoulder the darkest part of Hadrien.

AT THE END OF THE DAY, WHEN THE DEMINERS were packing away their equipment, Fabien spotted Vincent and smiled to see him returning so soon. This morning he hadn't been sure he would see him again. Plenty were tempted by the pay, the bonuses, and the coupons for gas, wine, cigarettes, and bread. But as they stepped out of the recruiting office, they heard a mine explode in the distance, tongues would be loosened, they'd be told some abominable story about a man blown apart in an instant, his body scattered to all four corners of the camp...and they would decide it was better to die of hunger.

"Did the recruiter mention the cooling-off period?"

"What for? That's just more administrative hypocrisy."

"Yeah, true. They're trying to say you had a choice. A lot of the guys here don't."

In springtime, finishing work didn't mean it was the end of the day. The sun was still high and gave all the men some relief. They stretched, came back to life, their strained faces instantly relaxing. Another life was possible now, a life in which they held their heads high, smiled with all the dazzle of their white teeth accentuated by their dirty, tanned skin, and defiantly looked people directly in the eye.

To reinforce Vincent's inclusion in the group, Fabien invited him to come for a drink with them. Max, a bundle of pure cocky energy, offered to take them in his Traction Avant. He'd found the thing goodness knew where and had passionately restored it to working order, sinking all his pay into the refurbishment. Thanks to this vehicle, he lent a party mood to the end of every shift.

Fabien climbed into the front while his three closest friends—Enzo, Georges, and Manu—got into the back with Vincent. It was quite a squeeze.

Vincent dreaded having to talk about himself, but he couldn't duck an invitation to a café. And anyway, he'd learned long ago the secret used by people who had something to hide: Getting other people to talk. It was all they wanted.

On the subject of mines, Enzo was unstoppable. Georges filled in any gaps, so that Vincent had the complete picture.

"It's a long list, what with antipersonnel mines and antitank mines, the bouncing mines like the S.Mi.35 and the S.Mi.40, the Schümine 42—activated by just two and a half kilos—then there's the A200 fitted with a chemical igniter…"

Their names sailed through the air: Stockmines, Tellermines, Holzmines, Panzer-Schnell mines, Riegelmines, Topfmines… and others whose names were lost in the thrum of the road or whenever Max honked the horn. There were so many of them.

"When they ran out of metal to make them, they started using wood."

"And then they made them out of concrete, ceramics, and glass."

"Easier and cheaper. Undetectable. Like plastic."

"And when there was absolutely nothing left, they cobbled them together out of papier-mâché."

"Basically, they made them out of anything they could lay their hands on, just so long as it exploded!"

The Treaty of Versailles had forbidden Germany rearming, but the Germans then invented all these mines, manufactured them by the millions, and perfected them year after year. And this was the end goal: making mines that couldn't be detected or disarmed, making them more powerful with broader reach, and making them explode. With mines, the perfection to strive for was very straightforward: It was death.

"They say you can't stop progress, but it's progress that stopped us!" Max concluded.

They hadn't yet reached the town when Fabien asked Max to slow down. A small crowd of men and children were doing their best to cordon off a section of road with wooden posts. Max parked and Fabien stepped out. He'd guessed right: The children had spotted a suspect piece of sheet metal sticking out of the ground with three metallic antennae. It must have been exposed by recent rain.

Three antennae on a W-shaped connector, cylindrical in form and small, barely ten centimeters in diameter—this was a Shrapnel 35, an S-mine, one of the most feared. By springing up from the ground to the height of the average man, it left no chance of survival withing a 25-meter range. Beyond that, up to 150 meters, it caused

life-changing injuries. Some said even up to 200 meters.
Two of the igniters could be triggered by traction and the
middle one by just three kilos of pressure.

Fabien loathed this mine. But he had no choice. He
would tackle it with the equipment at hand. He asked
everyone to back away then took his tools and a reel of soft
rope from Max's trunk. With its three ultra-sensitive igniters, there was no point hoping to disarm this mine; he'd
rather make it blow. Max reversed his car to block the road
behind them, and the deminers barred the way up ahead.
Vincent instinctively gathered the children in a huddle.

Fabien stayed alone with the mine.

He attached the rope to the Zug Zunder 35 traction
igniter and unwound it gently, walking backward for more
than 300 meters, with all the caution of a tightrope walker.
When he rejoined the others, he started breathing again.

With a glance he checked that nothing would disrupt
the ignition. He raised one arm as if about to start a car
race . . . then lowered it and gave the rope a sharp tug, triggering the mine.

Four and a half seconds later, the S.Mi.35 flew into
the air, a furious contraption with all the rabid force of a
geyser. As it sprang from the ground it hurled its incandescent steel beads in every direction with the power of
a fire hose and the demented intent of a sharpshooter on
amphetamines.

Barricaded in its metal carcass, the bouncing, dis-
charging mine started to create carnage from 30 centimeters off the ground, and continued up to 2.4 meters.
Theoretically, the only way to stay alive was to flatten

yourself on the ground and not move. Except that, in the space of four and a half seconds, including the time it took to realize the situation, there's rarely time for theory to be applied.

Seeing it from a distance was both strange and terrifying, like watching a jack-in-the-box. Everything about it fascinated the children: the sophistication of a magic trick, the weirdness of an automaton, and the terror of violent death.

Vincent heard someone mutter, Bouncing Betty. That was what the Americans called the S.35. Like Betty Boop. To make the war sexy—or for some reassurance—the men liked to paint pinups on their planes and give women's names to the most murderous weapons. Vincent had seen men turn into war machines, and he would now learn to be on first-name terms with mines. Men, women, mines, everything was now part of the same species: the human race.

∽

BY THE TIME THEY REACHED THE CAFÉ, THE team had almost forgotten that Vincent was new. The Bouncing Betty had been his baptism of fire. There was no more effective introduction.

True to his method, Vincent asked lots of questions to avoid being asked any himself, and the evening unfolded exactly as he'd anticipated: Each of the men was just as eager to talk about himself as to drink pastis.

Mostly with no dependents, they came from different backgrounds, a variety of horizons. They'd been sent on assignment to the southeast because it was a priority, but they could be from the north or central France and even farther afield, Spain or Italy. And then there were their social and political differences.

Max was a communist. Before the war he'd worked in a garage.

"I'm no egghead but if you need a mechanic, you won't find better than me!"

Fabien disagreed: Max had plenty of political knowledge. In the Party it was a prerequisite. A lot of Resistance fighters were communists. But that didn't stop him from ragging Max about the Communist Party's attitude at the start of the war when it had been trapped by the Molotov-Ribbentrop Pact.

Manu was the youngest in the group and had all the charm of someone who doesn't know his own beauty and all the hunger for knowledge of a student who'd had his studies interrupted and still bitterly regretted it. He didn't carry a card for any party but he'd demonstrated for peace before the war.

"I kinda got it wrong…"

He'd preferred listening to talking ever since. It was safer.

Next to him, Hubert mouthed off with his old-school ideas. He was a thin, athletic man and, even though at nearly forty he was the oldest in the team, he could plow through a lot of work without showing any signs of flagging. The others suspected some reversal of fortune, maybe he'd squandered it all for a woman. Unless he'd been soft on the enemy? It was a waste of time trying to get him to talk. He shrugged off any awkward questions by quoting a La Rochefoucauld maxim, often the same one: "Those who shout the loudest about morals are often those who have the least."

These words had become the deminers' favorite joke, but also their shield when other people judged them, their ultimate defense. Particularly for Jean, known as the Boss, sometimes the Lard, although he was more muscly than fat. As an ex-con, a former wrestler, and a newly reformed character, he too, in his own way, offered variations on the illustrious moralist's thoughts.

"I did some dumb stuff, but I have my honor. Not all crooks traded with the Boche, in case you didn't know."

"You still never said why you was in prison."

"Because I have the right to forget. Real sorry but I paid my debt to society."

"With what currency?"

"With years in the slammer, and they were no fun."

"Yeah, but you didn't spend those years fighting the war."

"Hey, easy! The war didn't last all that long, the fighting, I mean."

"For guys who weren't in the Resistance, okay, sure!"

And then there was Georges, who was from the southwest, where the coast was also peppered with mines. The whole Atlantic seaboard. But he'd chosen to exile himself in the east. What was he running away from? His family, bad memories, or worse?

As for Enzo, who knew the name of every mine by heart, he was married, adored his wife, and talked about her all the time. He'd joined the Resistance as one of the FTP-MOI, a branch mostly made up of immigrants. What was he doing here, with them? He would laugh and claim he was no good at anything else. Fabien would never betray him by explaining the real reason he'd joined the deminers: Enzo had come to France from Italy when he was five; he'd watched children throw stones at his mother and father. None of them had ever retaliated. He'd grown up in the Marseille neighborhood that people called Little Naples. When Italy sealed the Pact of Steel with Germany, all Italians had been suspected of collaborating with the enemy. But when the Germans invaded free France, they and the French police had rounded up all the Italians living in Marseille, imprisoned them in Fréjus internment camp, and demolished their homes. Enzo's family was among those who were now called "the evacuees" and who didn't dare protest.

Enzo wanted a fine future for his three daughters. He would never stop proving his loyalty to France. Being part of the FTP-MOI hadn't been enough: He'd come back for more with mine clearing. The Italians were often very good with munitions. Besides Fabien, Enzo was the only one who could neutralize and disarm a mine, and he had a rare encyclopedic knowledge of the multitude of ignition systems that triggered them. It wasn't only for his technical expertise that Fabien was so fond of him. They both had the same commitment to the Resistance, the same sense of honor, and they still managed to treat other people with undiminished tenderness.

Since he'd been demining, Fabien had seen all sorts: pro-Gaullists, antis, Resistance fighters, wimps and pen-pushers, Catholics, atheists, communists, anticommunists, aristocrats, classless vagrants, three Italians, two Spanish refugees, and rootless drifters. An extraordinary brotherhood held sway among this ragbag of men who, under normal circumstances, would never have met or would have despised one another. Only members of this disparate troop could understand what they were experiencing. The risks they took together formed a powerful bond. And so did their deaths.

Vincent was struck by their cheerfulness. No one around that table thought of taking issue with his fate. They were happy to be alive, happy to have food, happy to be together. They watched girls walk past in the street and, like everyone else, they thought the future was brimming with promise.

Being a deminer made you anything but a good catch. But that didn't stop them appealing to women. Desire has no rules, but it has some constants. Their bodies and their attitude brought together the magic ingredients that set sparks flying. And then there was all the rest: how offhand they were about facing danger, how gracious never to complain, the mystery that hung over them as if they weren't common mortals because they engaged in this unequal battle with death. Perhaps they had a secret, a particular aptitude, like the American Indians who were said to have no fear of heights and worked hundreds of meters up in the air building skyscrapers in the United States. Dancing with danger, taking it in your arms on the edge of the abyss and teetering on the frontiers of hell without faltering—it made them irresistible.

Léna, the café owner, brought their drinks and when they raised their glasses to every beauty they saw, their tanned, bare arms with pronounced muscles were clearly visible because they'd rolled their sleeves right up to the shoulder. The women returned their smiles. After all, the war was over here in the south. It was fine to smile at anyone.

Léna immediately noticed that Vincent was new.

"Did Fabien manage to rope you in?"

"I didn't have to push him, if that's what you think! He came of his own accord, like a big boy," Fabien replied for Vincent.

"I think you cast a spell on them. They'd follow you to the ends of the earth."

"I thought you were the specialist when it comes to magic spells."

Léna went off smiling to fetch the rest of their order.

It hadn't escaped Vincent that she was beautiful and had that indefinable something that catches the eye, but his only objective was to turn the conversation to the Germans.

"So, these Krauts," he ventured with all the nonchalance he could muster, "now that they're demining all the crap they left us with are they still convinced that '*Arbeit macht frei*'?"

From the roar of laughter, Vincent knew he'd been adopted by the deminers. On the other hand, the answer he was given was not what he'd been expecting.

"Yeah, well, don't fret about the Germans, they won't be here for long."

That didn't make him fret—it devastated him.

"It's late April," Max added. "I bet you Germany will have surrendered by May. And, you know, at the end of a war everybody usually goes home. With the faceful of bombing they're getting, they won't be disappointed with what they find when they get home!"

Vincent gave away none of his concern and turned to Fabien.

"What do you think?"

"In a nutshell: thirteen million mines, three thousand volunteers. You can see why we need fifty thousand prisoners in the equation."

"So they'll stay?"

"Aubrac even wants twice as many. But it's far from a done deal: It's all down to the San Francisco Conference. Gotta convince fifty countries to violate international law."

"Yes, but it's not like anyone's gonna take pity on the Boche."

"Damn right, everybody agrees the Germans have to pay! On their knees. Under the lash, even. And not only in France. So why not a bit of demining? Except our dear diplomats want us to do it without anyone knowing, under the table. Aubrac's against that and he's right: We'd be collared at the first opportunity. Getting prisoners to work out in the open on beaches and roads isn't exactly discreet."

"But the Germans are mine clearing here—"

"They're mine *detecting*," Fabien corrected. "The conference only just started—we're making the most of the gray area."

Léna was back with the rest of the drinks.

"I'd prefer it if it was only Germans risking their lives."

"Don't stress, Léna, we weigh the risks."

"You can never weigh a risk. That's the definition of it!"

"Léna, we're here to relax! And anyway, you know we have a lucky star."

Of course. Her views wouldn't change anything: The deminers didn't think they'd be killed clearing mines; the government thought they could clear them all without the Germans; and anyone who benefited from their sacrifice thought the mines cleared themselves.

As she poured a glass of white wine for Vincent, her gaze lingered a moment on his face. Perhaps this one was less reckless than the others and she could save him?

"Honestly, what made you sign up for this? Don't you have anything better to do than demining?"

"If we don't do it, who the hell will?"

The whole team raised their glasses to Vincent's answer, as if it were a motto, an act of faith, the musketeers' oath.

Léna was wrong—he was just like the others, clinging to his illusions. No one can live without denial, the only universal religion.

◇

TWO DAYS EARLIER, VINCENT HAD MET UP WITH Audrey at the bottom of the steps at Saint-Charles station in Marseille. The city was buzzing with a lust for life and a sense of pride reinforced by the commanding victory over the Germans, which had avenged the terrible roundups of January '43 and the dynamiting of 1,500 buildings in the Old Port neighborhood. Ordered by the Germans and organized by the French, these crimes had been traumatic, particularly as René Bousquet, the head of the Vichy French police, had personally gone far above and beyond the occupiers' hopes, as he'd done during the Vel d'Hiv roundups at the velodrome in Paris.

Marseille's inhabitants hadn't just sat and waited to be liberated. Like the Parisians, they'd risen up in arms just before French troops and the Allies arrived, and the exaltation of this victorious insurrection, the insurgents' irresistible and decisive conviction still hung in the air, on every face and in every smile.

Audrey was radiant. Eager to talk, she described the defiant spirit that had suddenly swept through Marseille: the rowdy crowds in the streets, women and children, a tide of people—happy, rebellious people confident of winning. Action had reclaimed its rights over the numbed city, the empty streets, the population diminished by fear. That was Liberation: The insurgents had triumphed over the collaborators' guilty cynicism and Nazi morbidity with their fervent longing to live.

Next Audrey talked enthusiastically about the new life that lay ahead.

"Everything will be different this time. And if you want proof: Tomorrow I'm going to vote in the local elections! Can you imagine? Women's votes will mean something. And not a minute too soon, right?"

Of course, Vincent thought this was inspiring. Of course, he was annoyed that he didn't feel as transported and buoyant as she did, but having heard about her excitement and convictions, it was becoming unbearable for him not to talk about Ariane.

"Have you heard from her?"

Audrey had been dreading this question since she'd spotted Vincent at the top of the station steps, looking perhaps even more handsome than she'd remembered. The burning intensity of his expression, which sadly didn't burn for her, had become even more intense and feverish. His eyes, which were black from a distance and green close up, flecked with gold for anyone who looked into them deeply, would stay pinned on her until she gave him an answer, told him everything she knew, offered up everything he wanted to hear.

What did she actually know? With Ariane you never knew anything, you had inklings, you got it wrong. And did Vincent really want to hear what she could tell him, what she was afraid was true? Audrey gathered her composure; she would take this conversation one step at a time, gain some ground, then they'd see.

"Last time I saw her was at my place."

"When?"

"Nearly two years ago…in June, June '43."

"That's when her parents stopped hearing from her."

"Are you sure?"

"Well, that's what they told me. She left the farm, and they haven't seen her since."

"But it was her parents who encouraged her to go back to her own life. Her mother was getting better, and they didn't need help with the farm anymore."

This was problematic for Vincent: Ariane's letters had continued to say that she was putting her medical dissertation on hold while she helped her parents. Her mother was sick and their apprentice had been killed at the start of the war. Another one then had to leave for Compulsory Work Service. What with the Germans' endless requisitions, they couldn't cope on their own.

Audrey could see that Vincent was thrown, but the handful of vague answers she gave him to win herself time to think did little to reassure him.

"I'm not the best person to tell you about Ariane. Maybe Irène knows more. I mean she's her childhood friend, Ariane told her everything," she suggested.

"Irène signed up to help repatriate prisoners. I've tried to contact her. Right now, she must be in the depths of Germany, or in Poland."

Audrey would have liked to know more about what Vincent had been through in the prison camps, but she didn't feel comfortable pushing him.

Vincent almost heard her unvoiced questions, but on such a glorious day it felt inappropriate to relate his grim time in captivity in those dire bunkhouses, a time impregnated with cold, with squelching mud, freezing skin and bones, violence and humiliation, as if all those years had been made up entirely of winter months. And who wants to conjure winter in the middle of spring? Perhaps that gave him an unintended air of mystery, but that was how it was.

Vincent realized Audrey was watching him and felt embarrassed for revealing his feelings to her. Still, he was grateful that she hadn't commented on the fact that his search was inevitably a little surprising. It wasn't his job to try to find Ariane. Audrey would probably have understood better if the man who'd come to see her today to find out why Ariane had disappeared had been the one Ariane had been married to when Vincent met her. No one knew that Ariane had left this man for Vincent, and Vincent himself would never tell anyone that they'd secretly been lovers.

~

THE FRESH AIR IN THE HARBOR, THE CHEERY clink of rigging, and the flapping of sails reminded Vincent of his student days and the cups of coffee sipped on café terraces, but to exchange confidences he needed to be alone with Audrey, in an enclosed space that wouldn't allow emotions to be whipped up by the wind.

He said he didn't feel comfortable surrounded by so many people, he wasn't used to it. And the harbor had changed so much since the Germans had blown up the huge transporter bridge. The technical prowess of that giant spiderweb and the modernity of its steel cables had been the pride of Marseille and much admired by the Bauhaus architects. Its absence was as outrageous as if the Eiffel Tower had been removed from Paris. And then there were the ruins over there, opposite the fort, so many streets and buildings in the Saint-Jean neighborhood demolished that it would take forever to rebuild, meaning no one could forget. Did she understand? He was only half lying, and Audrey looked genuinely apologetic.

"Do you want to go home?"

"Couldn't we go to your place?"

How Audrey would once have loved him to suggest that! She'd never guessed that she was the link between

Vincent and Ariane, but she now grasped that he was only there to talk about her.

She took him to the small apartment she'd inherited from her mother. Perched on the top floor, under the eaves, it opened onto a tiny terrace overrun with wild plants she'd gathered in the countryside. She served him a mediocre coffee, but at least she'd found some.

"Ariane stayed with me for three weeks. Then she left."

"Where did she go?"

"I don't know! I thought she'd try to go back to the hospital. I could have helped her. I work at Timone Hospital now and they would have hired her. But she didn't want to."

"And have you heard from her since?"

"It might be hard for her. One evening she mentioned possibly escaping via Spain to Morocco, then heading south in Africa. She also had connections who could smuggle people to Algeria from Saint-Tropez. She hated feeling like a prisoner."

Audrey thought she'd found the best possible argument to reassure Vincent: Ariane didn't want to let anyone dictate her life. She wanted to live now. With no better clues to help them understand, they just had to remember her passionate commitment to being happy. Ariane was terrified to think her life could just stop right there and she might not see any other countries before she died. He must remember how obsessed she'd been with going to Egypt to see the pyramids, if you please, dropping everything to go looking for Cleopatra's tomb. Perhaps she'd boarded a boat heading for these destinations that had fueled her dreams?

"Yes, of course I remember, but I can't see Ariane leaving her parents in the dark," Vincent kept saying, constantly baulking at that window of time when Ariane had been staying with Audrey but had told no one.

He found it easier mentioning her parents than talking about himself. It would have been impossible and presumptuous to say, "She would have waited for me. She wouldn't have abandoned me, even for the palaces of the one thousand and one nights, the streets of a souk, or all the gold in Babylon." But it's what he was thinking.

It was then that Vincent noticed a wooden sculpture on a shelf. Audrey had draped her jewelry over it in an appealing mishmash. In among the beads and trinkets, he was astonished to spot a gold chain he'd given to Ariane. He would have recognized it out of a thousand; it had been his grandfather's watch chain. It was a good enough length to form a long necklace, and Ariane had usually wound it twice around her neck so that it rested on her clearly defined collarbones. Sometimes, though, she'd kept it full length and the necklace had hung almost to her navel, the way flappers used to wear them in the Roaring Twenties to point out: I have a belly, you know, and it's alive, it's happy, it can dance…

Mesmerized by this discovery, he went over to the sculpture and held the chain between his fingers.

"Did she give this to you?"

"She forgot it. I found it in the sheets I'd put on the sofa for her."

Vincent closed his hand around the chain. The last thing he wanted to do was labor the point. Audrey really wasn't making this easy.

"Did you take any photos of Ariane at the farm?"

"I have some negatives, but I haven't developed them all. I didn't have the chemicals."

"And of the Germans who went there to requisition supplies?"

"I didn't go there much, you know."

"But do you have any?"

"Yes, not many, but..." Audrey could tell where he was going with this. "You think the Germans who came to the farm for provisions were the reason Ariane ran away."

"Well, if they were, I need to know."

Audrey now knew he would mire himself in an endless quest that would never provide him with any answers.

"How will you find out? They're either dead or in prison camps. There's a prison camp in Marseille and one in Aubagne, I think, and smaller ones scattered about all over the place, but no one's allowed in."

"I know."

"How do you know?"

"Well, I would guess. I'll find a way."

"I'd be very surprised if they let you in. Apparently, the conditions are terrible. They really weren't expecting so many prisoners. We don't know anything at the hospital, they treat them on-site."

Vincent found it hard to disguise his frustration.

"Say you do find something out," Audrey said, taking the conversation in a different direction. "What would you do?"

"What would *you* do?"

Audrey eyed him warily.

"Ariane always said that when you started answering questions with questions, it was time to fear the worst."

Vincent shrugged and smiled at her. "The worst? She overestimated me. No, I'm far too sensible, don't you worry."

ON THE BUS HOME FROM MARSEILLE, VINCENT ran the long watch chain that he'd given to Ariane through his fingers. On his altar to his goddess Ariane he now had her scarf, her necklace, and soon some photographs.

The bus was passing the Château des Eyguières, where the Germans had established a Kommandatura. He could see it up in the distance, built into the hillside, partly hidden by tall maritime pines. When he'd left Ariane's parents the day before, he'd stopped off at the château as if he might find answers to his questions. He hadn't been able to get near it. There were signs blocking the entrance: Before they'd fled, the Germans had mined their former headquarters.

Almost opposite him, across the aisle, a young woman was watching the countryside spool past. Her profile lost in contemplation against the window, the tilt of her delicate neck, her hair spilling over her disarmingly simple dress—they all captivated him.

She'd told the ticket inspector she'd come from Paris, and when he'd kept asking questions, she'd explained she was coming home. Vincent was intrigued by her one very small piece of luggage. He'd caught her name when the inspector had asked her to speak up. Saskia…he was just thinking he'd never heard anything like it when she turned toward him.

She was not coventionally pretty but had the most luminous pale eyes.

Pale gray and they seemed to fill the whole of her fine-featured face. She'd noticed that Vincent was surreptitiously watching her, and he was embarrassed but couldn't turn way immediately because he desperately wanted to understand the enigma in her face. It was so young and so full of pain, so fragile and so determined, anxious yet sometimes detached, flitting without warning between all possible emotions.

She seemed to be warming herself in the sun, which was streaming through the window and intensifying the smell of the moleskin seat. She wasn't happy to be coming home, that much was obvious. How old was she? Hard to tell.

When they reached the bus station, he reached out to help her step down, but she recoiled sharply as if the hand he'd offered her was a criminal's.

Struck by the vehemence of her reaction, he apologized for scaring her. He couldn't risk frightening her any more, but he wished he could tell her that he understood and for him too the war wasn't over just because that was what had been decided. Defeating the Germans was nothing compared to the injuries and bereavements everyone carried within them; and you had to keep listening to the signs left by the dead so that they knew you still respected and loved them—they were dead but not forgotten. He too was wary of the living.

EMBARRASSED BY HER OWN REACTION, WHICH was instinctive and disproportionate, Saskia looked aside and muttered an inaudible apology before walking away. From the bus station she set off down the main street and then turned onto the road she used to take on her walk home from high school before the war. Memories sprang up as she passed every house, every wall, every bench. Conversations she'd had with her brother and sister on their way home. The florist where she used to buy flowers for her mother. And the square where she'd first been approached by the boy she loved. His name was Rodolphe and they'd promised each other that one day they'd be married.

When Saskia finally reached the gate to her house, she was relieved to find it intact. The 1930s villa designed by her father was smothered in flowering wisteria, which filled the air with fragrance. In their absence, the garden had continued to flourish into gleeful exuberance. The purple-and-white clematises—the most beautiful and rare varieties that sometimes produce just one precious, temperamental flower—had proliferated. The May tree had filled out and transformed into a perfumed canopy of green and pink. It was all naturally harmonious. And that was the beauty of it: You could see the flowers, not the work. The ivy had also gained ground over the façade, attractively framing the windows in a marriage of nature and architecture. The grass was tall and dotted with self-seeded flowers, just as pretty as the more conventional ones. She could even hear the harmonics of frogs; it was their mating season.

Saskia pictured it all. Her father and mother reading together in the garden, her mother breaking off to reposition a jasmine branch, tie up a honeysuckle, or cut some lilac. Their evening meals by candlelight, their losing battles against mosquitoes, the heat of summer evenings— her favorite.

She wasn't looking forward to being here alone, but there was one thing she knew: Their home would help her start her life over, here, in this refuge created by her parents, a place that still testified to everything that her family had been.

All she need do now was find the key where her mother had hidden it, but…the garden was alive and she was afraid the house no longer would be.

A passerby stared at her oddly, and she made up her mind to go through the gate. It was then that she was struck by the sudden appearance of a woman on the doorstep. A beautiful, bustling, impeccably dressed woman in her forties who was staring right at her.

"What are you doing here?"

Stunned, Saskia couldn't utter a word. She didn't even think the woman was real.

"What do you want?" the woman asked.

"This is my home!"

"I'd be very surprised. I live here, with my family."

"But... Since when?"

Everything blurred, Saskia couldn't think straight, she couldn't even have said what date they were arrested, the starting point of all the despair and all her pain.

The woman stalked over to her menacingly.

"You're on my property and I'm asking you leave."

"This is my house! My parents bought the plot, my father built it," Saskia pleaded, her voice breaking.

"Can you prove it?"

Saskia was completely thrown, she could never have anticipated being asked this. The woman was already climbing the three steps back to the door to go inside. She had her back to her when Saskia managed to gather all her strength to say, "Excuse me, could I at least get a few belongings?"

"There's nothing of yours here."

"When did you move in?"

"Listen, I don't know you, and we see our fill of crackpots every day! If you don't leave, I'll call the police!"

The woman closed the door to end the conversation. Saskia wasn't sure how, but she'd managed not to cry.

By returning home, Saskia had been hoping to come back to her parents' books, annotated by her mother—never by her father, to him books were sacred—and into which Mila had also sometimes slipped little pieces of paper on which she'd jotted her thoughts or a citation in her beautiful, spirited handwriting. Saskia so longed to keep a conversation going with her like this. What other support did Saskia have now if not her books and her words?

Before the war when she'd wanted to finish a novel, she would race through her homework, turn down invitations to go out with her friends, and read under the covers with a flashlight until she was too tired to get up in the morning to go to school. At the time she'd loved reading as a forbidden pleasure. In the camp, it was all the other way around: Reading became essential to your survival, and remembering what you'd read, knowing it by heart—by heart, how accurate that expression was. And she blessed her mother and everyone who'd taught her literature, people who'd broadened her horizons, taking her much farther afield than the text she would have kept to had no one stimulated her mind and opened up the world of possibilities.

In class she'd hardly even noticed these apparently inaccessible lines from *Bérénice*: "Forever! Sire! Do you not feel the dread / A lover feels when that cruel word is said?" Only now did she understand what she'd read back then. Or rather, she'd tragically been given access to its meaning. She was not entirely alone today because Racine had written that "Forever." The depths of her despair, in a single word.

Late in the night, when she was trying to find somewhere to sleep, Saskia looked up at the sky. She saw the stars that are never more visible than when the moon is new and blends discreetly into the black of night, and they soothed her. She would fight. She swore it to her whole family gathered in a secret constellation whose meaning—as with books, plays, and poems—would be revealed to her one day.

THERE MAY WELL HAVE BEEN A THOUSAND WAYS to proceed to find Ariane and perhaps, amid this end-of-war chaos, Vincent should risk trying them all. From the simplest to the hardest.

The first thing he'd done was return to the small one-bedroom apartment on place Castellane loaned to him by an aunt, the space at the very top of a handsome building that had sheltered his secret meetings with Ariane. The key was still where they used to hide it, but he had trouble getting in: Mail had accumulated under the door.

Inside, nothing had changed. He'd hunted for a note she might have left him, a diary, something that would explain, but there's never a diary; in real life you never find anything to explain why someone has disappeared.

What he did find, though, were the letters he'd sent her from the prison camp, numbered by him then renumbered by her. He was moved by this. He hadn't been able to take her letters with him when he escaped. He decided to leave everything in the apartment as it was. Apart from a few books, there was nothing he needed. He wanted everything to stay exactly the same for the day when he would meet Ariane there again.

Then he made the rounds of all their old friends and went to see her parents. He even watched her husband, from afar. Ariane had been very young when she married, but Vincent was convinced she would never have chosen someone completely devoid of sensitivity. When Ariane had met Vincent she'd told her husband she was going to leave. He hadn't wanted to know his rival's identity, nor any details. He'd asked only two things: that she wait six months before reaching her decision, and that she discuss it with no one. If after this half year she was still determined, then he would give her her freedom. Ariane had sworn to respect his wishes. She'd asked Vincent to keep their relationship secret and he had promised to. And then war was declared.

Vincent couldn't dismiss the possibility that Ariane's husband knew something. He followed the man to his office, made inquiries, and when he heard that he'd made a new life for himself, Vincent arranged to meet him, claiming to be just a friend who wanted news of Ariane.

Ariane's husband was most likely not fooled. He shed a couple of tears. Perhaps they were heartfelt, after all. But as he saw it, the situation was clear: Ariane—the admirable young woman who'd unfailingly supported her parents day and night through the war—had died, too young, and it was up to them to come to terms with the weighty task of living. The arrival of his new girlfriend then interrupted his tender musing on life and death.

Vincent wouldn't truly live until he knew for sure.

The letters he'd received while he was a prisoner had alerted him to the fact that something wasn't right.

Correspondence had been restricted: Two letters a month. He'd had time to read and reread them, and to think.

The first letter had been from Irène. She was worried because Ariane felt threatened by a German officer who was billeted at the Château des Eyguières. He was one of the Germans who regularly came to her parents' farm. He was an insistent, intrusive presence, and the interest he so openly showed in Ariane was becoming dangerous. Irène was trying to persuade Ariane to leave the farm and return to Marseille. She wanted Vincent and all their friends to help convince her. Using well-chosen words, Irène had managed to get through the censors and make herself perfectly understood.

Ariane was furious that Irène had told Vincent and, to reassure him, she then wrote to tell him there was a German soldier at Eyguières whom she could trust. He was keeping an eye on her, protecting her, and would find a safe place for her if she really needed it. As a coded way of discussing the Germans, she'd used a sentence from Leibniz: "No two blades of grass are the same."

Vincent was not reassured: If Ariane needed protecting, that meant she definitely was in danger, far more than she was prepared to admit. And if she was putting her trust in a German, the danger was even greater: How could she be so unwilling to see the truth that she was prepared to take the word of an enemy soldier?

It was when he'd received this letter that he'd summoned the will to plan another escape attempt, the first one having failed. He had to find these two German soldiers whose names he didn't know. The officer who was a threat to her and this so-called ally.

Contrary to what he'd intimated to Audrey, Vincent had already researched the camps holding German prisoners. He'd started his reconnoitering in Marseille, at Sainte-Marthe camp, the largest, most overpopulated camp: Several thousand prisoners of war were crammed into the place. And more arrived every day from Germany. Next he'd gone to the camp in Aubagne. Same story. Several thousand. Even if he'd been able to enter the site, how would he have found the two soldiers he was looking for? Then there were also camps in Toulon, Hyères, Nice, Avignon...

He'd trawled through the archives of a regional newspaper for information about the Kommandatura that had requisitioned the Château des Eyguières. The Wehrmacht's entire garrison had been arrested by the French Forces of the Interior in 1944. There were photos of the cohort of German soldiers at the time of their arrest and as they were taken to the town square. All of them without exception had their heads lowered, their eyes looking evasively at the ground, as if wanting to avoid being captured by the lens too. The very opposite of their military parades, their marches through villages and on the Champs-Élysées. Hidden under hats tugged down to their eyebrows with the visors tilting over their eyes, their faces were impossible to make out.

And Vincent didn't even know where they were being held.

It was by chatting with some Moroccan guards that he drew up a list of other, smaller camps, Kommando prison labor groups scattered along the coast. Audrey was right. These too were off-limits: Even through the barbed wire, it wasn't hard to see that in these vast open-air prisons the penury that gripped all of France was hitting prisoners harder than the population. The authorities didn't need witnesses.

Vincent wasn't discouraged. Thanks to the information he'd gleaned, he eventually located the camp where the soldiers from Eyguières were being held. Then he identified one of the guards and got to know his routine and the café he frequented. Vincent managed, apparently casually, to strike up a conversation. How could he ever show enough gratitude to his pack of cigarettes! You don't smoke without chatting. Accepting a cigarette means accepting a chat. After the cigarette, he offered the man a drink, then another.

Vincent's patience in that smoky café was rewarded: The guard was quite prepared to talk.

"France has taken two hundred thousand prisoners! Not as many as the Allies, but still. Overall, you can count German prisoners in millions. Which is just as well: The Russians want a million of them and the English want some too. Everyone wants their share of Boche for rebuilding work. But well, that's not happening right away. For now, they're just waiting."

Vincent succeeded in steering the conversation toward more specific topics.

"What happened to the Germans who were at the Château des Eyguières?"

"All captured, all in one go when they were trying to escape!"

"And where are they now? Which camp are they in?"

"The one where I work."

Vincent managed to disguise his amazement and was especially careful not to show how eager he was when the guard divulged information he wouldn't have dared hope for.

"And they're not all just waiting for whatever's next. Some are working already."

It was at this point that the guard mentioned demining.

"They set all those mines so we're making them clear the things. And they sure screwed up the coast between Hyères and Saint-Tropez. It'll give them plenty of thinking time…"

It seemed almost unbelievable. Vincent couldn't go into a prison camp, but some of the prisoners came out!

"It's dangerous," the guard went on, "but that's how you have to start. We can't do anything if we don't demine first. Not put them to work in the fields, or in factories, nowhere. So some of them are moldering in the camp and some are out demining. And they'll be at it for quite a while. What the hell were they thinking planting all those mines?"

And while the guard confided his enduring opinions about the ways of the world, Vincent had a feeling that he now had his one chance of finding Ariane. Of all the options he'd imagined, he could now see no valid alternatives but this one insane idea of enrolling in a mine-clearance team to get close to the Germans who'd been at Eyguières. He'd be able to communicate with them, approach them in stages, start scraps of conversation, then, very gradually, soften them up. Slowly. Steadily. Earning their trust and their respect by working as an equal alongside them. Finally knowing what had happened to Ariane during the Occupation, why she'd vanished, where she was. And if he was lucky, among the team of deminers he might even flush out the friendly soldier Ariane had mentioned or the dangerous officer that Irène had.

He saw this as a clear sign that he was on the right track, and this was his chance of perhaps finding Ariane alive. It felt so completely serendipitous that he wasn't even aware that this longed-for opportunity was, at one and the same time, suicidal.

∿

THE GUARDS' YELLS SHATTERED THE NIGHTTIME silence. The prisoners had to drag themselves awake and out of the bunkhouses immediately: Two prisoners who'd escaped had just been caught, and all their fellow inmates had to watch the show.

Completely naked and lit by several floodlights, the escapees had to raise their right arms and run circuits around the prison's arena until they collapsed with exhaustion. The guards reckoned that the other prisoners, forced to witness this pitiful performance, would be sufficiently shocked to give up any idea of following their example.

Lukas clearly grasped the persuasive power of a staged event like this, but also the spirit of revenge that motivated it. No one came out of it well. All the prisoners had already had to parade bare-chested with one arm raised to prove they hadn't tattooed their blood group in the crook of their armpit—a distinguishing feature of the SS—or on their biceps like the Waffen-SS. This tattooing wasn't compulsory and some had even managed to conceal their damning affiliations.

Lukas moved over to the very young newly arrived prisoners. One of them was hunching his face into the collar of his pea jacket to cry. He was bone weary and thought they would all be made to run naked.

In the cool night air, the smell hovering around each prisoner was intolerable: Overpopulation in the camp meant they had access to the showers just once a week. Lorenz, the boy who was crying, was fourteen. He never removed his uniform, day or night, and he wasn't the only one. This meant that as the fabric became increasingly worn it grew stiff with filth and sweat. From this rough, colorless flannel emerged a dirty, pink, smooth-skinned face with terrified eyes that Lukas found very distressing.

He tried to reassure the boy. He was convinced that child soldiers would be released soon. They were minors. They didn't belong here. The group that Lukas looked after, and whom he'd taught to love the literature that their elders had scoffed at, clustered around him. Separated from their families and reduced to prey for every guard or fellow inmate who hadn't seen a woman for many long months, they moved about in groups as if conjoined. They listened to what Lukas said for warmth and guidance and to keep their heads above water.

In 1936 it had become compulsory for all children to join the Hitler Youth. Lukas had seen firsthand the staggering effects of their indoctrination. Long before his favorite authors had been officially blacklisted, brainwashed youngsters had stormed libraries and ransacked their shelves of books to cart them to the pillory. Not satisfied with hammering books onto stakes, like Christ on the cross, they then organized huge public burnings. But at just fourteen, what did Lorenz know of such crimes? What legacy had he been left by the ideological bludgeoning inflicted on Germany's youth? Lukas loaned him books, which afforded him some escape almost before they were opened. He watched the traumatized child devouring page after page and then, once the book was finished, rereading it so that he could stay sheltered within that paper sanctuary. When you love reading, you're saved.

The guards were still yelling to keep the escapees on their feet. The two men tripped, hauled themselves back up while the guards kicked them, then stumbled on. Their bodies sagged with effort. When the younger of the two collapsed, the older man fell to the ground too. Nothing could force them back to their feet now, not beating or shouting or the threat of weapons. They'd given up. The guards left them naked in the dust.

A prisoner called Klaus shuffled over to Lukas and muttered quietly, "See how they treat us, you know, they're as bad as…"

He was referring to the newsreel they'd been shown that afternoon which featured concentration camps being liberated. Many of them hadn't understood what they were seeing. It was almost impossible.

"Do you feel you're being crushed by a program of extermination?" Lukas snapped back at Klaus.

"No, I'm just saying that we're also—"

"Don't make comparisons. Never relativize. Relativizing is denial. And denial is killing all over again."

Lukas didn't have time to finish because the guards abruptly ordered the prisoners back to their bunkhouses. The two prisoners' failed escape had given the guards an excuse to indulge in one of their favorite activities: a search. The inmates had fewer and fewer personal belongings, but still there were checks. To reinforce the humiliation, each prisoner was asked to lay out everything he had left, not on his meagre straw mattress, no, on the ground, on the bare beaten earth. Watches, cameras, and gold chains had long since disappeared. What remained were wedding rings, letters, and photos. Occasionally a piece of fruit or some bread brought by kind souls and handed through the barbed wire.

The guards rummaged desultorily through these belongings with their feet. Lukas's amounted to a few letters and books. The guards had already read the letters. With the tips of their boots, they opened books by once blacklisted authors that Lukas had secretly saved by changing their covers. Disappointed not to find anything interesting, they crushed them by trampling on them, leaving the imprint of their heavy soles on the pages of Stefan Zweig's last book, *The World of Yesterday*. Zweig had written it in exile and had sent it to his publisher just before killing himself alongside the wife he loved.

When the guards had left, Lukas picked up his book, smoothed out its pages one after the other, and slept on it to finish erasing every crease.

The following morning all sorts of people thronged at the camp gates as if in a marketplace, thinking they could use the prisoners however they saw fit. The French Foreign Legion had come recruiting and a few German officers had rushed at the opportunity. Anything rather than staying locked up. Industrialists, storekeepers, factory managers, and smallholders all came to see if there was any chance of getting a few prisoners to work. They were disappointed to have to wait but reappeared the very next day to see if things had changed. Or if some agreement could be reached. In regions with fewer mines, prisoners were already out working. So in the meantime, they eyed the inmates, appraising them like goods in a shopwindow.

That was when Lukas spotted the group of teenagers that he kept a kindly eye on. The decision had just been made: They were to be transferred to another camp. Lukas had grown fond of them. He'd felt he was doing something that mattered in some small way, and this meant a lot to him. He gave one of his books to Lorenz, then tried to find out whether they would be repatriated. The guard shrugged. He'd be surprised if anyone could answer that.

The time had come for Lukas to escape.

CARVED UP BY VAST ANTITANK TRENCHES, strewn with barbed wire and blockhouses stranded on the sand like giant reinforced concrete excretions, the new beach they were to clear of mines looked like a hostile, abandoned wasteland, edged by a gray sea as lifeless as a gigantic puddle. The forest of centennial trees that once towered over it had been burned down by the Germans. All that remained were charred trunks; black was the dominant color.

Before the war this beach had been breathtakingly beautiful. Maritime pines, golden sands, and turquoise waters. It was now unbearably desolate. Burned land and a mined beach—who was there to remember that in the 1930s wealthy Americans, floundering writers, dandies, and gorgeous debutantes had sold their souls for the French Riviera?

This "Azure Coast" had been destroyed and its beaches were more dangerous than the seventh circle of hell. Only Fabien could envision their resurrection, because he'd known them as a child. And it was a beautiful day, you had to cling to the sun, which was still standing its ground.

Vincent wasn't the only person joining the team. There was also a shy young man called Thomas and a German prisoner replacing one who'd called in sick. Officially, he was genuinely unwell, but the translator confided to Fabien that in reality he was scared to death, so much so he'd made himself sick, much to everyone's amusement. As if he was the only one to be afraid.

Vincent had met most of the team at the café the day before. All except Miguel Ángel and Henri, who hadn't been there. Fabien introduced them.

Miguel Ángel had fled the Francoists with his family by crossing the Spanish border one winter night. He and his older brother had been cooped up in the Argèles-sur-Mer camp, sleeping on the sand and using their bare hands to build some basic accommodation. During the war they'd fought to free North Africa and had been among the first to enter Paris with La Nueve, part of General Leclerc's 2nd Armored Division. After Paris was liberated, La Nueve had headed for Germany to Hitler's Eagle's Nest at Berchtesgaden. Miguel Ángel had returned to southern France to be near his family. A fervent antifascist, his commitment—along with his brother's and that of every Spanish exile he knew—was truly heartfelt. They couldn't wait for the end of the war when the Allies would help them overthrow Franco and reestablish democracy in Spain. Miguel believed this would happen. Fabien hoped it would.

Henri, by contrast, was not very talkative. He'd fled the mines, but in his case they were coal mines. Anything rather than ruin his lungs as his father and uncles had done in the underground galleries of northern France. He wanted fresh air.

When he'd finished the introductions, Fabien came over to the newcomer who was standing close to Vincent.

"Are you even an adult?"

"Yes."

"Are you twenty-one? Really? Don't look it."

"Would you like to see my ID?"

"You were hired so I'm guessing you've made a good one."

"The recruiting officer checked it!"

"What that guy mostly checked was that you were listening to him. Apart from that he doesn't check much."

Fabien had already had to deal with cases like this. You couldn't stop people wanting to eat, but still. This boy looked very young to be risking his life.

"Do you know why there are inspections?"

The young man looked down and gave no reply, but didn't back away.

"What's your name?"

"Thomas, people call me Tom."

"Well, Tom, I hope the next inspection comes as soon as possible. Believe me, if your ID's fake, they'll know."

Vincent didn't move a muscle.

As for the German who was there for the first time, no one thought to ask him his name.

Fabien gave Vincent and Tom a bayonet each and a demining kit in a hemp bag they could hang from their belts: cotter pins, nails, wire cutters, and cone-shaped markers. He smiled as he acknowledged that this was as laughable as protecting yourself from lightning on a stormy night with a straw hat on your head. What really mattered, though, wasn't the accessories but the frame of mind.

He reminded them of their objectives.

"This beach is different," he said. "In these blockhouses here, there could be maps of the mines along the coastline. That means where they buried the mines and what type they are. Which will save us time and make our work safer. But they're also stuffed with explosives. I don't have to paint a picture, we need to stay completely focused. As soon as you feel the subtlest resistance to the bayonet, you stop and raise your hand, and either Enzo or I will take over."

The translator relayed this simultaneously to the prisoners, who showed no reaction. In fact, none of the men let any emotion leak out. Better to die than admit they'd give anything to be somewhere else. They bolstered themselves with the thought that there were plenty of other opportunities to die. After all, they'd survived the war; perhaps their lucky stars could protect them a little longer.

Fabien positioned himself between Tom and Vincent to show them how to hold the bayonet, tilting it at a forty-five-degree angle to be sure they didn't trigger a mine as they drove it into the ground every ten centimeters. They also had to stay in step with the others and mark out the terrain they'd already inspected. When all was said and done, it didn't seem that difficult. They skimmed the sand methodically in blocks fifty centimeters square, with perfectly synchronized movements. They scoured the ground for the tiniest length of wire poking through, then knelt to stroke the sand with the tips of their fingers and free any mines they found before calling Fabien. If everything went well, they cordoned off the checked areas with flax rope, dividing the beach into squares with braided fabric, creating a chessboard, and then they moved on.

Fabien had done his best to warn Vincent that the hardest part was maintaining concentration, but that was the first thing he lost. The silence, the slow footsteps, the monotony... How not to let your mind escape from this dawdling procession? This hypnotic, repetitive work?

It would take years to restore the shoreline's beauty and reinstate a mood of nonchalance to the Mediterranean, the legendary cradle of civilization, an Eden that the war had so quickly ravaged. Absurd enough to make a grown man weep. With these mines the war would never be over.

This wasn't the worst of it for Vincent. Now that he was doing the work, he realized it wasn't going to be as easy as he'd hoped to approach the Germans. The deminers and prisoners didn't mix. But it was only the start of the day, he mustn't despair.

Max suddenly raised his arm in warning. He'd just felt something with the tip of his bayonet. He could even have sworn he heard the characteristic spark of sound as the lance struck metal. A tiny clink that was completely inaudible under the sand, but that his imagination sent reverberating around his head with the same persistence as a funeral toll.

The whole group stopped as one. This was no time for talk. Confronted with danger, there were some who pretended not to be afraid, smiling and laughing exaggeratedly, and there were those who preferred to stay focused. There were some who couldn't help sweating profusely and would later put this down to the strong sun. And then there were those who crossed themselves surreptitiously, discreetly, some of them believers, others rediscovering a lost faith in the moment of truth.

With a lot of the men, it was impossible to know what they were thinking. There was Fabien, walking resolutely over to Max, and Max right by the mine, trying to stay calm and dignified, but who realized as he excavated the sand that this was a type of explosive he didn't recognize: a great long smooth surface on which it was impossible to locate the igniter. What the fuck was this thing? Max glanced around furtively to see where the guards were, as if to check there really was no means of escape, as if he too were a prisoner, like the Germans.

On a signal from Fabien, they all backed away the regulation twenty-five meters. Fabien stayed there alone with Max, who was trying to take a few small steps back himself; if the mine exploded, he'd be blown apart like Fabien, whether or not he'd backed away two or three paces.

"Doesn't look standard issue, this one," he said, justifying himself.

Fabien, still just as calm, waved Vincent over to explain the procedure.

"First of all, you have to see the whole mine, clear all around it, then work out where the trigger is. You have to do it gently, using your hands is best."

With his bare hands, Fabien swept softly around the contraption, which continued to emerge, a huge gleaming black shape in the wet sand, as implacable as a preprogrammed death.

The deminers may well have seen plenty before, but they were always awed by a mine looming out of the ground. As if each one had its own psychology and harbored a unique strategy to ensure their slaughter. This one was an unusual size. Far more imposing than anything they'd come across before.

As the mine emerged, the silence became more and more leaden. Max was particularly nervous because he was the one who'd found the mine, and because two minutes earlier he'd been talking to Manu...which meant he'd lowered his guard, paid less attention, so he could have been blown up along with the whole team. Like most of them, he fed himself the story of a lucky star. He hadn't set off the mine today, but he could see his lucky star as it really was—completely illusory.

Fabien had now been clearing around the explosive device for more than half an hour, and he'd far from finished. He alone had grasped what sort of adversary he was facing. "A sarcophagus mine!" he whispered to Vincent. And it suited its name: It had the grim outline of a coffin and was the same size.

∼

ON THIS BEACH, THEN, THERE WERE THE VAST terrifying contraptions that the deminers called sarcophaguses or tombs; devices that, like their namesakes, guaranteed a passage to the afterlife, except that anyone who died thanks to these particular sarcophaguses was rather less well preserved than Egyptian pharaohs.

These monsters, weighing in at more than 1,400 kilograms of steel and explosives, were spread out across the sand like mechanical sea lions, sprawling at leisure. Impossible to move. Now that the Germans had left, the sarcophagus mines stayed on thanks to their grueling inertia and their promise of merciless destruction.

Once the beast was revealed—powerful, arrogant, and ready to explode—you had to dig deeply around it to find the right angle to disarm it. But Fabien would prefer to entrust this final stage to more experienced munitions specialists. He wasn't sure he would get it, but he was going to ask for help from the army.

Fabien stood up and turned to the translator to explain the plan. Once the obese monster was neutralized, it would be wrapped in huge hemp straps, wound like the bandaging on a mummy. It would take several men to extricate the metal colossus from the ground, and they would then haul it overground using a system of pullies attached to a solid wooden crate. Building the crate was a job that was left to the Germans.

Meanwhile the deminers would continue checking over the rest of the beach. Fabien was prepared to bet that, from where they were now, the Germans had set mines in a strict grid pattern. The Germans always divided the ground up into regular squares, while the English and Americans introduced quirks that made demining more difficult.

So they needed to sweep the whole area for the munitions experts whom, Fabien hoped, the army would send. It was dangerous, and they needed to stay more focused than ever as they swam over such big sharks.

At the end of the day, they'd detected three more of these ruthless devices. They were still a long way from reaching the blockhouses that taunted them and that they would have to search cautiously to avoid whatever dangers were housed inside them.

Vincent watched the Germans assembling wooden beams to reinforce the crates.

How to talk to them? He'd have to get one on his own, but they stuck together. And how on earth would he identify one he could have an intelligible conversation with? Vincent was aware that if he approached the Germans, the other deminers would be completely baffled.

And why not? He despised the Germans too, all of them, including these former soldiers who were now keeping a low profile. And this loathing was irreversible, no accommodations were possible, with no exceptions. They thought they were the superior race, a race apart. An inhuman race capable of the unimaginable. But he needed to find a German who would trust him and could help him. His whole life depended on it.

He just needed to be patient and keep an eye out for any opportunity.

In captivity he'd dreamed endlessly about what he would do once he was free at last, how he would spend his first hours and, more particularly, his first nights. And now he was still being held back from moving on, from loving, from being free.

And yet he didn't regret being here: There was nothing else he could have done. He'd cleared only a tiny portion of the beach, barely a few square meters, but he could run his hands through the sand there with his fingers spread wide—there was nothing for them to catch on, the sand was clean, at least here in those few square meters, no longer dangerous.

He would have liked his life and his options to have been cleaned in the same way, and for the long threads of his memories to glide through his spread fingers in a wonderful, uncomplicated caress. If only it were possible to cleanse the past, to remove all its traps, and disarm all its ignitors waiting to explode.

Vincent could tell that mine clearance was going to completely consume him and channel his energies while he waited for answers that would take a while to materialize. He would move forward just like this, one step at a time and one square meter at a time. Surrounding each de-mined square meter with silk thread. He might even find a sort of serenity in it. And right now, that was all he asked to stop himself from losing his mind.

SOMETIMES THEY WERE THANKED. SPONTANE-ously. Warmly, even. As the men were packing away their equipment that day, a young woman and her husband gave them a basket of bread, wine, and olive oil. Two weeks earlier, Fabien and his team had cleared a road, which meant the couple could now reach their farm again. Touched by this grateful gesture, the head of the group took the basket and promised he would share it with his men. Except for the bottle of wine, he joked.

"We're not allowed alcohol," he then explained. "We're meant to stay sober."

"Even in the evening?"

"In theory, yes. Well, no one comes checking in the evenings, but during the day we need all our wits about us, believe me."

At this point another man came over to them. He looked anxious and awkward and clearly wanted to ask something of Fabien but didn't know how to go about it.

"I have a farm too, not far from theirs."

He stopped, hoping Fabien would understand. The first farmer came to his rescue.

"What Raoul's trying to say is his field's riddled with mines. He can't do anything with it. One of his cows was blown up and his dog. He wants you to come and clear it."

Fabien had several requests like this every week.

"I understand, but we can't, because of the regulations."

"How do you mean? You're here to clear mines, aren't you?"

"Yes, but *we* don't decide where. The ministry's given us priorities."

"The ministry isn't here, though! They don't see what's going on!"

"There's an overall plan: We start with things that everyone uses—roads, bridges, ports, beaches, key buildings…"

"What about Sundays?"

"Oh, on Sundays we have to rest. Not just our bodies. Our nerves too."

"Well, we work seven days a week, I can tell you. D'you think our animals rest on Sundays?"

"I know it's hard, but you'll have to be patient. We'll clear everywhere in the end."

"And when's 'the end,' then?" the farmer asked, then stepped closer to Fabien and lowered his voice to say, "I could pay you. It'd only need a couple of guys."

"Impossible," Fabien rejoined more firmly. "Two guys on their own would be dangerous. We'd be risking our jobs if we came. And our lives. Come on," he added, putting a hand on the man's shoulder, "we'll get to you as soon as we've done the rest."

Fabien hated having to say no. He was well aware of the hardship these smallholders were mired in when they could no longer work their land. But he just couldn't look out for everyone. He could see Hubert and even Manu listening intently to the farmer's offer. Fabien knew that some of his men were feeling the squeeze. Given that they were screwed either way, some wanted to go rogue and break the rules—quite a few had been doing it all their lives—and demine obsessively, every day and every night for the three or six months of their assignment, building up a nest egg and dreaming of a better life, one they'd earned. But couldn't be sure of.

The farmer wouldn't leave. He'd come with some friends who most likely wanted to make the same request. To demonstrate their disapproval, they spat at the Germans, then slung a few stones at them. No one reacted. After years of terror, everyone privately thought all was fair in love and war, as if anything was ever fair in war.

TUCKED INTO THE RECESS OF A DISUSED DOOR-
way in the wall opposite her house, Saskia had been waiting for the lights to go out. She didn't have a watch but
was good at gauging how much time passed. She waited
another hour. The whole wretched family must be asleep
by now. They wouldn't hear her.

She knew every detail of her garden wall and had
climbed over it enough as a teenager to know exactly
where the best spot was. She remembered each crevice,
each wobbly stone, where you could get a handhold, where
the ivy was strongest, the place where its trunk was thick
enough to hold on to before landing on the far side. This
wall was hers and it was going to help her.

Everything happened as she'd imagined it. The place
was steeped in darkness and the new moon stretched like
a narrow, glimmering parenthesis, too tenuous to light the
garden. Saskia knew her way around with her eyes closed.
She reached the pomegranate tree: This was where she
needed to dig.

She went about it with her bare hands, then with the
help of a stone. Her mother had buried the little box a few
days before they were arrested. She'd shown the whole
family to be sure they remembered. Saskia's father had

chided her for frightening the children—they were scattered about the four corners of town, who was going to find them?—but Mila had insisted.

On the train to the Camp des Milles near Aix-en-Provence, Saskia had noticed that a lot of people had brought their jewelry and fancy clothes with them, like shields. They'd been unceremoniously stripped of them as soon as they arrived. Had her mother anticipated this?

Mila had thought it all through. Anyone else would have buried the box under the chestnut tree or the Judas tree, for protection. But Mila wasn't just anyone. Nobody would guess that she'd chosen to bury treasure under a pomegranate shrub: It wasn't even a proper tree, just a bush, a luxuriant one, yes, but a muddled mass of branches barely the height of an adult. Her mother loved it precisely because of this modesty and cherished its discretion.

"You know," she'd told her daughters, "in Paradise it wasn't an apple that Eve bit into. There wasn't an apple tree. No, that would have been boring. In fact, in the oldest writings the real forbidden fruit that tempted Eve isn't named. But *I* know what it was: a pomegranate."

Saskia knew her mother was right. This sensual and mysterious fruit of desire that doesn't surrender its flesh easily, safeguarding its treasures inside its peel, the fruit that spurts and satisfies and quenches your thirst is a pomegranate. The color of sin has never been the straw white of an apple but red, a vermillion red, a passionate almost blue red, red and purple like blood, a red that springs out.

And there, sheltered under the shrub, Saskia heard the sound of metal against the stone: her mother's box. She continued to clear away the soil with her hands so as not to damage it.

All at once there was barking. It was coming from the house. The light went back on in a bedroom. Saskia could feel her heart galloping wildly. She worked away ineffectually at the dry compacted soil that resisted her efforts. Roots had wrapped themselves tightly around the metal case. When a first-floor light came on she hadn't yet finished extricating it. The door opened and the dog raced into the garden. Saskia abandoned her digging, ran to the wall, and climbed back over it.

Still frantic and with her heart pounding, she landed in the street, where she was blinded by a stark light trained on her eyes. She tried to run away but the bicycle caught up with her and its brakes screeched as it drew level with her. She felt a hand grasp her arm firmly and she shielded her face with her free arm.

Still dazzled by the headlamp, she took a while to make out the features of the man holding her. She recognized him. The man from the bus. The one who'd wanted to help her alight.

"I didn't do anything! Are you going to report me?"

"Not my style. Come on, jump on!"

Vincent hoisted her onto his bike and pedaled hastily away from the house, far from the dog that had been let out into the street and was barking at them.

As soon as they were a good distance away, he started pedaling more slowly and Saskia was able to explain herself.

"I'm not a thief."

"You can do what you want."

"It's true. It was my house!"

"Okay."

"Don't you believe me?"

"Of course I do. I do that myself when I leave home—send a dog chasing after me! Well, if I had a dog, that's what I'd do. Plus using the gate is just so boring."

"I'm not joking. It's my house. Some people moved in while we were...away."

"What were you planning to do?"

Saskia hesitated. She didn't know him. Could she trust him? He'd just trusted her and saved her from a difficult situation. What did she have to lose?

"I have nothing left. And my mother buried some jewelry in the garden. I started digging up the box, but I couldn't get it out because of the dog."

Vincent braked abruptly and made a resolute U-turn.

"Why didn't you say so before?"

"There's a dog—"

"They might find your jewelry box."

"What if they see us?"

"They'd never expect you to come back now."

"But if they do?"

"We'll cross that bridge if we get to it."

When the two of them were back in the garden, Saskia freeing the box and Vincent buttering up the dog, she wondered why he was helping her. But she had no choice. Everything she now owned was in that box, and it contained far more than jewelry; it represented the foresight that only her mother had had, her wild hope that all would never be lost and that—even if she, Mila, had to die—she could help those who survived. Saskia needed to be worthy of this powerful message and this gift that came to her from beyond the grave. With all her strength and all her love, Mila had wanted Saskia to live, to come through it, and Saskia now clutched to her the treasure that had been buried beneath the tree of a lost paradise.

VINCENT GAVE SASKIA A LIFT ON HIS BIKE BACK to his lodgings. Without asking her opinion, he spontaneously opened the rickety wooden gate and stepped aside to let her through. She stiffened.

"I don't think that—"

"Do you know somewhere to go?"

The last few nights Saskia had sheltered under the steps that led down to the beach. She'd thought it the best place to avoid seeing anyone. Who would think to venture there? During the daytime she'd seen the deminers at work and watched the routes they took, and she'd tried to convince herself that here, in the cramped space under the steps, she should theoretically be safe. She hadn't slept at all. She'd thought about her murdered family, her brother and sister and their truncated lives, their talents laid waste, about what she'd been through with them, what she found out about them and all their love, to the very end. As children they'd always said they would be there for one another, forever. And there under those steps, kept awake right through till morning by the whispering of the sea and the wind, she had once again—as she had on every previous night and as she would on every night still to come—experienced the painful realization of just how final it all was. The damage was irreparable.

Vincent felt as if he were waking her when he reiterated his invitation.

"So? Do you know somewhere to go?"

"I wouldn't want you to think..."

"I don't think anything, but I've a tiny room that I don't use. If you want to sleep here tonight, you can make some decisions in the morning."

To sleep, just for a night...yes, and stop all the thinking.

Everything inside the studio appealed to her. Its blissful simplicity and the purity of its white walls. Vincent offered her something to eat and she shook her head: Eating wasn't easy and could harm her. All the same, he put a few things on the table: two plates, two glasses, some bread, a bottle of olive oil, and some goat cheese that Mathilde had left for him. He tore off rough slices of bread and poured a thin stream of golden oil onto each piece. He handed her share to her. Watching her eat made him smile without realizing it, even though she nibbled at it painstakingly, taking small mouthfuls.

"Now that we're accomplices, you can tell me the whole story if you want."

"It's...complicated."

"You can also send me packing and go to bed. And anyway, you probably want to look at all the memories in that box."

Saskia froze. Was he putting her up for the night just for what was inside the box? When her family had been arrested, Saskia had been wearing a very fine chain as a bracelet. She'd miraculously managed to keep it until Birkenau, using endless different strategies, hiding it under her feet or in her mouth. And then one day she'd confided this secret. It was after her sister and mother had died. She needed a friend and friendships are sealed only with a secret. Her bracelet disappeared that night.

Absolutely anything can happen while you're asleep. Nighttime was dangerous. Girls in the camp had sometimes attracted the attention of the SS, the ones who didn't think it beneath them to rape a Jewish woman. You had to protect yourself from them. She instinctively hunched over and pulled at her flimsy cardigan to close it across her body.

Vincent sensed her discomfort.

"The best thing would be for you to go and get some rest. You needn't be afraid of me. There's a woman I love. Passionately."

Saskia knew she wouldn't lower her guard, but she still felt relieved.

"Won't she mind if I sleep here?"

"I don't think so."

She didn't dare ask more.

In the bedroom she found a mattress on the floor and a sheet. The mattress was a good one filled with horse-hair. Plump and welcoming. When she sat down on it, she felt all her resistance melt away. She was going to sleep alone, not clumped together with other bodies, not forced into a lack of privacy she'd loathed, and she would be on a mattress that looked clean and reminded her of her old life.

She pushed the only piece of furniture in the room, a small table, in front of the door, not that it would last long if anyone tried to come in, but it was something. She noticed a pile of newspapers and tore up a few of them, then folded the pages into a tight wad that she wedged between the door and the floorboards. That would stall anyone trying to open it by, say, two minutes, enough time to get organized and perhaps escape through the window, even though the thought terrified her. She checked: It opened onto roofs. She also pushed the mattress against the table, which meant she would get advance warning of any attempted break-ins. It was laughable, but it would have been far worse to do nothing.

Somewhat relieved by this latest idea, she now decided to open her mother's jewelry box. She carefully took out all the jewelry, fine necklaces, rings that had once belonged to Mila's mother, precious bracelets that she'd longed to wear to high school. She'd begged her mother, then her father to get him to persuade her mother, but in vain. Now she would have loved her mother to forbid her wearing the bracelets to avoid making anyone else envious. But even in this finery, who would be envious of her in her present state?

She put on all the jewelry. All of it, one piece after another. It smothered her but she had to. If she were ever threatened again, this is what she would do. She wouldn't wait. She'd escape overnight with all her jewels. Her mother's, her sister's, and her own. Her father's signet ring, the chain bracelet her brother had been given when he was born. The truth was they were modest items but their value to her was beyond measure. She was wearing a small part of the people she loved, wearing it close to her skin, warming it with the blood vessels that throbbed at her wrists and in her neck. Yes, inanimate objects do have a soul. Obviously. How could anyone doubt it? She hadn't known this when she'd studied Lamartine, and she would never have guessed that that line of poetry had any meaning, except for in an overexuberant way, but now she was convinced of it as she felt the glow radiating from filigreed gold, a medal, a tiny sapphire. The signet ring established a magical connection with her father, and she hoped that, wherever he was, he was happy she was wearing it. It was too big and swiveled around her thin finger, but she clenched her fist and it stopped turning. How could her mother have thought she could sell this beloved jewelry to survive? She would never part with it. She'd find other solutions.

She wished that, as well as the jewelry, her mother had put a letter into the box, words that Saskia could have clung to like the ones she used to slip into books, a letter that would have acted as her guide, would have explained everything to her, and would have consoled her. But Mila hadn't done that. Of course, she'd talked to her daughters in the camp, every day, until her last breath. But Saskia felt her mother could have taught her a thousand more secrets, she could have prepared her to be stronger, and not to miss her. Mila's words and thoughts, her passing on everything she knew and all her love...how could Saskia live without this? When we lose someone we love, two feelings descend on us simultaneously: the pain of not having had enough time with them, and the certainty that this insufficiency can now never be remedied.

VINCENT WOKE AT DAWN AND WAS SURPRISED to hear a door open—Saskia. And the sound of bare feet on the floor tiles reminded him of other bare feet in the summer on terra-cotta floors. The soft elastic sound as the sole of a foot peels away from the smooth, cool mosaic, a noise that's forgotten in winter but returns in spring to remind us that our bodies can be free in the summer.

Before the war, morning had been his favorite time of day, when he was lucky enough to wake beside Ariane, and could kiss her as the sun flooded in over the bed and its linen sheets; a moment suspended in time, his face slightly rumpled, his movements still clumsy, his thoughts not fully formed, and the joy of the day to come. More than anything else, he wanted to have mornings like that again. In the camp, he'd loathed mornings, because he loathed every day that lay ahead and only ever found respite deep in the night when everyone was asleep.

Saskia appeared in the kitchen, a shy, fragile figure. He was making some coffee with the ersatz version he'd managed to find in the cupboard. Nicely arranged on the table were the bread and olive oil—because that was all there was—along with two plates and two glasses.

"Early bird! Did you not sleep well?"

"I'm used to waking early," she replied when, in fact, she hadn't slept at all.

Vincent stayed standing to drink his cup of chicory.

"If you like, you can stay here while you try to get your house back. It's no trouble for me. I'm not here much."

"Thank you, but...what will people think?"

"Who gives a damn what people think these days!"

Of course, if she weren't so tired, she should have thought this too. In fact, what she most wanted to know was what *he* thought. But he was inviting her to stay so, for now, she should take that to mean he thought well of her. She accepted with a smile—the first on her face in a long time. She was surprised she could still do it without thinking. It struck her that she had clearer memories of the bumps on her childhood garden wall than of how to express gratitude to someone without uttering a word.

"Can I ask you something?"

Vincent nodded while he poured himself another cup of substitute coffee.

"I saw you on the beach, demining...Why do you risk your life like that? Wasn't the war enough for you?"

Vincent shrugged, as if it meant nothing to him.

"Does your girlfriend know?"

He hadn't thought of this, and that irked him. He ducked the question.

"I'll let the owner know that you'll be staying for a while."

"Don't you think she'll be angry with you when she finds out?" Saskia persevered.

He wasn't ready to think about this.

"I haven't asked you your name," he said, as if he hadn't overheard it on the bus.

"Saskia."

"Saskia?"

"It was Rembrandt's wife's name. My mother really liked his work."

"It's very pretty. Don't wait for me this evening, I'll be back late. I'll leave you the keys."

The cat was mewing at the door. Vincent let him in and then left straightaway. Mathilde was out in the street, trimming a wisteria that was desperate to spill over the sidewalk. Humans had been diminished but plants, no longer endlessly fussed over by the inhabitants, had broken free.

Vincent crossed the street toward Mathilde and she nodded as he explained the situation. He didn't know her well and couldn't yet identify what her half smile meant.

"Well, I think that's perfect! Thanks for letting me know."

Mathilde sure was full of surprises. A little taken aback that she hadn't asked any questions, he assumed he could leave, but she hadn't finished with him.

"It's good, we need to look after the living."

Struck by Mathilde's directness, he didn't know how to reply. He'd taken Saskia in without a second thought. Or rather, he'd offered what Ariane would have done quite naturally. And perhaps he would have too, given that he and Ariane always agreed on everything and, before the war, he'd been just as alive as she had been.

"We're all basically the same now," Mathilde continued. "We have our dead and we wish it was possible to go back to the old world. And we need to learn to live now…"

Vincent let her talk and then took his leave. Her words wormed their way insidiously into his thoughts. Yes, they probably all were the same, Saskia, Mathilde, Fabien, and all the men he would meet up with demining the beach. Each of them had their dead, people they cherished, begged, implored, and still loved, but he was different. He wasn't living for the dead, he was living for Ariane. He didn't need to learn how to live now. What was the point? So long as he didn't know where she was, he didn't give a damn about anything, about now or the old world or the new one.

WITH THE ADVANCE ON HIS SALARY THAT FA-
bien had secured for him, Vincent had bought chemicals
for developing photos, and Audrey was now preparing the
hydroquinone bath for the negatives in her apartment.
Vincent noticed that her films were made by Agfa...
German.

"Where did you get them?"

Audrey swept the question aside with a curl of her lip.

"Did the Germans give them to you?" Vincent persisted.

"Of course not, I bought it on the black market!"

Vincent acknowledged this possibility. Everything
struck him as suspect—he needed to calm down.

Audrey had set up a studio area in the corner of her
bedroom. Together they blacked out the window with
blankets, and their coordinated moves working to create
darkness, as she might have done with a lover, were torture for her. She slipped her negatives into the bath.

Vincent had to pretend to be interested in the hodge-
podge of snaps of men and women. The photos were simple, but they had a unique way of capturing expressions,
tense faces that should never have been so sorely tested
and so lucid but that you very often saw amid the torment
of war.

On one of those white rectangles a face appeared casually: Ariane.

Revealed by the chemicals in the bath, she looked supernatural, an evanescent Ophelia floating near the surface. When her features became clearer, her skin darker, and her eyes blacker, when the photo appeared in its full precision and entirety, Vincent realized the unthinkable: Ariane had cut her hair short.

Another photo in the same bath showed the radical nape of her neck in all its perfection.

This sharp haircut made her look unfamiliar to him, gave her something he couldn't quite identify, a quirkiness. She'd carried on living, without him, while he had lived only for her.

The more photos Audrey developed, the more distressed Vincent felt. He became obsessed with that insolent neck as if it were a sign of something he absolutely must decipher to understand the enigma of the woman he loved.

The photos of soldiers who came to requisition supplies at Ariane's parents' farm distracted him from these private speculations. The Germans had been perfectly relaxed as they posed for Audrey's camera. They were out visiting their colony and honoring the locals with their presence. Vincent found this even more repulsive. Did the Germans really think the French enjoyed their company?

Audrey described the dangerous game that Ariane had been forced to play—and to play it astutely because some of the Germans weren't fooled. At first, she'd acted shocked to see them there and had been reluctant to serve them, but not too much for fear of eliciting even tougher demands. This had established her baseline authenticity. Then she gradually let slip signs that she was starting to like them. Over time, they began to believe this. Once she'd been through this preamble, she could smile at them, possibly even laugh at their jokes, and not for a moment would they guess the hatred they inspired in her. They were so convinced that they were living gods!

"I know that game..."

Vincent had had to play it too. He knew the rules better than anyone. And he was planning to apply them again with the prisoners.

Audrey was now clipping the photos of the Germans onto a line to dry. Vincent hoped that among the soldiers he would recognize one of the prisoners who worked on mine clearing. Would that be possible? The prisoners he spent time with in Hyères no longer had these slick haircuts, the same panache. Their faces were altered by weariness, whereas in Audrey's photos their features were animated and their eyes shone with the happy conviction that they were entitled to everything and could reign over the world.

Stripped of their uniforms and their power, the Germans had shriveled. Under the southern sun, the deminers' skin took on a triumphant gleam, while the prisoners' skin withered and burned and spoiled. Their faces aged at a dizzying rate, and their eyes darkened. Even the natural world seemed to be hostile toward them and exacting revenge. The sun, the wind, and the sea air had cooked up a conspiracy to accelerate the destruction of the soldiers who had wreaked such long-term damage on the world.

"I'm struggling to remember their names. I think this one was called Klaus. And he was Kurt. That one was Frantz... I'm really sorry, I've forgotten, I'm jumbling them up."

"Was there one that Ariane was especially wary of?"

Looking at the photos, Audrey started to remember.

"Some of them were very respectful, you know. Others, obviously—"

"Like who?"

"When everyone was dying of hunger, I saw one of them take the farm's entire reserve of butter. Then he casually ordered someone to grease his vehicle's axel with it! Can you imagine. Another one gobbled down ten eggs in one sitting, just like that, out of nowhere, in front of everyone. For obvious reasons, I didn't dare take photos of them—"

"That's not what I mean, Audrey! I want to know if there was one who tried to seduce her, who wouldn't give up and scared her."

Audrey hesitated, then told him that they all used to try to get a smile, a date. And Ariane didn't look away bashfully—she quashed them. She would always be in a hurry, and where her blouse was unbuttoned at the neck it afforded glimpses of a cross in tiny pearls that she constantly fingered. Even if the Germans didn't respect anything, she just wanted to come across as pious and boring.

"Audrey, come on, did she never tell you which one she was more scared of than the others?"

"You know what she's like, she didn't want anyone worrying about her."

By serving all those soldiers, Ariane had been exposed to the front line, and Vincent was horrified by the flimsy self-protection strategies she and all the other women had used. He tried another tack.

"Who did Ariane get along with?"

Audrey showed him a picture of a slender young man with a fine-featured face and a disarming expression. It seemed completely absurd that he'd had to put on a uniform.

"Him. He was a musician before the war. One time he surprised Ariane by bringing a violin to the farm. It was timeless, like a pocket of time nothing to do with the war. And suddenly we had beauty in our lives again, we came back to life. But the others treated him badly. It was horrible."

Vincent studied the photo: He looked like a teenager. This couldn't be him, the ally Ariane had mentioned, the one who could have protected her from danger.

"You really can't think who she could have put her trust in? Who kept an eye out for her?"

"Apart from him, I can't think of anyone."

Vincent was getting nowhere. He wanted to break away from those dark times and be woken by the salty winds in Marseille's Old Port. He left with the photo of Ariane and her boyish crop, the photos of the Germans, and more and more questions.

Audrey accompanied him to the door and as they reached the second-floor landing, they met a woman returning to her apartment with all her suitcases. She greeted Audrey and gave Vincent a kindly smile, thinking he must be her fiancé.

"He's a friend," Audrey corrected her. "We were in the same group of friends before the war, with Irène, Ariane, and a few others."

The woman's face clouded at the mention of Ariane.

"Oh, Ariane…"

Vincent reacted immediately.

"Did you know her?"

"She came to see my husband. He was a doctor."

"Do you know why?"

The woman hesitated before replying, regretted having said too much.

"She wanted to ask him for something…and he had to refuse."

Vincent looked at Audrey questioningly, but she was dumbfounded.

"What are you talking about?" she asked.

The doctor's wife seemed to haul herself away from a punishing memory.

"I shouldn't have…We owe our patients the strictest confidentiality. And I owe it to my husband…even if he's no longer with us."

"I'm so sorry," Audrey said.

Vincent didn't have time for condolences. He was in purgatory. Was this woman sadistic or just thoughtless? Audrey decided to appeal to her better nature.

"I understand that you have to respect patient confidentiality and you don't want to betray your husband, but Ariane's disappeared—"

"We're desperate."

"What's to say you won't feel worse when you know?" the doctor's wife asked.

Vincent couldn't take any more and the woman could tell. Neither could Audrey so she kept going.

"The worst of it is not knowing," she said.

"Well, I did warn you...she wanted my husband to give her digitalis. But he wasn't fooled."

Vincent's anxiety escalated further.

"How do you mean fooled? Maybe she found out she had a heart problem!"

"So why didn't she want my husband to examine her?"

"Ariane had done her residency. She could make her own diagnosis and—"

"And ask for a dose that could just as easily cure her as kill her? I'm sure you know that the same dosage of digitalis can be remedial or lethal."

Of course, he knew. But he couldn't answer and think at the same time. And the doctor's wife, who hadn't wanted to talk, now couldn't stop.

"She was strange, very agitated, almost incoherent. She came back several times. She even snuck into the office once after the last consultation to try to steal some from the cabinet."

Audrey tried to reason with the woman, but she kept on talking.

"She wanted to kill someone. For sure. Perhaps she wanted to kill herself!"

Ariane wanted to die? All the hypotheses that Vincent had envisioned had left no room for this one.

Audrey brought an end to the conversation and her neighbor's flights of fancy, and led Vincent outside.

He was pale and silent. His mind was racing toward other theories for his own protection. It was wrong to demonize digitalis: This substance extracted from foxglove was a miracle heart treatment. Ariane may have wanted to treat someone who couldn't afford it. Or needed to hide. If she'd been sick herself, she wouldn't have let herself die. She would have fought.

But what if she'd wanted to kill someone? Yes, it was possible. The soldier who was terrorizing her. Or someone else. Ariane had always been brave. With the necessary recklessness to be courageous. Obviously, she could have wanted to kill a Nazi occupier. That was more the sort of thing to imagine. Had she paid for this with her life? She would have planned everything to try to stay alive.

Every time he tiptoed close to the theory that she could be dead, he backed away from it as quickly as possible. Because if there was any chance, however tiny, that Ariane was still alive, he absolutely mustn't give up hope, not now, and he must keep searching for her. He owed it to her, and to their love, the magnificent, secret, abruptly interrupted love that they'd shared; he owed it to that luck, that privilege.

And yet a shadow hovered over his reasoning. They'd both faced ordeals they could never have imagined while they'd secretly swum together in their cove. He himself had changed shockingly in captivity. What did he know of the woman she'd become?

VINCENT'S MIND WAS NO LONGER ON WHAT HE was doing on the beach. He was the boxer who has a delayed blackout several hours after being struck the fatal blow: He walks out of the ring and it's only that evening, during the celebrations in his honor, that he collapses.

He was haunted by the notion that Ariane could have killed herself. He'd rejected this theory the day before, but he'd been woken by a nightmare in the middle of the night and hadn't stopped thinking about it since. By morning, he was no longer looking for the German who would help him find Ariane, but for the German he was going to kill.

His entire body, which had burned with desire for Ariane's body while he was in the camp, now burned with a longing for revenge. He couldn't live in a world in which Ariane had been harmed, damaged, killed, or driven to suicide as he was starting to envision. Life couldn't just return to normal as if nothing had happened. Anyone who believes that the courts should settle things rather than individuals knows perfectly well that justice is simply a hypocritical, regulated version of raw vengeance. Not to mention the mistakes it makes. Why delegate?

He would never have reasoned like this before the war, but now everything seemed clear to him. Retaliating meant not giving up, it meant single-handedly accepting the consequences of his actions, taking every risk for himself, it meant honoring their love, declaring war on destiny, and joining the ranks of those who act rather than those who sit and wait.

Fabien was watching Vincent. His jerking movements and distracted manner would almost have been funny if this hadn't been a question of life and death. He saw him trip once, twice. On the third time, Fabien decided to bring forward their lunch break. His men were surprised but delighted, reverting to schoolboys when the bell rings for recess.

While they took out their packs of Gitanes before reaching for their plates, Fabien took Vincent to one side.

"Listen, Vincent, you can talk to me. If I can do anything to help…"

"I'm fine. I just didn't sleep well."

"You're putting the team in danger."

"I'll pull myself together."

"No, you can take the day off. We'll say you're sick."

"Look, I need to work, Fabien. I really need to."

Fabien thought quickly. He couldn't devote all his time to Vincent. A team, even made up of experienced men, is a family. Everyone has a right to the same attention.

"Let's see how things are after lunch. If you're no better, you're going home."

The town hall had set up some trestle tables for their meals. Fabien and Vincent joined the other men, who were laughing and talking loudly. Fabien hoped the group and its team spirit would help Vincent get a grip on himself.

Within two minutes, the deminers had shaken off the tension that weighed on their shoulders. Some of them stood to call out to a coworker at the far end of the table, occasionally they even sang. The most impressive of them was Enzo. Everyone said he had a good pair of lungs. He also had talent. He intoned "Una furtiva lagrima" in his tenor voice, and all the other men had tears in their eyes. They laughed and tried to join in, even when Enzo came to "Cielo! Si può morir!" which they all sang very badly, particularly because they were laughing so hard.

Perhaps they would soon forget it, but for now every minute mattered, every mouthful of bread was a feast, every look exchanged, a moment of intense brotherhood. The war had taught them this. They weren't allowed to drink alcohol, but the fresh air was enough for them. And singing. And talking.

During the Occupation, it had been the Germans who talked in public, who gave orders and shouted and made their presence felt. The French stopped voicing opinions; they replied if they were asked something, but could no longer argue, protest, object, stake a claim. Speech was no longer free. People had to be careful what they said—in front of the Germans but also in front of one another. The spoken word could betray, it could condemn. It had lost all its joy.

Now people could say what they wanted in front of who they wanted and have nothing to fear. They laughed about the Germans and, when they were feeling good, even laughed at themselves. Talking made people happy again. It could be enjoyed at any time, while they ate, when they drank, talking with friends was the spice of life.

Over on the far side, next to the crates that they were building, the Germans sat on the ground eating without exchanging a word. Yes, they were doing the same work, but that was the deal, it was their turn to carry a shame that keeps your head lowered and your mouth shut.

And they were particularly keen to stay silent that day. The prisoner who'd made everyone—including the Germans—laugh because he'd ducked out of demining by claiming he was ill had killed himself the night before. Without a sound. Without disturbing anyone. The guards and other prisoners didn't realize until dawn. Everyone had jeered at his lack of courage, but he'd had the courage to decide his own death. And none of the deminers wanted to talk about it. They may not even have known. Not that it was the first time a prisoner had taken his own life, but what did that matter?

Lukas saw it as an incontestable sign that he needed to escape. He too had thought a lot about suicide. But somewhere he had a son he would do anything to find, and this son who knew nothing of war might be able to love him as a normal father who might never have been German or a prisoner.

He couldn't bring himself to eat. He looked over at the bunkers. Like Fabien, he couldn't wait to reach them. Inside them was his grail: American grenades that the Germans had stolen from the Resistance and for which he had high hopes. When you took the pin out, they let off clouds of blinding white smoke that stung the eyes. Perfect circumstances for disappearing. No one would be able to follow him in that thick fog of tear gas. He knew exactly where they were. If he was to make it to the little fort, he mustn't let Fabien suspect him. Or better, he must secure his trust. And Lukas knew how to do that.

At the end of the day when the Germans were about to climb into the truck and return to their camp, some locals turned on them. As often happened, they spat at the prisoners and insulted them. But this time, although he couldn't tell exactly what was going on, Fabien noticed an unusual amount of commotion, like a cockfight, goaded on by laughing, clapping, shouts of encouragement from passersby and the few deminers who'd reached the road ahead of the others. At the back of the truck a tight circle had formed around the scene of the fighting. It was impossible to see the prisoners now. Fabien and Vincent both ran over to the truck. They then spotted the smallholder who'd come to ask them to demine his field. Out of sheer frustration he was taking it out on the Germans.

He lashed out at them haphazardly with a rifle which, if it had been loaded, could have killed anyone, French and German alike, deminer, prisoner, passerby, or farmer. He'd been drinking and was sobbing, and no one intervened, out of fear but also because he was enacting what everyone around him had always wanted to do: Lynching the Germans just as they had lynched, massacred, hanged, machine-gunned, raped, burned, executed, terrorized, and tortured. At last! About time they paid their dues for all that. No, no one pitied these prisoners who, only yesterday, were still parading around in uniform. Everyone hated them and would continue to do so until the end of days.

And yet these prisoners submitted to everything that was asked of them. True, they sometimes tried to escape, or they took their own lives, but they didn't rebel. They worked hard, unsparingly, conscientiously. Everyone thought this was only natural, the least they could do, and it was a good thing they were helping rebuild and repair what they'd destroyed. But it wasn't enough. The crowd that was growing around the original circle would have liked to see them work themselves to death, dying in the most appalling agony, endlessly begging forgiveness. And for them to die but not find rest or peace. Because even death wouldn't be enough. Ever. The crowd wanted to stone them, crush them, bury them under rubble, annihilate them over several generations, and once they were dead, the crowd would demand that their enslaved ghosts rise up and continue to work tirelessly, putting France back on her feet again.

So when they saw this poor smallholder—and some of them knew him, they called him Raoul—all the people who'd spontaneously gathered to watch the altercation couldn't fail to encourage him. If he killed a German, it would be legitimate defense after the fact. And it wouldn't be doing any harm, quite the opposite. Who would ever criticize him for it?

Fabien persuaded the men to back off one by one to break up the frenzied crowd that was still massing around the farmer and a German who'd tripped. The prisoner was on the ground and Raoul was strenuously pummeling him with all the energy of his despair amid spiteful encouragement from the onlookers. The prisoner was curled up into a ball, not defending himself. Fabien and Vincent could see only his bloodred back and his dirty blond hair.

The situation was complex because of the shotgun. Fabien tried to drive back the furious farmer's last few supporters, but that only aggravated their rage.

It was then that Vincent stepped between the farmer and the German. He'd recognized Lukas, although he didn't know his name. Lukas was a choice target: Blond with blue eyes and a face structured by high cheekbones, a straight nose, and a square jaw, a body sculpted like a statue by Arno Breker—he was the caricature of an Aryan seen in propaganda. Of course, skinny as he was and in his prison-issue clothes that were falling apart and his dilapidated shoes he was a far cry from representations of a sporting god, but there was certainly no mistaking what he was.

Fabien made the most of Vincent's brave—insane—intervention to disarm the farmer and drag him away.

Vincent extended a hand to the German to help him up. Lukas was surprised; it was probably the first time a Frenchman had looked him in the eye. And he was speaking to him in German without exaggerating each word and waving his hands about, which was what the others did, the ones who'd only half learned German at school or during the Occupation and made fools of themselves while implying their occupiers were half-wits.

Lukas should have been grateful but—and this was another habit from the war—he was wary. He couldn't believe the Frenchman was doing this without a motive. Although there wasn't much to be gained from a prisoner. What did Lukas have to offer him?

Lukas could have replied in French, but keeping his secret made him slightly less vulnerable. And it might help him with his escape plan.

Vincent couldn't take the exchange any further: The guards were already using the lull to yank Lukas by the shoulder and bundle him into the back of the truck. They were now running late and were in a hurry to get home.

"Hell of a day," said Fabien, returning to where Vincent was. "Are you coming for a drink?"

As they passed the people whom Fabien had driven back from the wildcat fight, Vincent felt the full weight of the incomprehension in their eyes. Helping a German was almost an act of collaboration. Although it wasn't an occupier that he'd helped but a prisoner. And that reaped no kind of reward. Except for the way the crowd was looking at him now.

∼

IT WAS WORSE IN THE CAFÉ. OTHER THAN FABIEN, few of the men viewed Vincent with the same goodwill as on the first day. The verbal attack wasn't long coming.

"So you don't have a problem helping a Boche, then?"

"I'd have had a problem if he'd been killed in front of me and I hadn't done anything."

Max, Thibault, and Enzo took their glasses, stood up, and moved to the next table. Fabien raised his voice, a rare occurrence, and called everyone to order.

"This work's tough enough as it is, if we start fighting among ourselves, it's not going to help!"

"I thought we were all in agreement about—"

"We're all in agreement about demining and putting this country together again, not about behaving like criminals, otherwise we're no better than the Germans."

"Oh, come on, he wasn't going to kill him!"

"There aren't that many of us, even counting the prisoners. If they're not here to help us tomorrow, we'll never finish this demining."

"It's not a joke, then? The Krauts might leave?"

Vincent held his breath. Fabien clearly had some news and hadn't had a chance to pass it on to him. And he was probably aware of how interested Vincent was in the subject.

"Apart from the army and Raymond Aubrac, nobody gives a damn about the prisoners. Not Dautry, who's the minister of reconstruction, or Bidault, the foreign minister."

"What do they want?"

"They want the mines to be cleared in record time but with no personnel to achieve that."

"Taking the prisoners away from us would be just great!" Georges exclaimed with exasperated sarcasm.

"We're not *supposed* to employ them at all," Fabien reminded him.

"Really? But there's even talk of putting them in factories! And coal mines. It makes me mad: Bosses will have a free and totally exploitable workforce, and nobody will say a word against it!" Max protested, fueled by his party's concerns.

"But if we don't have them, who's going to walk along the roads and over the beaches when we've finished the job?" Manu asked anxiously.

It was one of the most dangerous phases in mine clearance. Despite all the protocols, despite every possible imaginable precaution, you could never be sure there were absolutely no mines left after demining. What they needed was tanks, but those were being used elsewhere. And no farmers wanted to sacrifice their livestock. So the prisoners were sent out. And everyone blazed through a cigarette and thought about something else. Because as much as they hated the Germans, seeing someone blown up by a mine was never a pretty sight. They'd lost a lot of Germans like that. It was a tricky subject. But they all agreed on one thing, and Thibault articulated it.

"It's for them to do! I refuse to."

Fabien looked at him wryly.

"I don't understand. Five minutes ago, you were happy to get them off our hands with the butt of a shotgun, and now you'd be sorry if they weren't here?"

Fabien was standing by the table to which the mutineers had retreated. He brought them back into line.

"Okay, we don't like them. But you have to remember we don't have the worst of them with us here. Can we agree on that? The war criminals were winkled out to stand trial."

"D'you really think they found all the war criminals?" Enzo asked. "And there are none hiding among the prisoners?"

"And anyway, the way I see it, all Germans are war criminals," Max added.

"And I would remind you that some soldiers are civilians and never asked to be here," Fabien said.

"To think you were in the Resistance!"

"In the Resistance we fought the Germans but also Vichy France. It's not always straightforward."

Fabien caught the waiter's eye to place their order and bring the conversation to a close after a final cautionary reminder.

"Here's what I think: We're here to clear mines so that everyone can get back to normal without risking their lives with every step they take. You're brave but there aren't enough of you. We need the Germans. So let's all calm down, getting wound up doesn't achieve anything."

The waiter arrived just at the right moment, and Vincent was relieved that Fabien's intervention had deflected the conversation away from him.

When the two men headed home together at the end of the evening, he thanked Fabien, who admitted he'd been glad an opportunity had come up to set a few things straight. He even allowed himself to share a more personal opinion, something he most likely wouldn't have confided to the rest of the team.

"I hate the Germans, but sometimes I hate the way some of our guys look at them even more."

"It's hard to criticize them for feeling like that. The Boche really are the dregs of humanity," Vincent replied, hoping to bury the fact that he'd broken one of the group's unwritten laws by talking to a German.

"Yes. But...you know, apart from Enzo, the guys on the team haven't all been great role models. Who knows, we could even have some who took advantage of the general chaos. If you dig deep enough, we're sure to have some informers, some antisemites—statistically, we can't not. They don't see themselves as the dregs of humanity, but I'm sure you'll agree they're not the cream either. We've also got guys who did fuck all, didn't help, just waited for the storm to pass. And waiting for a storm to pass means allowing the storm to rage."

They continued in silence for a while, Vincent pushing his bike and Fabien walking beside him. It was a warm night. It would have been glorious if they didn't have to clear mines in the morning.

Vincent asked why he'd chosen demining, and Fabien thought a while before replying.

"After the south was liberated, de Gaulle came to see the Resistance of the Interior and asked us to enlist alongside the Allies for the campaign in Germany. He said it would be a continuation of our commitment to resistance."

"Hmm," said Vincent, "what he mostly wanted was for France to have some of her own dead so that he could sit at the negotiating table with the others."

"Exactly. I don't really like being told what to do. It was a good thing he was here because, no two ways about it, if I was going to die it might as well be on home territory. So I put up my resistance here. Especially as since then we've seen what he thinks of us. Oh, there's plenty of talk about the Normandy landings! But there was hardly a single Frenchman involved. There's less talk about the Provence landings, when we were very much here, we did all the groundwork, joined forces, and recaptured towns. But hey, that wasn't de Gaulle's landing, so he kept nice and quiet about it…"

There were things Fabien was telling him and things he wasn't telling him. Vincent felt he was confiding in him but not saying everything, and there was some other reason for his commitment to mine clearance. But he didn't press the point.

They walked past the beach, which by night regained some of its eerie beauty. They watched the sea in silence. Fabien had noticed that Vincent wasn't one to try to impress the girls in the café, and guessed that he too had some absent woman who filled his thoughts. So, after a while he started talking about Odette.

He'd met her at college in Aix-en-Provence, where she was doing a triple major in math, physics, and chemistry. She'd given it all up without a second thought so that she could systematically sabotage the Germans who were swaggering around Marseille.

She'd been arrested once, but on that occasion the Germans found nothing on her and let her go. From then on, she'd worn her calm smile with all the conviction of an Ausweis, a German ID card. One day she didn't come home.

After waiting more than three months, Fabien had to face the unbearable fact that he would never see Odette again. He went back underground: The strong kinship within the Resistance network became his center of gravity and his source of strength.

When the fighting ended, returning to a normal life without Odette was unendurable. He felt he was becoming a diluted version of himself. In demining he rediscovered the adrenaline of his former life. To answer Vincent's question and to be completely honest, that was why he did it. People thought he was strong, but he hadn't been able to protect one of the two people he loved most in the world. Demining stopped him thinking about that.

One of the two people, Fabien said, but he didn't talk about the other. He was maintaining his mystery. There was no denying how much Vincent liked him. He envied the way Fabien could come out and say the things that made him terribly vulnerable and keep to himself others he didn't want to discuss. He understood the humility that this took and how much trust Fabien was putting in him.

When they parted, Fabien gave him a few ration tickets in advance, they might be of help. He didn't resent Vincent for helping the German, and their conversation had crystallized his thoughts. He was under no illusion that a little speech could bury the animosity between the two camps, but at least if there wasn't such palpitating incandescent hatred in the group, a force he could almost visualize like the air shimmering above an asphalt road in the heat of the midday sun, then they'd be okay.

But despite his best intentions, Fabien advised Vincent to avoid talking to the prisoners again. Frankly, for the sake of the team, it was for the best.

LIKE THE CONTINGENT OF PRISONERS, VINCENT arrived on the beach early. He didn't want Fabien to catch him approaching Lukas and offering him a cigarette.

He took Lukas to one side and quickly got to the point.

"Tell me, were you at the Château des Eyguières during the war?"

Lukas didn't want to admit he'd had accommodation at the Wehrmacht's headquarters. Yes, he'd been forcibly enlisted, but who paid any attention to that? He was afraid of this peacetime arbitrariness, of the summary justice that comes just after a defeat.

"What's the Château des Eyguières?"

"The place you spent part of the war. Why are you lying?"

"Ah. That's not what we called it."

Lukas could see that his feeble explanation hadn't worked, but Vincent seemed conciliatory.

"Look, I can see why you're wary of me. You're not always treated well here."

"It's only natural, we're prisoners," Lukas conceded.

They each advanced their pawns cautiously with a combination of mistrust, courtesy, and measured empathy.

"I was a prisoner too. I know what it's like."

"Is that how you learned German?"

"I also learned just how alone prisoners are, abandoned by your own country. France hates you but Germany's forgotten about you. It was the same for us."

Lukas was surprised that Vincent was speaking so openly to him.

"Oh yes. When a government can't stop talking about the mother country, the ungrateful mother is never far behind."

No prisoner could understand it: They'd been sent off to be killed and now, nothing, no news. Neither official nor private. Their mail had been stopped several months ago, and no one had turned a hair.

Vincent would have liked to get to know this German to gauge whether he would be able to help him approach the prisoners and have access to their secrets. But he could see the first deminers arriving, and Fabien wouldn't be far behind. He didn't have the time or the choice. So, going against all the plans he'd put in place, he cut straight to the chase.

"Did you know the farm near the château, the Jourdans' farm?"

"Yes."

"So you knew the farmers and their daughter, Ariane?"

It was imperceptible but when Lukas nodded his assent, Vincent could tell that he'd made contact with the right person. But then again, how should he interpret that slight hesitation, the way he'd held his breath? Vincent remembered that when you're a prisoner, you're dogged by fear and weigh each word before speaking.

"She's disappeared," he continued. "I want to know what happened to her."

"How am I supposed to know?"

"Find out. Everyone at your HQ was taken prisoner and they're in the same camp as you. I'm relying on you."

"And if no one talks to me?"

"You're prisoners, you talk. There's nothing else to do in prison."

Vincent noticed the other Germans watching them inquisitively, time for him to move away. In fact, he might have said too much and too loudly. But there was something Lukas desperately wanted to know.

"Is that why you stepped in to save me?"

"Like I said, I was a prisoner too."

"And one of the soldiers at the castle could be responsible, is that what you think?"

"Most likely. I want to know who."

"What will you do if I find him?"

"I don't know."

Then Lukas took another step in the strange relationship developing between them.

"This woman, Ariane, did you love her?"

"I still love her."

Why did Vincent tell him that? Tell a German he didn't know? More important, Fabien had arrived and was coming over to them. He needed to end this conversation. Vincent had a joker and he needed to use it now.

"Listen, I have a proposal for you—"

Too late: Fabien, still some distance away, was teasing him.

"Hey you, I know you don't give a damn what the guys think, but I'd say it's kind of soon to be championing Franco-German friendship!"

Vincent roared with laughter.

"Franco-German friendship? What a thought! It'll be an eternity before we're reconciled!"

He didn't know where he'd found the energy to laugh and he hoped it didn't sound false; he was desperate. By dragging him away from Lukas, Fabien had stopped him from producing his trump card.

Could he trust this German? Would he really question his fellow prisoners and push them when they were at their lowest ebb? Vincent had a feeling Lukas wasn't like the others and he'd been right to choose him. This hunch was based on the slenderest signs: He'd seen him reading during their breaks, and Lukas sometimes made pencil sketches in the margins of books.

He was sorry he hadn't been able to come at the problem in a more roundabout way, approaching Lukas in subtle stages, raising more general topics first and gaining his trust by offering him cigarettes, reemphasizing their similar experiences so that Lukas sensed a natural affinity with him. Instead, the German now knew that Vincent needed him.

Just before Fabien rallied the troops to start work, a man ran over to give him a telegram. Fabien opened it and read it in silence. As soon as the porter had left, Fabien told Vincent he wouldn't be there the next day.

"Not what I wanted at all. It's really not the time!"

He'd asked the guys to work hard to reach the goal of the first bunker, and he wouldn't even be with them. And in any event, when he was away, the men took advantage and slowed down while Enzo, with his zealous perfectionism, went the other way, taking initiatives that overburdened all of them.

To complicate things further, they were supposed to be taking on a team of reinforcements the next day. Fabien wanted to watch how the newcomers worked—there was no training so everyone had their own techniques and routines—and give them some pointers to standardize what they were doing.

But he had no option: Raymond Aubrac was summoning him to meet Raoul Dautry at the politician's home in his stronghold of Lourmarin.

Fabien carefully organized the following day by giving precise instructions. He encouraged Enzo not to take any risks; he trusted him completely, but the team needed to continue sweeping the ground around the sarcophagus mines. And even if they found other, easier devices, they would neutralize them later, once Fabien was back. In fact, they'd entrust them all to the army specialists who would be dealing with the sarcophaguses. This beach was dangerous, and Fabien couldn't relax.

"Do you know what they want?"

"I hope they're not going to tell us we need to manage without the prisoners."

Vincent realized that time was running out for him. He spent the day watching Lukas, waiting for an opportunity to talk to him alone. It was only at the end of the afternoon that he snatched a moment when Fabien wasn't watching to brush past the German and quietly offer up the proposal he'd been going over and over in his mind since he first came up with his plan.

"If you have any information at all about what happened, if you can find out who did something to Ariane, or who was closer to her than the others, if you have a name... tell me. You have my word as a former prisoner: I'll help you escape."

SASKIA DIDN'T DARE COME OUT OF THE STUDIO. She'd taken refuge in her bedroom to think, and then sleep had caught her by surprise. She hadn't slept like that for three years—not for the terrible two years in the camp or the strained months when her family had been in hiding. She woke disoriented and couldn't even remember where she was. She very quickly gathered her wits and the first thing she did that morning was consider all the possible ways she could protect herself. Like a hunted animal, she explored every little corner of the studio to work out where she could hide. No, hiding was really the worst option. She wouldn't last two minutes if anyone came looking for her. What she wanted was to be able to escape.

From her bedroom window she could get onto the roof of a lean-to. The tiles looked robust, and Saskia banked on the fact that her very thin frame wouldn't break them. She was frightened but she needed to be sure: Was this solution workable, a possibility? Would she make a noise if she walked along there? Would she be spotted? She had to try it out. It was a question of life and death but, despite her efforts to reason with herself, nothing could stifle her mounting panic. She'd heard that there was still fighting in Saint-Nazaire and Germany. The enemy hadn't surrendered, there'd been no peace agreement. Why was everyone behaving as if it was obvious the Germans were about to capitulate? Anyone who said that didn't know the Nazis as she did.

France—and Europe as a whole—had such a capacity for self-delusion. No one had anticipated the blitz. Her father had told her that this same delusion had held sway at the start of the Great War. Troops had set out naively to teach the Germans a good lesson. The war to end all wars. But no one ever taught a good lesson to the Germans. Or to anyone else. The only lesson was that there was never a war to end all wars; war begat war.

In the camp she hadn't known what was going on in France, could no longer even picture her country. The Nazis were the horsemen of the Apocalypse. She wondered whether France, as she'd known it, still existed.

And if they returned now, she needed to have an escape plan. When the men had come for her family, her mother, in a desperate bid to save her, had said Saskia was one of her pupils, a Catholic, called Sophie—look, you can see the initials on her hankie—and that she had an ID card to prove it.

Saskia was the only one who'd had a false ID card on her. She only need show it. But she was struck by a searing flash of intuition: If she didn't go with her mother, then her mother would die. She threw down the card and contradicted her mother: She *was* her daughter, her name was Saskia and she would go with them.

Saskia now had no one left to protect. This time she would be prepared and know how to get away. No one could hurt her now—she would run away before they had the opportunity. And even if the country was destroyed, completely laid waste, she would never stop walking. On a piece of paper she'd written down the route she needed to take to reach Spain and, from there, how to get to Morocco. She would stitch the jewelry into the inside of her dress. She'd heard that the king of Morocco had refused to hand over his Jewish subjects. She would go there, to the sunshine, and find work. Her father had friends in Mogador who'd not been disturbed at all. And the name filled her head with dreams, Mogador...

For the plan to work perfectly, she must be able to walk over this roof. She couldn't try it at night. Too risky. She'd noticed the day before that the studio was on an unlit street. And she suffered from vertigo, terrible vertigo. It made her head spin, cut her off from her own body. But she had to try out this route now.

Climbing out of the window was the easiest part. She'd done it at home once with her brother before the war. He was smoking cigarettes and they'd sat on the windowsill. She watched him smoke and felt happy—she so adored him. He incarnated a sort of natural distinctiveness: When he walked into a room, he was noticed. Sitting on that windowsill next to him, she was afraid of nothing, she was the happiest girl alive.

Now she edged along the gently sloping roof. The tiles were rough and held firm under her. Her supple bare feet adhered perfectly to their slight curve; she wasn't in danger of slipping. And yet she already felt off-balance, her eyesight blurred, and her mind reeled. Blindsided by memories of her brother, she fought with all her strength to reject the overwhelming draw of the void below. Then her mother appeared to her; her mother in all her tenderness and forgiveness, her loving mother, her mother who was above any judgment, her mother laughing, the teasing way she reminded everyone to be more modest, and then her mother humiliated on that first day in the camp, when she was forced to undress in front of her daughters.

Saskia had never seen her mother naked. She so loathed the Germans that day that there was no possible way back. But she needed to blot out this image. She didn't want to kill herself, just stop all the nightmares. And hers weren't really nightmares: They were soul-destroying, intrusive memories of the years she'd endured, the hideous deaths she carried everywhere with her.

She couldn't let herself be swallowed up into the void now, she had no right to, and she didn't even want to, but how could she rekindle a lust for life when the people who had been—and still were—dearest to her in the world were no longer there? *One single person is missing and the whole world feels empty.* One single person ... If it had been this sort of grief, she might have been able to share it and talk about it. But when the numbers go beyond that, there's no poeticizing. Everything around her had been ravaged, and standing on this roof now she couldn't contain the macabre forces infiltrating her mind and body. They were stronger than she was. She could no longer reason with herself and calm her thoughts. Torn between the pull of the void and her duty to live, she froze, her mind numbed, and her body deadened, quite unable to move.

Her legs were shaking. Reality had stopped existing. She was no longer in the South of France under a cloudless blue sky. She was terrified, transported into the churning gray abysses of her memory, so far from the warmth and the springtime. She was cold, freezing even. How had she ended up here? She'd known she would be overcome by vertigo and yet she'd stepped out onto this roof. She had survived, she'd crossed Poland, Germany, and France from north to south in order to get here, to this place she'd dreamed of returning to for three years, and now here she was, four meters above the ground when a fall of half that distance would have been enough to shatter her weakened bones. Why fly in the face of danger? To escape? To punish herself? Escape what? Reality? She'd been told often enough she needed to face up to it. Accept it. But reality must have been ashamed of what she'd become, reality must have wanted to escape.

They say vertigo is a fear of heights, of the abyss. Saskia knew it wasn't that. Vertigo wasn't the fear of falling into the abyss, it was the fear you would throw yourself into it.

◆

THE RUMOR WAS EVERYWHERE. THE GERMANS would be surrendering in perhaps a matter of days, and the prisoners would stop coming to demine. In early May 1945, the dance of diplomatic negotiations in San Francisco did not favor France.

To steady himself, Vincent had gone back past the Château des Eyguières, as if just seeing those old walls would give him clues, some inspiration.

He'd also lingered around the prison camp. What was he hoping for? That Lukas would call out to him from behind the barbed wire, telling what had happened and giving him a name?

He was angry with himself. In order to soften up a German, he'd had to admit that he himself had been a prisoner when that was a stain he never wanted to discuss. An inexorable chain of events that led him to hating the whole world.

And what for?

Wouldn't Lukas tell him whatever came into his head and denounce whomever he wanted just to get Vincent to help him escape?

He hadn't seen Lukas when he was near the camp but had spotted Mathilde handing food and clothing to the prisoners through the fence. When she saw Vincent, she smiled at him as if it was perfectly natural to help the Germans.

The prisoners threw themselves on what she gave them. Shoes were the first to go. Such extreme privation, privation that precludes any sense of honor, that wipes out any vestiges of dignity, degrading privation. He watched them fight over clothes that would replace their rags, clothes they would wear down until they too were rags, and he found he had a small measure of compassion for them. He'd had that same glint in his eye for a very old coat that had been too big, too rough, too thick, and had a horrible, persistent smell. He hadn't wanted to know what the smell was, but the coat had saved his life through the winter. He soon swept any fellow feeling from his mind: They were Germans, it wasn't the same.

When he went over to say hello, Mathilde already anticipated his questions.

"I know what these soldiers did, but I know what the French did too. Before the war. During and after. I don't trust anyone, but there are children in this camp, and I want to believe in them."

While he bicycled home, Vincent thought that, yes, Mathilde had been right about the children, but he couldn't weaken. It was as he reinforced his resolve that he spotted a figure swaying dangerously on the roof—Saskia.

VINCENT DROPPED HIS BIKE, RAN INTO THE studio and raced upstairs to the window.

Paralyzed with fear, Saskia had turned to stone. Vincent's voice woke her, and she turned to look at him but couldn't take a single step. She didn't need to explain: He threw himself at her, covered the distance that she'd walked toward her dead loved ones, and brought her back inside.

She was amazed by the comfort she felt from his hands on her shoulders, barely even noticing that they were as rough as the tiles beneath her bare feet. He was embarrassed by this abrasiveness that wouldn't soften. He'd hoped that by returning to a normal life—yes, he'd caught himself seeing demining as a normal life—his hands would revert to how they'd been before, but no. Despite his shame, though, his hands were tempted to close gently over Saskia's, as if they had a will of their own, their own innocent and spontaneous desires. Not something he was really controlling.

He restrained the urge, instinctively dropping his hands back by his sides so that Saskia didn't notice. She did. She'd spent her time in camp hiding everything: her bracelet so that it wasn't stolen, scraps of vegetables pilfered from the kitchen to eat, and—by some miracle she still didn't understand—a coat for her mother in the middle of a very cold winter. So she wasn't going to be fooled by this little strategy of Vincent's: In the camps she'd succeeded in hiding her body even when she was naked.

Of course, Saskia couldn't tell him why she'd gone onto the roof. Vincent usually defused every situation with his outlandish rejoinders, as he had done the day he'd seen her outside her house. But now he kept his eyes locked on her without a word. He didn't ask her anything and he asked her everything, because he didn't want her to die.

Try as she might to deny that she wanted to kill herself, Saskia felt that none of her denials convinced him. Besides, she couldn't really convince herself. She was no longer sure of anything. She'd probably never been such a stranger to herself. She didn't want to see her own body or question her own mind. And none of her decisions seemed to make sense. Thinking things over had become difficult and it certainly didn't lead anywhere.

"Don't ever go out onto that roof again...I forbid you."

"Well then, you stop demining...I forbid you too!"

"I'm not joking."

He poured her a glass of water and in the same deep, serious, emotional voice reiterated, "Don't risk your life again."

"That's ironic coming from someone who risks his all day long."

～

ANY PRISONER WOULD HAVE SEEN VINCENT'S offer as an unhoped-for opportunity. Not Lukas. Escape was what he wanted most in the world, but he had his own plan and didn't want to deviate from it. He couldn't trust a Frenchman, or play with fire. This help might be invaluable or it could be his downfall. But why had the Frenchman come specifically to him? How should he interpret that?

So far Lukas had been discreet, and the guards didn't have him in their sights. The camp director had even invited him to lunch when he heard that he'd worked in a bookshop in Berlin. They'd talked about literature and blacklisted authors, Thomas and Heinrich Mann, Stefan Zweig. It had been the director who told Lukas that Zweig had taken his own life in Brazil, and he'd obtained a copy of *The World of Yesterday* for him. This memoir had profoundly moved Lukas. And it was this same book that the guards had trampled underfoot, not knowing how he'd come by it.

Lukas's escape mustn't fail; he had too much to lose. And the Frenchman could easily denounce him once he'd secured the information he wanted.

The offer made Lukas reconsider his planned tactics, calling them into question. He couldn't exclude the possibility that he might need Vincent. Even if only to help him when he was on the run. Stopping him being recaptured. But he was exhausted at the thought of introducing new parameters into his decision-making process, of hovering between two options.

Other prisoners fired questions at him. They wanted to know why the Frenchman had come to talk to him. Lukas was evasive and that intrigued them even more. They pestered him. In all the weeks they'd been clearing mines, no Frenchman had ever come and offered a cigarette to a German. Had Lukas heard anything that they all should know?

Lukas was saved from their questions by the arrival of a French official who summoned all the prisoners to the yard: those who'd been captured several months ago and those who'd recently been transferred from Germany or other prison camps. They were ordered to stand in silence.

The official had come to do an unpleasant job: Recruit more deminers. He came regularly, every time there were new arrivals at the camp. The way he presented the situation, it sounded as if the prisoners had a choice when in reality they didn't. Besides the fact that there were not enough Frenchmen signed up for the work, most of the job's victims came from among the prisoners. They needed replacing. But the recruiter didn't reveal this. Just as he'd done when Lukas himself had been recruited, he opted to showcase the opportunity for early release.

If the men demonstrated "a good work ethic and courage," they could submit a request to return home earlier, and it would be considered fully and attentively. Since he'd been demining, Lukas hadn't seen anyone return to Germany. Or rather he had: Those who'd been horribly injured on a job, who were no good to anyone—they'd been sent home. Then they could die without overstretching the statistics for Axis prisoners of war.

Three detainees came over to Lukas.

The first was Hans, the tallest of them, such a colossus that it seemed almost inconceivable that he'd been captured. His torso was like a great barrel, and no one could have put their arms around it. He'd torn an old sheet into strips to fashion himself something like a boxer's body belt, and he drew on this intact, powerful body's resources every day to find reasons to believe in his survival despite the impossible conditions. And he wasn't only strong: He'd studied to be a lawyer in Munich. He knew their rights and would ensure that they were upheld.

Then there was Matthias, the youngest and slightest, a musician with transparent skin that afforded glimpses of his veins. He was fragile, crippled with anxiety. He'd been so terrified for five years and no longer had music to sustain him.

And lastly there was Dieter, who wasn't even blond, wasn't even proud, and seemed to accept everything. Here or somewhere else...

They all listened closely to the translator relaying what the recruiter was saying as fast as he could.

"Gentlemen, the Ministry of Reconstruction has decided to offer prisoners an opportunity to redeem themselves and reduce their sentences."

"Oh yes, a wonderful opportunity," Hans muttered under his breath.

"As of today, as many volunteers as would like to can step up to the great mission of mine clearance."

"And what if they don't get any volunteers to be blown up?" quipped Dieter.

"They'll just keep on forcing us to demine without actually calling it demining," Lukas reminded him.

"They've won, what more do they want? When do we get to go home?" Matthias asked desperately.

As well as the risky prospects threatening them, the prisoners identified something in the way the French official hammered home his words, labored his points, and glared at his audience: the full weight of his contempt.

"Any questions?" the recruiter eventually asked no one in particular.

"How long before we can secure an early release?"

"It all depends on how brave you are."

"Why do we need to be brave if you've said we wouldn't be demining?"

True, where was the bravery in clearing away rubble or detecting and removing disarmed mines, which was how the recruiter had described the role? The recruiter didn't pick up on the paradox but simply explained they would be judged for their attitude. The questions became more insistent.

"How many deminers will be entitled to early release?"

"And how long will it take for applications to be processed?"

"Who handles them?"

"Will there be quotas?"

So many numbers—the recruiter kept quiet about those. When the mine clearing was well advanced, the organizers planned to select ten Germans across the whole country each month. Ten out of fifty thousand. In other words, they had a better chance of being blown up by a mine than of going home.

The recruiter was dodging the questions, so Hans rammed the point home.

"We're not war criminals," he said, "just regular soldiers. We can't be used for dangerous tasks. Doesn't sending us to clear mines violate the Geneva agreement? Articles thirty-one and thirty-two."

His question didn't need an answer. The recruiter abandoned the paternalistic mood he'd adopted while singing the praises of demining and switched to a more menacing tone.

"We're granting you a huge favor by viewing you as men with whom we're prepared to work rather than monsters. Think it over."

Matthias turned to the others and said, "We'll never go home."

～

WHILE THEY WAITED FOR THEIR EVENING MEAL, or what passed as one, Matthias, Hans, and Dieter tried to get more information out of Lukas during a private conversation.

"What exactly do you do when you're demining? I mean, we're all supposed to have been given information about mines when we enlisted, but, you know, it was kind of basic, and we definitely weren't taught to disarm them!"

"In the last five years we've all done plenty of things we never dreamed we'd end up doing, right?"

"Yes, but in reality?"

"I adapt."

Lukas studied Matthias. He was the one he wanted to talk to. He knew who Matthias was and had already identified him in the distance when they were at the château, but Matthias had only just arrived at the camp and this was the first chance Lukas had had to speak to him.

Hierarchy had been strictly observed at the headquarters, as had social differences. All that had been blown apart in the prison camp. Lukas was not alone in taking mischievous delight in now addressing officers as *du* rather than the formal and respectful *Sie*. And Hans, who, during the Occupation, had never mingled with those he deemed beneath him, now talked to Matthias with genuine interest, completely unaware that they'd already come across each other at the château.

"What did you do before the war?" he asked Matthias.

Matthias, on the other hand, very much remembered Hans, whom he'd loathed at the time, but he didn't mention it.

"I was a musician. I started learning violin when I was three."

"Oh, we're in the presence of genius!" Hans said enthusiastically.

"I even had an offer from the Berlin Philharmonic. But five years without playing... I can forget that."

"And it's not over yet! How long are they going to keep us here? A year, three, six?" Dieter asked.

"Everyone's saying we've lost. If we surrender, the war will be over and we'll be sent home to Germany," Matthias suggested optimistically.

"Except that the guys who are being captured in Germany are being sent here," Lukas reminded him.

"The Americans can't let them do this," said Hans.

"Everyone's doing it. All those nations in San Francisco are discussing how to make use of us. We're beaten, we're prisoners, that's just how it is! If we want to get out of this situation, we need to find solutions... otherwise we could die here," Lukas announced gloomily.

"So Mozart gets sent out to be blown up by mines?" objected Hans. "It's absurd!"

Imperceptibly the conversation evolved into sparring between Hans and Lukas.

"It's war."

"It's illegal!"

"What are those articles thirty-one and thirty-two that you cited?"

"Article thirty-one states that it's 'forbidden to employ prisoners in the manufacture or transport of arms or munitions of any kind' and article thirty-two adds, 'It is forbidden to employ prisoners of war on unhealthy or dangerous work.' There you are, demining contravenes the Geneva Convention."

"Do you think Hitler respected it, this Geneva Convention?"

"We're not responsible for everything. And the war's over."

"Not for us."

Lukas was right and they all knew it. For a moment they stood in stricken silence.

"But did you hear the recruiter?" Dieter asked, hoping to raise their spirits. "You can get an early release by demining."

"If you don't die first!" Hans pointed out.

"Either way, you won't have a choice," Lukas warned.

"There's no way I'm being taken in by their supposed trade-off!"

"You'll see!"

"Look, *I* didn't decide to have this war. No one wanted it. Remember how happy everyone was about the Munich Agreement. We wanted peace in Germany. Even Hitler wanted peace!"

"Except that he was lying," Lukas said grimly.

Hans looked at him, surprised. "Well, in the early days at least, he certainly kept saying he wanted peace."

"His writings tell another story."

Lukas was referring to that cursed book, the book no one wanted to talk about, the book whose very name had become taboo. *Mein Kampf.*

"He didn't even believe it himself when he wrote that book," Hans countered. "He was young and in prison and angry."

"But he must have believed it. He applied everything he wrote to the letter."

"How would anyone know—no one's read it!"

"No one? A million copies were sold in 1933. Four million in 1938! That's unheard of!"

"It was at least seven hundred pages long, no one can read that."

"What about extracts, installments, and abridged editions? People used to queue up for them at the bookshop where I worked. Do you honestly think no one knew what was in that book? Some people agreed with him, some just accepted it, and others turned a blind eye, didn't want to think about it, but everyone knew. Hitler had it all mapped out, he'd announced it, and nobody did anything. And that's the truth."

Deep down they were well aware that Lukas was right, but they didn't like discussing it, not like this. Pretending that no one knew was just another survival technique. Lukas did not add that the book had been read in France too. Despite Hitler's efforts to stop its publication in France—because he was afraid of being smoked out—the

International League Against Racism and Anti-Semitism had distributed the book to congressmen, ministers, journalists, anyone whose opinion mattered so that the necessary measures could be taken. And yet, just like in Germany, not one leading French figure, with the exception of de Gaulle, had really believed the program would be implemented. Or had wanted to think about it. Or had taken offense to it.

Later that evening, Lukas came to find Matthias to talk some more. The violinist was ravaged by doubts. If he didn't go home to Germany, he could say goodbye to music. But if he joined the deminers, what chance did he have of returning to Germany?

"They want us to be brave, but what does that mean? Being blown up by a mine to help France get back on its feet? It's so dangerous."

"What's dangerous is staying here. You can see for yourself, they haven't got the resources to give us decent sanitary conditions. The only time the Red Cross visited, the guards hid the sick!"

"Hans says they can't keep us here."

"Like that's gonna bother them!"

"Aren't you scared?"

They'd now walked to the far end of the yard in which prisoners were made to take a few minutes' exercise before returning to their bunkhouses.

"Of course, I'm scared," Lukas replied, lowering his voice, "but I'm doing it for a reason. If you come demining with me, we can get out of here. We won't ever actually do their missions."

Matthias looked at him, not grasping what he meant.

"You mustn't talk to anybody about what I'm about to tell you…"

Matthias nodded silently, impressed by Lukas, who was putting his trust in him even though everyone saw him as the weakest and least useful of them all.

"There's a bunker we're going to demine on the beach. Inside it there are grenades and arms. I need someone to create a diversion. Do you want to escape with me?"

"When's it happening?"

"It's tomorrow or never."

FABIEN HAD RISEN EARLY. MAX HAD LOANED HIM his car for the trip to Lourmarin but he had about a three-hour drive and Aubrac had warned him: The minister, Dautry, was a morning person.

Sure enough, Raoul Dautry arrived at his office at five o'clock every morning. By way of breakfast, he annotated all the newspapers, and his brain was firing at its best during his morning meetings. He was a graduate of the prestigious École Polytechnique as well as a discerning man of letters, and his library comprised hundreds of novels whose cracked spines proved he had read them attentively.

Raymond Aubrac knew that he must come to terms with the stringent demands of this man who had declined all the Vichy government's offers before returning to work without a moment's hesitation when de Gaulle had asked him to. Other ministers were responsible for arranging the sweeping reforms that the general was calling for to restore pleasure in life—votes for women, social security, recognition for trade unions, and the establishment of works councils. Meanwhile, Raoul Dautry had been given the most thankless task. Except that the facts were inescapable: Without demining, it was impossible to envision rebuilding France.

On this particular morning, Dautry was in a bad mood when Fabien came into his office. He was reading out loud passages he'd underlined.

"'These deminers have come from who knows where, or rather we do know, we know only too well. These inexperienced nobodies have hastily signed up to erase their own disturbing behavior during the war and to wipe their slates clean…'"

Aubrac had anticipated the minister's anger when he'd read the paper before coming to the meeting.

"Luckily, we usually get good press… Because this time…"

Fabien felt that, having been summoned, he had a right to contribute.

"Perhaps we should try to find out exactly what *he* was doing during the war," he suggested, and then he even recycled the aphorism that Hubert kept quoting to them, "You know La Rochefoucauld's maxim: 'Those who shout the loudest about morals are often those who have the least.'"

"For sure," Aubrac agreed.

"This man's never asked to meet the deminers, he doesn't know what he's talking about, and here he is hurling insults at them!" Dautry protested in disgust.

"It's libel," said Fabien.

"Should we ask for an amendment, a right to reply?" asked Aubrac.

"We'll send him out into the field," Dautry replied.

"He must be the sort who sits and barks safely from behind his desk," Fabien joked.

"He won't have a choice, believe me," Dautry said heatedly.

Raymond Aubrac and Fabien smiled. They were pleased Dautry was angry. Dautry never compromised and he hunted down any whiff of criticism of the deminers. Plenty of journalists unwisely wrote that their work was too slow, poorly executed, badly targeted, disorganized, and used a ragtag of ex-convicts and former collaborators. They were immediately summoned and Dautry asked them to cite their sources and prove they'd investigated the facts—they couldn't. Dautry then reminded them of the principles that he and General de Gaulle had fine-tuned to help the country undertake the vast and dangerous mine-clearance operation. After the Great War, reconstruction had been entrusted to private companies. Everyone realized that those companies had filled their own coffers and done a botched job. General de Gaulle had a different vision of France, one that demanded that the state and no one else should take responsibility for putting the country back on its feet.

And oh, the disgrace of it. Deminers devoted themselves to this work at the risk of paying with their own lives—it would be no bad thing if journalists did *their* work by paying with a proper investigation on the ground.

Fabien was happy to see that their minister in this terrible mission was not washing his hands of the deminers' honor. But he still needed to discuss the requests he'd submitted through Aubrac. They were all short of time, so he came quickly to the point.

"On the question of disarming all the large-scale mines, the sarcophaguses, tombs, Goliath bombs...do you have any news?"

"We've passed on your request to the commanders of the armed forces, we'll keep you informed."

"And electric detection equipment?"

"The Allies have promised us some soon. And we're trying to replicate American, Russian, and British prototypes. We'll have to cope as we are for now."

"What about the deminers' status? Will they be recognized as war wounded in the event of accidents?"

"It's being considered. But that doesn't sit well with our combat forces. I'm sure you understand—"

"We're fighting just as they did, we're risking our lives just as much as they did. My commitment to demining is an extension of my commitment to the Resistance."

"Fabien...not everyone has your impressive track record."

"My men are building their own impressive track records now."

Aubrac agreed with Fabien and was fighting furiously for deminers to be granted the status they deserved. If they were wounded, they should be guaranteed a pension as war wounded. If they were killed, their widows should be confident they could raise their children in decent conditions.

There were other points Fabien wanted to raise.

"Any maps of the mines?"

"Still none."

"Do you have any leverage with the army? If the Germans are negotiating the terms of their surrender, they should give us the maps."

"It's not easy."

"Neither is demining without maps."

"You know what these army types are like, they love secrecy. Mining maps will be classed as defense secrets before we know whether they can be made public."

Aware that Fabien was losing patience, Aubrac intervened.

"The problem," he said, "is that it's not just the Germans who set mines. So we need the Allies' mining maps...But I have good contacts in the military. If this doesn't happen through official channels, it can be done under the table. That stays between the three of us."

"What about the German prisoners?"

"Now that I've managed to persuade Bidault to plead our case at the San Francisco Conference, he'll need to do the job well!" said Dautry.

They'd often discussed this controversial topic. Aubrac had plotted out the subject from political, moral, strategic, and pragmatic points of view and had eventually convinced Dautry. He couldn't give a damn if he didn't have the diplomatic seal of approval. They needed to hold on to the Germans to help with mine clearance. Mines were a new manifestation of war. The warring parties were being confronted with this problem for the first time, and they would have to adapt their principles to ensure it was the last. If the nation that had transformed a whole country into a huge minefield didn't take responsibility for removing the mines, then there would never be an end to it. Hence the need to enact it in law.

"Yes but, as predicted, the International Committee of the Red Cross has not looked favorably on that. Which isn't a good start."

Not wanting to be discouraged, Fabien moved on to his final—crucial—request.

"We need a mobile emergency first-aid unit. When a mine goes off we're often a long way from a hospital. If we had someone with us, to administer first aid, we could save lives."

Aubrac and Dautry were embarrassed. It wasn't easy to tell men who were risking their lives for the sake of others that there weren't the resources to help them.

Disappointed, Fabien said quietly, "Well then, fight to get hold of those mining maps."

They nodded solemnly. They'd worked through all the questions, but Dautry wasn't indicating that their meeting was over. Fabien wondered exactly why he'd been summoned. If they were just going to say no to everything, then ... but Aubrac and Dautry were looking at him oddly.

Dautry offered him a coffee.

"You know, Aubrac paints a very flattering picture of you."

"Thank you."

"If all our men were like you ..."

"They just need training."

"We're working on that. We're currently finalizing our training project for this summer. But you're too modest.

It's not just a question of technique; it's also about ethics and commitment. So, you see, we thought you'd be perfect to work with us, at the ministry."

"Excuse me?"

"Yes, we're inviting you to come and work in Paris, at the demining project's central office," Aubrac explained.

"Obviously, you'd also have go out to see various sites," said Dautry. "Like Aubrac, you would spend three days a week out on the road, with the men."

Fabien hadn't been expecting this. His first thought—as brief and devastating as a flash of lightning—was that he must tell Odette. He'd never lost this impulse, but it took him by surprise every time.

Thoughts jostled in his head. He needed to give Aubrac and Dautry an answer as soon as he'd finished the cup of coffee that he allowed to dawdle in front of his mouth. Why didn't he accept enthusiastically and unreservedly right here and right now? He had a lot of time for Aubrac; he liked him. He was young, eager, rigorous, and honest. As a civil engineer, he had the necessary qualifications for his job, and he was still a modest man despite the pivotal part he had played in the "Secret Army." Working alongside him was bound to be motivating. And when it came to Dautry, Fabien admired his vision and his capacity for hard work.

At last Fabien could take a job in which he didn't constantly put his life on the line but was still useful. Surely, he deserved this? What was the shadow hovering over it?

He was thinking about his men. How could he break the news to them without appearing to abandon them? He even felt bad for not being with them today.

"You don't have to give us an answer straightaway."

"It's an honor. Thank you. Before I make a decision, I'd like to finish demining the beach that I've started, and its bunkers."

"Perfect, we'll wait to hear from you."

Of course, he was more tempted by this offer than he would have liked. When Dautry gave him the address for the demining office—6 rue de La Trémoille in the eighth arrondissement of Paris—he remembered that he'd dreamed of living in Paris with Odette, of being in the city that came alive at night, so he could take her dancing in jazz clubs...

SASKIA HAD MANAGED TO GO OUTSIDE. SHE'D found it very difficult, but walking along the street was even worse. And yet how she'd dreamed of this freedom when she'd been deprived of it. Now even this simple pleasure was being denied her; she couldn't shake off her fear.

When it had become clear to her parents that they were facing deportation, the family had dispersed among the households of friends, and Saskia was no longer allowed out. They did still meet at home once a week, and it was during one of these clandestine get-togethers that they'd been arrested.

On that fateful day she'd had a feeling she was being followed. For a long time, she wondered whether the arrests had been her fault. No, it was worse than that: She was utterly convinced she was responsible. One of her friends in the camp had said, *None of it's your fault, it's the Germans' fault*, and she knew she must cling to those words for the rest of her life, although she wouldn't always grasp the truth in them.

Now she was walking along a street again and she couldn't be sure that nothing would happen to her. She was no longer endangering the lives of her loved ones, but endangering her own life meant risking wiping out her family because she was all that was left of it.

And so she walked with the caution of those who are alone in the world. The threat can't have evaporated. Where were all the people who'd insulted them and wanted to see them dead? All the henchmen in the French Popular Party and the National Popular Rally, the hotheads in the Milice who'd viciously ferreted out whole families, including children, to send them off to the camps? And all the invisible eyes who'd spied on them and denounced them? The snitches must still be alive, happily going about their lives unscathed, with no cloud to darken their thoughts. Apart perhaps from a nostalgia for the nonsensical days when their hatred had been seen as right. Where were these people?

Perhaps she was walking past them right now. That man in the tight-fitting suit, the woman with her hair pinned up who was staring at her as she crossed the street... What about in that group chatting and laughing over there, could one of them have denounced a family, just like that, out of jealousy or revenge or so they could take over a shop, perhaps even for nothing, unthinkingly, for the sheer pleasure of snitching, to feel all-powerful?

And then on the sidewalk opposite she spotted not these carefree enemies but... her mother! Her mother from behind in the pink viscose dress that danced with her as she moved, the dress with the hazy print of evanescent roses, the one that cinched her waist and flared over her hips, her dress with a belt she'd made out of a different fabric because she didn't have enough of the rose print, but they went so well together. Saskia ran to catch up with her.

The whole time she was engaged in this exalted pursuit, she was bathed in the enchantment of the apparition, spellbound in her mother's wake. Perhaps she could catch her by the waist and press herself to her mother's soft body as she had done as a child. She breathlessly inhaled great lungfuls of the illusion.

The woman turned around.

As soon as she saw the woman's kindly face smiling at her, Saskia abandoned the realms of fantasy and was back on the sidewalk.

The woman was young, a little taken aback by Saskia, who had caught hold of her and was studying her feverishly.

"Can I help you?"

Saskia was out of breath, but she managed to tell her that the dress she was wearing was one her mother had made and the cheap little brooch pinned up near the shoulder was hers too.

The young woman was deeply moved by Saskia's emotion. She unpinned the brooch and handed it to her.

"I'm so sorry...I didn't know..."

How could she? But Saskia could feel rage rising inside her. Her house inhabited by people devoid of humanity, their belongings confiscated, her mother's dress worn by some stranger... Had everything they owned been dispersed? And what if, thanks to this dress, she could trace back to the informers? Could she prove that the new occupant of their house had lied? She must have been the one who gave—or sold—the dress to this young woman.

"Where did you get it?"

"I bought it in the market. An older woman had a little suitcase of dresses and a few knickknacks. I thought it was pretty, I didn't know it was stolen."

Her mother's dresses peddled in the market from a little suitcase...

"If you tell me where you live," the young woman said, "I can give it back to you."

Where you live... such an everyday question, but Saskia hadn't anticipated it, and it filled her with dread. She was completely incapable of giving her address—which wasn't in fact hers, anyway—as if she might still be denounced, as if she had to live in hiding for the rest of her days. It was better to say nothing. This would have seemed ridiculous before the war, but it now struck her as the most sensible course of action. Try as she might to think on her feet, she couldn't come up with a solution. She wanted the dress, she desperately wanted it—she'd have gladly found a discreet corner where the woman could have undressed and handed it back right now—but she couldn't say where she lived.

"Could we arrange to meet on the Place de la République? Outside the café? That would work better for me."

The woman agreed and suggested late afternoon the following Wednesday because she'd have more free time then. They said goodbye.

Saskia envied her: She had things to do and knew where she was going.

Still dazed, crushed, shaken by memories of her mother, Saskia watched the dress walk away. She couldn't remember where she was. She started following the woman from a distance, as if wanting to intoxicate herself on the mirage for a while longer. Then a man coming in the other direction smacked straight into her. She instinctively screamed and put up her arms to protect her face.

"Oh, I'm sorry, did I frighten you?"

Saskia had now completely lost her composure. She'd exhausted all her reserves in the camp. She was always frightened first and foremost, and it was only afterward that she analyzed a situation. The young man was mortified, then his face broke into a smile.

"Say, are you coming to the party this evening?"

He had an irresistible accent, a confident expression, an American smile.

"The party?"

"Yes, there's a dance, didn't you see the stage in the square, outside the café? There's going to be a band."

"I didn't know."

"Come, I'll be there..."

His enthusiasm flustered Saskia. She tried to smile back at him, then walked away. A party. Music. A band. Going dancing...Impossible. She was grieving for too many people. And she might run into Rodolphe. Obviously, that was all she wanted, but she was anxious about seeing him when she was so thin and worn down. She needed to get some color back into her cheeks. Or perhaps an hour in the sun would do the trick, like in the old days? But she also needed some strength. And to achieve that she had to move on.

Out of nowhere she remembered that one of her mother's pupils had found work at the town hall before the war. He might be able to help her. Édouard... Édouard something...

She was right. Édouard Maillan still worked there. She had to wait to see him. A long time.

"I'm very sorry," said a secretary when it was finally her turn, "but we're about to close. If you could be quick..."

Too busy filling in a form, Édouard Maillan didn't immediately look up at her when she stepped into his office.

"What are you here for?"

"Hello, Édouard. Saskia..."

He didn't recognize her. Last time he'd seen her, her face had still had childish curves.

"Oh. Saskia...Forgive me. You've changed so much...How old were you when you left?"

"Seventeen."

"And...your mother?"

Sitting very upright in her chair, her eyes misted with tears, Saskia made a great effort not to cry and slightly averted her eyes. Embarrassed and unsure how to react, Édouard pushed aside the pile of papers he was annotating as if to clear the space between the two of them, and then he gently tried to break the silence.

"I'm so very sorry. I was very fond of your mother, as you know. I owe her so much. Without her, I would never have passed my diploma, that's for sure."

Saskia was still unable to reply so he tried to deflect her emotion and speak more breezily.

"So, are you moving back here?"

"Well, I'm...I'd like to go back to our house but someone's living there. I saw from the letter box that their name's Bellanger."

"Ah, the Bellangers...Yes, they came to introduce themselves here. They seem...decent people."

"But it's my house!"

"Of course! Have you spoken to a notary?"

"I only just got here, Édouard. I haven't been able to contact anyone. Make any headway. All my papers stayed at home, but the woman I saw claimed there was nothing left of ours...I thought maybe you could help me."

This clearly put Édouard in an awkward situation.

"Of course, I'll try, but...Your family had it built if I remember right."

"My father drew the plans and oversaw the construction."

"The problem is before the war people didn't need permits."

"We bought the plot. Isn't that enough?"

"Actually, it's not, it's complicated. In fact, that's why the Vichy government tried to introduce a construction permit a couple of years ago. Even if, between you and me, no one really followed the law...Anyway, some municipalities want to introduce them now, Ramatuelle, Saint-Tropez...It'll be easier to get your bearings then."

"What about me, what can I do?"

He sighed and pulled the pile of paper back in front of him.

"Poor Saskia. And it's terrible timing. We're so busy! You see all this? They're compensation claims."

"For what?"

"For war damage. Houses were occupied or destroyed, farmland was ruined. Here, look, this one, the de Charvil estate, they lost six hectares of vineyards. And the Barjaval estate lost eighteen! And their house was badly damaged by the occupiers. Someone has to pay."

"They want to be compensated... for the war?"

"Yes! And we're so behind schedule." He stood up, opened a cupboard. "Look, I'm not lying! You see the problem?"

Yes, she could see well enough. Those big estates, all those hectares, naturally they took priority over her. One of the claims featured an image of a huge country house printed at the top of the notepaper. The writing was expansive, and the ink had faded to sky blue. The letter was dated August 6, the day after the landings. The owners hadn't wasted any time. The damages they were asking for were astronomical. Saskia felt very small.

"Do you think you'll be able to do something?"

Édouard thought for a long time, then opened a drawer. Saskia hung on his every move as if he had the power to give her back her old life. He took out a few pieces of paper.

"Here, maybe these'll help."

Ration tickets.

Saskia had no family left, no house left, and he was offering her ration tickets? She mumbled an embarrassed thank-you and tried once more.

"Tell me when I can come back."

"Give me some time..."

Then, as if by some bizarre equation this might be of consolation to Saskia—ration tickets traded for a house—he took more tickets from the drawer and handed them to her. This time there was a voucher for a pair of shoes.

"Here. And if you want my advice, don't make a fuss."

DON'T MAKE A FUSS...

It wasn't the first time she'd heard these words. She was presented with them in every tone of voice, sometimes as a warning, sometimes a friendly tip. When the camps were liberated, political prisoners were evacuated first—*First those who fought for France, then everyone else*, they were told cruelly, and the exit was barred to Jews—and Saskia had begged to be allowed home as soon as possible. She was told sternly: *Everyone will be evacuated. Don't make a fuss.* When she and three other young women had managed to make their own way back to France in a truck and then wanted to describe and explain how they'd been treated, they were met with polite evasiveness, disconsolate headshaking. *Now's not the time to make a fuss.*

When she reached Paris, it happened again at the Hôtel Lutetia...When she refused to undress for a medical checkup, *Come on, don't make a fuss.* When she didn't want to be doused with DDT or to answer the endless questions, *Did she really want to make all this fuss?* And then, just before she fled from that nightmare hotel, she was given a few ration tickets and a few francs as if she were being offered a fortune, along with this atrocious instruction: *Take these, and don't make a fuss.*

No one wanted to hear. But what she had to tell wasn't just a story, it was History with a capital H and all the other little letters to go with it, History at its most repulsive, History going against the tide of progress, and against the image we like to have of humanity, History that should never have allowed such hell to happen, History that must never be forgotten.

The first time she'd heard this demoralizing directive, she hadn't known that it would follow her everywhere. No one was interested in their story. The Resistance fighters' story, yes, but not theirs. People wanted heroes, not victims. And yet she'd seen nothing but heroines around her at the camp. Why pit deportees against Resistance fighters, and political prisoners against so-called racial prisoners? When the Nazis were ruthlessly implementing a monstrous, implacable program of total extermination, trying to stay alive had been an act of resistance that used all your imaginable and unimaginable strengths.

And to imagine the strength you no longer have, that no one could have in the face of such insurmountable opposition, that takes stories.

It was stories that had saved Saskia herself and some of the others—too few of them—who liked listening to her narrations. Before the war she'd told stories to her brother when they'd shared a bedroom. She'd continued when she was in the camp. Her knack for taking twists and turns to avoid the homestretch that would wind up a story meant she could keep her friends going for several consecutive evenings. She always chose stories that ended well. Otherwise, she would change the endings. And why

not! Their lives had become sufficiently unbearable, they
didn't need to be burdened with sad fiction. The stories
should be something they could believe in, something
to bring them back to life, raise them up. Even tales that
she adapted from Zola and Maupassant became cheerful.
Gervaise ended up finding a job and a good husband and
moving into a lovely house. Boule de Suif was cheered by
her fellow travelers and turned her back on prostitution.
Kafka's cockroach metamorphosed a second time, revers-
ing the alteration, like a frog into a prince, and his life was
full of meaning again. As a bonus, she embellished stories
with other tales, by the same author or another, it didn't
matter so long as the story—and the authors' lives—could
be extended: Kafka enjoyed a long happy relationship
with Milena. No one would have guessed that the real
Milena was slowly dying in another camp. Those who'd
read Zola or Kafka didn't protest. Besides, they preferred
Saskia's versions.

Now that she was alone with no one to talk to, she
still had novelists to constitute a family of sorts for her.
The novels she'd read that had helped her to survive felt
as if they'd been written for her, as if they'd been waiting to meet the one person who would truly understand
them. And Saskia put so much faith in this, in these elec-
tive affinities, this mystical communion. Victor Hugo
talking to his dead daughter turned the tables so that
Saskia became the living daughter whom he addressed
from among the dead. She had no confidence in herself,
but this was a powerfully held conviction. It was neither
delusional pride nor arrogance, it was her belief system.

They were her gods, literary avatars of the God in whom she didn't believe.

When she left the town hall—still fuming—she inadvertently wandered to the square where the stage was being set up for the dance that was to take place that evening.

The exuberant bustle of the laborers assembling the wooden planks and hanging lightbulbs, the smiles on the faces of passersby—everyone wanted this party. Except for her.

It was definitely too soon to see Rodolphe. But could she wait? And what if he thought she was dead?

She dropped in at the perfumery that his parents owned to ask for news. The salesclerk was unpacking boxes and arranging bottles on shelves. It certainly wasn't a scene of abundance, but Saskia still wondered how anyone could buy lotions and beauty products now, how these luxuries could coexist with the destitution she saw around her, and how such things could follow on from the privations that so many had suffered.

And then, on one of the shelves, she spotted the perfume that Rodolphe had given her. A single flower fragrance based on jasmine that came from large plantations that a branch of Rodolphe's family owned in the heights above Grasse. She was moved by this perfume bottle. She opened it delicately, then carefully dabbed her wrist with the frosted glass stopper. It all came back to her. The day he'd first given it to her and the day she'd seen those great expanses of flowers, as far as the eye could see. And the smell, and those white stars perfuming the night...the salesclerk came over to Saskia briskly and took the bottle from her, afraid she might break it.

"I can apply the fragrance for you, if you would like."

"I'd like that."

The clerk saw the look in Saskia's eyes; perhaps she anticipated her questions.

"Perfume is a luxury but for a Frenchwoman it's also a way of life. The Germans didn't take everything from us!"

Saskia made the effort to give her a little smile. She'd lived so far removed from such sophistication. And yet, even though luxury seemed ridiculous to her, perfume was quite different. She understood its power. Its secret pact with memory. Its protective strength. One young woman had managed to keep a bottle of perfume hidden all the way from the Camp des Milles in Aix-en-Provence: a bottle of Guerlain's Vol de Nuit. When she arrived in Birkenau, the kapo discovered it and asked her for it. Amalia looked at her defiantly, applied the perfume to her neck and wrists right there in front of her, then passed the bottle to Saskia, who did the same before handing the bottle to another girl. It passed through a whole string of them until it was empty. The kapo beat Amalia, but the clothes they'd been given when they reached the camp—stinking, unwearable rags—kept that fragrance for weeks. Saskia had read Saint-Exupéry's novel after which the perfume was named, and she became friends with Amalia. When they huddled together to sleep, Saskia escaped into that enduring fragrance.

Saskia drew on her memories of this friend who was no longer there to embody the audacity she herself had never had. She asked the clerk if the Delambre family still lived in the city. She made a point of listing their first names, with particular emphasis on Rodolphe. The sales-clerk changed once she realized Saskia knew the family. She said that they had taken exile in the United States during the war, but Mr. Delambre had stayed behind. Rodolphe and his mother were due to return any day. They might even be here already. Saskia thanked her. She could feel herself coming back to life.

She stepped out into the street bolstered by this news. The band was rehearsing for the dance, and the music offered the town the melody of happiness, the return of spring.

She walked past the café L'Envol. Her mother had been close to the owner, Léna, before the war, but Saskia didn't dare go in to see her. She came across the young man who'd told her about the dance, and he waved to her and called out his name as they passed each other: Michael. It was actually quite uplifting, having American strangers smile at you like that.

∾

ON THE CAFÉ TERRACE, IN THE FRONT ROW OF seats, where they could see the preparations for the dance, Léna and her waiter Aurélien were watching the musicians.

"If you pick the right time, I'll let you go dance. You're allowed to have a good time too."

"Except I was too young five years ago and now, I'm probably too old."

"Nooo, the war years don't count! Our ages all start back where they were. Otherwise, it's just not fair," Léna joked.

"Yes, but thanks to the war, I can't dance! I'll have to watch you."

"I won't stop working. It's going to be our best evening."

"Why are you wearing makeup, then?"

"To get you talking."

Their conversation was interrupted by a woman who drew up outside the café in a car. A real beauty of about thirty, dressed as a man, not in a suit but rather ready for work—she was quite eye-catching. She seemed to be looking for someone to ask something.

Léna went over to her, and the woman, relieved to find someone available and approachable, came closer and handed her a photograph.

"Hello, do you know this man? He's a friend of mine and I don't know where to find him."

Léna took the photo to have a closer look, screwing up her eyes to focus; the image wasn't very large. It showed a young man playing tennis. Svelte, moving with impeccable coordination. It wasn't a portrait but a full-length shot. His face was slightly shaded—hard to get a strong impression. And yet Léna felt she'd seen him before.

"He looks familiar…"

"The photo's from before the war. He's bound to have changed. He has brown hair, green eyes, a really beautiful voice."

Léna noticed the young woman's distress. She seemed both agitated and exhausted, holding a table for support.

"Are you okay? Would you like to sit down?"

The woman dropped onto a chair.

"I've been running about all over the place since this morning. I think I've been to every café there is."

"Is he your fiancé?"

"No, but…I know him very well. I really need to talk to him."

"And you think he's here?"

"If he's alive, I'm sure he will be. He's looking for a woman called Ariane. I need to talk to him about her."

Léna concentrated. It was possible to see Vincent in the photo, a younger version, before he'd been marked by the war, but she didn't recognize him.

"But...that face. Green eyes, you say...a beautiful voice...What's his name?"

"Hadrien. Hadrien Darcourt. He's a doctor."

The name finally convinced Léna that she'd never seen the man.

"No, I don't know a Hadrien, and certainly not a doctor, but I'll make a note of his name. And what's your name?"

"Irène. Ariane is my best friend."

Discouraged by this search that was leading nowhere, Irène stood up, thanked Léna for her help, and returned to her car. Léna called out to her once she was back at the wheel.

"There's a dance tonight. There'll be lots of people around. If he's here, you're sure to find him."

Irène thought for a moment, hesitated, then smiled. "That's a good idea. I'll try to delay my trip until tomorrow."

Léna tilted her head inquiringly.

"I'm heading to Poland with a group of five other women to bring home our wounded."

"Just women? That's dangerous."

"If we don't do it, who will?"

"Funny, I've heard those words before..."

As if driven by an intuition that she didn't yet understand, Léna stopped Iréne just before she started up the car.

"If I happen to see him and you don't, do you have a message for him?" she asked.

Irène considered this for a while. Perhaps she was evaluating how trustworthy Léna was in the light of all the experience she'd accrued over the five years of war, when the most regular and most essential question was always whom you could trust.

"Tell him Ariane wants to be forgotten," she confided, almost in a whisper.

WITHOUT FABIEN, SOMETHING DIDN'T FEEL right on the beach. Yes, the deminers knew his instructions by rote but they still felt they'd been left to their own devices. The backup team had arrived, and the men had taken some time to smoke a cigarette with them, crack a few jokes, get to know them. They all had their stories to tell. They'd started work quite late in the morning, which had set a strange rhythm to the day.

As Fabien had anticipated, the team was slacking. Even Enzo, which was strange. And because everyone was using him as the pacemaker, the group advanced more slowly. With no warning, Hubert simply hadn't shown up. And then there'd been the break that had lasted longer than was reasonable, and the sun beating down on them, and the story Max had told to no one in particular. He'd chatted up a girl to get her to meet him at the dance later, then he'd chatted up a second girl, because you always need a plan B.

"You made a date with two girls? That's risky, my friend—if they find out, you'll be paying the price, for sure."

"You're not kidding! My plan B was my plan A's sister! So the net result is I have no plans for this evening. I'll just have to improvise."

Manu also had a date, but his discretion meant the others had to drag the details out of him. She had dark hair and green eyes. Like him, she'd been a student before the war but had been forced to drop her studies. He came in for some ragging: An intellectual…she wouldn't stick around with him for long. In any event, no one was concentrating without Fabien there.

Vincent had been watching Lukas all day, waiting for a sign. The German must have spoken to his fellow prisoners. He was bound to have something to tell him about Ariane. After five years of war, what sort of prisoner would refuse help to secure his freedom at last? Still, Vincent couldn't catch his eye, as if Lukas were trying to avoid him. But Vincent remembered the German's reaction when he'd mentioned Ariane—a minimal reaction that would have seemed negligible to pretty much anyone. Yes, anyone who hadn't known Ariane. From that subtle reaction, Vincent could tell that Lukas hadn't told him everything. Why not? Was he afraid? Was he hiding something unspeakable? Did he want to negotiate? To manipulate him? Or perhaps this just allowed him to believe he had a vestige of power, the pitiful power of those who know over those who don't.

Truth be told, Lukas didn't mean to play on Vincent's nerves. He didn't want to think about him, consider his offer, be at his mercy. His attention was entirely focused on the bunkers. His dream was right there, within reach, and they were getting no closer. Lukas cursed their breaks, the never-ending lunch, the French with their jokes; they would never get to the blockhouse today. In fact, nothing was going as planned. He was meant to be securing Fabien's trust and Fabien wasn't there. Could he apply the strategy to Enzo?

Lukas kept an eye on Matthias, who repeatedly glanced at him anxiously. Lukas had promised him that he would have to clear mines for just one day and wasn't sure he could hold out any longer. He was also aware of how tense Vincent was, doggedly watching him, which didn't help at all.

Too bad, he had to go ahead with his plan. If he had one chance of escape, it was today, for at least three reasons: There was the dance this evening so the deminers weren't so focused. Plus, his aim was to reach one of the blockhouses and, even though they hadn't made as much ground as he would have liked, they were getting closer. Lastly, it wasn't actually such a bad thing that Fabien wasn't around. Fabien was the most difficult person to fool; he was a mind reader.

Despite his misgivings, Lukas had managed to convince himself that everything was in his favor. During a break, he went over to Enzo and, with the help of a translator, told him what he'd been planning to tell Fabien.

"Next time we have a mine to disarm, I'd like to learn how to do it."

Enzo looked at him, unmoved.

"I want to take the risk," Lukas explained. "It's not heroism—just, we were told that if we're brave we could be released."

Vincent had discreetly edged closer. He couldn't understand what Lukas was trying to do. Was he not taking his offer of help to escape seriously?

Meanwhile, Enzo was staring sternly at Lukas. He should have taken an interest in this German's initiative, which could have encouraged other prisoners to follow suit. Instead, he snubbed him with: "Look, Kraut, *we're* the deminers. You just stay where you are, we'll be fine as we are."

A large part of Lukas's plan was in danger if he couldn't get close to the lead deminer and the blockhouse. He was sure Fabien would never have responded like that. And to make matters worse, Vincent was making the most of the fact that Enzo was mouthing off to the other deminers—*I mean, who do these Boche think they are, like we're all best buddies!*—to sidle up to him, ignoring the fact that Matthias was standing right next to him.

Vincent offered them a cigarette and pretended to embark on a normal conversation. He would come up with a roundabout way of letting Lukas know he wanted an answer, however fleeting, that would give him hope of finding out a little more. He ended up with something better. When he heard that the newcomer, Matthias, had been a violinist before the war, Vincent was buffeted by a tide of emotion as he remembered the scant information Audrey had given him. He reacted immediately.

"Did you play violin at the farm next to the château? Did you know Ariane?"

Matthias backed away instinctively, terrified that Vincent had such detailed information.

"I just want to know if you can tell me anything about Ariane," Vincent reassured him. "Did you know her well?"

"I think so," Matthias replied. "I would even say I knew her best."

So was he Ariane's ally? Perhaps Audrey had been right.

Enzo interrupted them to get the men back to work—they'd spent the whole day on breaks—and just as Vincent was finally going to have news of Ariane, game-changing news, Enzo suddenly wanted to get on with it!

Vincent found it hard to keep calm. He'd made this a personal discipline in order to avoid attracting attention, but this was especially difficult. He reluctantly resumed his impassive expression and his place among the French deminers while Lukas and Matthias returned to the other Germans. And they all advanced in silence.

From where he was, Vincent could surreptitiously watch Matthias. He would have preferred a stronger, more robust man. He couldn't see how Ariane had felt protected. Matthias was younger than she was, and probably physically weaker. But Ariane's letter had said that her ally could take her to safety. Perhaps he knew a secret place. This violinist would be able to reveal where...

And then he started wondering just how far their connection had gone. He remembered what Audrey had said, Matthias's concert in the farmyard, the magic that had made them feel alive. The German had fine features. Vincent had to acknowledge that he was good-looking. It broke his heart. How could he compete with a musician? He played the piano so badly.

"Mine!" Enzo had just come across a device. And the routine started all over again. Everyone twenty-five paces back. Manu took out the twine and markers. As Fabien had asked the day before, he would cordon off the mine until the better-equipped military munitions specialists arrived to neutralize it. But Enzo was still scouring the ground. It wasn't an antitank mine but a very small explosive, an antipersonnel device. A Behelfmine W-1. Absolute child's play alongside the others they'd found. It comprised a salvaged mortar shell 50 millimeters across and a Buck chemical igniter on a plastic connector. Not all the mines were melted down over concrete, but this one had been—perhaps to make it more stable in the sand.

"It's okay, this is gonna be easy. A piece of cake!"

Enzo was keen to defuse it. Everyone heading to the dance along the seafront lingered to watch the demining operation, shuddering at the vicarious danger. Enzo loved having an audience. It electrified him. He would end the day on a high.

It was at this point that Fabien arrived. He'd been thinking about Aubrac's offer all the way back from Lourmarin, constantly wavering between the two options before him: staying and demining alongside his team, or starting a new life far away from the south, where everything reminded him that Odette would never come back. He'd hoped that the answer would become obvious over the course of the journey, but he'd been driving for three hours and still didn't know what he should do.

As he walked across the beach, his instincts warned him of danger. The guys hadn't made much progress— Fabien had expected this, but still. After facing physically exhausting, nerve-shredding trials every day, a degree of attrition creeps in. It was palpable today. His men were rattled. The dance had started, and they could hear tunes, some familiar, others that they'd forgotten. Manu and Tom hadn't even noticed that Fabien had arrived and were chatting. He startled them with a big slap on the back each.

"So, when I'm not here you get free time?"

They were all glad to see him.

"Okay, guys, okay, it's party time tonight but you need to be at the top of your game on Monday, we're expecting a visit from a journalist!"

Then he turned to the youngest of them and added, "If you lied about your age, Tom, you'll be caught—he'll be looking at everyone's records. And the ministry also wants to start checking IDs to stop any bad-mouthing."

This wouldn't make things any easier for Vincent.

Fabien watched Enzo in the distance, still doing battle with the mine. Enzo was one of the best deminers Fabien had met, but he'd have preferred it if they'd stuck to his original instructions—cordon them off and wait for the military experts. And anyway, it was strange: The beach was bristling with powerful antitank devices, so why was this discreet little antipersonnel mine all on its own by the bunker? Like a solitary shooter making the most of the diversion caused by swarming troops to strike the fatal blow from where it was least expected. Like a second front. Fabien was annoyed with himself for going to Lourmarin. He should have stayed with his men and the new team. He could smell danger. The stench of it filled his lungs. He tried to reason with himself, but reason sometimes meant listening to his instincts.

THE BAND HAD DECIDED TO BE DARING, TO BE jazz, to be swing. The city had so longed for this dance that the musicians had struck up before it was even dark and, to release all the pent-up energy of this first party, romantic tunes could wait until later. Some men and women were still eyeing one another, but most had already formed couples, not waiting, magnetically drawn together and now twirling. The air was full of desire—intense, joyous, irresistible. The night would be sweet and wild, unpredictable.

Léna flitted from one table to another on the café terrace, her lithe body weaving, bending to pour a drink, straightening, arching supplely, her hair rippling about her face. She wasn't serving her customers but waltzing with them, and she was eagerly awaiting Fabien's team. The terrace was her dance floor. She called out to her waiter, who appeared with a very full tray in his hand.

"Strange that they're not here yet…"

"They must be sprucing themselves up. You know what they're like. Never on the back foot when it comes to showing off."

She smiled. He was right. They could even be dandies in their own way, with their white shirts, their rolled-up sleeves, and little kerchiefs around their necks or in their jacket pockets, if and when they wore jackets. She liked their attitude, the look in their eyes, their uniqueness. But when she realized what the time was, she started to worry, or rather it was stronger than that: She couldn't help having a nasty sense of foreboding.

All of a sudden there were loud detonations, whistling, explosions...

Léna dropped her tray, her heart pulverized, while all her customers were gripped with terror and tipped over tables and chairs as they fled without even knowing where the danger was.

The detonations didn't let up. A wave of panic swept inside the café, like during the grimmest times when the warnings had sounded, and people had to hole up in cellars.

Léna was captivated by a glow up in the sky: a rocket exploding. Then another, and another. Luminous, powdery clusters of wisteria tearing through the sky. Fireworks! They'd all been frightened by cheeky, mischievous, improvised fireworks. Léna could have kicked herself. Of course! Berlin had surrendered three days ago. They needed to celebrate the peacetime to come, it was within touching distance!

Relieved, the customers laughed as they returned to their tables. The trauma of bombings was still there, but on an evening like this they were prepared to forgive the thoughtless individuals who'd reignited their wartime fears and reflexes.

"Well, they need to have their fun! It must be some youngsters..."

Conversations buzzed again happily, but one young woman was still feeling shaky. Léna hurried over and helped her sit down. The woman was upset for ruining the party.

"Oh, my God, I'm sorry, I was so scared."

"No, don't be, I understand, it really wasn't a good idea! What were they thinking? I thought it was forbidden. Here, have some water."

"I was in Paris, not far from Boulogne, when combined Allied forces bombed the Renault factories . . . and I was in Saint-Tropez when the Germans blew up the harbor."

"Come on, all that's over now, we need to get used to being happy!"

A distraught-looking young woman arrived at the café. Léna recognized her. She was wearing a figure-hugging black shirtdress and had undone a couple of buttons at the top and the bottom. Her low neckline and the slit in the dress revealing her slender, already tanned legs left no room for doubt about her intentions for the evening. She was beautiful and that wasn't going to be a problem on a night like this.

"If you're looking for Manu," Léna said with smile, "you'll have to wait. They're not here yet."

"I heard an explosion."

"Don't worry. Just some youngsters messing around."

It was seven o'clock and the deminers still hadn't shown up. At seven in the evening in April on the French Riviera the light is softer, tending toward pink. It's stunning but it's no time to be clearing mines. Deminers start early so they can finish early. They should have been there.

Ever since she'd known them, Léna had always dreaded
bad news, fretted when they were late, interpreted any
sign. The music struck up again, even more rousing than
before, couples danced and drank, but those poor souls
were still demining.

ENZO'S NERVOUS TENSION HAD CRANKED UP further because of the fireworks. Fabien was furious that he couldn't take over from him. Too risky: The mine that had supposedly been easy to defuse had in fact been connected to another, which had itself been linked to a third, and so on for more than two hours. Enzo had started to quaver on the third, but he hadn't let it show.

Just to spice things up, each device and trigger mechanism was different. In the very early days of demining, people like Fabien and Enzo who took all the responsibility had been given a simple leaflet by way of background information; it was a very incomplete list of different devices and igniters. When he'd studied it, Enzo had never guessed that he could end up disarming so many different mines in one go, as if flipping through the pages of that booklet, as if a psychopathic instructor wanted to pummel every diagram, every instruction, and every operating mechanism into his head, into the sweat of his fear. Gripped by exhaustion and tension, he shook as he recalled friction triggers, the four different release models, the four pressure models, the one that used just traction and the one that used traction and release, the chemical igniters...

There was never anything straightforward about mine clearance, and Max regretted believing Enzo and staying close to him. Besides, wasn't it bad luck to say it was going to be easy? They should have been at the party several hours ago. A piece of cake? No one dared move.

Fabien was on edge. He knew about Enzo's pride, which could lure him to the best of situations or the worst. He would never give up in the face of a mine or the team or the passersby who'd gathered as if at a show. He just couldn't, even though it was a high-risk situation and this chain of devices sitting there waiting to explode was interminable, infernal. There was nothing Fabien could do about it. Confronted with a mine, Enzo was fascinated. He liked guessing what the trap was, predicting it, anticipating how it would respond, cradling it exactly the right way and then undoing the screws, slipping in a decoy, sliding it open, pressing, cutting, in exactly the right place, at exactly the right time. Did mines think they could crush him? He mastered them. Thanks to them, he could resume his unvoiced conversations and quash his shame, focusing it where he wanted: on each mine that needed disarming. He was proving to all the people who'd thrown stones at his mother that he'd risen above humiliation. He would triumph over them all. With fury. And nobility.

This was possibly one of Fabien's last days with his team and it wasn't going as he would have liked. His men had been looking forward to this evening's party for such a long time and they were now prey to this mounting anxiety. Along with the men from the team that had joined them. One after another they'd flattened themselves on the ground to protect themselves from danger, and Fabien could tell that this was only increasing the pressure on Enzo's nerves.

For Vincent, this waiting for the end of the day without moving and without approaching the Germans was becoming unbearable. He wasn't thinking about Enzo or the vicious medley of mines but about Matthias, this unhoped-for acquaintance. With equal measures of anticipation and dread he was eager to hear what the German had to tell him. Would they be able to talk before Matthias returned to his prison camp? Vincent didn't take his eyes off him, waiting for a sign that never came. It was Saturday. If he missed this opportunity to speak to him, he would have to wait all evening and all day on Sunday wondering whether Matthias would give him conclusive information. The waiting was unendurable. It was all he could think about. As for the rest, the mines, he had faith in Enzo and Fabien.

Meanwhile, Lukas was now sure he wouldn't reach the bunker this evening. His plan was screwed. Fabien was back and everyone was watching Enzo's every move: The circumstances were no longer favorable. Unless, in all the confusion when they headed to the dance, when the tension dropped, if it ever dropped, he could try something desperate. The sky was starting to glow, shifting from pale pink and pastel blue to angrier colors. Violent yellow and glowering pink, bloodied orange and purple clashing against turquoise. Before disappearing, the sun was parading its most exalted colors, and in less than an hour it would be dusk, when the light would descend into midnight blue. Under cover of darkness, Lukas would be able to sneak over to the bunker if Matthias caused a diversion. He stayed vigilant, watching out for any opportunity. The men were completely wrung out, and the band's jaunty chords plaguing their ears didn't help. Perhaps that was a good thing.

And then, unexpectedly, Enzo looked up slowly and glanced despairingly at Fabien and the others; he couldn't do it.

"I'm so sorry, I shouldn't have—"

Any who weren't yet on the ground, threw themselves down.

But Enzo himself jumped to his feet with a roar of laughter.

"Come on, let's pack this all up and get to the party! I wish you could see your faces!"

As he brandished his arms triumphantly, an extraordinarily powerful explosion knocked him down. It was contagious: A string of connected mines exploded, racing furiously to the blockhouse. The explosives inside took over and tore the blockhouse apart. Clods of sand were hurled into the air, filling it with a powdery mass. There was zero visibility in this tornado of fragmented rock, ash, and sharp metal. Fabien had dived on top of Georges to protect him. Lukas could make out Matthias being launched into the air with some of the other men, and time seemed to be distended.

Vincent had to close his eyes, the sand was burning them, and he felt as if his whole being was compressed inside his skull. The shrill whistling of an intolerable music resonated in there, bouncing off the inflamed boundaries of his brain. Other than this deafening music, everything had slowed excruciatingly. Nothing belonged to him now. His body that he couldn't move, his actions and his malfunctioning senses, his heightened hearing, his shadowy vision, his stifled breathing—hadn't it stopped? The overpowering, piercing, all-consuming music kept spiraling into his eardrums, and his every neuron exploded into myriad shards of razor-sharp crystal. He was struck down by a madness that had always been there waiting for him, now ripping savagely into every crack as searing pain took possession of him.

The blast.

The violence of its exhalation, so powerful and oppressive. The excessive brutality of the shockwave. Vincent is in such pain that he doesn't know where it hurts. The worst of it isn't the agony from his wounds but the unfathomable and enduring pain of not being able to breathe the opaque air. His ribs are blocked into a vise, his body shattered, and exhaustion is winning. He descends into the darkness, welcoming it, calling to it. Just like the others.

No one is moving now. The apocalyptic outburst is becalmed.

Sharp, jagged pieces of concrete have flung a hostile, futuristic landscape over the beach. Sand mixed with dust has covered the scene in a thick powdery gray carpet, making it look pitifully desolate. The bodies are shapeless. Skin is no longer the color of skin. The war is still with them, persistent, insistent, and insulting.

And there on that beach, on that day, how to distinguish the living from the dead in among all these near-naked bodies, their outlines etched by a now gray sun as they lie under the fallout of this hurricane of sand, dust, metal, and stone?

THE FURY OF THE EXPLOSION WAS FOLLOWED BY silence, which was just as terrible. Nothing moved. Birds had vanished in an instant; the wind had suddenly dropped. After such stupefying violence, the very elements seemed to be paralyzed.

The first of them, the men farthest from the blockhouse, started to stagger to their feet. To rally together with the living. They would be grateful to those who had survived. This need to feel life around them urged them to move despite their pain. But what their battered bodies and souls really wanted was to stay there in peace for all time, not to be touched, not to be asked any questions, nothing that required a superhuman effort of them. Plagued by thirst, they didn't want to drink, bringing a flask to their lips was inordinately difficult. Thinking a colossal effort. They had reached absolute suffering. And so some of them thought of death as their only refuge and opted to let themselves go.

That was the effect of the blast, the long-dreaded blast, that destroys everything inside, mercilessly.

It took courage to extricate yourself from this deep, dark place. Jolted by survival instincts, Vincent emerged from the depths and battled to open his eyes. The post-eclipse sun blinded him. With injuries to one arm, his torso, and his face, he managed to make a small movement with one hand, then the other, then—cautiously—with his feet. He tried to stand. He hadn't anticipated how badly his suffering body had been paralyzed by the powerful shockwave that had compressed his stomach and lungs, and transmitted its formidable, explosive power into his every bone. Breathing was impossible, his lungs seemed to be trapped in a tight clamp. And yet he struggled to his feet, not really believing he would achieve it, and started to walk as best he could through the identical suffering bodies covered with their uniform of ash.

Matthias had given him the strength to get up: If Matthias was alive, then surely now he would tell him the secrets he hadn't yet revealed. With his last breath. Out of compassion.

It was impossible to find him in this tragic, dusty chaos. Vincent drifted from one body to another, and what did he care if people tittle-tattled that he'd helped a German first. He hadn't taken all these risks only to miss a chance to talk to the one person who could tell him about Ariane. His survival depended entirely on Matthias.

Lukas had hauled himself painfully to where the young musician lay, and he was the one Vincent saw first. He was murmuring German words that Vincent heard only in fragments. He was begging for Matthias's forgiveness. Matthias must hold on. He was so young…

Vincent dropped to his knees beside them. Matthias was losing blood. A lot of blood. The flow sprang from his inert body, and its wide, dark red tide through the gray powder was a striking sight, as if the beach itself were bleeding. Vincent's eyesight was still obscured by the shock and the sand irritating his eyes, but he adapted his vision and forcibly pulled himself together.

He quickly assessed Matthias's condition, took his pulse, and examined him frantically: Matthias was breathing weakly. Vincent pulled off his shirt, tore up the sleeves, and, with the leather strap from his water flask, tied a tourniquet to stem the bleeding.

At the far end of the beach, Léna had just arrived. When she saw Fabien lying inert with his eyes closed, she raced over, calling his name. He didn't respond. She panicked, not knowing what to do other than gently, despairingly slapping his cheeks. She was so frightened. He absolutely must wake up. He couldn't go, it was impossible, not now, not like this.

Fabien managed to open his eyes feebly, his expression blank and his pupils peculiarly dilated.

"Fabien, say something!"

His jaw was locked, and he barely articulated the words, "A chain of mines...all linked...a filthy trap."

"Aurélien's called the rescue squad."

"The team...Enzo...Max...Vincent?"

Léna noticed that a German prisoner had got to his feet and was walking away as if to escape. Fabien looked in the same direction to see what had caught her attention. With immeasurable effort, he tried to get to his feet to stop the prisoner escaping. Léna persuaded him not to.

"Hush, you must stay lying down."

Contrary to Fabien's fears, the prisoner was going over to save Thibault, who lay prone under some rubble, and he called for help. Fabien dropped back down to the ground, his eyes fixed on the sky. The clouds were stretching and resuming their slow journey. The light shimmered. The setting sun exhibited all its splendor and majesty, completely unfazed by death.

Fabien asked again about who had survived, but Léna couldn't bring herself to let go of his hand and check on the others. She had plenty of courage and wasn't afraid of blood, but she had a feeling that if she left Fabien, if she took her eyes off him even just for a minute, he could be gone forever. She recognized something in his face, a weariness that shifts toward surrender, a fixed expression, defeated eyes, the outline abruptly diminished, and the dark expanse of shadows under his eyes taking over. She didn't like it.

The rescue squad was trying to work methodically. As the deminers had before them, they worked across the beach in sections, looking for the wounded. In almost every instance it was too late. Despite the danger, they ran from one body to the next, deciding against covering them with sheets, then running to another man in the hope of saving at least one. Léna raised her arm to attract their attention.

Fabien stopped her by squeezing her hand. He didn't want their help. The others first. She nodded, reassured him, yes, she would do whatever he asked, and continued to send discreet signals to the rescuers with her free hand.

Then, rising above the moans, came a harrowing, soul-destroying scream...Matthias. Vincent had made the decision to cauterize his leg wound: The tourniquet hadn't stemmed the flow of blood because there was another wound near his groin. Vincent had removed the knife from his bayonet and Lukas had lit a fire. Using the incandescent blade heated by the flames, Vincent burned the young musician's raw flesh. Georges, who'd come over to them, had offered his flask of cheap whiskey. Even he couldn't bear to hear the German's screams. Lukas made Matthias drink, tipping his head back and holding his mouth open with his fingers to pour the lifesaving liquor down his throat as best he could, a drop of alcohol in an ocean of pain, but he would have done anything to relieve the suffering of this boy to whom he'd promised freedom. Matthias passed out.

Vincent took his pulse. Nothing. Matthias's heart had stopped. He wasn't breathing. They were losing him. At the risk of breaking one of the boy's ribs, Vincent started vigorously massaging his heart. No choice. He gave him mouth-to-mouth, anything to save him. He battled on, he knew what to do, and didn't even notice Fabien watching from a few meters away, surprised by his recruit's unsuspected abilities and then collapsing again from the effort he'd put into getting up.

Matthias came around howling in pain. Vincent had succeeded—but for how long?—in bringing him back to life. The musician studied his own hands: Nothing about them looked like hands anymore, and he howled all over again. The nurses who were now beside them lifted

Matthias and slid him onto a stretcher. Every move revived his searing pain. A nurse gave him two doses of morphine. Should she give him a third? she asked the doctor beside her. They were rationed, of course, and they needed enough for everyone but this, the level of pain … The doctor didn't do it gladly but said the decision should be deferred until later, in the prisoners' medical center.

Vincent intervened, making one final bid to help, and speaking with an authority that left no room for procrastination.

"Their medical centers aren't as effectual as the hospital. If he's not taken to Marseille, he has no hope of making it. And he'll need the best orthopedic surgeon for his hands."

Vincent's authoritarian tone seemed strange to the doctor who studied him, his distraught expression, tattered clothes, and bleeding body. It wasn't in the regulations … but Vincent wasn't giving him a choice.

"They take all the same risks as we do demining. This is no time for hesitation. Otherwise, he won't make it."

Vincent's conviction was indisputable. The doctor signaled to the stretcher-bearers to take Matthias to the hospital.

Lukas was still kneeling in the sand, motionless, he didn't even startle when Vincent put a hand on his shoulder.

"I'm so sorry."

Lukas looked at Vincent, not sure whether he was being sincere or was still trying to get information. Vincent sat down next to him with some difficulty.

After thinking for a while, Lukas took a very battered book from his pocket. He flicked through the pages before choosing one and feverishly making some notes in the margin. He tore out the page and handed it to Vincent.

"Could you take this to Matthias at the hospital…if…"

He didn't finish his question. No one wanted to talk about death, ever, as if a few simple words alone could conjure it by some curse still more lethal than the explosion. Vincent didn't look away, still looking into Lukas's eyes, which seemed an even paler blue than usual, almost transparent, his expressionless face, his jaw clamped to keep his emotions locked away: Lukas was fighting back tears. It was the first time Vincent had seen a German with tears in his eyes, and he almost couldn't believe what he was seeing. He found himself thinking—although it was a very fleeting thought—that in another time, in different circumstances, Lukas could have been his friend, and there was a good reason it was Lukas he'd first approached.

"I promise."

∾

WHILE LUKAS HAD BEEN WRITING ON A PAGE OF
his book, a wild thought had come to Vincent: The message was for him, he was sure of it. Lukas must have spoken to Matthias, and he must know where Ariane was.

Even when he realized that the message really was intended for Matthias, Vincent was convinced it had a double meaning, or that there was coded information within
the text itself, waiting to be deciphered.

He went home to the studio and was relieved not to
find Saskia there; he wanted to read and reread the note
Lukas had confided to him. He didn't clean his wounds,
didn't pay attention to the pain. He went to his bedroom
to find the photos of soldiers that Audrey had given him.
Matthias was definitely the soldier Audrey had had in
mind.

Then Vincent immersed himself in reading the few
lines scribbled into the margins of a book, as if trying to de-
code the hieroglyphics on the Rosetta stone. But the words
were in fact simple. Lukas was apologizing to Matthias. He
would never forgive himself for what had happened, and
he promised Matthias that, if they both survived, he would
help him get into the Philharmonic orchestra, he knew

people who could help. Reading between the lines, Vincent gathered that Lukas had persuaded Matthias to enroll in the mine-clearing team. Why, Vincent wondered, but unless he was insane, there was no possible double meaning he could detect, no message intended for him.

As for the original text on the page, it was a poem by Heinrich Heine. What did the Germans think of it? Heine was a major poet, but a French-speaking one; he'd lived in France in the nineteenth century, been married to a Frenchwoman, was banned in his own country and despised by the Nazis. Was Lukas hoping the French would think he loved France because he liked Heine?

One thing Vincent did know for sure was that Lukas hadn't chosen the poem at random. Granted, the much-read book tended to fall open near this poem, but Lukas had leafed through and torn it out specifically.

"I told you you had to stop!"

Vincent looked up. Saskia was back and she was shaking with fear and rage. She'd only made up her mind to go and look for Rodolphe very late and it was then, long after the explosion, that she'd grasped what had happened. She'd then gone straight to the beach to look for Vincent and hadn't found him. She'd been told that three seriously injured men had been evacuated and about ten were dead. She'd thought he was among them.

Saskia was spitting with anger that Vincent risked his life clearing mines. She was so beside herself that she wanted to hit him despite the injuries she could see through his torn clothes.

"Do you think you'll somehow get out every time? That you're luckier than everyone else?"

Vincent didn't reply. He could tell she hadn't finished. And she hadn't. She'd found out something else that profoundly offended her.

"I heard that a Frenchman saved one of the Germans. Was that you?"

She didn't need him to reply. She knew.

"Why did you do it?"

"Because he was going to die."

Saskia noticed Vincent move to hide the poem Lukas had entrusted to him, and she snatched it from him.

"It's a message I need to give to the injured German."

"And you read it? I didn't think you'd be so prying."

"I think the note is for the German, but the poem is for me."

She scanned through the text.

"And you're taken in by this? He's hiding behind Heine—it's a lie! He's making you think he loves France, but you can't trust a German!"

"Don't you believe Heine?"

"I don't believe *him*!" Saskia snapped.

"You don't know him."

"So, now are you going to tell me he's a good man, he's not like the other Germans, they're not all the same? Those are lazy, cowardly arguments!"

"I didn't mean to offend you. I'm sorry."

Saskia had forgotten that a man could apologize. She tilted her head to indicate that she acknowledged his apology.

"Okay. But you won't be going demining on Monday."

"I'm very sorry. I will go."

"So you'll die too?"

"Don't say that."

"If I don't say it, I'll never be able to forgive myself."

She hadn't dared admit to him that her sister had died right beside her, on the same thin mattress, and she'd witnessed the transition from life to death, in a sigh, a transition no one can do anything to stop. And yet she had a feeling that if she'd reacted one second before the moment when everything turned upside down, the moment when everything became irreversible, she would have managed to save her sister's life, their lives. It haunted her. Occasionally she stopped cursing herself and in these rare interludes was angry with her sister for leaving her alone. Then the next minute she was angry with herself for being angry with her sister.

She couldn't tell Vincent all this, but he could feel her fury—it enveloped him, oppressed him, made him feel guilty.

He got up to drink some water by cupping his hands under the faucet.

With no reaction from him, Saskia couldn't help grabbing hold of him. His silence filled her with a rage that she'd been containing for too long. The rage she had inside, ready to explode at any time since her family had been arrested, her rage on the trains and in the camps, her rage when she'd seen her mother naked, her rage that anyone could humiliate the person she loved most in the world. She hit him to make him stop, make him wake up, make him understand. He had to live. He couldn't go on thinking his life wasn't worth anything, and let himself be blown apart, more pitiful than a tire exploding on burning-hot asphalt. He couldn't accept this fate. And yes, it was selfish too; she didn't want to see him die. This wasn't something she wanted to divulge but she'd seen death at such close quarters that it felt like a stranger she could almost see and touch. It prowled around her and took away everyone she loved. There are some people who escape it. Some who don't acknowledge it. Some who don't want to talk about it because they refuse to accept it or they're superstitious. Saskia wasn't like them. She would meet it head-on. This was personal—she wouldn't let death win every time.

ON THE BEACH, THE FIVE POSTS USED TO RAISE the sarcophagus mines looked like five gallows, and it was hard to tell whether they were there for the explosive devices or the deminers. Five, like a sinister portent of the five men who'd died the day before, not to mention the reinforcement team, the Germans, and others still to come.

On this morning after the dance and the disaster of the night before, the ruins of the disemboweled blockhouse were still there on the beach, a debris of cement with arteries of steel, along with shreds of clothing... and of human beings. The eye would grow accustomed to it. The craters left by the explosions made a lunar landscape of this scandalous postwar cataclysm that hardly anyone would ever mention.

After ensuring that the rescuers examined Fabien, Léna had taken him back to her apartment above the café. She'd undone his bandaging which the sand had infiltrated, disinfected his wounds, and wrapped his arm and leg with clean cloth. Then she'd fed him and given him clothes for the night. He'd fallen asleep and later had woken with a start: He was freezing, he was burning. He was incoherent.

And so she'd practiced her own form of medicine in the night. She knew how to quash a fever and minimize pain using extracts from willow bark that she'd gathered from the best trees. She made poultices with clay and plants. She boiled water and threw in dried flowers and leaves. She strengthened his body with oil extracted from junipers on the heath that were said to be descended from the burning bush in the Bible. She used her entire pharmacopeia, she used arnica and everlasting. She coated his arms and legs with a maceration of Saint-John's-wort—the flowers were still in the bottle—which produced an oil as red as grenadine. When he woke, she told him that these flowers could heal bruises to the body but also bruises to the soul. He let her tend to him and slipped back into sleep.

Léna went to his apartment to collect some clothes and to find the number for the Mine Clearance Department in Paris to let them know.

He'd asked her to go there, but she felt she was breaking and entering. She knew Fabien only from the snatches of deliciously annoying conversations they'd had at the café; overnight she'd to some extent come to know his body, his fever, and his skin; and now she was entering his world like a thief. Books, poetry (mostly the surrealists), jazz records (almost all American, but she recognized the sleeve of *Mademoiselle Swing*, which made her smile), a record player, a radio. Letters in their envelopes sorted into small packages carefully tied with ribbon or string. Photos of his parents, of a younger man who looked like him and must have been his brother. Fabien didn't talk about him. Just as he never talked about this young woman whose picture caught Léna's eye and stealthily crushed her heart. Everything Léna wasn't. Léna would have given anything to have the same dazzling smile, the curly—very modern—hair, and those pale eyes that struck her as infinitely more attractive than her own dark eyes.

The photo that most hurt her had been taken in a university courtyard. The gentle but bold young woman was surrounded by twenty-year-old men who were probably all in love with her. She had more than just a fashionable haircut, she had quite the head on her shoulders: She must have been a scientist, a pioneer, the only woman among a future elite. Léna's entourage was her customers on the café terrace...She too, though possibly in a different way, felt like a pioneer. She hadn't been able to go to college but had taken her future in hand; she wasn't dependent on a man, and no one had ever told her what she should do. She had rejected her mother's polite, elegant, desperate form of submission, even though she adored her and didn't judge her. Every woman in her family had allowed the next generation of women to progress. This was how women would cope. So Léna felt like a sister to this young woman who was probably no longer alive but whom she would respect.

Then, under the pile of clothes she gathered up for him to change into, she found something she would have preferred not to see. A memento that Fabien must have been keeping of the Resistance, along with its ghosts, its nightmares, and its nostalgia. It was kept inside a small metal pillbox. Nothing was written on the box, but she was in no doubt: This was the dose of lightning-swift poison that Resistance fighters kept on them at all times, the tragic release to stop them talking under torture, to stop them betraying and screaming, allowing them to die. Why had Fabien kept this cyanide pill like a precious possession?

WHEN LÉNA RETURNED TO THE CAFÉ, IRÈNE, the woman she'd talked to briefly before the dance, was just getting back into her car.

"So, did you find your doctor…What was his name again?"

"Hadrien? I waited all night for nothing, I didn't see him. I need to leave now."

"Can I help at all?"

Irène handed her the photo she'd shown her the day before.

"If you ever see him…Do you remember?"

"I remember. He's looking for a woman called…"

"Ariane."

"But Ariane doesn't want anyone looking for her."

Irène nodded. Léna promised to ask whether her waiter or any of her customers knew him and she wished Irène good luck with her mission. As she walked through the café, she showed the photo to Aurélien, who studied it again; Irène had spoken to him too.

"Do you know who he reminds me of, but bulkier and younger?"

"I can't think."

"The new deminer, Vincent."

"Except this guy's called Hadrien and he's a doctor! I'd be surprised to see a doctor in this café, but you never know. It seemed to be important to her."

She handed the photo to Aurélien, and he looked at it again, more doubtful now.

When Léna walked into the apartment with Fabien's clothes and a few records, he was awake. He was looking at the vials, dried flowers, and plants around him. She was afraid he would take her for a witch, but he smiled at her. She gave him some hot broth to drink and started applying her unguents again. Sometimes he would recognize the smell of thyme, sage, or rosemary, but at other times nothing, he didn't understand and put his faith in her, allowing the aromatic vapors of ancestral magic arts to go to his head. He closed his eyes and his pain melted away under the warm, fragranced facecloths, the balms, the wax perfumed with eucalyptus and mint. He didn't know it, but she intoxicated him with valerian, the herb that sends cats crazy and soothes the mind. It meant that he could briefly escape the terrible fear, the irrepressible fear of the blast. He stopped trying to picture the invisible and irreversible damage inside his body, in the secrecy of his lungs, the meanderings of his organs. He'd felt pulverized, now he was alive again. Terror was followed by tiredness, a beneficial sort of languor. Fabien had no religion. No word from any god could heal him. The skin of Léna's hands on his own skin—that could. He didn't believe in miracles, but Léna knew how to make them happen.

She didn't say, I told you so.

He didn't say, I've been offered a job in Paris.

They didn't need to talk, just to discover each other. When Léna worked at the café, she was always on the move, looked people dead in the eye when she spoke, and laughed in great peals. At home, her movements were soothing, her voice muted, everything was gentle. And he, the restless Fabien, surrendered to an unusual sense of boundless tranquility.

She had given him her bed to sleep in, and she herself slept on a bench seat in another room. When she woke in the night, she found Fabien lying on the ground. Now that the fighting had stopped, he hadn't been able to re-adapt to the comfort of a bed. He claimed it was out of habit. She understood that he wasn't allowing himself to.

Fabien couldn't get back to sleep. He dreaded the morning. Not because the pain would return—he would ignore that—but he was head of a team and would have to handle administrative details for the dead, gathering their few possessions and, the hardest part, breaking the news to their families.

In the morning they didn't exchange a word about what had happened the night before, Fabien abandoning himself to Léna's care, the alchemy between them. She redressed his wounds, and they ate breakfast in silence. When she got up from the table to go and open the café, she gave him a *See you this evening* without even thinking. He replied *See you this evening*, and when—out on the street—he realized what had happened, he smiled.

IN THE GUESTHOUSE WHERE THREE OF THE dead deminers had lived and the farm that had taken in the other two, there was no rent to pay off: The landlords had asked for payment in advance. They justified this to Fabien, saying there was no glory in asking for money from a man because you were afraid he would die before paying his debts, but Fabien had to understand their point of view: Giving credit to a deminer was risky. Fabien cut short their excuses and said he just wanted to be sure the landlords returned all the men's belongings. The dead men no longer needed them, but their families did.

Fabien piled up his teammates' few personal effects in Max's Traction Avant. The town hall would take care of returning them to the families.

One of the landlords ran after Fabien in the street. Full of remorse, he handed over a canvas bag that he'd found under one of the deminers' mattresses. In it were some money and a notebook. He swore so furiously that all the money was there that Fabien was sure he'd taken some of it. When Fabien opened the notebook, he was amazed to see it belonged to Hubert.

"Did Hubert live at your place?"

The landlord nodded. Apparently, he was cheaper than the previous place Hubert had been and provided better meals. Hardly surprising, since the landlord was a baker. But Hubert hadn't had long to enjoy them. He never came back, and the baker assumed Hubert had died in the accident on the beach.

Fabien thanked him and left. He was worried: Hubert hadn't been there when the explosion happened and hadn't told anyone where he was going...

Did he not dare come back to the team after deserting on such a crucial day? Or had he made the most of Fabien's absence to abandon the job and go home to his family without having to explain himself to anyone? Others had done the same before him. Something could also have happened to him in an accident or a fight...If that was the case, Fabien would hear about it eventually. He couldn't linger over Hubert, he had work to do.

He did the rounds of the other landlords, then went to the prison camp. He was well acquainted with the director, a former Resistance fighter from the Maures, and respected him. They spoke about the Germans for a while; Fabien wanted to know more about each of them. Their families would have to be informed. It would be difficult. The war was still going on in Germany and the country had descended into chaos—all communications had been broken off.

This was the first time Fabien had seen at close hand the conditions in which the prisoners were kept. He could understand why some of them wanted to get out and clear mines rather than stay behind this barbed wire.

Then he had to make up his mind to go and collect the administrative files for the dead and injured deminers. He was not looking forward to this. He had to wake the recruiting officer to get him to open his office. The recruiter, awash with cheap wine from the party, had passed out for most of the weekend and still didn't know where he was when he heard knocking at his door.

Pulling himself together, he swore that, yes, he'd warned all prospective deminers of the risks when they were hired; he was duty bound not to downplay the risks.

"But what's the point? We can tell them as much as we like, how many injured, how many amputees, how many killed, not one of 'em thinks it'll happen to him! What a tragedy!"

"Can I see their files?"

They were factual, minimalist; reading them was an ordeal. Age, marital status, number of children. The replies to these simple questions used so few words to sketch a heartbreaking life. A few numbers told the whole story. Tom, an only child, was responsible for both of his parents at just twenty-one. Twenty, in fact. Fabien had retrieved Tom's real ID papers from his landlord and, as he'd suspected, Tom had lied about his age. At twenty-three, Valentin, who'd come as part of the reinforcements team, already had two daughters and a son, which had exempted him from enrolling in the army. With three children, Valentin had avoided the war, but not death. How would these families manage without their breadwinners?

Fabien shook as he read Enzo's file. His wife, whom he mentioned so often and still adored, had borne him three daughters. He too could have avoided going to war, but he'd joined the Resistance. He'd never spared himself, never gone into hiding. He'd given his all. Fabien was devastated by the names he'd chosen for each of his girls to express how much he loved them, the names of princesses and goddesses—now orphans.

Even the men's signatures were moving. Two of the men who'd died, Valentin and Tom, had filled out their forms in fine handwriting with impeccable upstrokes and downstrokes: They'd passed their school certificate. Their families must have been proud of this qualification, but it hadn't put food on the table or protected them.

And then there was Henri, who'd fled the north for fear of a firedamp explosion in the depths of a coal mine only to be caught out by a mine exploding in the open air. Did he think about this cruel twist of fate as he hovered between life and death in the room next to Max's?

For his own peace of mind, Fabien asked for Hubert's file. His wife and children lived in Corrèze. In a château. The recruiter had raised an eyebrow, but Hubert had told him he was financially ruined, and the château was just a big old house with a leaking roof. And anyway, he had a big family. Fabien didn't say anything, but when he'd glanced at Hubert's notebook, the key thing he'd discovered was that Hubert had *two* families...

In the margins, the recruiter had occasionally written comments in pencil. "Is he reliable?" "Too hard on himself, one to watch," "Liar." What was the point of mistrusting men who were being sent to their deaths? And worse than that, who went of their own accord?

"How are you getting on with recruiting?"

"I'm not gonna lie, we don't have many coming forward." He handed Fabien just two forms. "We do have these two. Because of their age, I gave them a couple of weeks to think it over. I can try asking them to sign up sooner. But with the explosion it'll be tough to keep up their enthusiasm."

Twenty-one and twenty-two. Fabien didn't like it. Even if the war had aged everyone overnight, that was still young. Did he have a choice? Two recruits wouldn't even be enough to get his team back to where it had been, he'd have to wait until they were up to full strength before they returned to work.

His sad round of visits ended at the town hall.

While Fabien sat at a desk in the administrative offices writing a letter to each next of kin, a very emotional but very discomfited mayor mumbled a few condolences. His words tripped over one another as he expressed not only how terribly sorry he was that Fabien had lost so many men but also how urgent his task was. Demining must be resumed as soon as possible: It was crucial that his citizens were safe.

Then the mayor let Fabien see what was in the box he'd just received. By way of equipment to counter the dangers of demining, the ministry had sent new brochures explaining the job. A stricken Fabien leafed through it listlessly. As with previous brochures, barely half the different models of mines were mentioned.

Lastly, the mayor told him that, given the circumstances, the journalist dispatched by Dautry to come and see for himself and rectify his disastrous appraisal of deminers would not be making the trip after all.

As if this wasn't enough, Fabien was rudely collared by some locals as he left the building. Thanks to the explosion on Saturday evening all their windows were broken! Blown in just like that! The guys needed to be careful—accidents like that were expensive. And dangerous: What if a kid had been injured?

Without losing his temper, Fabien reminded them that it was precisely in trying to secure their safety that several deminers had lost their lives. The gaggle stopped its onslaught for a few seconds, and then they remembered why they were there, and asked the mayor who would be paying for the damage.

On his way back, Fabien wondered how to go about talking to his men. He didn't want to prepare a speech. Truth be told, he couldn't. Having lost five teammates, he would find it hard to motivate the survivors. Hadn't they done their fair share? And how had that been recognized? Maybe he should encourage them all to head off to other opportunities. He would say whatever came to him at the time.

Then out of nowhere, when he'd stopped thinking about him altogether, he realized what had happened to Hubert. And if he'd guessed right, it wasn't good news.

WHO ON EARTH COULD BE KNOCKING AT THE door? Paralyzed in her bed, Saskia endured the sound of knocking downstairs as it grew faster and faster. Vincent wasn't there. Fabien had come for him at the end of the morning, with a conspiratorial air and muttering quietly as if they were still at war, as if there were still secrets that could be the death of them. As soon as they'd left, she'd gone back upstairs. She was tired and had lain down, not to sleep but to clear her head and gather the strength to fight. Try as she might to think it through, she couldn't see what to do. Her whole thought process was numbed.

When she'd been in constant danger in the camp, she'd been able to think with astonishing speed. Now that the Nazis couldn't get her and she had plenty of time to think about things other than making herself invisible, she couldn't do a thing.

And still this banging on the door. Harder and harder.

The last time she'd heard knocking like that was at home, with her family, when they'd met in secret, with the lights out, whispering to one another. The knocking had been so violent that the front door had been broken down. A furious, shouting, black tornado had swept into their home, devoid of any shred of humanity, words had made no difference. Savage, gratuitous violence drunk on its own power had bombarded them. The men had beaten her mother, her father, the whole family, and then taken them away.

She buried her face in her pillow. She didn't want to hear this hammering at the door. If it was for Vincent, they could just come back later. The day after she'd first arrived at the studio, a man had come knocking at the door, prompting insurmountable terror in her. Miraculously, he'd given up. That afternoon, Vincent had told her the man was Mathilde's cousin, who'd come a long way in order to tune the piano. She'd claimed she hadn't heard a thing. But this time the knocking wouldn't stop.

She reasoned with herself: The Germans hadn't been in the south since the end of last summer. The militiamen were in prison. No one would come for her here because no one knew she was here.

But this insistent knocking, going on and on . . . In Vincent's bedroom there was a window that overlooked the street. From there, she'd be able to see who was knocking without being spotted herself. Impossible. She'd have to lean out, she'd be seen. Why wouldn't the knocking stop?

Since she'd returned, getting out of bed had become one of her most difficult trials. She hoped she'd been forgotten, but perhaps someone had followed her and knew where to find her. Her legs shook. The horrible feeling that she was heading for another arrest. Perhaps, as she'd threatened to, Madame Bellanger had gone to the police to ensure Saskia didn't return to her house again.

But what if it was someone who mattered to Vincent? She knew intuitively that he spent every day hoping for news of the woman he loved.

So she made herself go and look out of the window.

A young woman was waiting outside. Not for Vincent. For her.

It was the woman she'd met in the street, the one who'd been wearing her mother's dress. She'd arranged to meet Saskia outside the café on Wednesday. What was she doing here?

Saskia went down to open up. Still as dazzling, elegant, and cheerful, the young woman was wearing slightly oversize shorts belted at the waist and a white shirt with the sleeves rolled up. She looked spectacular in this simple outfit. Saskia was ashamed to greet her in the same dress, but it was the only one she had. She washed her clothes every evening, blessing the warm southern nights that dried them in less than fifteen minutes.

"I'm sorry for knocking so hard, but I wanted to bring you your mother's dress today so you could have it as soon as possible." Seeing Saskia's astonishment, she anticipated her question. "People said this was where you lived. Everyone knows everything in this neighborhood."

Saskia was aware of this. Her family had paid too high a price for her ever to forget. She felt more and more overwhelmed. Now that she was cornered, her mind started whirring again. People know I live here, if the Germans come back in force tomorrow, they'll know where to find me, and if it isn't the Germans, it could be antisemitic neighbors, or the Bellangers...

"Your mother's very talented. This dress hangs just perfectly. I'll miss it."

Saskia still hadn't said a word to her shorts-wearing visitor. She now invited her in, hoping she would refuse, but the visitor accepted and thanked her for the invitation.

At least Saskia wouldn't have to stay on the doorstep. Even if *everyone knew everything*, she didn't want people to see her there. She felt embarrassed behaving like the mistress of the house in this studio whose rent she couldn't contribute to.

"What a pretty place you have."

She didn't even know what to do with these simple words, spoken completely spontaneously. Did her visitor want to know whether the place really belonged to Saskia? Did the "you" mean Saskia or did it include the man who lived here and who'd left a pair of shoes by the door? They'd caught the visitor's eye, although she may not have meant to pry but had simply been filling the silence by glancing around the room.

There must be some purpose behind every sentence. And if there wasn't, or if it wasn't ill-intentioned, then Saskia really had lost the knack of understanding other people. This woman was probably her age, but *she* wasn't thin, her hair was nicely styled, her makeup glowed, she'd already embarked on life, while Saskia still looked like a feral child.

Saskia stalled for time by boiling some water on the hot plate, and this gave her a chance to think about what she would say, to formulate a semblance of conversation. Thanking someone for a dress that was hers seemed abhorrent, but she did it anyway.

"Oh, it's only natural, the dress is yours."

Saskia smiled at her for the first time. At last, someone who understood.

Now feeling more confident, the woman said, "I'm Éléonore."

"Saskia."

"Oh, what a gorgeous name... quite unusual."

Saskia smiled again. Hearing her name spoken out loud resonated through her, waking something familiar, something she'd forgotten long ago but that came rushing back, and now seemed so obvious: I'm being named therefore I am. It was a long time since she'd been called by her name. And she'd so missed having a friend.

Saskia liked Éléonore's chatter: Her aunt Ida had been a *zazou* before the war—oh, the very word *zazou*, the people who coined it to describe a movement of young rebels were geniuses!—so she loved anything provocative and jazz and outsize English clothes. Éléonore hoped she herself would have Ida's courage: Like many *zazous*, she'd joined the Resistance. Basically, Éléonore adored Ida.

She punctuated all of her sentences with Saskia's name, like a child who's learned a pleasing new word and keeps endlessly repeating it. In the natural course of things, she became bolder and started asking questions. Which school did Saskia go to before the war? Did Saskia enjoy schoolwork? Had Saskia been to check her results for the baccalaureate? Even if she took the exams two years ago, the results would still be recorded at the Board of Education. She could look into it if Saskia wanted. Oh, look, a piano! Did Saskia play? She so wished she could.

Saskia listened to the uninterrupted flow of her conversation—light, gracious, peppered with generous and astute remarks and observations that made Saskia smile. She was so grateful to Éléonore for not surreptitiously trying to spot the stigmata of camp life, or not asking "What was it like?" as if a normal conversation was any place to share the horrors of deportation. And anyway, the people who did ask never really wanted to hear a single detail. At last, someone was seeing her as an equal, without being suspicious, afraid, or contemptuous. Saskia started to relax; she was becoming like other people again.

When Saskia had finished making the tea and was walking over with the teapot, Éléonore felt she could now say, "Seeing as we're the same height, I thought it would be okay to bring some of my dresses. I thought you might need them."

Saskia didn't know how to react. Should she thank her? She poured tea into Éléonore's cup without a word.

"Don't worry, they're not ones I wear anymore!"

The scalding tea strayed from its trajectory and poured straight onto Éléonore's slender hand, making Éléonore snatch her hand away.

"Put your hand under cold water! It'll stop the burning!"

Éléonore ran cold water over her hand for a long while, which gave her time to think. Whatever made her say she didn't wear them anymore? They weren't worn or unfashionable. She just hadn't wanted to embarrass Saskia but had been terribly untactful. She couldn't think how to salvage the situation.

Meanwhile, Saskia was annoyed with herself. She hadn't done it on purpose, but what was this? Did she deserve to be given used clothes that people didn't wear anymore? When she'd reached Paris, a friend from the camp had given her a dress that she'd bought before the war and had never worn. Now, that was a real present. It was the one she'd been wearing ever since. But how could she accept this? The dresses were bound to be pretty, and Saskia wanted to wear different things. But she'd pictured herself becoming friends with Éléonore ... No, she couldn't bring herself to accept them.

"Is it any better?"

"Yes, thank you. Cold water was a good idea."

"For the dresses, it's very kind, but it would be better if you gave them to someone who needs them."

Saskia turned her back on Éléonore as if she urgently needed to empty the teapot and rinse it out. Éléonore understood that her visit was over. When she said she wouldn't keep her any longer, Saskia didn't stop her from leaving.

∽

FABIEN HAD COME TO FIND VINCENT AT THE studio but hadn't wanted to explain the reason in front of Saskia. Why had he chosen Vincent? Instinct, most likely, but that wasn't all. If his theory about Hubert was right, he would need this business to be hushed up, and who better than Vincent to keep something quiet? The man clearly had things to hide, this would just be one more.

They drove far into the scrubland with the car bouncing along the stony tracks, and Fabien had no trouble finding the place he was looking for. Before Vincent had been recruited, Fabien's team had demined a road that led to several farms. It was called chemin Conil, which means "hillside path" in Provençal. He very soon found the smallholder and his wife, the couple who'd come to the beach to thank them so warmly and give them oil and wine. They were delighted to see Fabien, but when he asked where he could find the other farmer who'd wanted his field demined, their faces darkened.

Vincent hadn't forgotten the man either: He'd fought him when, in his despair, the man had lashed out at the German prisoners.

Seeing how uncomfortable the smallholders looked, Fabien knew he'd guessed right. The farmer had successfully persuaded Hubert to clear his field of mines. Perhaps Hubert had even come forward willingly and offered to do it to earn extra money. He'd made the most of Fabien's absence and must have promised to do the work over the weekend.

The couple swore they didn't know anything, but when Fabien and Vincent drove to the neighboring smallholding, a gaping crater betrayed the size of a recent explosion. Fabien had been hoping that Hubert was just injured and was hiding somewhere on the farm. The diameter of the crater banished any such hope, as did the farmer's refusal to open the door to them. Fabien and Vincent had to force their way in.

Confronted with Fabien's insistent questions, the farmer came up with a story and stuck to it doggedly. The explosion in his field? His cow had stepped on a mine.

"And where's the cow now?"

The farmer shrugged, refusing to reply.

"Do you know what you're risking here? A prison sentence."

"For a cow setting off a mine."

"For poaching a deminer."

"But I never saw your deminer!"

"His name's Hubert. Where is he?"

The farmer wouldn't talk. Fabien had to threaten to call the police before he admitted that he'd dragged Hubert's body to an oak forest and hid it in the undergrowth.

When the three of them reached the area, they were hit by the smell. Vincent suggested a cigarette. Then another.

Once their noses and throats were saturated with tobacco, they were able to go over to the bushes...

As they pushed aside dead leaves and brambles that ripped their skin, Fabien and Vincent reopened their own wounds. Vincent's shirt and bandages were torn, Fabien's forearms bleeding. They were too committed to turn back. When the farmer eventually showed them Hubert's body, they recoiled. He had no face or hands. His body was stiff, hunched, his arms crossed over his chest, frozen in a pathetic attempt to protect himself from the explosion. The farmer hadn't decided to remove him from the field until several hours after he'd died. It had been too late; the body couldn't be straightened. After their initial shock, Vincent and Fabien felt great compassion. Hubert had broken the regulations to earn enough to feed his two families. He wasn't the most talkative or the friendliest of men, but no one deserved to die like this. He'd thought he could get the better of the mines. No one ever could.

Neither the farmer nor Vincent knew how Fabien would act on this. With his eyes still pinned on Hubert, he told Vincent, *We're taking him with us.* The three of them smoked another cigarette, then carried the body to the car.

Hubert was so rigid that he wouldn't fit in the trunk so they put him on the backseat. Before returning home, the anxious farmer took a piece of thick sacking from the back of his little truck and gave it to them to cover the body. But there was still the smell. They would have to drive with the windows open.

Once Fabien and Vincent were alone again, Fabien explained his plan.

"We'll 'repatriate' the body to the exploded bunker, and we'll tell the authorities that Hubert died in the explosion."

There was no one on the roads, but Fabien was worried about going to the beach. They would have to wait until it was dark. There was another—sizable—problem: The beach was now under guard night and day to ensure no one went near it.

So Fabien and Vincent spent the day together, hiding in a forest with Hubert in the car. It was their first opportunity to spend a good deal of time together, and they weren't surprised to find their conversation flowed easily. After a few difficult days, it did them good to talk. Vincent was no doubt hiding a lot from him, but no one chooses who they eventually talk to. The words come out, when they find a chance, when they want to, a meeting of two minds. Just as thoughts are formed as they're spoken, friendships are born of confidences. Fabien wouldn't have been able to say why he liked Vincent.

Vincent asked for no explanation about Hubert, but Fabien supplied one anyway.

"The thing is, if they find out he was demining somewhere else while he was under contract, he'll be stripped of all his rights."

"Does a dead man have any rights?"

"If Aubrac secures the deminers' status, and I can tell you he's fighting hard to do just that, Hubert's widow will get a pension. The problem is he has two widows, but we'll have to deal with that later."

Over the course of the afternoon, Vincent noticed that Fabien was careful not to talk about Enzo. They still hadn't mentioned his name, but he was all they could think about. Enzo had welcomed Vincent with open arms, with an Italian's instant, intense brotherliness, and he was probably Fabien's closest friend. For now, it was all but impossible to accept that he was dead. It was the first pain they'd shared.

Still, Vincent knew that sooner or later Fabien would talk about Enzo, because he often mentioned the dead who were a part of his life, both deminers and fellow Resistance fighters. Fabien felt responsible for them, and Vincent had noticed that, to keep them alive, he talked about them whenever an opportunity presented itself. When he started a sentence with a smile and the words *I had a friend who*, it wasn't unusual for his voice to become gradually strangulated as he spoke.

In Enzo's case, Fabien needed to defer the pain if he was to avoid drowning. He'd learned to do this in the maquis.

When it was dark, they went to the beach. They'd found clothes to change into in the trunk: Max always had a couple of clean shirts in case he was lucky enough not to go home for the night.

Fabien offered to take over from the guards for a couple of hours. They could go to Léna's, he'd pay for their round. The guards didn't need to know the details, they were happy with the offer.

It was a dark night. After checking a safe route with their bayonets, Vincent and Fabien were able to put Hubert discreetly into what was left of the bunker. They covered him with sand and rubble. Tomorrow, Fabien would "find" his sandy body, and—thanks to him and Vincent—justice would be done to Hubert's wife and family...at least, this was justice as Fabien saw it and friendship as he understood it. To each their own laws.

There was no escaping the fact that some people had to fight the war that came after the war. This one was waged with no newspaper headlines and no mobilized army, and those who died weren't crowned with glory but were quietly disappeared.

SINCE SHE'D RETURNED TO THE SOUTH, SASKIA kept finding herself wondering what her mother and father would think, what would make them happy and what would disappoint them. Every apparently insignificant detail felt like a sign from beyond the grave. And she clung desperately to these signs.

Wasn't Éléonore proof of this? Saskia hardly ever went out; the two women should never have met. Surely, her mother had made them meet so that Saskia would know she would always be there for her. And so that she could find this dress, this particular one that Saskia loved.

The dress was perfect for first seeing Rodolphe again. She couldn't wait until she'd recovered her house and some peace of mind or had started to recuperate physically: She'd never achieve anything like that. She would be so much stronger with him. She remembered how he'd always encouraged her in everything she did. He'd enjoyed talking to her, and she'd always been eager to read the long letters he sent her regularly. She should trust him. Even though she'd changed and was weak, he would still love her. She shouldn't be in any doubt, that was unfair to him.

Saskia readied herself excitedly in the bathroom. She pressed crushed poppy petals to her lips—something she'd seen her sister do. The splash of red on her still-pale face looked to her like a savage wound. She tried to rub it off, but the color was tenacious. She wasn't used to seeing her face with any color in it. She smiled as best she could and managed to sustain the smile for a few seconds; Rodolphe would believe it.

She took her jewelry from its hiding place and chose a gold chain with a small pendant shaped like a dove.

Now for the hardest part, which she'd left until last.

Did she dare to wear her mother's dress?

Having rejected Éléonore's offer, she had only this one and the one she'd been wearing when she arrived. She might as well look as good as possible, and her mother's dress was definitely the prettier of the two. But wearing a dress that her mother had worn on her own body? And could no longer wear? Saskia felt she would be breaking a taboo. No, that taboo was ridiculous, she'd just made it up. What was stopping her? If she could bring herself to admit it, it was probably that her mother hadn't particularly liked Rodolphe. Relying on her mother's dress to charm a young man she hadn't really liked didn't seem fair. But perhaps Mila had appeared averse to their budding relationship simply because she thought her daughter too young. She'd so wanted Saskia to go to college, have a job, and be independent, as she herself had learned from her own mother.

Saskia was twenty. She would be an adult in a few months. Éléonore was right: She should check whether she passed her baccalaureate. Then she would start studying again. She would make her way thanks to university, she would work. No question Mila would have been reassured to know her daughter had a job. And had been reunited with Rodolphe knowing where she was headed.

She put on the dress, happy that it fit her, heartbroken that her mother could no longer wear it.

As she'd expected, the dress was magical. It accentuated the curve of her back, made her want to move so that the poplin, softened from so many washes, caressed her waist and hips. She could see the effect it had when she walked. Then she twirled a circle, once, twice...

On the third time, Vincent was there in front of her.

Saskia stopped dead. He was standing in the doorway. He had a wound on his temple, his arms were covered in large lacerations, as if he'd been attacked by a wild animal, and the cuts were soaking his shirt with blood.

She ran to fetch some old sheets that she could tear up to make bandages. She didn't think he'd noticed that she was dressed up to go out—which reassured her about the color of her lips.

When she returned, Vincent was stripped to the waist and was sluicing himself clean. The water pooled red in the basin and his hands were red with blood, but Saskia stayed calm, and Vincent was grateful that she didn't ask any questions. She offered to help clean his wounds, but he refused. He could do it himself.

"Anyway, you were getting ready to go out... Go on, don't keep this boy waiting..."

⁓

ALL THE WAY TO RODOLPHE'S PARENTS' HOUSE, Saskia kept rubbing her lips to get rid of the poppy ink that seemed to have tattooed her mouth. The sight of the roofs over their wall calmed her. She'd come here frequently before the war. She remembered the first time: She'd been so impressed—every time in fact. She walked through the entrance gate, which stood wide open, and went up the path edged with flowering lavender and olive trees flecked with white; it was their short-lived flowering season. Nothing bad could happen in a big house like this.

When she reached the house, a woman in a smock was sluicing the front doorsteps with water. Saskia didn't recognize her; she must be a new servant.

"Hello, I'd like to see Rodolphe. I think he's back from the United States…"

"And you are?"

"Saskia."

Saskia thought her name would have been a door opener, but the woman just smiled, apparently waiting for more information.

"We were at high school together…and…we studied for our baccalaureate together," Saskia explained, not daring to expand further.

"I'll let him know."

The woman disappeared inside. Saskia saw a young cat and bent to stroke it. The one at the studio hadn't been home for a couple of nights, and she was starting to worry about him.

She glanced around the magnificent grounds. Nothing in this surreally beautiful garden had been damaged by the Germans. Everything was as it had been, which did her good.

As she gazed at the garden, she didn't notice that a young man was watching her from a window on the second floor. He smiled, his face thoughtful. When Saskia put down the cat that she'd picked up and turned toward the house, he took a step back, afraid she might see him.

He was not alone in the room: A ravishing young woman who wore her refinement to the very tips of her fingernails was lining up small perfume bottles and items of makeup on a dressing table. She was moving in.

The servant knocked and entered.

"An old friend of yours has come to say hello. Saskia…"

"Who is it?" the young woman asked quickly, thrilled at the prospect of meeting another woman her age.

"A friend… well, we were at school together."

"Invite her to tea!"

"Maybe another time. Aren't you tired?"

"Not at all! I can't wait to meet some people. You know everyone here, but I don't know anyone."

"You're right. But later… All I can manage right now is a siesta."

The servant withdrew. Rodolphe put his arms around the young woman and led her to the bed; she no longer had a single thought about meeting anyone.

She hadn't noticed Rodolphe's discomfort, but the servant had. Accustomed to decoding what she wasn't being told, she'd grasped who Saskia really was. She found her by the fountain in the garden, with the young cat in her arms again.

"Monsieur is indisposed to see you. He's exhausted from the journey. He's sleeping and I didn't dare wake him."

"Oh, of course … I'll come back …"

Saskia put the cat back down. From the way this visitor slowed her movements, the way she breathed, the servant found herself pitying her. The worst thing was being kept in ignorance.

"His fiancée was awake. She'd be delighted to see you. She's very keen to make friends. She doesn't know anyone here."

Saskia absorbed the shock, then put on a brave face.

"Oh. I see … I would too. Of course …"

Distraught, Saskia gave the woman a smile she didn't know she could muster, heard herself say some words that didn't feel like hers, and fled. She was angry with herself for wanting to cry. What had she expected?

She didn't notice that Rodolphe had come back to the window to see her one last time. He'd truly loved her and had often thought of her while he was exiled in America, wondering what had become of her. There was something indefinable about her that he liked. Her mind and her eyes. And they'd been so young and carefree together. The high emotion the first time he'd gone to meet her outside her house, when she'd climbed over the wall, and they'd talked all night. He'd felt listened to as never before and hadn't found the same intensity with anyone else. He missed her.

If Saskia had known this in that moment, would it have changed anything? She'd just reached a decision. She'd lived with the illusion of this love that would resume when she was out of the camps, and the illusion had helped her stay alive—that in itself was extraordinary. Now she needed to shake it off and face the world. She took a deep breath and, right there and then, forbade herself to think about him again. And anyway, it was better that way: After what she'd been through, would Rodolphe ever have understood her? It was simply not an option to suffer because of him, even for a moment. It would make her no stronger or happier, and she just didn't have a right to suffer for nothing.

Strangely, the decision wasn't hard to reach, and it wasn't even a question of will. This attitude simply seemed the only right course to take, and the easiest.

Occasionally, people enjoy the privilege of being thunderstruck by love. A unique, fundamental, astonishing experience. This was the same revelation, just as physical and mystical and freighted with promise. This particular thunderbolt didn't commit, it released. It too was a state of grace. A privilege. And she discovered this fact on that day. As swiftly as a dream melts away come morning, Saskia fell out of love.

ON MAY 8, 1945, GERMANY SURRENDERED. FINALLY. The Allies had won, and Fabien now needed to find the energy to continue. While everyone was jubilantly celebrating the victory, his men were bedridden, utterly drained, trying to recover, and wondering what they should do.

Not one of the deminers stayed away when Fabien summoned them to the beach a few days later: Everyone who had survived was there, with the exception of Max and Henri, who were still in the hospital. There were only five of them—Georges, Manu, Miguel, Vincent, and himself—but Fabien had asked the guards to come over so that they felt less alone.

The few German prisoners who were still able-bodied waited some distance away. The surrender left them with a bitter taste in their mouths. Not only because Germany was defeated but because on that eighth day of May 1945, nothing had been negotiated about the return of prisoners.

Fabien wasn't surprised that Miguel had arrived first. He wasn't the sort to give up. He'd been fighting almost constantly since the start of the Spanish Civil War in 1936. On the side of the republicans in Spain, then with the Resistance in France. In two months' time, in July, it would be nine years... He had dependents but remained a man of his convictions.

Georges was still in a bad way, silent, traumatized. His injuries, his whole body hurt. He would never admit that he'd come close to not showing up. Then he'd remembered why he'd run away to the southwest, and that had driven him to get up good and early to be here on time.

Manu's face was gashed with a red-and-blue scar that only emphasized his good looks, more unusual now but still just as striking. He preferred not to talk about it, but one of his eardrums might have been perforated: He couldn't hear much except for intermittent, strident whistling. Others hadn't been as lucky, he wasn't going to complain. He hoped it would pass.

Vincent had hidden his injuries under his shirt, and, in a superhuman effort to reassure the others, Fabien seemed to have overcome his. They'd all aged almost overnight, and they hugged affectionately like long-standing friends, powerful hugs that lasted several minutes.

They were devastated, shocked, they needed to talk over what had happened and, as they gathered in a circle around Fabien, to talk about the dead, honoring their finest qualities. What did their past history matter—no one cared about that now. Whatever fights there had been, whatever differences of opinion and occasional insidious suspicions, death glorified their lost teammates with its veil of absolution.

They hadn't had time to get to know the members of the new team but respected them just as much. Then there was the problem of Hubert. Fabien was planning to lie to the authorities, but all the survivors knew full well Hubert hadn't been there on the day of the explosion. He needed to play a tight game. If a secret is to be kept, it mustn't be shared. Fabien told them that Hubert had decided to return home, and Vincent confirmed this. Miguel didn't think this odd: It happened, even to the best of them. No one guessed that he was lying a few meters away, well covered in sand to mask the smell. Hubert had shown some intuition by leaving before the explosion...

No one resented Enzo. On the morning of the disaster, he'd come across a cohort of Italian prisoners on a road. Someone had teased him and, although he had a sense of humor, the Italian occupation of southern France had been a personal injury to him. This pain alone had meant he started the day reluctantly, but then hadn't wanted to stop. Enzo had been passionate, raw, sometimes unpredictable, but they could all tell how sorely they would miss him. And without his voice leading theirs, they'd never be able to sing again. They would mangle *L'elisir d'amore*. To prove the point, but mostly to pay homage to Enzo, Georges and Manu mumbled rather than sang "Una furtiva lagrima." There was more than one tear, and they weren't furtive. Fabien, his throat tight with emotion, still couldn't talk about Enzo.

There were the wounded too. As far as others were concerned, people who'd danced all night in the square and heard of the tragedy—many were calling it "the accident"—when they'd sobered up in the morning, the wounded didn't count. They were less serious, anyway. At least if you didn't think too much about how badly they were injured. But to the deminers, being injured often meant something worse than death. It's not easy for a strong man—happy to expose his burnished skin to the sun, enjoying the way women want to nestle in the crook of his shoulder, against the reassuring bulk of his body— to come to terms with pitying looks.

They'd protested loud and long that they would never agree to amputations. No longer whole...they'd rather die. But when the cut needed to be made, it was a whole different story. They found they were more tenacious than they'd thought, shockingly attached to this life, the only one they knew, one they weren't prepared to give up for the sake of a leg. Or even two.

Fabien gave them what little information he'd managed to glean from the hospital. Max was the only person he'd been allowed to visit on the ward. Max was the most spirited of them all; it was impossible to imagine his injuries getting the better of him. Or so they tried to convince themselves. Besides, all of them were quietly forming scar tissue under their clothes, and they would pull through with no long-term consequences, for sure. A tricky phase but nothing to worry about. They were tough, thick-skinned.

Fabien impersonated Max: "Okay, Fabien, what really matters is...Are you listening to me? Take the Traction out and drive her around. She mustn't get out of the habit. I went to enough trouble getting her back on the road! So you keep pampering her and getting the prettiest girls to sit on her leather seats. That car doesn't run on gas, she runs on women's perfume."

Even potentially mortally wounded, Max didn't change, and everyone was grateful to him for this. Adding a typical gesture to his words, Fabien bounced the keys to the Traction in his hand. Generosity incarnate, old Max. Well, if it helped toward his recovery...

Their conversation was interrupted by the arrival of a truck covered with a khaki tarpaulin. A different group of guards let out a new batch of German prisoners to replace those they'd lost. Hans had sworn he would never demine but had now been enlisted. Dieter had too. They both looked at Lukas with weary resignation. Lukas had been right; there had been no way out.

Fabien waited until the new men had reached them to start his improvised speech as he handed out the booklets he'd been given at the town hall.

"Mine clearing isn't an exact science. Particularly in terms of how much we know. We paid a heavy price for our ignorance of enemy weapons on this beach. While we wait for the team to be up to strength again, we're going to try to broaden our knowledge. I've been given some booklets by the ministry. They're not much but, along with what we've learned on the job, they should mean we can train new deminers."

Lukas stepped forward to take a booklet and nobody commented. He leafed through it quickly while Fabien finished what he was saying.

"Yesterday, we lost the whole of the new team and five of our men: Thibault, Jean, Tom, Valentin, and Enzo. Henri and Max are fighting for their lives."

Fighting for their lives. The words had just come out. And the guys who'd laughed at his impersonation of Max now felt the brutal force of this reality.

It wasn't only the French who were feeling the strain. The prisoner who was quietly translating for the other Germans had come to the end of the speech: *Und wir haben fünf Menschen verloren...* As the man spoke, Fabien noticed Lukas's feverish, intense, lacerating expression. He pulled himself together and continued.

"It's not just our men we lost. We also lost German prisoners."

"Yes, but that's not the same!" came a voice from behind him.

Who said that? A deminer? One of the guards? Fabien didn't even try to find out—plenty of them shared this thought—but kept going, unfazed.

"No one can deny that the prisoners take just as many risks as we do and we'd never get our work done without them."

This didn't stop Georges minimizing the effect of what Fabien was saying by adding, "Except that one of them used the explosion as an opportunity to attempt an escape."

"Wouldn't you have done the same in his shoes?" Fabien asked coolly.

"Plus, he didn't actually try to escape," added Manu.

"That's bullshit!"

"I should know. I saw him try to save Thibault."

Georges didn't pursue it any further, and Fabien paused to clarify a point to him.

"I spoke to the camp director, and he confirmed that there were no SS in the group. And you can believe him—he's a rogue agent for the Resistance, he doesn't joke about stuff like that."

The deminers fell silent. Meanwhile, Fabien went up to each of the Germans and looked him right in the eye, starting with Lukas.

"We will never forget what your country did to us," he said, "but today I feel closer to you who are with us on this beach to repair the damage caused by the war than I do to the people who watch us and don't do anything. I often say that demining's an honor for us. For you it's dishonor. Yet you have the good grace not to hold back in this difficult work. From now on we'll all eat lunch together. I want us to remember there were lives lost on both sides, for the same cause."

Hearing muttering from the guards behind him, Fabien turned around; the talking stopped. He could have added that his team had more in common with these Germans than with collaborators who were discreetly slipping through the cracks in the name of some putative national reconciliation. That they had more in common with them than with the people who'd complained about their broken windows. And anyone who'd hidden or profited from the war or been informers. And everyone who, at the earliest opportunity, as soon as they'd regained a liberty for which they themselves hadn't fought, had labeled all Resistance fighters "last-minute fighters" to tarnish them, put them in the same bag and then toss the bag into the sea.

The team could sense the tension he was containing, and there was no more muttering.

Lukas made the most of this pause. Leafing through the booklet, he'd quickly seen how rudimentary it was and he asked the translator to translate the offer he wanted to make.

"There are lots of models missing from this. I could draw the ones I know that aren't featured here."

"Excellent. We'll send the information back to the ministry so they can send it out around the country."

On the strength of this, Fabien handed the remaining booklets to the Germans.

"What's your name?" he asked each of them and they gave their first names. It was the first time the team had heard them. They were Hans, Dieter, Franz, Rainer…When Fabien came to Friedrich, he recognized him as the German who'd tried to help Thibault and put a hand on his shoulder. He came to Lukas last.

"Matthias has had surgery. He's not in great shape but he's in good hands and we'll keep you informed."

And, just as the deminers had hugged one another, Fabien gave a brief but heartfelt embrace to Lukas, then to each of the other German prisoners. He didn't expect the rest of the team to do the same, but hoped that, given time, they would all come around to it.

"DO YOU KNOW HOW YOU CAN TELL A CRACK shot? He fires first, then aims, and last of all he thinks."

It was one of Max's favorite jokes. He inevitably followed it by making a comparison with their demining work. They'd started by clearing mines, they hadn't learned how to do it, and as for thinking about it, they weren't there yet...

With the war everything had been done the wrong way around. They'd demined straight after the landings, when they didn't know anything about mines: There had been colossal losses. But while waiting until the team was complete again, Fabien planned to start over, the right way around this time. The correct order meant binding the team together and then training it. If they had to wait until the promised teaching unit was built...

With help from town hall, Fabien had found a training ground in an abandoned quarry a long way outside of town. The prisoners and deminers climbed into trucks that drove them far away from the beach and its tragedies. They would never have imagined being so happy to go back to school.

Fabien kept Vincent behind; they would join the team after lunch.

As if they hadn't had a hard enough time with this grueling return to work, they had to find a safe place to stow the mines they'd stored along the edge of the beach right at the start of the project. Some had been disarmed, but others were waiting to be destroyed. They'd judiciously put them close to the access point, a long way from the blockhouse and the sarcophaguses; it wouldn't have taken much for the carnage to have been even more radical.

"Do you have a safe place?"

"The town hall's loaning us a warehouse. Somewhere discreet."

"The two of us'll never manage it alone."

"But we have to. The storage place needs to be kept secret."

They had to load up the devices with great caution: There were enough of them to blow apart the lives they'd just managed to wrest from the blast a few days earlier.

They placed the mines into wooden crates filled with sawdust. The ones they couldn't disarm had to be slipped carefully into containers full of sand. Fabien had borrowed a truck, and every crate of mines that it transferred was a testament to the work they'd all done. When they reached the warehouse, Fabien went to take the key from under a stone a little farther on.

"Are you sure about this?" Vincent asked, dubious.

"I don't have any other solution. And we need to do this quickly...before the army comes asking for them."

"*They* didn't do the demining."

"But they want their share of the haul…and they're not the only ones. This shit fetches a high price. We already had some stolen from the old shed we used."

They unloaded the mines and left. They still had several return trips to make—at least three. When they'd finished and were alone on the beach overseen by town hall staff, they pretended to find Hubert's body. The town hall employees informed the authorities. There was no one to dispute what would be the official line: Hubert died a hero.

Fabien was quite pleased that he and the team were in the quarry starting this training, and he had high hopes for it. Not just to spark a sense of vocation; he also needed to put some distance between them and the tragedy, to reassure them with know-how, to give them confidence by teaching them how to go about the work and—with experience and proficiency—how to establish that man is superior to the mine.

He wanted to make this apprenticeship a forerunner to a true craft, so that it was no longer a question of submitting to miserable circumstances that forced the men to risk their lives for a pittance. Of course, he had to make a show of knowing all the ins and outs. But wasn't that what it meant to be a man?

Fabien himself may have been familiar with everything in the booklet, but the other members of the team were not. By contrast, the German prisoners knew virtually every different model: They'd been trained to use them during their military service, regardless of their duties and rank. The German general staff had put a lot of store by mines and had prepared its troops accordingly.

It was a pleasant surprise for Fabien that the prisoners were now sharing their knowledge. Boosted by Fabien's speech, they were confident enough to come forward and point out the particulars of a triggering device or a mine that had been produced in several different variations, making it even more complex. But although the Germans knew how to set them, they didn't always know how to disarm them.

Fabien had made a point of selecting mines, grenades, shells, and a variety of explosives from the warehouse. He'd lined them up on a wooden table or buried them to reproduce real-life conditions. Theoretically, disposing of shells was the army's job, but this was a completely artificial distinction. They were sometimes called in urgently when a shell had been found and of course they were lumbered with the work.

Fabien started with a wooden crate the size of a large shoeshine box: a Panzer-Schnell mine A.

"This is an antitank mine that I've disarmed and put back together without the explosives. Who's first?"

No one moved. Even though the device was neutralized. Knowing how to demine was one thing; they also needed to be prepared to actually do it, and Fabien would show them how. Wouldn't it be better to stay ignorant and never be called on? Who cared if the pay was better for the guys who actually handled the mines; Enzo's shadow hovered over them…

Even though Fabien had brought them far away from the site of the disaster, it was perhaps too soon to be tackling the problem head-on. He went back to discussing theory.

"When we're given detectors, we'll be able to spot devices like this because of the metal handle and the nails inside. The charge consists of 5.9 kilos of picric acid wrapped in watertight paper. This sort of mine can be set very quickly. Hence the '*schnell*' in its name."

As he talked, he demonstrated how to neutralize the mine. This model was triggered when a tank went over it—a pressure-sensitive ignition distributor was screwed into the block of explosives. The cover had to be opened very carefully with no downward pressure, then the ZZ42 ignition distributor had to be unscrewed and the detonator removed. As simple as that.

Fabien then moved on to a more intimidating mine, perfectly sealed in a plastic coating. A Topfmine. Containing no metallic materials, it was virtually undetectable. Fabien had buried this 9 kilogram cylindrical pot with a diameter of 33 centimeters, and this time he insisted on having a volunteer.

The team still seemed numb.

Lukas was the only one to step forward. Stunned, the deminers waited to see Fabien's reaction as he studied Lukas briefly.

"Prisoners aren't allowed to disarm the mines. That's the regulation."

"If I ever want to be released, apparently I have to be brave. If I don't defuse mines, how can I show my bravery?" relayed the translator.

Fabien hesitated. There weren't many people applying for the work; there was no guarantee the recruiter would be able to reconstitute the team quickly. Lukas was certainly willing, he'd proved that. What did the regulations matter; there were only ever one-off cases. If they wanted to make a success of this postwar period, they'd have to adapt.

"Okay, Lukas. First of all, you clear the soil away from the mine to find where the igniter is and, in this instance, whether it's booby-trapped. You have to do this carefully, very carefully, like you're sweeping it with feathers on the ends of your fingers."

Lukas patiently stroked the earth around the device with his bare hands.

"Watch out because the Topfmine has a second housing for an extra igniter. Keep your wits about you. Run your hand all over the mine. You do it blind. Your hands and the tips of your fingers are your eyes."

Fabien had to take Lukas's hand and guide it in order to show him what he meant. He hadn't thought about it beforehand but as he took the other man's fingers, there was an awkward moment. No one on either side had anticipated this. Talking to the enemy was one thing—even the hug had been okay—but taking his hand, feeling his skin, his evil skin, that was something else altogether. It was as if a taboo had been broken... so Fabien talked technicalities.

"These mines were delivered disarmed and the Germans filled them with 5.7 kilos of explosives on-site. Lukas, make sure it isn't damaged. That's the problem with plastic mines. Lift it up, gently, yes, like that, put it down straightaway and unscrew the primer. The last thing is to take the igniter from its housing. To put your mind at rest, this mine isn't loaded."

Lukas relaxed.

"Now, you have to disarm it. You unscrew the protective casing on the second detonator, take out the detonator, and put the casing back in place."

Vincent had watched Lukas throughout, his concentration, his precision. Seeing this bookish man handle mines was so absurd, but Lukas went about it with an impressive attitude and application, not rebelling. Vincent himself hung back, where he could smoke with the others.

He'd never felt such a hostage to his own decision. Sweeping a beach, road, or railway track with a bayonet— yes, why not? But to go from there to delving into the entrails of these monsters laden to the gills with explosives... He could always quit. But he could hear Georges and Manu wondering who would be next, he could see Fabien and Lukas. He remembered the children who'd almost been caught by a bouncing Betty.

The war had profoundly changed him, but he still had some jolts of personal morals; he couldn't leave the others to take on all the risk on their own, not now.

He stepped forward to take over from Lukas. Fabien stood next to him reassuringly, but nothing was reassuring when you were confronted with a mine. Humbled, Vincent made a mental note of the information. This was a Tellermine 35 N1 fitted with a T.Mi.Z. 35 igniter. A gray-green aluminum saucer with a 30-centimeter diameter, whose lid was attached to the main body of the mine by a coil spring. Weight: 9 kilograms. Charge: 5.4 kilograms of TNT, which exploded under 90 kilograms of pressure.

All those who weren't in Vincent's shoes joked about their respective weights: Too skinny to make it blow. Then they thought about Jean "the Lard" and reverted to listening to Fabien in silence. This mine was intended for tanks but with a pressure tolerance of just 90 kilograms, it went off too soon, with the very first pressure from the caterpillar tracks. So it was fine-tuned as the Tellermine 42, which was designed to explode under a 200-kilogram weight when the whole tank was over the mine and the blast could destroy the floor of the vehicle. And the Tellermine 43, which shouldn't be touched. They were very often booby-trapped, right from the word go in the factory, and even military specialists didn't want to disarm them. They had to be blown up in a safe place.

As for the Tellermine 35, you first had to check it wasn't booby-trapped by pulling on a cable attached to its transporting handle. Then, once it was freed, unscrew the T.Mi.Z. 35 igniter. Using your thumb and index finger, you gently pushed the safety lock in its housing. Whatever you did you mustn't keep going if you met any resistance. Then you turned the screw on top of the igniter until the red dot lined up with the white "*sicher*" mark. If it didn't turn easily, same again, you didn't push your luck. And because it could be booby-trapped, you definitely didn't try to lift the mine with your hand until any extra igniters on the side or underneath the explosives had been removed. To do that you had to make the device safe by using a small iron rod to stop the pin from going down, then rotating the cam shaft attached to the *"scharf"* frame so that it was under the cocking hammer.

It was all about memory, dexterity, awareness of what you should or shouldn't do, right down to how much pressure to apply to the screws, the pins…

Even in the quiet of that quarry it took a lot of concentration. With training, you could do the work more calmly, at least that was what Fabien was trying to tell them. But in reality—and Vincent was well aware of this, having studied anatomy for several years before operating on anyone—there's what your brain registers and what your hands remember. There's learning and there's instinct. There's what you predict and the unforeseeable. Faced with the unpredictable, we have the resources given to us by experience, concentration, and measured audacity. And sometimes there's nothing.

At the end of the day, as promised, the mayor came to offer his condolences. He was escorted by an English officer and an American officer. In the maquis, Fabien had been in contact with a good many Anglo-Saxon paratroopers. He liked their courage, their humor, their selflessness. Their commitment. The two men smiled and spoke French with familiar accents. Aubrac had dispatched them here to deliver the technical information that was cruelly lacking.

Their expertise would be valuable. When the British and Americans had realized the Germans were making alarming advances in mine production, they'd concentrated all their efforts on swiftly redressing the balance and had succeeded in catching up, both in analyzing enemy mines and in manufacturing their own.

That evening, everyone was willing to extend the day's work by chatting over a meal that the town hall had laid on for the deminers and the two Allied instructors.

They were all galvanized by a delectable feeling of having fought and won together. Allies. It was a strong word, a powerful one. Miraculous given the risks that had been run. And their shared story. The French and the English had fought against one another for more than two hundred years. The Americans, with the support of the French, had gone to war to shake off England's control of their territory. Everyone had fought everyone, and yet here, in this quarry, there were only frank exchanges between men who were happy that they were now living free and in peace. A moment of grace. This sense of restored freedom that needed to be protected meant they were all in agreement and could joke together, including with the Germans. Neither the Englishman nor the American was shocked that Fabien had decided to form a united team rather than prolonging rifts with the prisoners. It was like a presage of peacetime. In this small group of men who were in such close contact with mines, risks, sacrifice, self-denial, and death, brotherly feeling carved out its own small path. The war had been a barbaric, all-consuming transgression and yet, within these demining teams, the concept of a shared future for European countries was already taking shape.

Fabien, the Englishman, and the American were swapping stories, describing the landings, throwing out names: Operation Dragoon, the various forces—Romeo, Garbo, Alpha, Delta, Camel, and Rosie—that had landed on the eighteen beaches between Cavalaire and Saint-Raphaël,

the liberation of Saint-Tropez, the close coordination between the French Forces of the Interior, the Allied forces,
the French Liberation Army, volunteers from North Africa, Guinea, Senegal, and the Ivory Coast, and resistance
fighters from overseas. Yes. Those quick, efficient landings
based on flawless cooperation had been a miracle.

Vincent envied them. At the time of the Provence
landings, he'd still been a prisoner. Several years of his life
had been stolen, and he was angry with himself for this.

The day was coming to a wonderful close when the
American and the Englishman got up to go and look at
the mines laid out on workbenches as if in a small museum
of horrors that everyone hoped could be relegated to the
past, a cabinet of outdated curiosities to frighten children
in years to come. The deminers wished they could believe
that the lesson had been learned and that this had been the
first but also the last time that warring parties would use
these instruments of death.

But the two instructors picked up each of the mines
and told the men that they now had an equivalent model
for every one of them. Their engineers studied German
armaments, copied them, reproduced them, modernized
them, and honed them to perfection.

There in that quarry, they all started to grasp that what
they most feared was already happening. It was the end of
the war, but the world was far from finished with mines. It
was only the beginning of a long history.

∾

AUBRAC HAD BEEN RIGHT: THE AMERICAN AND the Brit were efficient and explained things clearly. True to the Anglo-Saxon reputation of not muddying work with qualms and soul-searching, they got straight to the point; they needed to keep going.

As the work progressed, they became increasingly friendly with the team. They planned to have dinner with the deminers, buy them a round of drinks, and visit the area. Professional but also slightly extravagant, concentrated on their work and still enjoying a joke—they'd charmed the whole team.

Fabien made the most of having them there to slip away at the end of the day and take Vincent to the hospital to visit the wounded. Vincent wanted to give Lukas news of Matthias. They went their separate ways in the hospital lobby.

"Meet back here in an hour?"

Fabien walked off, keen to see Max. He was relieved to find him alive. Lying in bed, hooked up to a drip, and with his arms and trunk completely swathed in bandages, Max still managed to dredge up renewed energy when he saw Fabien. And Fabien was conscious of this: A leader can motivate a team, restore strength to his men because they don't want to disappoint him, like a father, even a father the same age as they are. Driven by this strange energy, Max gripped Fabien's arm.

"Don't leave me here, will you!"

Fabien was struck by Max's forcefulness, the strength in his hands—he'd been told the man was dying. He had nothing to offer to match the faith that Max had in him, and this weighed on him. He tried to make a joke.

"Are they not taking care of you? Come on, I saw a couple of nurses I'm sure you'd take for a trip in your car, right? And at least here you don't have to compete with Manu."

"Manu? Even now they've trussed me up like a mummy, he's no match for me!"

"Well, make the most of being here, get some re—"

"I want to get out," Max interrupted.

"If there's anything you're not happy with, I'll talk to the doctors, I'll tell them who they're dealing with," Fabien said, still joshing but with little conviction. He knew where Max was going with this.

"I'm dying of boredom in here. I can leave now, I'm fine."

"Max…I don't think so. You need specialized care."

"We were just altar boys back in '35. The Germans were manufacturing mines by the millions and we let them go right ahead!"

"Don't stress, they lost in the end, once and for all."

"But that's not enough! The Boche need to understand who we are. Next time we won't be caught out."

"Next time?"

"We won't have any more accidents. I can't wait to get back to work."

"You had me worried—I thought you meant the next war!"

Fabien hoped he sounded playful but, try as he might to tune in to Max's denial, he was struggling to hide his doubts given the extent of his friend's bandages, which spoke volumes about all the injuries that had shattered his body. The doctors had warned Fabien that he might not make it to the end of the week. Max was clearly not in the loop.

Fabien heard himself reply that he couldn't wait to see Max back out with the others and of course everything would be fine next time. They'd learned from their mistakes; that was their strength.

Max had been his first recruit. They'd started demining together and—along with Gauthier, the poor wretch in a problematic coma on the next floor up—he was the only survivor from Fabien's first pioneering team in the heroic days when the war had still been in full swing. It was only a few months ago, but those few months seemed like an eternity.

He felt he knew Max better than anyone, and yet he knew almost nothing about his early life. He'd only just learned from Max's file that this serial seducer was married and had a son. Fabien suggested arranging for them to visit.

"Nah-ah! I don't want them to see me like this."

"How long is it since you saw them?"

"That's not the point. I don't want to scare my son. Plus, you see, I never told my wife I would be demining. I told her I had a steady job that paid better than others. If she sees me like this..."

"Do you love her?"

"Like hell I do!"

In spite of himself, Fabien gave the beginnings of a conspiratorial smile.

"Oh, I know what you're thinking," Max was quick to correct him, "but when I ask women out for a drink, it's just that, for fun. I'm not doing anything wrong. My wife's different. She's so beautiful, you can't even imagine. And guess what, she can sing. Not like Enzo, she's more into new popular stuff. She sings those songs better than any singer on the radio. And the best part is she doesn't even know it!"

"Well then, we'll get her here and you can tell her."

"Not now...As soon as I'm back on my feet."

So Max really thought he'd pull through.

In a different ward on the floor below, Vincent was watching Matthias sleep. His hands were bandaged and the dressings, which were huge, didn't reproduce the shape of hands that could hold a violin and a bow. The temperature chart at the foot of his bed hadn't dropped below 104 or 105 degrees. Matthias must have a serious infection.

When Matthias woke, Vincent jumped straight to the only question that mattered to him—where's Ariane?—clinging to Matthias's every word, but he spoke only of melodies and sheet music. His fever and the morphine were making him delirious. He was grappling with the unrelenting terror that he would never be ready for a concert in Cologne the next day.

Swimming through the befuddled waters of his opiate semi-wakefulness, he waved his arms around to grab hold of a bow hanging before him and a violin that hovered over his bed, then he rehearsed for his intransigent upcoming concert with his bandaged hands.

Vincent was crushed by a huge feeling of remorse. He'd tried to find out what the relationship had been between Ariane and Matthias, he'd even envied him, but he could see that Matthias was now prey to a ruthless solitude: Unarmed and barely conscious, he had to square up to a fight with death that he didn't understand. Vincent promised him—could Matthias even hear him?—that he would speak to a doctor. With the endless comings and goings all over the hospital, he knew it would be difficult to corner one. Matthias was still sweeping his arms through the air when Vincent showed him the note that he'd promised to bring.

"It's from Lukas."

The name produced no reaction from Matthias, who now looked like a hypnotized ballerina, lost in musical hallucinations.

"He really cares about you, you know."

Matthias was softly singing a tune Vincent didn't recognize. Pointless talking to him, a wasted effort. So he pulled a chair up to the bed, took a notebook and pen from his jacket, and started writing quickly.

He was interrupted by Fabien calling to him from the doorway. Vincent went and joined him in the corridor.

"How is he?" Fabien asked.

"Not great. I guess that's to be expected after his operation…"

The stark reality was that Matthias's infection could claim him, and Vincent knew he needed to act fast. He had no choice.

"He dictated a note for Lukas. I need to take it to him."

Vincent tore the page from the notebook on which he himself had just hastily composed the message. Fabien paused; he hadn't heard Matthias speaking.

"And how's Max?" Vincent asked, quickly changing the subject.

"All he can talk about is next time he's out clearing mines."

"You mean he wants to go back to it?"

"It's all he can think about! I've got another one like him. Gauthier, from the previous team… who'll never get out of this place. But if they ever do get out, even if they were told they only had a month to live, they'd still go and clear mines. They'd go in a wheelchair! And it's not like they're not scared. They just can't help it. They don't want to admit they're defeated."

Vincent wasn't the right person to judge another man's obsessions. He knew there was no controlling them.

They stopped off to see the doctor who was overseeing Matthias and gathered that they shouldn't hold out too much hope. But they made a point of asking the doctor to do everything to save him. Back out in the corridor, they didn't speak but neither of them would have gambled much on the young musician's survival.

It was when they'd almost reached the hospital's main entrance that Vincent very clearly heard someone call out a name that he dreaded hearing. His own.

"Hadrien!"

FABIEN TURNED AROUND AND SAW A VERY PRETTY woman in a white coat coming toward them. Vincent didn't look back but hurried toward the door too desperately for it not to be noticed.

"Are you okay, Vincent?" Fabien asked, surprised.

"I don't really like hospitals."

The woman had almost caught up with them. Vincent had recognized Audrey's voice: In his obsessive need to talk to Matthias, he'd completely forgotten that she worked at Timone Hospital. She said his name again and touched his arm to attract his attention, he turned to her coolly and gave her his most charming smile.

"You must be mistaken," he said. "My name isn't Hadrien, I'm very sorry to say."

A dumbfounded Audrey didn't know what to say, but she soon gathered her wits.

"Oh, sorry... you look like someone I knew before the war. From a distance, I thought... but up close, you don't look like him at all."

"Please, don't apologize. Have a nice day."

She walked away, completely baffled, while Vincent continued toward the door. Audrey had suspected that he would try anything, but not to the point of changing his identity…and making her look a fool in the process.

Vincent could feel Fabien studying him; he must keep acting calm, as if there was absolutely no reason for the incident to have ruffled him.

"Hey," he said, "do you think I could stop off to see Lukas to give him Matthias's note?"

"You can give it to him tomorrow."

"Matthias wanted me to get his news to the other Germans, who aren't demining."

"You can't walk into a prison camp just like that."

"But you know the governor. And I promised Matthias."

Fabien hesitated, seemed to calculate something privately, then replied in a neutral, offhand voice, "I'll write a little reference for you. That should work."

Vincent was amazed to get off so lightly and suspected Fabien had some secret design that he couldn't identify. He needed to be vigilant. They reached the Traction Avant, climbed in, and Fabien started driving.

"Speaking of letters but on a totally different subject, a friend's going to send me the ones that d'Estienne d'Orves wrote just before he was shot by the Germans. His lawyer managed to circulate them. Apparently, they're exemplary."

Vincent had been right to be wary and there was one thing he knew for sure: Fabien chose his every word carefully.

"Do you know who I mean by d'Estienne d'Orves?"

In his oflag in Germany, Vincent hadn't had the opportunity to know anything of the sort.

"An incredibly courageous naval officer. He resigned, joined the Resistance, and set up a network. He was caught…"

"How did they get him?"

"He'd taken a young sailor with him. A radio operator. He trusted him but the boy shopped him to the Germans."

"You mean the radio operator talked under torture?"

"No, he went to see the Germans to sell them the information. And you want to know the worst of it? D'Estienne d'Orves had been warned that this cabin boy had a loose tongue in bars and couldn't be trusted. But he didn't want to believe it. He'd put his trust in him and didn't take it back. He was shot at Mont-Valérien. He'd just turned forty."

Fabien had said "on a totally different subject," but he was in fact talking about only one thing, about the nagging question that obsessed them all and would continue to do so for the rest of their lives: If it all started again tomorrow and there were Nazis, fascists, and barbarity, if there was war and mortal danger, who could you have faith in? Who would you trust with your life? Who would say nothing under torture? Who wouldn't betray you? Who would never betray?

The question of betrayal would go on to haunt all relationships. And if Fabien thought that Vincent might betray him, Vincent's days on the team were numbered. He needed to work fast and get information out of Lukas now, if indeed Matthias had given him any.

Mention of the Resistance fighter felled by a firing squad had created silence between them. Fabien lived in a celestial cemetery, taking his dead everywhere with him. His dead were more alive than all the people who wrangled their way through life, compromised themselves, and came to terms with everything around them. He erected enchanted tombs for them. With him, all the dead were welcome, even those who hadn't had his political leanings or been in his maquis. Even if he hadn't known them. It didn't matter where they were from. All that mattered was what they'd achieved.

Fabien would read the letters to his team as soon as he received them. He was torn between wanting to keep the words to himself like a personal conversation, a conversation only possible between people who bathe in the same clear waters, and the urge to share them in the hope that they would sustain the others and slake their thirst.

They were coming into an age when keeping company with the dead seemed more commendable than with the living.

FABIEN STOPPED OFF AT THE CAFÉ. HE NEEDED to see Léna. Urgently.

"You know that photo you mentioned? Where is it?"

Léna was cashing out.

"The photo..." she thought out loud.

"The one that a woman showed you on the night of the dance. She wanted to talk to a man. You told me that she said he was called Hadrien."

"Yes, I know. It's just I gave it to Aurélien. Where did he put it?"

She had a look around behind the bar, opened a drawer filled with things that had been left in the café. The photo was in there and she handed it to Fabien.

"Do you know him?"

"Yes, and so do you. It's Vincent."

"Are you sure? Aurélien thinks it looks like him too. I can't see it at all. Mind you, it's hard to tell with the shadows."

"It was taken before the war. If you add five years, fear, hunger, and time in a prison camp—it takes less than that to change someone."

"Why would Vincent lie about his name? And anyway, the man in the photo's a doctor. Why would he lie about that too?"

"That's what he's going to have to explain."

Fabien was keyed up. Léna put her arms around him and spoke to him gently.

"Fabien. Promise me you'll let him explain. Don't go blaming him till you've heard what he has to say. I know that's not easy for you to hear, and in the maquis a lie was often as good as murder. But you're not there now. Believe me, people sometimes have good reasons to lie."

"To lie to me?"

"Don't twist things. You know what I mean. All I'm asking is that you don't do anything in the heat of the moment. Even if that's hard. When you see him, at least wait till the end of the day."

"Why'm I listening to you?" he asked, affected by her words.

On the back of the photo, as well as the name Hadrien, there was the name of the young woman who had spoken to Léna: Irène Zeller.

"Did she tell you anything else?"

"He's looking for a woman called...Ariane, I think. But I think this Ariane wants to be left alone."

Fabien froze and Léna understood immediately.

"Do you know her?"

Assailed by a wave of violent emotion, he nodded in silence.

"I've thought she was dead for such a long time. I'd be happy if she's still alive."

~

SINCE THE EXPLOSION, LUKAS HAD BEEN haunted by that twilit evening; it went around and around in his head right through until dawn, and would be the nightmare of all his nights to come. He so wished he could have saved Matthias, helped him escape and seen him play the violin in all the great concert halls in the world... or even just play for Ariane again.

He relived every minute, over and over. Just after the storm of steel, he'd looked at the wrecked blockhouse that had housed weapons and his now atomized dreams of escape. His plan had almost come through and now there it lay, just a few meters away, pulverized amid the rubble. And then he'd seen Matthias and he'd been crushed by an inexpressible sense of guilt for sacrificing the young man for his project. He would have given anything to see him pull through. He'd given Vincent all the help he could, had held Matthias's arm and not averted his eyes when Vincent cauterized his wounds with the searing hot blade. When Matthias was taken away on a stretcher, Lukas was devastated, talons of guilt embedded themselves in his heart, tearing him apart, and yet now he found he was thinking of escape again.

He hated himself. The problem with escape was that it was impossible not to think about it—not to think about it all the time—without driving yourself insane. The whirlwind of possibilities left Lukas with no chance of returning to a semblance of peace. Subjected to the oscillations of a runaway metronome, he was tossed between wildly contradictory thoughts. Insurmountable fear and absurd hope. His negligible chances of success and the terrible repercussions of failure. His heart raced frantically. He now found it impossible to decide with any certainty on when the right moment would be to make a move. Worse still, to be incontrovertibly sure that it would be right to make a move at all.

And yet he couldn't back down, even after suffering the most disastrous defeat.

Preparing an escape was in itself an escape. Dreaming of what would come later. Demolishing the guards' smug assumptions that the prisoners had given up. Contradicting the French who thought all the Germans felt helplessly overwhelmed. Setting straight the Germans who believed their prisoners would agree to be forgotten and would never hold anyone accountable.

Lukas vitally needed the dreams in which he projected his future self, after an escape. He replaced reality with his longings, and that suited him just fine. It was either that or dying. Where would he go? He'd considered this a thousand times and his indecision was like a premonition of freedom.

Before the war, he would have chosen France without any hesitation. Paris, to open a bookshop near the banks of the Seine. Or there was the south, maybe near Hyères, Ramatuelle, or Saint-Tropez—how ironic. Now, he would choose Italy. But Italy was going through a terrible time; he wouldn't be able to stay there. He'd have to run away again.

Spain was still under the yoke of the fascists; Greece was prey to confrontations between the British and the communists. He'd had so many dreams of the Mediterranean and now it was a scene of devastation.

Why not go farther afield? To Morocco? Or Algeria? He remembered Delacroix's paintings and the thought alone was enough for him to feel the hot dust of these red-soiled lands. He pictured himself beturbaned with cotton as protection from the heat, eating delectable fruit, finding an oasis in the desert...

These dreams gave him the strength to concentrate on the technical aspects of escaping. He couldn't put anything down in writing because the guards regularly searched their bunkhouses. A shame, writing allowed him to think. He'd noticed this with the letters he'd written to his beloved girlfriend but been unable to send. Eight months with no news, can love survive that?

He couldn't wait. He had one opportunity left, just one. To achieve it, he would need to organize a chain reaction of crucial events, triggered one after the other like the mines that had been their undoing. It seemed impossible, but he had no choice: He must return to the Wehrmacht's former headquarters at the Château des Eyguières, which was out of bounds and heavily mined.

It was the only place where he would have an advantage over the French. He knew where to find weapons there, and gold, and a secret escape tunnel.

Lukas knew every corner of the château. He'd had access to all its secrets, all its disguised closets, its rooms and secret passageways, its hidden doors. He liked every aspect of the château: the architecture, the grounds, the furniture. The sense of a past that was still within reach delighted him, as did the general mood in the place, despite the German occupation. Centuries of sophistication had resisted the occupiers' behavior, in the refinement of its furniture and paneling, in the majesty of its ceilings and mirrors. The monumental scale of the reception rooms, corridors wider than whole apartments, the sumptuous main staircase, chandeliers hanging four meters overhead—everything about the place crushed the arrogant uniformed men with its finery. They thought they were completely in control, but the château came out the victor in this clash.

In the final moments, their leader had made a last stand, but one that was quite unrelated to honor: He'd set mines in every nook and cranny of the château. He could just as easily have burned it or blown it up, but no, his primary aim was to kill the French.

And therein lay the big problem with Lukas's escape plan: The château was a powder keg waiting to explode and no one dared set foot there. It wasn't like a road, a railway line, or a beach, where you could scratch at the soil with the tip of a bayonet, no, in this instance there were explosives everywhere, beneath the floorboards and stair treads, even in the bookshelves and wardrobes, the china closets and vases, under cushions...

Lukas had overheard a couple of conversations between Fabien and Enzo: The Mine Clearance Department was holding off while it waited for more sophisticated equipment. Even though the château was a prime strategic target, the powers that be would rather not send their deminers into such a diabolical trap.

The equipment might take a while to arrive. There was little of it and it had been earmarked for the army teams who were busy demining the Eastern Front to bring the fighting to an end. Who knew how long the château would be condemned to sleep?

The only thing Lukas had up his sleeve was not a major piece but a pawn: Vincent.

He would need to win Vincent over, then Vincent would have to convince Fabien and—once that much was achieved—Fabien would have to find a way to persuade the mayor, who, in turn, would almost certainly have to refer to some prefect and the Mine Clearance Department and the Ministry of Reconstruction at a time when France still had an interim government and everything, by definition, was susceptible to change at any moment.

That was a lot of people, but he was reasonably confident he could convince Vincent, and Fabien had become so indispensable to the region's safety that no one could deny him anything.

Was he crazy to think he'd be able to do it? His plan was complex, but then plans were never easy, so why not?

He needed to think about the best way to manipulate Vincent. So long as Vincent believed Lukas could give him something, the plan would work. But that meant luring him with some vital information that would sufficiently arouse his interest for him to drop his guard and take risks without even realizing it.

Lukas had what he needed. In chess, you must learn to sacrifice some key pieces. At the risk of putting your queen in danger.

VINCENT REACHED THE PRISON CAMP AND WAS disappointed not to find the guard he'd managed to soften up with a few cigarettes at the café. Too bad, but he had Fabien's note, which he showed to a security guard he didn't know. His heart was pounding as if he were preparing a reverse breakout, from the free world into the prison. While the guard went off to check whether he could admit him, Vincent studied the prisoners through the fence. He always expected to feel nauseous at the sight of all these soldiers cooped up in a lobster pot of barbed wire, but it reminded him of his own lobster pot, the oflag where he'd just spent too many years of the war. He could see himself in his shapeless clothes, with fear in his belly but still obsessed with the thought of reassuring Ariane about how he was doing. In all his letters he'd described how the Germans respected the rules of war and treated officers well. This was in fact true of the German doctor with whom he'd worked, a brave and desperately humane anti-Nazi. Other than him, Vincent obviously wondered whether Ariane had believed him.

He then noticed three prisoners walking slowly up and down the prison yard, their bodies hunched over the ground. This posture would have been incomprehensible to anyone who hadn't spent time in prison during a war, but not to Vincent: He instantly knew that the men were casting about for the tiniest blade of grass in the dirt. For months they'd had only liquid food, soup or tea—at least that was what they were called but the taste bore no relation to the names. They had to find something to bite into. It could be a weed, a snail, anything. They would add it to their broth. When Vincent had arrived at the Cassel camp in central Germany, he'd never guessed he would be reduced to this. It came to them all, and quickly.

He felt stifled.

He didn't want to keep thinking about the camp.

He backed away, turned around, and saw that in the distance, yet so close by, life had reclaimed its freedoms, people were out for a stroll, a couple of lovers were laughing out loud.

A hearty smack on the back startled him. The guard he knew scolded him for not asking for him personally. Vincent gave him the pitch that he'd fine-tuned with Fabien: He was in possession of the last words from a gravely injured man and must give his news to the other prisoners. Yes, the patient was German but they all had to be human. He didn't need to try any further persuasion with his "friend," who was taunting him for being sentimental, because the duty guard was coming back to fetch him.

He took Vincent into the camp, passing the officers' quarters that were kept separate, affording them, if not privileges, at least a degree of distance. When they reached Lukas's bunkhouse, the guard left him.

Memories came flooding back and his instincts as a doctor took over. In among the fit and healthy—like those who worked on mine clearance—Vincent saw men who were starving and sick. The slightest illness, however minor, could cause rapid deterioration. He'd learned how vitally important state of mind was. In Germany he'd treated French, Belgian, British, and Russian prisoners. He remembered one young Russian whom the Nazis wouldn't allow him to treat, but he'd helped him all the same. He wondered whether the boy had pulled through.

Vincent felt compassion rise within him, completely against his will. He asked Lukas which bunkhouse the soldiers from Eyguières were in, wanted to know exactly where to find the senior staff from the headquarters, and then handed him the letter that he claimed was from Matthias.

"How is he?"

"It's too soon to tell."

"And his hands?"

"He won't play again."

Lukas looked away in anguish. "I told him he'd get home to Germany sooner."

"He made the choice."

"I pushed him."

Lukas folded the note and put it in his pocket, then thanked Vincent and turned as if to return to his quarters. Vincent stopped him, exactly as Lukas had anticipated.

"You know the promise I made you, I'll keep it. Do you know anything?"

Lukas turned to face him. "Do you want to know?"

"More than ever."

"It's going to hurt."

"What have you heard?" Vincent asked feverishly.

Lukas looked down and dropped his voice. There was still time to say nothing. To pretend he knew nothing. But he was peculiarly determined to continue.

"Matthias didn't meet Ariane at the farm. He met her at the château, at Eyguières."

"Ariane went to the château?"

"She worked as a waitress sometimes, when there were receptions."

Vincent had always known that the Germans came to Ariane's parents' farm for supplies but not that she had been made to go to the German HQ. When he'd met her parents, they hadn't mentioned this. He'd had a feeling they were ducking some of his questions. They must have felt bad: She'd stopped studying medicine in order to help out on the farm and take care of her mother. So if she also had to wait on Germans...!

"Did that happen a lot?"

"Quite a lot. She didn't go willingly. She was made to."

"Who by?"

"I don't know. Probably a high-ranking officer. She was scared it would be taken out on her family if she refused." Lukas dropped his voice again. He was getting to know Vincent; he would take the bait. "One evening, after a party, she disappeared. We never saw her again. Something bad happened with an officer who wanted to...charm her."

"Were you there?"

"I wasn't invited to receptions like that."

"Can you find out who the officer was?"

"I've done everything I can to."

"When was this?"

"It was the commandant's birthday. June 8, 1943."

The date reverberated like a thunderclap. It tallied with when Ariane had left and taken refuge with Audrey in Marseille. He needed to rethink the whole scenario. So far, he'd been looking for a wolf in the sheepfold, but Ariane had ended up surrounded by the whole pack.

Lukas suggested what Vincent had been dreading all along: Ariane had been assaulted or worse by an officer at the château and had decided to disappear. Why had she agreed to wait tables at the château? She should have run away sooner. Her parents would have understood. Questions swirled in Vincent's head, but he had a feeling that an important part of the puzzle—the setting—was falling into place.

He had taken a notebook and some pencils from the studio, and he handed them to Lukas.

"I want portraits of all the German officers who were at the HQ and are in this prison with you. Ariane had a girlfriend who sometimes came to the farm. She'll recognize the officer who put Ariane in danger."

"I'm not good enough at drawing."

"If I could take photos I would, but I'm pretty sure I wouldn't be allowed."

"I'm happy to try, but there's a better way to find out more." Lukas was about to deal his decisive blow. "Our archives are in the château. We used to film everything during the war: Official ceremonies but also outings, Sundays, parties, there are thousands of images, kilometers of Agfa film. It's all well archived—German orderliness coupled with propaganda initiatives."

This was beyond Vincent's wildest hopes! Images of Ariane, animated images of Ariane alive. He found it hard to conceal his emotions.

"It all stayed at the château?"

"We were short of time, we had to get out. Nothing was moved and nothing was destroyed. You'll be able to see the last party where Ariane worked. And almost certainly the guy who wanted to take things too far."

In this hellish game of dominoes in which he needed to convince Vincent, who would then convince Fabien, who, in turn, would have to convince the mayor, and so on all the way to the ministry, Lukas had overcome his first hurdle.

Vincent knew that he was in a weak position and didn't like the fact that Lukas was aware of his dependence on him. So he now affected some doubt, but in the negotiations of a desperate man, doubt is a paltry subterfuge.

"It's not up to me alone. I think I've heard that the château isn't a priority. Too dangerous."

"I was there when they set the mines and everything else. I could help you."

"I'll have to persuade Fabien."

Lukas had thought about this long enough to have alighted on the domino that would knock down all the others, the right piece of information, delivered at the right time.

"There's also something at the château that Fabien might be interested in, something he's been trying to find for a long time…"

SASKIA HAD RETURNED TO THE TOWN HALL TO ask Édouard if he'd made any progress with her file. She had the distinct impression she was bothering him.

"*I* will contact *you*," he'd said. A thinly disguised way of telling her not to come back.

"I don't have a home now, you know. I don't really have an address either. How will you contact me?"

He'd been caught out by this question, which she'd voiced in clear, measured tones although it was full of insolence. He hadn't troubled himself with wondering where she slept, hadn't offered to help her, but her question had blunted his hopes of keeping her at arm's length.

Whenever she tried speaking to neighbors, local shopkeepers, or children playing in the street, she felt she was being a nuisance. She'd been to see a notary—she seemed to remember he'd been the one her parents used—but he'd said he couldn't help her. He hadn't even told her how she should proceed. He'd been offhanded with her, doing nothing to hide a slight curl of his lip.

Saskia was exhausted, but she wouldn't give up now; she just wouldn't accept yet another injustice. This was essential to her but meant nothing to other people, and she had to live with that.

She'd found some notebooks at the studio, something
with which she could start a diary of her investigations
to make sure she kept going. She tried to be methodical,
not to let her emotions run away with her. She'd survived
far worse. But she was crushed by the awkwardness she
seemed to produce wherever she went. She wanted to
disappear, didn't want people to see her anymore. Didn't
want to have to ask any questions. Perhaps the only person
who didn't feel uncomfortable around her was Vincent,
but he didn't really see her, and she couldn't rely on him
forever. And what would happen to her if he was blown up
by a mine? She didn't want to think about that. The only
people she could truly trust were those who'd helped her
family to hide. She kept delaying the day when she would
go to see them: She didn't have the heart to tell each of
them in turn what had happened after her family had been
arrested.

She tried to organize her thoughts. Who had stood to
gain from denouncing her loved ones? It would be intolerable for her to live in a world, a town, a street where the
people who'd sent her family to their deaths might be living in perfect impunity, basking in the joy of newfound
peace, never really wanting to know the impact of the
murderous words they'd jotted on a piece of paper. Who
had despised them that much? Surely people could only
ever have loved her parents?

There was bound to have been some obvious fact that
her family hadn't considered. Some pragmatic reason,
someone's self-interest. It now seemed clear to her that
whoever wanted her family arrested had just wanted to

appropriate their house. But not one of them had thought of this explanation while they'd been in the camp.

It could be the new occupants, but there was something about that line of argument that didn't stand up. The children in the street had told her that the Bellangers had been living there only since the previous summer. Why denounce a family two years ago and not take over their house until a year later?

Even if she couldn't completely dismiss this lead, there must have been others.

When her mother used to come and pick her up from high school, Saskia had spotted men trying to make advances to her. Could they have felt so humiliated by her rejection that they wanted to punish her, along with her whole family? Mila and Ilan had been the perfect couple. There must have been many people who envied their happiness.

In fact their neighbor, Madame Morin, loathed them. She'd never shown the least trace of shame in hurling insults peppered with antisemitic insinuations. And she would come around to complain at the least opportunity: The noise the children were making playing in the garden, the shade that their trees cast on her flower beds, the ivy that was overrunning her wall and would surely damage it. For a long time, she'd been quite hysterical about having a cedar tree cut down because she was afraid it would fall on her house. Mila hated the thought of felling any tree, and certainly not a cedar. It was at least two hundred years old. Was it to be cut down just like that to satisfy the ill will of a sour-tempered neighbor?

Ilan and Mila had been staggered that Madame Morin managed to obtain signatures from a few neighbors. Had they signed against the cedar or against them? Saskia's parents hadn't wanted to make the situation any worse: With heavy hearts, they'd had the majestic tree felled.

Saskia thought about the signatories on that contemptible petition. Should she add their names to the Bellangers and Madame Morin on her list of suspects? Her father had always said that not all the French were antisemitic. And despite everything they'd experienced, she herself hadn't been able to believe that they were hated for being Jewish.

It made no sense; they didn't go to the synagogue, believed in nothing but the Republic and the France of philosophical and intellectual endeavor. Her parents had come to France from Poland and had abandoned all the trappings of a faith they'd never had along with the last snows of Warsaw. And what if her parents *had* been believers? In France there were Catholics and Protestants. They'd fought violent wars for many years and were now reconciled. She'd learned this at school, and in the towns and villages of Provence she'd seen churches and temples built very close together, sometimes on the same street.

Perhaps Saskia should think about something else; her questions would never find answers. One of her teachers had told them about the concept of carpe diem, seizing the day. As she saw it, this was the only sensible route to take. But who could be sensible now? Carpe diem was a luxury for anyone who hadn't experienced prison camps. How could you seize the day when you've lived every day as if it were the last of the Apocalypse?

On her way back into the studio, Saskia met the owner coming out. They hadn't been introduced so she felt awkward, but Mathilde smiled and she was the one to apologize.

"I'm so sorry. I did knock and no one answered. I wanted to bring you some clean linen for the beds and for you."

"Oh, thank you…"

"A young lady came and left a message for you. Éléonore. She's looked into your baccalaureate and managed to find you because of your lovely name. You passed! Congratulations!"

Saskia felt unsteady on her feet. Her parents had always thought she'd passed but she still would have loved to share this news with them. Two years ago.

"So, to celebrate I brought you some bottles I had in the cellar. And I've left some fruit and vegetables from the garden on the table. Oh, and also Éléonore wanted to apologize, I don't know what for but she seemed very genuine."

Saskia listened, not knowing how to reply, but with the day she was having, she was comforted by this small sign of human kindness and consideration. When all was said and done, she thought Éléonore rather brave after the way she, Saskia, had treated her. She must see her again. Perhaps she could give her some piano lessons. And then there was Mathilde standing right here with such rectitude, such graciousness, and such thoughtfulness. Her words soothed Saskia. She seemed to understand everything. Vincent had mentioned that Mathilde talked in enigmas and it wasn't always clear what she was getting at. As the two women finished their conversation, Saskia wasn't really sure how but Mathilde didn't break with this tradition.

"You know, Saskia," she said, "it's only in times of war that we see the worst of mankind so starkly. But it's also in times of war, and only then, that some people become sublime."

AFTER AN INTENSIVE CAMPAIGN MOBILIZING local town halls to send new demining candidates, Fabien was able to reconstitute a team. They'd been joined by four young Frenchmen who could protest with plenty of bravura that they had no God or master and did as they pleased, but they weren't free: If they were doing this job, it was because they were hungry.

As Manu had before his injuries, they had physical grace, an unselfconscious beauty, and generous smiles. Youth. But Manu was secretive and nostalgic where they were chipper and still had plenty of enthusiasm in their eyes. Even the most hardened members of the team found themselves thinking it would be appalling if it was these boys who were blown up by a mine.

There was also an older man, Andreï, with gloomy eyes and black hair. He'd been among a group of Americans whom the Germans had forcibly enlisted in the Ost-legionen. They had retaliated against the Nazis and, as well as disclosing crucial information, had carried out key acts of sabotage with extraordinary courage. Fourteen of them had been found and shot by firing squad. The others had joined the Free French Forces and played pivotal roles in the liberation of Hyères. Fabien had heard about

Andreï and guessed that, like himself, he wanted to melt into a new team in order to cope with the terror of having survived.

Each recruit was aware of how difficult it would be to join a decimated unit. They had a peculiar sense of stealing dead men's places, as if tipping them into oblivion.

To dismiss this notion that there were two groups—the old and the new—as quickly as possible, Fabien took the time to talk to them and listen to them. And so that they could all move forward, he'd decided it was time they finished with the damn beach. That would establish cohesion in the new team.

It was difficult returning to the site of the tragedy. Fabien had secured assurances from the army that they would send weapons experts to disarm the sarcophagus mines. And, if they found any mines that hadn't been triggered in the series of explosions, he'd been given permission by the authorities to blow them up in situ. He'd been granted this permission relatively easily, which astounded him: The relevant town hall should have taken into account the disturbance such noise levels would cause to locals—not to mention the potential for shattered windows. It was a favor, and Fabien knew only too well that all favors come at a price. He would see soon enough when and how.

They went right back to the start, sweeping the beach in sections. To finish the work as quickly as possible, the guards followed a meter behind them, clearing rubble from the areas they'd covered. It was an opportunity for the guards to redeem themselves: When the explosions had happened, they'd stood by and watched, not knowing what to do. They'd been so paralyzed by the violence of it that they hadn't even had the presence of mind to contact the rescue squad. Since then, they'd been keeping a low profile, including with the prisoners, making a point of going easy on them out of respect for the risks they took.

Whenever a deminer's bayonet touched something suspect that wasn't a lump of cement or the vestiges of an exploded mine, Fabien took over. Or Vincent. Sometimes Lukas.

As anticipated, there were very few devices that had escaped the first sweep and the explosions, but there were some, around the edges. Every disarmed mine was taken away carefully and put with the others, neatly lined up, before the final explosion, which would be their revenge for the fatal blast on the evening of the dance. They were now in control of the situation, deciding where and when...

Vincent derived a strange satisfaction from having to concentrate so intently. In the early days, when he'd been detecting, he hadn't achieved this, but now each disarmed mine, each victory over metal and powder boosted his confidence and found a resonance in him that he couldn't define but was related to adrenaline and pleasure. A poisonous pleasure. Addictive. He'd hardly finished disarming one mine before he wanted to find another and start again. Having to concentrate on an explosive device, using a watchmaker's precision and a marksman's composure as he used to when operating on a patient, created a diversion from his obsession. It allowed him to breathe a little more easily until he could get into the château.

Vincent had waited until the midmorning break to speak to Fabien, but this time Fabien was the one sharing his cigarettes with the Germans. Vincent then waited until lunchtime but was thwarted again: Fabien was sitting with the new recruits asking them about their first impressions and Vincent wasn't able to catch his eye. During the afternoon break it was still the same: He couldn't approach Fabien.

Thanks to Lukas, Vincent knew what to tell Fabien to persuade him to demine the château, but couldn't work out how to tell him or when. Fabien had been avoiding him since they'd seen Audrey at the hospital. Or rather, he was giving sideways glances, then looking away. This made Vincent very uncomfortable, but he tried to convince himself it would all be fine.

At last, it was time to detonate their haul. Fabien started the countdown, and they all joined him in chorus. Children who'd seen signs warning of the explosion had congregated above the beach with their parents to watch the drama. Fabien hadn't anticipated that the warnings, designed specifically to keep people away, would attract such a crowd.

When the mines exploded in geysers of sand, there was clapping and whoops of joy, the clear voices of the youngest onlookers blending with the deminers' cheers. Everyone was caught up in the children's infectious glee. As Fabien had hoped, these controlled explosions acted as a catharsis, exorcizing their trauma.

After this volcanic demonstration of pleasure came the final test. Theoretically, all the devices had been detonated and there was no more risk, but this was the protocol. With mines, nothing was ever guaranteed. Some could have become more deeply embedded in the sand or could have been missed by their sweeps. It was up to the Germans to advance in a tight-knit line, treading every square centimeter of the beach with the full weight of their bodies to check that no mine had been missed.

Everyone who'd watched the explosion stayed to see the Germans risk their lives. This solemn spectacle raised no cries of joy, but the crowd was fascinated by the strange sight.

"If we were civilized, we'd use tanks to do this," said Fabien.

"Do we have the funds to be civilized?" Vincent asked pointedly. He could see that Fabien was lost in thought during this tense and sobering process, but this was the only opportunity to catch him alone.

"You know," he ventured, "thanks to you, I got to see Lukas at the camp. He says he can tell us where the mines are in the château."

"The château?" Fabien asked, not really listening.

"At Eyguières...the German HQ."

"Really?" Fabien said, at last interested, as far as Vincent could tell.

Fabien was in fact merely replying automatically. He offered another enigmatic response: "I've thought about the château, but...as things stand, it's complicated."

Complicated...the word that made everything impossible. Vincent wanted to press him but was careful not to show that he longed for a glimmer of interest as if for a source of water after crossing a desert.

Fabien was no longer on the beach with him but way up above with the crowd behind the railing, fascinated by the sharp contrast between the nervous impatience of the people watching and the impassivity of those risking being blown up. The spectators and the deminers. He intuitively sensed a latent danger, without knowing exactly what it was.

Then his gaze settled on Lukas, who was advancing slowly with the other prisoners. They were now coming to the end of the beach. All the markers had been removed. Lukas and Hans caught each other's eyes and breathed, relieved.

Vincent made up his mind to broach the subject again with Fabien.

"He can draw us plans of the château and gardens, showing where the mines are."

Fabien wasn't listening.

In a rush, the people who'd gathered behind the railing, frustrated by so much waiting, raced down onto the beach, laughing, hastily stripping off to throw themselves into the water.

They didn't know that the seabed was carpeted with mines. Right under their eyes, weever fish made of metal were buried in the wet sand and jellyfish of steel floated menacingly, waiting for the softest touch to explode.

Fabien bellowed to stop them, but every sound was smothered by children's laughter. Even their parents were laughing along.

Instinctively, the French and Germans linked hands to form a chain and stop the onslaught of would-be swimmers. And this time there wasn't a flicker of hesitation, their hands had no nationality. German, French, Spanish, Armenian, their hands were strong, broad, human, and protective, all working together. The chain was robust, but the swimmers themselves were unchained. They didn't want to hear anything. Besides, they were squealing so loudly, they couldn't hear a thing.

Held back by the strong arms of the deminers, prisoners, and guards, the bold adventurers were forced to listen to what Fabien was saying. He explained that, although the beach had been made safe, the sea hadn't. To stop Allied landings, the Germans had deployed sea mines powerful enough to blow up tank transporter ships. So bathers in swimsuits...

The danger should have driven them back immediately, but they were watching Fabien suspiciously. They'd waited so long for this. What with the Italian occupation and the German occupation, they hadn't been allowed onto the beach for three years! Three years without a dip in the sea! When Fabien told them that the water would still be out of bounds this summer, some of them were downcast, others enraged.

"That's still two months! Isn't that enough for you to clear up our beaches?"

Seeing Fabien's determination, the more reasonable of them eventually persuaded the more recalcitrant. They climbed back up to the road, muttering about the deminers as they went.

The lull at the end of the day seemed like a good time to Vincent. Once the equipment was packed away, he approached Fabien, but found him preoccupied with something rather than heading home: He suggested to the guards, who had nothing against the idea, that they could stop off at a creek that they'd demined a few months earlier. It was still out of bounds to the public to avoid causing any confusion, but, thanks to the rocks and the shallowness of the sea, no boat could navigate there so there were no sea mines. Fabien had had this checked by divers when they'd demined the area.

And there, far from the prying eyes of passersby, he organized a fishing trip. The Germans lit a fire. Manu lobbed two or three grenades into the water and the small explosions brought enough fish to the surface to make a feast.

The Germans were so hungry that, without any discussion, the deminers all let them eat first. The wood fire, the grilled fish, some shellfish found among the rocks, and the pleasure of being together to celebrate their victory over the beach that had claimed their friends made them want to prolong the evening.

Meanwhile, Fabien took Vincent aside.

"I can see you want to talk, let's talk. But we'll do it at your place. I don't want anyone to hear what I need to tell you."

∼

VINCENT SHOWED FABIEN INTO THE STUDIO. HE thought he had only a bottle of wine and some fruit he'd picked up in orchards when he bicycled home, but found everything that Mathilde had left. He opened the bottle and put the fruit onto a plate. Fabien didn't sit down; he watched Vincent, then threw the photo of him playing tennis onto the table.

"Can you explain?"

Vincent had gathered that Fabien had his doubts about him. Since their hospital visit, he'd had time to think of a defense.

"Who's Vincent Devailly?"

"A prisoner who betrayed me in the camp. We'd planned to escape together. He ratted on me to the guards and escaped without me."

"That doesn't explain why you changed your name."

"I'm a doctor. A military doctor. I couldn't pay for my studies and the army paid them for me. I owe them ten years of my life in exchange, but I don't want to go back."

"You don't want to go back to the army but you're clearing mines?"

"You didn't want to fight in Germany either, and you're clearing mines."

"It's not the same, Vincent. You're demining because you want to mix with the German prisoners. You're looking for Ariane."

Vincent was visibly shaken.

"You know her?"

"I think so. Do you have a photo?"

Vincent raced upstairs, grabbed some photos, and tore back downstairs. He handed several portraits of Ariane to Fabien, who looked at them for a long time without a word. Was that because he'd been mistaken? Because Ariane's beauty broke free of the black-and-white image to pierce his heart and he was enthralled by her face? It was as if she were looking at him and him alone from her backdrop of glossy paper. Vincent hung on Fabien's reactions to interpret them. He had a feeling, from Fabien's obvious emotion, that he knew something but was hesitating to tell him.

"Ariane," Fabien said at last. "Yes, that's definitely her."

Fabien didn't want Vincent to latch on to a few snatches of information that might plunge him into despair, but he decided not to lie to him.

"I didn't know her well. She came to offer her help."

Why did Vincent see it as a betrayal that Ariane had enlisted in the Resistance without telling him? Of course, his mail had been monitored, but she could have found a way of telling him in veiled terms, as she always did.

"Was she in your network?"

"Not exactly. But she did things for us."

"Such as?"

"She found out what the Germans in the region were up to. She was in touch with quite a few officers."

Vincent was all too aware of this, but he wanted to know more.

"Did she say anything before she disappeared?"

"Nothing. And I was worried. I had to take security measures and make my team lie low for two weeks."

"How come?"

Fabien knew that what he was about to reveal would frighten Vincent. He knew full well how it felt to be scared for the woman you loved, to be aware of the risks she was taking and not be able to protect her. Vincent could tell he was hesitating, and he understood why.

"Ariane didn't just give you information...she went further."

"She'd offered to poison the commandant at the HQ. It was a very unusual idea, but she persuaded us. She was very determined."

"I know she tried to get hold of some digitalis."

"Exactly. She was meant to pour it into his glass at the end of the evening at his birthday party. But he didn't die, not him nor any of the others. We didn't see her again after that. No one knew what happened. Did she fail? Did she decide against it? Did someone manage to turn her?"

"How could you think that?"

"I had to go through gymnastics like that to protect my men. We couldn't trust someone we didn't know well. But mostly I was just really worried, obviously. Everything about her screamed honesty and generosity. You only had to see the way she looked at people. When she was listening to you, she made you feel like the most important person in the world. In fact, you felt chosen, but she wasn't choosing any one person. In her eyes, everyone was fascinating."

Ah, so he'd noticed that too...

"And this commanding officer at the HQ that she wanted to assassinate, where's he now? In the camp?"

"He's in bad shape. He'll probably be transferred."

The door opened and Saskia came in. From outside she'd seen through the window that there was a bottle of wine on the table, photos of Ariane, and nostalgia hanging in the air which, like a genie from a lamp, must have emanated from the wine bottle along with talk of this woman whom they probably both loved in their own way. Nostalgia for love in one case and for a network in the other, and for a time when he'd shared great risks and every tiny victory with men and women whom he felt all deserved to be in the Pantheon.

She didn't want to intrude, so she said hello and went up to her room. Fabien already knew that Vincent had offered her a room until she could reclaim her house.

"Listen," he said, picking up their conversation, "here's what I suggest. I've told you what I know about Ariane and I'm not sure you'll get much more out of the prisoners but go ahead and try. I think that if she's alive, she'll come back and explain, I have faith in her. As for demining, I shouldn't think you're really interested..."

"I want to finish the task I started with you."

Fabien thought for a while, then said, "I'm going to be very pragmatic. I trained you and I don't have many recruits, even fewer who know about mines. As for the army... You were a prisoner and not everyone's come home from Germany yet, which still gives you some time. I think you're more useful here than you are there. So that's a yes."

Vincent couldn't have hoped for better. He was relieved. Fabien poured himself a glass of wine and almost whispered to lend some solemnity to his words because he'd never been afraid of a bit of gravitas when he deemed something important.

"People who think the fighting stops when you lay down your arms are wrong. The Resistance is the opposite of a lightning war, it's a constant battle. I hated carrying a weapon, but we had to. And I would do it again, exactly the same, if there was another war. But we must never come to that again. They often say, if you want peace, prepare for war. But I think it's the other way around now. To avoid war, we need to prepare for peace."

Vincent didn't dare raise the subject of the château again.

∾

VINCENT DIDN'T IMMEDIATELY GRASP WHY, AT the end of the last training day, Lukas bumped into him, then apologized and walked away. What he'd actually done was slip a note into his hand, saying that he'd finished his drawings.

That same evening, Vincent went to the camp to collect them. He handed some food over the barbed wire to Lukas: Some bread and a few early strawberries he'd picked in an abandoned garden. Lukas didn't wait to eat them, not wanting to make the others jealous. He devoured the piece of bread and Vincent wished he'd brought more. He had such clear memories of hunger taking up all the available space in your days, to the point of distraction. When Lukas had finished and checked that no one was watching, he passed the sketches to Vincent.

A whole gallery of suspects was captured in the small book which Vincent crammed into the inside pocket of his jacket, next to his heart that beat faster and faster, as if all these hypothetical criminals who were still alive might infiltrate him through the book's covers.

He stopped by the side of the road, eager to see the portraits. As he'd suspected, Lukas was good at drawing. With swift, very elegant strokes he'd sketched the faces of some fifteen of his fellow inmates. And yet Vincent was disappointed. He'd expected it to be instantly clear—from the evocative power of the drawings—which of the officers from the German HQ could have been a threat to Ariane. Who was criminal and who wasn't. Except that Lukas had drawn men where Vincent wanted soldiers. He'd brought out their humanity when Vincent was looking for their violence.

Lukas had penciled in only their faces and shoulders, and these faces didn't look like officers or Germans. Not with their anxious foreheads and lines around their eyes, their pale eyes, but pale gray like the gray of the pencil that he must have smudged with the pad of his thumb. His draftsmanship blurred the differences. Vincent resented Lukas; he felt he'd been played. But then when he'd watched the new members of the team on the beach, he'd caught himself confusing some of the Germans for Frenchmen.

During the war with their uniforms, it had been different. There had been no risk of confusion. There'd been such conformity in the way they held themselves, their attitude, the expression on their faces, the arrogance and indifference. And their icy stare. A stare you didn't want to cross for fear of being done for, but that you had to meet for fear of being suspect. A stare that single-handedly symbolized the Nazi project; a stare that scrutinized, evaluated, dissected, scorned, judged, filtered, selected, and condemned; a stare you would never forget; a dead-eyed stare that made you hate eyes even though it's through the eyes that we first communicate, it's the eyes that save every species from their darker side; a stare full of hatred that twisted the very vocation of eye contact, channeling the most hostile part of a human being. So yes, you could conclude that all Germans were the same because variations in body shape and features were erased under the strictures of their uniforms, their military hats, and this stare that governed everything else.

When they were working on the beach, at the lowest point of their defeat, the Germans had abandoned that arrogant stare and adopted a different expression, almost touching in its humility. When they'd lost their uniforms they'd also lost their defiance, as if their military trappings had been acting as their skeletons and muscles. Bare chested in the sunshine, their liberated bodies held themselves differently, and each of them went along with its own inclinations, like flowers in a vase.

And now these faces couldn't tell him anything about the evils these men may have committed. But the man who'd so dramatically changed the course of Ariane's life was almost certainly hiding among them. Could ignominy be smudged away like these pencil strokes?

Audrey would be able to tell him more. She would recognize the German he wanted to find.

When he reached her apartment, she wasn't there. He could knock at the door all he liked, he didn't hear a single sound inside, even though he'd sent word ahead by calling the woman who ran a shop on the ground floor and had a telephone. He waited on the landing for an hour, then went and walked around for a while and came back. She still wasn't there.

It came to him in a flash: Audrey knew he was coming and was avoiding him. So she did know something about Ariane and was refusing to tell him. He remembered her reassuring words the first time they'd seen each other again, words that now made him despair: *What do you think? If I knew Ariane was dead, I wouldn't be here in front of you wondering where she is! It would be the first thing I'd tell you. Or I'd avoid you. I hate being the bearer of bad news.*

Audrey was avoiding him, she was afraid to see him... Clutching his book of sketches, Vincent was filled with despair. He was so close, he could find the man who'd attacked Ariane, and maybe none of it meant anything now, maybe it would all collapse into infinite chaos when he found out that Ariane was dead...

On the sidewalk opposite Audrey's building some prostitutes were sharing a joke. They had a hint of flamboyance about them, and Vincent admired them: He knew the application it took to preserve your dignity when everything is conspiring to destroy it, and the discipline you had to impose on yourself to appear happy when the whole world views you as negligible. He couldn't do it anymore.

And yet he knew the virtue of this self-discipline: If you faked happiness, you almost achieved it. He'd tried this technique in the prison camp. He hadn't come up with the idea himself but had seen it in another prisoner called Jules. Jules spoke German and knew the right jokes to make the officers laugh. He smiled and made other people smile so much he ended up as one of the winners; you couldn't smile the way he did if you were defeated.

By managing to convince his jailors that he felt no resentment, Jules had avoided any punishments for several months and had even secured some small rewards: He'd been sent to work in the kitchens, which was one of the most coveted positions. But when he came down with some sort of flu, the guards were annoyed that he'd stopped making them laugh, as if he wasn't trying hard enough. Within three days he was dead from a bullet in the back of the neck. You have no right to be sick when you're the local jester.

As he walked along the street and made his way toward the harbor, Vincent realized that he would never be able to see his life today other than through the prism of his previous life. There was a huge area of darkness, Germany, and there were sunny shores, Ariane. If he hadn't met her before the war, he wouldn't have made it. While he was a prisoner, she'd helped him overcome every difficulty and achieve his freedom. Now that he was free, she made his life bearable, even if he still felt he was a prisoner.

Ariane was everywhere, so powerful that her radiant presence supplanted all his darkest thoughts and gloomy reflections on the human condition and war. He still had conversations with her. He knew what she would have thought, said, and done; he knew her so well. Sometimes he was surprised by a comment she seemed to make, like in a dream when you're taken aback by the events even though you're aware that it's a dream.

Before losing someone, people imagine it takes great strength to keep the departed by their side, stopping them from flitting away into the vastness of the heavens or just evaporating. They couldn't be more wrong. The absent have the gift of being everywhere at once and their presence is powerful. Ariane allowed Vincent to continue to find meaning in his life. Her opinion still mattered. What she would have said, thought, or done would always guide him. He need only let his mind drift for a moment and, without having to summon her, Ariane was there before him immediately. She laughed, talked quickly, was vivacious, and—much more so than he was—was alert to life's possibilities and to people, all of whom she found equally fascinating. Never faking that interest. She used to say that all living beings have learned something unique in their lives, and they could pass it on if only we were prepared to listen.

He could see her expressing this idea, and the vision of her saying these words hadn't come to him by chance. Something was niggling him. Something imbued with Ariane's thoughts was wafting in the air and had been following him since he'd left Audrey's building. A tenuous but obsessive, penetrating impression that kept coming back but was just beyond his grasp, seeming to sidle before his eyes, almost reach his mind, then evaporate with the volatility of a perfume smelled in the street which conjures someone you've known or loved with such intensity, but you'd need to smell it for longer to work out who, and you try desperately to catch it again, sniffing the air, prepared to follow anyone anywhere.

And then it suddenly came to him. It was so obvious! How hadn't he thought of it before? The prostitutes! As a young intern, Ariane had treated several of them when no one else would give them an appointment. She didn't make them pay, didn't judge them, and Vincent had often heard them laughing together.

He ran back to the street where Audrey lived.

They were still there, lined up like fragile reeds, their slight bodies made all the narrower by wartime shortages, their scanty dresses and bare legs with a line drawn onto them to imply stockings, and an elegance in spite of everything, in spite of poverty, the graciousness of women who still smile when everything should make them weep.

Ariane must have talked to them. For sure. Vincent went over to ask them a few questions. After the first few moments of confusion when they thought he was a customer, they told him that they did know Ariane. She'd even helped some of them. When they realized that Vincent was searching for Ariane day and night, they told him the secret she had confided to them.

Sensing that she was in danger where she was, Ariane had returned to Marseille but hadn't stayed there: She'd decided to run away, had said her goodbyes to them and said she would never ever return to France.

Vincent was knocked sideways. Ariane was alive—at least she had been when she'd talked to them—but she would *never ever* return…What did that mean? Had she lost all hope of seeing him again or did she no longer love him?

People have an enthusiastic way of saying it's a small world. Now that Ariane could be anywhere in it, the world had become vast, and Vincent was completely lost.

SASKIA NEEDED TO MAKE PROGRESS EVERY DAY without faltering, so she returned to see Édouard at the town hall. Even if she found it hard, she would wear him down. He would eventually relinquish some information. And she had another good reason to see him...

Once she was in his office and before she'd even said anything, he gave her the crucial piece of information she'd wanted since arriving back. But it was the exact opposite of what she'd been hoping: Her house wasn't in her parents' name. In the absence of a title deed or a license to build, there was nothing to establish Saskia's legitimate claim to it.

She couldn't believe it. What name was on the deed? Had there been a change of ownership? When? Her father had bought the plot, drawn up the plans, and overseen the construction! Could she have a look at the file Édouard had there?

Édouard snapped it shut and admonished her gently. These files were confidential. Would she like it if her personal information was circulated to all and sundry? As he'd hoped, Saskia didn't raise the subject of the land registry, clearly unaware that it existed and how it operated. This allowed him to make a show of compassion, feigning distress at such injustice. Lord knows none of us wanted this... What misery the war caused! And the world's full of inequality! If only we could do something about it! But we can't and we don't know everything!

He was extremely surprised when Saskia then changed the subject. Thanks to Mathilde, she'd discovered that she could apply to be a ward of the state. Both of her parents were dead, she was not yet an adult—she had a right to this status. It would allow her to pursue her studies. Édouard nodded in agreement: What an excellent way for her to start over! He realized that he would have to help her and, all in all, wasn't displeased to be useful in his own small way, in honor of Saskia's mother, Mila, who'd played a pivotal role in his securing a diploma. Even though he wouldn't handle this directly and didn't really know the procedure, he would see whether there was a template for the application process somewhere, a form, something to fill out. He went to ask a colleague.

Saskia darted to his side of his desk, opened her parents' file, and memorized everything she could.

When Édouard returned she was back in her seat. She managed to betray none of the emotion that had gripped her when she'd spotted a very familiar name in the file. She thanked him calmly for the forms she needed to fill out, asked for details on a few points, and told him she would ask for further help if need be. Relieved by her apparent willingness to accept the bad news about this grossly unfair title deed without a fight, Édouard saw her to the door.

Outside there was an enveloping, chill little wind that seemed to be blowing with the sole intention of driving her forward. She now had two pieces of information: The name of the owner of her house, and the name of the village where the Bellangers used to live.

The first name was not new to her and had put her in a state of turmoil. Bunley. Her father's associate. They'd set up their architecture practice together, they were friends, and—a rarity—they'd stayed friends. Could he really have usurped the title deed? Betrayed her father in the worst possible way?

Ilan had always talked of him as his benefactor because Bunley had had the capital to set up the practice on his own and he'd allowed Ilan to benefit from this. But hadn't he in fact benefited from her father's talent? From his sheer hard work? Ilan had been so grateful that he'd always been determined to secure more commissions.

All at once she could only see the dark side of it. Bunley's friendship? Faked. His affection for Ilan and Mila's family? Self-serving. Their professional partnership? A con.

She remembered that when in September '41 the law had forbidden Jews to work as architects, Eugène Bunley had suggested that her father put the practice entirely in Bunley's name. He'd promised to return Ilan's share when the war was over. Had they done the same thing with the house? Had he really intended to keep his promise or had he suggested the substitution to appropriate Ilan's share? These questions were monstrous and the worst of it was that Saskia's parents had hidden in the Bunleys' house.

Léna had a telephone and a directory. When Saskia arrived Léna was out, but Aurélien let her use the phone booth. And there at the back of the café, perched on a barstool covered in deep red moleskin, she learned that Eugène Bunley and his wife were dead. Murdered for acts of resistance. Meanwhile, their son had lived in Ilan and Mila's house to protect it from looters but had been arrested shortly after his parents were and was deported.

She still didn't know who had informed on them, but it wasn't the friend whom her father had venerated. He and his family had wanted to help them, to the very end. She remembered what Mathilde had said. She was right. You had to look at everything properly. Forget nothing. The worst of it as well as the sublime.

THE FOLLOWING MORNING SASKIA WOKE EARLY to go and see the village where the Bellangers had lived before the war. She took a bus up into the inland heights around Grasse. It was a long journey, but the village was charming. She had no trouble finding the Bellangers' former house: a large property surrounded as far as the eye could see by fields of jasmine, cabbage roses, and tuberose. Intoxicating crops. How could the Bellangers have left a place like this to live in a much smaller house in town? These estates were passed down through generations and stayed in the same families.

She had to do it: She would speak to the locals. After all, there was no reason for anyone to take it badly. She need only pass herself off as a friend of the Bellangers who wanted to know where they now lived.

It was the worst tactic she could have chosen. People looked at her as if she had the plague and talked to her as if spitting in her face.

"No one knows where they took themselves off to. Let's just hope they were caught and thrown in prison. Or better still, shot!"

Saskia was sickened to hear that collaborators had taken refuge in her house, but she now had her first valuable information—this would make Édouard relent. He hadn't helped her much, but now he would be obligated to. Indisputably. Him or someone else. No one could allow these traitors to go unjudged.

She took the first bus back, ran to town hall, and arrived just as the staff was leaving. She caught up with Édouard in a nearby street and blurted out everything she'd discovered, speaking so quickly that he didn't understand at first and had to ask her to start again. She was so enthused she wasn't finishing her sentences, but he eventually understood and summarized the situation to show that he'd grasped it. And added that if the Bellangers were collaborators, then he would inform the necessary authorities.

She felt for the first time that she was changing the course of events. She'd exposed the Bellangers. She would win. Édouard, however, seemed less enthusiastic than she was. He must have been tired. But she felt a nagging doubt, which she immediately tried to dismiss.

VINCENT WOULD HAVE PREFERRED NOT TO ASK anything of Fabien, but he had no alternatives left. Every lead he'd followed ended up in the same place: the château. He went to the café and found Fabien there, sitting alone on the terrace, which was more convenient than Vincent could have hoped. Vincent went and sat next to him and ordered a glass of white wine.

Fabien said he didn't have much time: He'd been asked to go to the town hall, where the mayor was expecting him. This wasn't a good start for Vincent. Particularly as this wouldn't be an easy subject to broach. He was now familiar with Fabien's perceptiveness: Fabien would know he was there for a reason. So Vincent didn't waste any time, he came straight to the point as if it was perfectly natural to pick up a conversation they'd started two days ago.

"There are huge arms stores at the Wehrmacht's old HQ. If we manage to demine the castle, we might be able to trade them with the army in exchange for detectors."

Fabien stiffened at the mention of the château, as he had at the beach the first time Vincent had talked about it. His only response was to order another glass of wine.

"Plus, their archives are there. They could be useful for the trials."

Strangely, Fabien didn't react. Not to the arms nor the archives, which were so important as evidence against war criminals. Vincent now went on to reveal one of the pieces of information that should clinch Fabien's support:

"And Lukas has promised me that we'll find mining maps of the region at the château."

Fabien was obsessed with these plans, but he listened in silence, as if none of Vincent's arguments struck a chord with him. He was on edge. Maybe because of his meeting at the town hall? He wasn't talking about it.

"The Allies have reached Berlin," he said eventually. "They're bound to get their hands on the plans."

This didn't suit Vincent's ends. He still had the most persuasive argument that Lukas had given him, but he couldn't make up his mind to use this final string to his bow. In the archives there was a list of Resistance fighters who'd been interrogated, files on all the undercover fighters who'd been taken prisoner, and a summary of the interrogations. Fabien could most likely find out what had happened to Odette. But even tiptoeing gently around the topic and using considered words, Vincent would prefer not to tread on such thorny territory. He decided against it.

Fabien downed his glass in one go, ordered a third, and confided quietly, "If we go to the château, I'll find out. I don't want to find out."

Of course. Fabien didn't need Vincent or Lukas to think of this. He knew exactly what he might find at Eyguières.

"I've waited a long time for Odette..."

Deportees who'd escaped had told him about the special measures reserved for women in the Resistance. The reason they'd been deported rather than killed on the spot was so that their murders would go unseen. Because they were killed in the obscenest way. He'd have preferred not to know.

His wife was a dancer, always on the move—in her words, her gestures, her body—and he would always picture her like that with her pretty face and curly hair and her peppy comebacks. The Nazis wouldn't put any other images in his head. Like him, she'd kept a cyanide pill hidden on her at all times; she'd killed herself, he was sure of it, or she'd fled, very far away, and they would never have had the repulsive satisfaction of murdering her.

When Léna came to clear away the glasses and bring them some slices of fougasse that she'd made to go with aperitifs, Vincent noticed that there was no more casual banter between them, no barbed remarks or teasing, but eye contact and a way of talking that was for the two of them alone, a discreet exclusivity that brought them closer and created a space all their own.

He watched this evidence of life picking up again, something from which he'd excluded himself, and he envied them. Even though she hadn't heard it, Léna was worried about the conversation they'd had because she'd noticed the sadness clouding Fabien's eyes. He reassured her with a smile.

Vincent felt pitiful for failing to notice sooner, and for upsetting Fabien by stirring up murderous memories. He wanted to leave, but as he mounted his bicycle, Fabien suggested he come to the town hall with him.

"You're right, we need to fight to get hold of those mining maps. We can't wait for the army to show us some crumbs of goodwill. But you can be the one to get the files from the château. I don't want to go rummaging through their shitty archives."

Vincent wasn't proud of securing what he wanted like this. He thought about the expression that people always used without really gauging its terrifying recklessness, its terrible scope: The end justifies the means. But when all was said and done, if someone used despicable means, what did they lose and what did they gain?

Vincent would never forgive himself for waking a sleepwalker who still dreamed of his wife dancing.

IF FABIEN HAD TAKEN VINCENT TO THE TOWN hall, it was because he wanted a witness. His years in the Resistance had taught him to anticipate dirty tricks and given him a complete aversion to last-minute meetings. During the war they'd constituted a major risk of being ambushed. And in this instance, he sensed a trap...

A map hanging on the wall in the mayor's office showed the advances made by the deminers. Red thumbtacks indicated danger, and green ones marked out reclaimed territory. It was like the war; it was like a game with the Riviera gradually being covered in different colored tacks. There had been some fine victories, but there was still work to do: There were more red tacks than green.

While the mayor offered them a drink, Fabien kept his eyes pinned on the two men in impeccable suits standing off to one side with files and leather briefcases under their arms. They would most likely come forward later, when the mayor had paved the way. For now, he was joking amiably.

"So tell me, I hear you go fishing with the Germans! I've had quite a few complaints. 'The shame of it! Fishing with the Boche! And using grenades!'"

"Looks like the informers have gone straight back to work," Fabien replied calmly.

"Oh, it's to be expected, no one's surprised, are they... Still, don't you worry. You know what you're doing. I have full faith in you. I mean, look, I let you have your big blowup on the beach! I took plenty of criticism for that, but well, I don't regret it."

Fabien had always known he would have to pay for the controlled explosion. The time had now come. The mayor's words were intended to be friendly, grateful, but Fabien could spot the calculations going on behind his avuncular joviality, and he was waiting to be handed the check. Having performed the preliminaries, the mayor produced gifts like a colonist placating an indigenous tribe.

"I have good news! These gentlemen have brought us the magnetic resonance detectors you've been so keen to have!" Then he lowered his voice as if discussing a state secret to add, "We don't know how they got their hands on them, and we don't want to know. All that matters is we now have them!"

Good news—Fabien didn't like it. Especially when it was sold to him gift wrapped. What came next proved him right: The team must now demine an area that didn't feature in their schedule. What's more, the mayor insisted—with some diplomacy, it has to be said—it needed to be done immediately. Rebuilding programs were whetting people's appetites.

Thinking Fabien would agree to this with no objections, the mayor casually showed him a place on the map.

"I'll take you there. You'll see, it's very beautiful."

Fabien studied the map, apparently interested.

"I know it. It's near the two prettiest beaches in the area. Nicely south-facing but sheltered from the mistral by the hillside and the forest of maritime pines. There even used to be palm trees."

"That's right! I can see you know the area."

"Oh, I do. It's idyllic," Fabien said, unfazed. "The Germans burned it all down, but the pine trees will grow back eventually, and you can always plant more palms."

The mayor turned to the two men in suits. "I told you, he's very quick, don't need to waste time explaining things to him."

"Which is why he doesn't like being referred to in the third person when he's in the room," Fabien snapped.

That put a damper on things. The mayor was in no mood for hostilities.

"Come, come, Fabien, I was doing nothing but complimenting you."

"Don't butter me up. That area isn't a priority."

"Forgive me, but everything will have to be demined eventually."

"We're a public service, not a private company. We're waging this fight in everyone's interest, not in these gentlemen's interests. The land is mined so I guess it has no value and they've bought it for a song from destitute smallholders. And then, thanks to us, and at no cost to them, it will be worth a fortune again. Wheeling and dealing are back—if they ever stopped!"

Fabien turned to the two businessmen. "What do you want to build on the plot? A hotel, a villa?"

"An apartment blo—"

"It can wait," Fabien said curtly.

"But you *are* paid for what you do. And not just peanuts. I've heard you have substantial bonuses."

"Nothing could compensate for the risks we run."

The mayor gestured to the two men to show that he would take over from here.

"Fabien, rebuilding France really does mean what it says. If we don't do any building, it doesn't make sense."

"If we don't prioritize public safety, it doesn't make any sense either."

"It's just a simple plot."

"Which will earn these gentlemen a lot of money and may cost my men very dearly. So please give us some choice about why we're risking life and limb."

The mayor understood what Fabien meant because they'd talked about this many times before. The worst of it was that he agreed with him. But this was over his head: The businessmen had powerful local support. There would have to be some negotiating.

"We could give your men extra ration tickets."

"That's an insult! My men are risking their lives for France. Not to scrounge for ration tickets!"

"What about the Germans? Couldn't they come outside working hours?"

"The Germans are just like us—physically and mentally exhausted. And to make matters worse, they're undernourished. If we ask them to work on Sundays, we'll lose them. Besides, it's against the regulations. But I may have a solution."

He paused for a while, pretending to think, and the mayor and the two men relaxed during this pause.

"First of all, I'm going to tell you a story."

They all held their breath.

"You know Saint-Exupéry, a wonderful writer, but also a poet, reporter, and aviator, one of the pioneers of the French airmail service. He lived in New York, with a wife he loved. He could have stayed there all through the war, but he chose to come home to France to fight. He was advised against it, he was told he wasn't young enough to be called up, he was injured. He wouldn't hear it. Every morning he took off in his plane from the far side of the Mediterranean. One morning he flew out of Corsica with enough fuel in his tank for six hours in the air. Despite antiaircraft defenses that could have brought him down at any moment, he flew very low along the coast, as low as possible. Probably too low. And do you know why? Because as well as the antiaircraft defenses, he was spotting minefields, and you can't make out signs that say 'ACHTUNG MINEN' at higher altitudes. He drew up accurate maps of minefields to prepare for the landings. His final mission was on July 31, '44. He was forty-four. When he stopped sending out a signal after six hours, they knew he wouldn't come back. He was somewhere at the bottom of the sea, with his plane. He died for his mission. So you see, mines sacrificed him too. Is what you're asking today worthy of his sacrifice?"

The atmosphere was icy. No one dared talk of ration tickets now. The lesson was clear: Deminers are paid, not bought. The silence was so awkward that the mayor

poured more drinks for everyone, to give himself something to do. Then he approached Fabien again, his voice
trying to sound detached when it was desperate.

"Didn't you say you'd thought of a solution?"

"We'll demine the Château des Eyguières, then we'll
clear your plots. I'll let you think it over."

Vincent admired Fabien more than he ever could anyone else. And in such grizzly times, it felt good to admire
someone for who they were, with no ulterior motives.

The two businessmen were furious. They wanted to
reply, but the mayor made it clear that it would be better
not to. Fabien put his jacket back on to indicate that the
meeting was over, and looked the businessman who'd insulted him in the eye as he said, "We think we're dying for
our country when we're dying for industrialists."

"I didn't know you were so grandiloquent."

"It's not mine!"

"Who said it?"

"Anatole France. And it's not grandiloquent. Eloquent,
yes, but also important. And it's never been truer!"

IT WAS ONE OF THOSE MEETINGS ON WHICH YOU pin all your hopes. One that would finally give her a chance to change her life. As soon as she stepped into the office, Saskia knew she would come away disappointed: Édouard was smiling at her, but smiling as if to defuse legitimate anger, as if to say, Come on, it's not that bad, there'll be other solutions...

She thought she'd brought to light incendiary information to annihilate the Bellangers, information with the scope of weapons of mass destruction. Not a bit of it. Édouard had done some research and told her that the Bellangers had already been tried. Their lawyer had judiciously relocated their trial to Aix-en-Provence, where no one knew them, where no one from their own town had gone to bear witness; and there, thanks to the distance of just over one hundred kilometers, their crimes hadn't seemed so serious, just as mountains start to look like hills when you travel away from them, until they gradually disappear in the distance. They'd been acquitted.

Édouard thought it worthwhile telling her that the Bellangers weren't the only people to have benefited from a court's leniency. In the early days, yes, justice had been harsh, implacable, expeditious, but gradually—and even de Gaulle had been in favor of this—verdicts had softened.

Saskia, who'd listened in silence, horrified, latched on to this last word. Édouard couldn't say verdicts had *softened*! They weren't soft—they were outrageous! The Bellangers had collaborated with the enemy while her family had died in a camp! Where was the justice in that? They were blithely living in her house when she was seen as an intruder there—in her home. It was so unfair... hearing herself say those words, Saskia was aware of how pitifully inadequate they were in proportion to her emotions. Was the French post-Liberation justice system no better than the one under the Vichy government had been?

Given that no one wanted to consider her legitimate claim, she would cling to her continued education. She would find a job that matched the hopes her parents had had for her. And that she herself had had. Perhaps a lawyer, to give other people the help she hadn't been offered. Or an architect. Like her father. She would resurrect his practice.

Next, Édouard handed her the reply concerning her application to be a ward of the state. Saskia read it several times. It was a short letter, but she couldn't register what it said. It was absurd: She must have misunderstood, or the words were badly chosen, or ambiguous. She looked up and Édouard's downcast expression gave her no room for doubt: She could not be considered a ward of the state because there was nothing to prove to the French authorities that her parents were dead. She needed to provide irrefutable proof that they were deceased and not just missing.

Prove they were dead? Saskia's head was spinning.

Even Édouard sympathized and tried to comfort her.

"I know it's not easy, but sometimes we have to forget, turn the page, and start afresh. It's what we're all doing."

Saskia almost pitied him. It was easy for him to turn the page in a book he'd never read.

LUKAS WASN'T FAR FROM HIS GOAL NOW BUT WAS in danger of going under. At the San Francisco Conference, the French minister of foreign affairs, Georges Bidault, had—by the skin of his teeth—secured the right for France to use prisoners of war for any task, including mine clearance. It was now official: Everyone had forgotten them.

And, a fatal blow, he'd just heard that Matthias, the man he so wanted to protect, the only person he felt like talking to, would not be returning to the camp. He wasn't dead, not yet, but was to be repatriated to Germany to die in order to avoid further compromising French statistics. Lukas had succumbed to despondency and, as everyone in the camp knew, despondency was the beginning of the end. He needed to be fired up by his escape plans again. It was vital. But what was the point of escaping when you have no one to go with and probably no one to return home to?

The others can't have felt as alone as he did. Hans had received a parcel, something they'd all lost hope of seeing. His parents, friends, and fiancée had finally found out where he was. In the parcel, which had miraculously found its way to him thanks to connections, they had sent wine and beer, dried meat—lots of dried meat—and dried sausage. The guards, who usually helped themselves, hadn't dared appropriate it, afraid of a furious outburst. Hans was intimidating thanks to his sheer physical strength, and to the element of madness everyone sensed in him.

When he'd opened the parcel, the other prisoners had been overwhelmed by the smell of cooked meat. As well as the hunger that gnawed at them constantly, and their taste buds that made them salivate, they'd been hit by a wave of nostalgia. Hans hadn't shared his treasure. Worse. He took frugal little portions of the meat to prolong the pleasure, and the prisoners found themselves dreaming every night not of women but of seasoned pork.

Another inmate, Kurt, had been visited by a woman. She'd come from Germany and had brought clothes, a blanket, and a stout pair of shoes. She maintained her dignity despite all the whistling and lewd comments from the prisoners. Kurt was so moved to see her that he didn't even bother trying to quiet the other men. He couldn't take his eyes off this woman. His woman, his wife. Through the barbed-wire fence, she'd told him calmly that she and their daughter were coming to live here, to be as close to him as possible. She didn't give a damn about the way the French looked at her, didn't give a damn that she couldn't speak the language, didn't give a damn about the likely unfit conditions in which she would live, a conquered woman among the conquerors, with no work for now, and so far from her family. Germany was in chaos. She'd seen German prisoners sent to Russia, England, and France. She'd heard that they would stay outside Germany even when the peace treaty was signed, perhaps for longer than was reasonable. She didn't want her daughter to grow up so far away from him. She'd referred to her daughter, but Kurt was overcome with emotion that she too, who was still so beautiful, couldn't live without him, even though he was now nothing. As soon as the rumor spread, and it spread very fast, that the visitor had left Germany to settle in France, in hostile territory, to be by her husband's side and support him, the prisoners no longer saw her as a doll but as a heroine.

Like the others, Lukas envied Kurt. Of course, he did. The only thing he had left that was in the least unique, and he was well aware of the terrible irony of the situation, was his relationship with Vincent. But it was in danger of losing its uniqueness. All the prisoners on the demining team had guessed that the Frenchman had made some sort of offer to Lukas, and they were prepared to fight to take up that offer instead of him.

The previous day, Hans had made the boldest move. He'd approached Vincent and had asked him a few questions, which Vincent had answered without much enthusiasm. No doubt he didn't want to run the risk of letting everyone know his plan. But it also seemed likely that it had suited him that Lukas had been watching. Lukas suspected that Vincent was banking on this desperate competition. He must have learned this when he himself was a prisoner. Truth be told, there will always be rivalries, even among the most oppressed. And therein lies the sick genius of the oppressors: Encouraging the humiliated to fight among themselves, rather than with their humiliators.

Lukas had, therefore, deliberately isolated himself from the other prisoners in order to avoid inconvenient questions. But he needed an accomplice and that wasn't easy. Dieter wasn't shrewd enough to keep things to himself, and Kurt wouldn't want to escape now that his wife was here. As for the others, he didn't trust them.

While he was working from memory but, thanks to his flagging hopes, with little conviction on plans of the château, he heard a rumor making the rounds: They would be demining the old HQ the very next day. His hopes rallied—he would have his chance to escape. And in that surge of optimism, he was driven to a conclusion: Hans. Hans was far from stupid and didn't adhere to Nazi ideology. He wasn't keen on the French either and refused to be made to feel guilty, but at least you could have a decent conversation with him. And anyway, Lukas was no better than the others. He was exhausted, he needed to build his strength...and he just couldn't stop thinking about the stuff. The idea humiliated him, but he was dying to do it: Perhaps, while he and Hans discussed things, he could negotiate for a snick of dried meat...

THE DEMINERS WERE HAPPY THAT MORNING. After stressful weeks working on the beaches in direct sunlight and trying to forget the terrible explosion that had decimated them, making the château safe seemed the most exhilarating task they could have been given. They felt more necessary than ever: The building's former glory would ennoble those who restored it.

The HQ that the Germans had chosen was a serendipitous combination of a medieval tower and a Renaissance building influenced by nearby Italy, along with a more recent extension that dated from the nineteenth century. When the Germans requisitioned it, it had become the most feared site in the region for the local population. It was no longer a château—their château—but a despised fortress, a macabre lair that they envisioned being transformed into a decadent rathole come nightfall.

Even after the Germans left, it was still the incarnation of the antechamber to hell: No one could forget the seven children who'd tried to venture inside and had died on the grounds.

The château was mined, booby-trapped, stuffed full of explosives from floor to ceiling, a site of horror in a fairy-tale setting, but the thought of seeing inside the building made the deminers feel important. Without their intervention, the château would never be anything again.

Fabien saw this as a valuable opportunity to get his hands on the mining plans, Vincent as the promise of knowing why Ariane disappeared. And for Lukas, it was his last chance of escape.

To mark the occasion, the mayor had made the trip along with a few local grandees who hoped to play a part in the future administration of the region. They congratulated the mine-clearance team, assured them of their boundless admiration for them, and even managed a ripple of applause. It didn't cost anything and was a reminder of the first hesitant and heroic days of demining, when no one had dared believe anybody would come out alive.

As soon as the officials left, Fabien set out the plan of attack. Even though everyone wanted to get inside this château that fueled so many fantasies—there might be gold coins and spoils of war for them to share—they urgently needed to make the approach to it safe. First, the central driveway, with all of them working together. They would then divide up the château's grounds, the areas immediately around each wing, followed by the surrounding gardens. Once every access route, every part of the façade, every door and window had been carefully cleared, a team could begin work inside.

Paper was in short supply, so the mayor had used the back of Vichy posters to reproduce Lukas's plans. Before pinning them to wooden panels at the gates to the grounds, the shocked deminers read Pétain's propaganda:

THE BAD TIMES ARE OVER, DADDY'S WORK-
ING IN GERMANY. FRENCHMEN, GO WORK IN
GERMANY, GERMAN WORKMEN ARE INVITING
YOU TO JOIN THEM. They knew it hadn't been German workmen who'd invited the French and that even
some French citizens themselves had used violence to
force their fellow countrymen to go there.

Fabien brought an end to their comments and asked
Lukas to describe the basic outlines of German mining.

They all started concentrating again—their lives
depended on it—but they couldn't stop their emotions
bubbling back up to the surface. The French had gradually come to like the Germans in their team, but now here
was Lukas explaining in detail how they'd sabotaged the
château and its grounds, mining every corner of this ar-
chitectural wonder that awakened childhood memories of
enchanted fables and dreams of national grandeur.

As Lukas talked, he became aware that their anger
was mounting. And resentment. The French who'd had
to submit all through the Occupation, who'd had to cope
with the misery and fear, the demands and injustices,
were now drawing themselves up to their full height
again as if, all of sudden, it was too much. It was ridiculous after all those years of war. But the insanity of this
scorched-earth policy disgusted them. Even those who
weren't local had grown fond of these old walls, these
slices of history, and were outraged to think that just one
step taken into the grounds could pulverize men and ancient stones alike.

A few acerbic remarks started to fly. Lukas stayed impassive; he wasn't supposed to understand what they were saying. But to ease the tension, he changed his speech and ended with a smile.

"We spent so long setting traps in this château that we ended up being trapped by Resistance fighters ourselves! German engineering's a wonderful thing!"

The deminers were disconcerted by his self-mockery, but some of them laughed and their laughter was contagious. On the other hand, the prisoners found it hard to take: Lukas was going ahead and explaining how the Germans, convinced they'd be able to escape with no trouble, had been caught almost before they'd closed the gate behind them.

Fabien wasn't laughing; he was alarmed that the tension between the French and Germans was so ready to rear its head again at the least strain. This site symbolized the Occupation and could trigger an emotional release that he'd been dreading from the start. He indicated that it was time to get to work.

Vincent watched Lukas, who had gone back to join the other prisoners. He seemed to have picked the most astute of them. He hadn't chosen him by chance but because of a look, an attitude... The books he read during their breaks, the way he talked and kept away from the others, as Vincent did himself. He'd read that, according to Edgar Allan Poe, intuition isn't a magic power but endless recorded pieces of information combining in synergy and eventually crystallizing into a revelation. He was also quick to remind himself that his instincts weren't infallible. The first time he'd tried to escape, he'd put his trust in the worst of men. Since then, he'd sworn never to give in to his intuition. He was starting to like Lukas, which meant he should be extra wary of him.

THE FIRST DAY ON THE CHÂTEAU'S GROUNDS WENT well, and the work was quicker than anticipated. Having Lukas's information generated a confidence that made the men more efficient. They learned a lot about how the Germans set mines and caught out the French.

Lukas continued to earn Fabien's respect as he explained their strategy. He indicated a line of clearly visible explosives that they should blow up to get straight to the château. A hillock landscaped with trees some distance away would protect them from the blast...

Two deminers prepared the controlled explosion while the others waited for Fabien's signal to climb to the higher ground. When everyone was ready to start, Lukas stopped them: In anticipation of this move from the French, the Germans had also mined the hillock. The deminers laughed again but it was different this time; with the exception of Fabien, who'd seen a similar setup before, they would all have instinctively taken refuge on the higher ground and been killed.

Lukas could have exploited his familiarity with the terrain to create a diversion but preferred to stick to his plan. He had to ensure that he and Vincent were on the team that would work inside the château in a few days.

The next day they were all happy to be returning to the château. Planning ahead using Lukas's maps and cooperating with the Germans made the work less of an ordeal. On top of this there was a wonderful surprise on that second morning, an offer that astounded the Germans and French alike: Hans wanted to share the huge parcel he'd received from his family. At the rate he was eating the contents, he had enough to last several weeks if he kept it to himself, but he would prefer to offer it to the whole group.

It was a bold offer. The German prisoners resented it and the French deminers were suspicious. What was it hiding? Who did this German think he was? Who was he to play the host like that? Did he think he could buy them with his sausages? François backed away and spat on the ground. He wouldn't so much as touch his disgusting charcuterie.

Hans maintained his dignity. Fabien came up to the baskets, crouched down, and sniffed them. Then he smiled and nodded—he was won over.

"It's a pity for you, François, but now there's more for us. This is quality."

All the men were staring at the cold meats. Deminers were better fed than most people, but many of them sent their ration tickets to their families and their staple diet was about as appetizing as metal staples. But everything about this appealed to them—the baskets brimming with food, the comforting smell coming from them, and the rarity value of something they no longer ate.

As far as Fabien was concerned, the decision was made.

"It looks excellent to me," he said, smiling at Hans. "Come on, guys, if we manage to clear a quarter of the grounds today then, just this once, we'll stop thirty minutes early for an evening drink!"

The atmosphere was relaxed, and Vincent discreetly suggested to Fabien that the teams should be mixed. Rather than working with the French on one side and the Germans on the other, perhaps they could work together. Fabien agreed.

As planned, Vincent picked Lukas to be on his team. In the cool shade and with the tangy smell of maritime pines, the men felt something that came close to being glad they were alive. The spring was gently asserting itself and brought everyone together in agreement that they needed to be happy and to leave behind old hostilities so they could fade away.

It was almost summer, and Vincent had never been so close to finding the truth.

ON THE THIRD DAY, FABIEN DECIDED TO ACCEL-
erate their progress: He was increasingly sure that it was
going to rain, and demining in mud was extremely dangerous. It was one of the instances of emergency conditions
that necessitated a halt. He needed to come up with a plan
B so the team could work inside the château, out of the
rain.

Before that, they must clear the access routes, the hallway, corridors, and staircases, to prepare for the arrival of
the whole group. With his phenomenal recall of the mining plans, Lukas clearly needed to be in the advance party.
Vincent, because he spoke German, would lead the very
small team assigned to do this. They needed a third person, and, at Lukas's recommendation, Vincent suggested
it should be Hans.

The atmosphere inside was strange. Since the children had died on the grounds, no one had been into the
building. On the one hand, there were traces of the explosions that had left their mark on windows, chandeliers, and ceilings; and on the other, there was evidence
of the German occupation, a degree of untidiness, the
vestiges of life. The Germans had left their HQ in a hurry,
and despite the dust, it looked as if they'd only just left

and there could be two or three terrified stragglers holed up like rats.

A coat still hung on a hook by the door. Lukas took it down carefully; underneath it a small Bakelite mine, not unlike a pot of cosmetics, was ready to explode. Their haste hadn't hindered this careful piece of staging. Lukas disarmed the device.

As he had for the outside, Lukas had deftly sketched plans of the whole layout. In the hallway they started by lifting the floorboards to flush out explosives hidden under them. Lukas's visual memory proved as accurate as ever.

"Our commandant gave instructions to put mines along this line in the parquet, perpendicular to the staircase, but not blocking access to it, just in case."

"Just in case what? Did you think you could come back?" Vincent asked, amazed.

"We had bad intelligence. We were getting contradictory messages. Hitler had asked Toulon and Marseille not to evacuate. Our chain of command was terrified of reprisals if the situation was reversed."

"But did you personally still think you could win?"

"Well, I'm different. I wanted us to lose," Lukas replied calmly.

Hans stiffened at this.

"Didn't you?" Lukas asked him.

"I just wanted it to be over," Hans replied, trying to be as neutral as possible.

Lukas realized he'd upset him so, having knocked Germany, he allowed himself to knock France. After all, it would prove he was speaking candidly.

"Germany didn't deserve what happened to us. But…France didn't look like its old self anymore either, wouldn't you say?"

"I wasn't in France during the war," Vincent replied. "I wouldn't know…"

Lukas had thought he would be allowed to engage in debate, among equals and in complete sincerity, but Vincent was refusing to engage. Fine. They stopped talking, intently focused on the blocks of parquet. This meticulous work at ground level didn't give Vincent a chance to get a feel for the building as a whole. While he worked away at the waxed wood, dowels, and battens, he wondered when he would be able to reach his grail. Lukas was estimating that it would take two days; the archives were on the third floor at the end of a very long corridor riddled with mines.

When they were close to each other, Lukas returned to his subject.

"There were resistance fighters in Germany, you know. Just like here. From the left and the right."

"Not many, I wouldn't think," Vincent replied flatly, not keen to wrangle over it.

"It's not how many that matters. How many deputies and senators in the Vichy government refused to vote for Pétain to have full power?"

"Eighty."

"Out of how many?"

"I don't know. Five hundred fifty. Five hundred seventy."

"Eighty out of five hundred isn't exactly heavyweight."

"You're right. We can't say our honor was salvaged."

"No, but we can say it's not all screwed…"

Vincent was struck by Lukas's reasoning. Rather than condemning the French representatives for their cowardice in tackling Pétain and Laval, and for personally abandoning the tools of democracy and the values of the Republic, he was more interested in this small minority, these eighty individuals who'd opposed Pétain, courageously, in the name of honor. Interesting when it would have been so easy for him to have used this failure of democracy.

"Everyone condemns the Weimar Republic, which lost its way, but the French Third Republic also died with Vichy, and without any sort of coup. We'll make the staircase safe then I'll show you something…"

Vincent glanced over at Hans, who was concentrating on the baseboards.

"With the others outside he wouldn't get far," Lukas reassured him.

Propelled by the thought of finally getting his hands on the archive films, Vincent checked the stairs one by one in record time. He'd never been so focused. When Lukas ascended the staircase that would now do no harm, he explained how the HQ had been organized.

"On the first floor we had reception rooms, on the second offices, on the third more offices and a sickbay, on the fourth the commandant's apartments, and in the attic…"

The château's attics were crammed with old furniture, trunks, files, a nameless administrative shambles that was yet more proof of the Germans' hasty departure. Lukas forced the lock on a trunk. The lid sprang open with the pressure of envelopes spilling out from inside. These weren't the archives Vincent had been hoping to find.

"Denunciation letters," Lukas explained. "Thousands of them. By the end, we'd stopped opening them. We didn't have time. I found it sickening. And I wasn't the only one."

Vincent took one at random and read out loud: "'As an honest French citizen, I have the honor to denounce by this document...' The *honor* to denounce..."

"Before the war, I wanted to open a bookshop in Paris. I dreamed of France... and then I watched dozens of letters like that come in every day."

Lukas didn't need to say, *And that's it right there, the France I no longer recognize.* Vincent didn't recognize it either. The question they all pondered—Would France have been capable of what Germany had done?—was partly answered by these trunks full of hatred. It wasn't just the informers, there had also been people who'd pointed out all those innocent souls, arrested, confined, and overseen them, and bundled them into trains to send them to their deaths. And the survivors who returned home now weren't shown any consideration, any respect, any love. German philosophers, writers, and scientists, their Nobel prizewinners, all of German culture had served no purpose, but the brilliance of French Enlightenment had also been extinguished. And no one understood.

Vincent would have liked to talk with Lukas, it turned out. No one could resolve this unbearably probing question of the origin of evil. But they heard the signal for the end of the day and Vincent threw the letter back down with the others. As they descended to ground level, Lukas pointed to a door at the end of a corridor.

"That's the office where the films are..."

WHEN HE SAW THOSE TRUNKS OF LETTERS, VIN-cent had immediately thought of Saskia. But now that he was leaving the château, he was no longer sure he should tell her about these letters, which could destroy her with the chilling efficiency of a time bomb. Perhaps she was like Fabien and didn't want to know? He stopped off at the café to give himself time to think, and had to order several glasses before he reached a decision. In the end, it was the first subject he raised with her when he returned to the studio, and Saskia didn't hesitate—she asked him to take her to the château. It was a Saturday and the team had finished work early so there was still time to go.

There were No Entry signs, but Vincent now knew better than anyone which route to take to reach the attic, where there were trunks filled with all those written testimonies of personal disgrace.

As she stepped over the dismantled slats of parquet and deconstructed stair treads, Saskia was able to gauge how difficult Vincent's work was. With him guiding her, she felt emotional about sneaking into this huge, mined building: She was sharing some small part of his experience. And, strangely, she wasn't afraid.

When they reached the attic, Saskia felt overwhelmed, as if she were in the very pit of evil once more. She held her breath. She'd heard that there was a section in the National Library of France where they kept all the banned books; it was called "hell." But hell was right here, in this château's attic.

It was enough to make her break down and fall apart, but the time had come to find out the truth. The man or woman who had picked up a pen to target her loved ones would have to answer for his or her crimes. Saskia would take as long as it took, not leaving this dusty space that had accumulated the day's heat under its stifling roof.

Vincent set to work on a trunk filled with letters that had been opened. Saskia's gaze strayed to another one that was brimming with unopened envelopes. She couldn't help envying the families whose names had stayed inside those sealed envelopes, and who may therefore have escaped deportation.

How were they going to do this? Even if Vincent helped her, it would take days and days. It seemed an impossible task. He told her about the thirteen million mines that needed clearing. That too seemed impossible, but there was no choice. The team dealt with it one step at a time. Well, they would do the same with these letters. Trunk by trunk. Envelope by envelope. Line by line. She would find out.

Saskia sat in front of the trunk, next to Vincent. Every now and then she read a name out loud. She knew the family being reported, or the letter writer, someone she would never have believed capable of such infamy. She read the letters in their entirety. Out of respect for the families, she felt that she could briefly pay homage to them by conducting a mental trial of the person who'd denounced them. She wanted to understand. And then it was too much. There are a thousand types of love, but hate shows little variation. The letters were so alike, all of them breezily intending to annihilate the families they named. If someone was jealous of a neighbor or wanted to get their hands on another person's business, could they envision their whole family being deported? And the turn of phrase used again and again: "I have the honor to..." She had to skim through the letters, her eyes becoming like radar that homed in on the names of the families being denounced.

As she read, she became aware of an unanticipated problem and was gripped by another fear: Most of the informers "had the honor" of denouncing others, but not of signing their own names...What if the letter that had triggered her own tragedy was anonymous?

When they finally stopped at the end of what had been a sun-filled Saturday and they'd almost been capsized in the maelstrom of handwritten loathing, they hadn't found anything. The incalculable number of letters had burdened them with poison. The ink had dirtied their hands. Their bodies were exhausted, and their minds trapped in profound sorrow. It was now two o'clock in the morning. Devastated both by what they'd read and by what they hadn't found, they really had to stop, and there was a risk they wouldn't have the strength to return.

Saskia had one of the most important pieces of information of her life within reach, but to find it, she would need the courage to dive into the abyss once more.

THEY DIDN'T SPEAK AT ALL ON THE WAY HOME. Vincent drew indefatigable strength from his need for revenge, but Saskia was crushed. He could tell she was faltering and he was annoyed with himself for taking her to the château. When he told her so, she set him straight: On the contrary, she needed to be brave. It was her duty, and not just to her family.

Vincent watched her; she was so slight, so fragile, and so determined despite being overwhelmed. Grief for a dearly loved person is unbearable. But mourning all the people you've most loved, how can you survive it? How long can you hold on when you're left alone in the world, a world you no longer recognize and that doesn't view the loss off your loved ones as unendurable?

They passed a poster about the interim government. It talked of reconciliation and encouraged resuming a state of calm. And it was their job to calm down? Really? So all their lost loved ones meant nothing? It was too much for Saskia; she couldn't hold back her tears.

Vincent suggested that, before going home, they make a detour to the creek that Fabien had demined. The sea would soothe them. They wouldn't find it easy getting to sleep, anyway, so what the hell...

When Saskia saw the creek and the myriad silvery glints on the quiet sea barely creased by the nocturnal breeze, she was overwhelmed by its beauty—something that had been missing from her life for many years. In the camps, there was no grass, there were no flowers, no colors. But you could see the stars. Now that she was back, she needed water and wind, fields of wheat and wildflowers, pure air, nature, and—particularly—places like this where there were no people. And she needed magic. Vincent asked if she'd like to walk along the beach. She said yes. Evil hadn't won the day: Saskia was smiling at him.

When they'd taken the path down and reached the narrow crescent of sand between the rocks, Saskia wanted to walk barefoot. Here was a freedom, a sense of childhood that no one could confiscate: The exact moment when you take off your shoes and feel the sand under your feet. They walked along the water's edge and were surprised to find it was still warm. It was impossible to resist the urge to swim, to immerse themselves in this mysterious harmony, to feel insignificant under the stars. A privilege. Vincent undressed; Saskia couldn't. So he handed her his shirt. She hesitated for a few seconds, then put the outsize shirt over her dress before slipping the dress down and stepping out of it. And they swam in silence, side by side; they swam a long way with the moon in their sights, as if trying to get closer to it.

When they turned around, Saskia was tired and afraid she wouldn't make it back. She put one hand on Vincent's shoulder for support, and they headed back to the creek. She trusted him and he found it peculiarly moving. He concentrated on swimming, wanting to be as silent as possible, to disturb nothing.

Back at the studio they went to their separate bedrooms. Something had changed, but they didn't want to think about it. Exhausted, their hair wet and their bodies salty, they fell asleep very quickly. Despite all the different contradictory thoughts milling in their heads...the night would take care of sifting through them and would set aside their questions, including those to which they couldn't find answers.

VINCENT AND SASKIA HADN'T EXCHANGED A WORD since waking. They finished drinking their ersatz coffee in silence.

Saskia couldn't make up her mind. Should she return to the château and be torn apart by an abhorrent letter? And then there was the fact that most of the letters were anonymous. If the one that had sent her family to the death camp wasn't signed, it would feel as if the informer was still taunting her and was winning every battle.

Vincent could sense her apprehension, although they hadn't been able to discuss what they'd found at the château. Nor had they talked about the beach and the awkwardness they'd experienced when a tired Saskia had moved closer to Vincent. When she'd put her hand on his shoulder, he'd felt her grow weaker, had wrapped his arm around her waist and taken her back to the beach as he swam, their bodies tightly intertwined, synchronized with such fluidity, such self-evident rightness that—far from hindering his progress—Saskia's body had propelled him toward the shore. He had drawn new strength from this contact. A strength that meant he needn't exert any effort. The very opposite of the endurance he had to demonstrate in order to stay on his feet for eight hours on a beach, his back bent double as he cleared mines. A spirited strength that allowed for new departures, and generated more energy than it expended. It was impossible for Saskia not to have felt its heat. But it was clear they would never talk about it.

As she got up from the table, she asked whether he would mind returning to the château. He had to work the next day; it bothered her to see him sacrifice his Sunday. Perhaps he could take her there and leave her so as not to waste his whole day? That was out of the question for Vincent. He would be with her all the way.

In the attic she took a deep breath to muster her courage. She wished she could take all the signed letters, brandish them in front of the people who'd written them, and insist that they express their regret and repentance, perform endless acts of contrition. She so hoped they would be consumed with remorse.

Her mother had been right. No one delighted in other people's happiness, not ever. And Saskia now had a better understanding of Mila's obsession with modesty and discretion. But now wasn't the time to keep her head down. She needed to find who had envied their simple, harmless happiness which they would have liked to share, but it had still filled someone with envy and hatred, chipping away at them until one dreadful night they'd indulged themselves, taken out their finest paper and, with references to honor and other obscenely bombastic words, written that her family was a stain on the glory of France and that they were pariahs who didn't deserve to stay there.

All of a sudden Vincent stopped reading. Saskia understood immediately. He handed her the letter. They'd been named as targets on handsome, heavyweight vellum paper.

As Saskia had feared, the infamy wasn't signed.

She'd spent more than five hundred days and five hundred nights wondering who had denounced them, she'd just inflicted more than twenty hours of these despicable missives on herself, and the letter wasn't signed.

Meticulous handwriting, no spelling mistakes, formulaic text. In other words: No hint about the author's identity. No way of knowing to whom the crime should be ascribed. It was just everyday hate. Self-interested hate would have left a trail back to the person feeling it, but with hate for its own sake, what was there to do?

Vincent tried to reassure her. He thought they could compare it with the Bellangers' handwriting, or Édouard Maillan's, or her neighbor's, the woman who'd wanted the cedar tree felled, or all the neighbors in the petition. It shouldn't be too hard to get examples of their handwriting. Saskia doubted they would ever be able to prove anything.

Even so, there were some clues; granted they would be hard to use, but they might offer the beginnings of a lead. The man—he'd used the masculine form of the words "proud" and "delighted"—was very well informed about Saskia's family. He knew their true identity and that their name was false, Gallicized. He knew where Mila was hiding; which family had taken in her brother, her sister, and herself; and the dates of their secret get-togethers. It must be someone who knew them well. Someone very close. Intimate. But Saskia didn't recognize the handwriting.

She couldn't stay in that attic. She stood up and took the letter with her. It was still daytime outside. Beautiful fluffy clouds were piling high and diffracting golden sunbeams with the brilliance of a divine manifestation. Perhaps the sky was consoling her and the sun sending her a sign. The air was a transparent stained-glass window offering her this arresting spectacle, but the letter burned her hand. She passed it to Vincent. Now she would never know. Would she recover from that? Or perhaps it was just as well...

Way up high, gliding steadily, two clouds parted. No more slanting sunbeams from the heavenly kingdom, now the sun was blinding her.

And that was when Saskia had a thunderbolt of intuition. She took the letter back from Vincent and held it up to the sun. Now backlit, a watermark appeared, impeccably clear. She didn't recognize the handwriting in the letter, but she knew this watermarked paper well. She checked her hunch by holding the envelope up to the sun: Initials in sophisticated calligraphy were embossed onto the flap. Two intertwined letters: D and R. D for Delambre. R for Rebattet. Delambre-Rebattet. It was the monogram of Rodolphe's family.

In this envelope, on this vellum, she had received the very first letter from the boy she loved...this same paper with its monogramed letters that she'd feverishly longed to find in her parents' mailbox had indiscriminately played host to her first love letter and the death sentence of her loved ones.

SASKIA HADN'T RECOGNIZED THE HANDWRIT-
ing in the letter because it wasn't Rodolphe's. The writing paper belonged to his father, and the writing was most
likely his. All the things she'd never wanted to contemplate,
mostly because she was reassured by Rodolphe, flooded
back into her mind. Carried away with the zeal of her growing love, she hadn't felt like lingering on the tinge of disdain
when Rodolphe's father looked at her; or Rodolphe's embarrassed convolutions when he explained that the lunch
to which he'd invited Saskia wouldn't actually be taking
place, but then he didn't give her a new date; or the way
their parents avoided one another at high-school events.
There had never been a dinner for their formal introduction. She'd swept this all under the carpet of their passion,
which was bound to win over the parents in the end. The
man who mattered in this wonderful relationship they
were going to have was Rodolphe, not his father.

It pained her to realize that if she hadn't been in love
with Rodolphe, perhaps none of it would have happened.
She clung to what her friend at the camp had told her:
None of it's your fault, it's the Germans' fault.

What was she going to do with this letter? There were
no certainties in this confused postwar period. What

fate would be reserved for collaborators and informers? Some of the most obvious and active collaborators had been lynched or arrested. At least, that's what people said. But there were still plenty of them, like the Bellangers, who were well hidden and safe, skulking in the shadows of the protectors they'd judiciously indebted to themselves. They were slipping with impunity through the cracks of the national reconciliation that Fabien had told Vincent about one evening. Saskia had heard it all. De Gaulle wasn't prepared to see France divided again. And if notorious collaborators were getting away with it, the same would go for informers. Informing was an abominable crime that represented the best ratio between zero risk and maximum consequences. A few words written with relish, put into an envelope, and hey presto, it was done . . . How to put on trial everyone who had sent thousands of innocent people to their deaths thanks to a simple letter, and who would surely cry, "Oh but we had no idea!"

But this time, Vincent promised her, there would be no impunity. They had to do something. And it was Sunday—perfect timing.

He stormed his way into the Delambre-Rebattets' home. The housekeeper was unable to withstand his thunderous intrusion. He then forced his way through a magnificent door at the end of a sumptuously decorated corridor, the door to Rodolphe's father's study.

Terrified, the man leapt to his feet to square up to Vincent.

"Who are you?"

"And who are you?"

"I beg your pardon."

Vincent left no room for doubt about what he knew. He was used to keeping quiet but now produced an un-interrupted stream: Yes, who was this man who'd knowingly sent a whole family to their deaths so that his son wouldn't marry Saskia, and was now continuing with his life as if nothing had happened? Jean-Robert was unable to sustain a defense for long on the basis of *You're making a terrible mistake* and *I don't understand a word you're saying* because Vincent was holding the shameful letter under his nose with one hand while, with the other, he grabbed the writing paper and envelopes neatly piled on the fine leatherwork of the tray on the man's desk. The paper, the envelopes, the handwriting—it was all identical to the defamatory letter Vincent was holding. He looked the man right in the eye. Jean-Robert looked away.

Vincent didn't moralize for long. It would have been pointless. What had made Rodolphe's father avert his eyes wasn't remorse but fear. Vincent wasn't prepared to listen to any more of his pathetic lines of argument—*I was afraid for my son's future*—or his justifications—*I didn't know what would happen in Germany*—and he didn't believe these excuses.

What Vincent did insist on, though, was that Jean-Robert must arrange for Saskia to return to her home. Straightaway. Deal with the thorny problem of the title deed. Evict the Bellangers, who were almost certainly his friends—perfumers and owners of large flower-growing estates all knew one another.

Rodolphe's father crushed out the cigarette that was burning down in the ashtray. He was backed into a corner.

"How do you expect me to do that? I'm not a judge or the mayor or the police!"

"But you have a rare asset that few people own: that magnificent black Bakelite telephone. You're going to use it to resolve this situation."

"You're overestimating me."

"You know everyone, and you have lawyers. If you don't want your son and the whole population of this town to know what a disgusting little snitch of a criminal you are, then find a way. Fast."

Feeling out of his depth, Jean-Robert Delambre-Rebattet hesitated before putting forward the argument Vincent had been expecting from the start.

"I didn't know they would die."

"You didn't know or you didn't want to think about it?"

"They were strange times, it was—"

"When," Vincent interrupted him, "do you think it's acceptable to rip a family away from its home, its country, its life?"

Rodolphe's father couldn't meet his eye.

"It's not the strange times that produce bastards, it's too many bastards tainting our times."

RODOLPHE'S FATHER ACTED SWIFTLY: THE BEL-
langers moved out without further ado and Saskia could
finally go home. Something that had seemed so natural
when she was a child, that she had so longed for while she
was in the camp but had been impossible when she'd returned to Hyères, was now within her reach. If she wanted
to be a little more like other people again, she need only
step through the front gate, walk down the path, turn the
key in the lock, and open the door.

In a final act of thoughtlessness, the Bellangers hadn't
bothered to close the door when they left, and it stood ajar.
Saskia was afraid she would find the house looted, but
nothing appeared to have been ransacked. She had no illusions: They definitely wouldn't have left the place intact
willingly. They must have been fiercely admonished by
Rodolphe's father, who feared for the future of his honor
and was dependent on Vincent's goodwill.

During the several months that they'd spent in the
house, the Bellangers had changed the layout of the rooms.
The house had been so perfectly conceived by Saskia's father to be happy, with areas for reading, others for talking,
and huge windows in the right places to let in the sun; it
had been their paradise but it was now also a space that

had been sullied by people she despised and she entered it as cautiously as an uninvited cat.

She was surprised by her own instincts. When she went into her brother's bedroom, she automatically looked over to the left of his bed, to the spot where he used to sit on the floor to do his homework, as if she might find him there. She'd already looked for him on the sofa in the living room, where he used to lie full length, as if on a chaise longue. She didn't dare go into her parents' bedroom, just as she hadn't dared to while they'd been alive, out of respect. Her own room and her sister's were in an indescribable mess.

On the landing, she opened the linen cupboard. At first glance, there seemed to be some sheets missing, and their familiar smell was gone. When she'd lived here, the closet had been filled with sheets from top to bottom, and they'd smelled wonderful: Mila felt there were better things to do than ironing, and she hung their linen sheets in the garden, where the warm wind took care of smoothing out the creases as well as perfuming them with wafts of jasmine or wisteria.

Saskia then remembered that her mother had been keeping to one side beautiful sheets skillfully embroidered by her grandmother and monogrammed towels for when Saskia herself and her sister were married. She'd kept them in the almost invisible drawer at the very top of the closet, a plain ledge with no handle or lock, disguised trompe l'oeil style.

Saskia had to climb onto a chair, grip the drawer from below, and pull it toward her. It wasn't easy, the drawer was stiff, and she started to worry: Either the Bellangers had forced it or the wood had swollen. At last, it slid out and there the sheets were. Her mother had won this small victory.

On her way downstairs, Saskia was surprised by the sound of recent rainwater dripping slowly down the gutter next to the kitchen window. As it always used to. And this was the same kitchen where she'd enjoyed watching, unseen, as her parents told each other about their day over a glass of wine, thinking they were out of their children's earshot.

She found the pretty earthenware crockery for everyday use, and the porcelain set with its fine gold edging. The Bellangers hadn't looked after it; some of the plates were chipped.

She felt a sudden stab of disgust at the thought of the Bellangers eating off her family's plates, using their glasses and cutlery. She had an urge to clean everything. The house, the crockery, the linen. She ran back upstairs, took the sheets from the closet, and carried them down to the massive stone basin in the garden that they'd used for washing.

A sound made her turn around. She'd heard something, very clearly, like footsteps on the gravel, even a twig snapping. It was the Bellangers. She was sure of it. They must have been spying on her. They were bound to have kept a set of keys. She would never be safe: They could come back, just like that, with no warning, maybe even when she was asleep. She ran and locked herself in the house.

She was only just home but was already trying to find a way to escape, as she had in Vincent's studio. It would never end. She checked all the windows, just as frantic as she'd been in the studio. Could you jump into the garden from her parents' bedroom? Hold on to the shutters to soften the fall? Where was the least dangerous place? There must be a means of escape in this perfectly designed house.

The question had been haunting her since the camps: Why had they taken refuge with people they didn't really know? You never truly know anyone. They should all have stayed together, at home. Her father could have devised a system to hide them—they would all have helped him—a secret, undetectable room. They would have left the lights off in the evenings. No one would have known they were still there. She would have gone out shopping by slipping, unnoticed, over the neighbor's wall. She would have changed her appearance, cut her hair, even disguised herself as a boy. No one ever noticed her anyway. And when they had to run away, like the evening they were arrested, then it would have been planned, a passageway out of the cellar, or at least something that required them alone, because they could trust only the five of them, no one else. Escaping from this house would have been possible together. They would have taken turns, keeping watch like the crew of a boat sailing day and night.

She was filled with memories for which she was now the only custodian and she clung to them—"I have more memories than if I'd lived a thousand years," how that line of poetry resonated with her—and she felt alone in the world. Now more than ever. Here more than anywhere else. And there was no point trying to find an escape route on her own. What would she do if she came face-to-face with the Bellangers thirsty for revenge? Perhaps they'd only pretended to leave, apparently complying with the injunctions, but they would come back to kill her and reclaim her house. She tried to reason with herself. Everywhere she went, in the streets, in every conversation, on every lip, she heard the words *We've won, the Allies are in Berlin!* She could see that people were smiling again, but even if the war was over, would she ever be at peace again?

She had to leave. It would have been inconceivable to her as child because the house had been such a refuge, but she was safer outside. What had protected her once was trapping her now. She felt suffocated. She was where she most wanted to be in the world, and it felt impossible to stay. She wasn't afraid of the ghosts she might find; she was afraid that even they wouldn't be there.

MAKING THE SECOND-FLOOR LANDING OF THE château safe seemed to Vincent to take an eternity.

"Your archives must be horrific for you to have spent so long protecting them."

"And to think no one ever felt they'd end up being compromising!"

"Did you know everything that was going on? I mean did your forces here in France know what was happening in Germany, and Poland?"

"We knew we hadn't been fighting a normal war for a long time. No war's ever normal but this one, given what we're now finding out...I don't know what you'd call it. It was a project against the whole of humanity."

Hans listened to them, not joining in but frightened of what Lukas was admitting. He hoped it was a tactic to make the Frenchman less vigilant, but after all the conversations they'd had in the yard of the prison camp, he knew that Lukas meant what he was saying. Lukas could think what he liked—he wasn't alone, after all—but why discuss it with Vincent? Why let the French feel that everything they were inflicting on the German prisoners was legitimate by implying that the Germans were despicable? If the French had won the war in 1940, if they'd occupied

Germany, would they have behaved any better than the Germans had? Since the Allies had granted the French permission to use prisoners of war in whatever way they saw fit, Hans had been hanging on only thanks to thoughts of escape. So he had to listen, appalled, to the conversation between the two men.

He was released by Vincent who, once they'd finished demining the landing, asked him to work his way back down to the hall checking that everything was safe. He could join them again later.

Lukas and Vincent were now alone outside the office where the archives were kept. All Vincent could think about was the films he would find in there. As Lukas had expected, he'd forgotten his responsibilities, forgotten Hans, forgotten everything.

Inside the office, Vincent found three of the four walls covered floor to ceiling in numbered boxes and neatly stored files, all carefully labeled and dated. The most recent date was from the day before their rushed departure. So, even in those final chaotic days, the Germans had still kept organized records.

"Is it all here?"

"All of it. Photographed, filmed, documented, archived... Hitler wanted an epic in honor of the German nation. And our commandant wanted memories of his reign at this regional Kommandatura. We didn't miss anything."

As Lukas had already told him, there were also recorded memories of birthday parties, Christmases, and all sorts of receptions.

"Why the private films?"

"Because of our unique communications program. Our newsreels regularly featured Magda Goebbels and her children and their various adventures—in country meadows, having picnics, baking cakes, drinking milk, feeding donkeys, playing with dogs. It was part of the overall scheme. It was about showing that, even within families, even when they were having fun, the German race, the superior race, was best."

Lukas started studying labels more closely, opening boxes and leafing through the files in which all the information had been stored. Vincent too was searching, feverishly.

Down in the hall, Hans, who always seemed to keep a cool head in every situation, was now full of doubts. Should he go along with Lukas's plan? With the whole demining team around the château, wouldn't he risk being shot while trying to escape?

He tried to reassure himself: There was no such thing as an infallible plan, but this one seemed well thought out. Taking weapons from a closet hidden behind paneling, going back to the upstairs office, neutralizing Vincent and escaping with Lukas along an underground passageway built during the Wars of Religion in the sixteenth century—that would get them more than a kilometer away and it seemed perfectly feasible, but he had to seize the opportunity. It was now or never. Tomorrow, they might no longer be alone inside the château.

Lukas had assured Hans that the passageway was clear, but hadn't told him where it was. Hans was entirely reliant on him.

He was alert to the slightest sound, delaying putting Lukas's plan into operation whenever he thought someone was coming close, then starting to believe in it again after a few seconds' respite. He caught himself trembling, pulled himself together.

Inside the closet set into the woodwork was a whole arsenal: rifles, revolvers, ammunition, in great quantities, all neatly stored.

He took two revolvers, loaded them, and wrapped them in rags before slipping them into his thick canvas pants in the small of his back. To keep them hidden, he pulled up his shirt and made it billow over them. This operation took only a few minutes, but it had taken such concentration that his impression of time passing had dilated and he was afraid he would be behind schedule.

Meanwhile, in the office on the second floor, Vincent was jittery with nerves. He too was in a hurry. He was afraid Fabien would come into the château to check how they were getting on.

"Are you sure that party was filmed?"

When he realized that not all the archives matched their labels, Lukas was starting to have his doubts. Behind the apparently perfect classification system, there was in fact terrible mayhem. An eloquent metaphor for what had happened to the Nazi regime... He felt uncomfortable. Particularly as he had a hunch that Vincent was armed. He thought he'd seen a metal butt between his shirt and his pants. He tried to convince himself that his imagination was playing tricks on him.

And then, in a drawer, Vincent stumbled across what he was looking for: photos of the party on June 8, 1943, with serrated edges where they'd been cut with a notched guillotine, a pile of them in a box.

Lukas tried to stay calm. He had to give Hans enough time to come back up to join them, so he started giving a running commentary of the photos.

"That's the commandant, it was his birthday party. And I would guess those are the films you're looking for. We can hold the film up to the light."

But Vincent snapped the boxes shut. He would come back for them later. He didn't want Fabien to know that he wanted something here. In the meantime, they needed to hurry up and get out of this office.

This was inconvenient for Lukas. How would Hans react if they were already back out on the landing? If Vincent was standing facing him and not caught out, cornered in this cramped space? And anyway, Vincent would then have time to see Hans coming, to anticipate. And if he was armed...

A change of plan, even a tiny one, can knock everything off course. Lukas didn't want Vincent to be killed, he'd really stressed the point to Hans. But with the element of surprise, he wasn't sure either how Hans would respond or how the Frenchman would defend himself. And Vincent had already opened the door to the office; the plan was falling apart.

Lukas decided to knock over a stack of boxes. It collapsed noisily onto the parquet. Photos scattered as far as

the corridor. Apologizing for his clumsiness, he started
gathering them up. Vincent knelt to help him... and it was
then that they came across a photo that chilled them both:
a picture of Hans with Ariane.

It was Hans, there was no room for doubt, even though
he'd lost weight since then. He was dancing with her, in
the reception hall, which was almost empty, very likely
at the end of a party. There wasn't just one photo. He'd
clearly monopolized Ariane at the end of the evening.
Blindsided, Vincent closed the door to the office that he'd
just opened and moved closer to Lukas.

"Did you know?"

"No, I swear to you."

"I've heard she wanted to poison your commandant.
But could it have been Hans instead?"

"How do you expect me to know?"

The only thing Lukas now knew for sure was that Vincent was beside himself and the situation was about to get
out of control. Hans needed to show up very soon. Vincent was already opening the door with the photo in his
pants pocket. Lukas had to follow him. As he walked, he
tried to make a noise to warn Hans. Please let him realize that the plan intended for the second floor would now
have to happen on ground level...

When they reached the entrance hall, Hans was gone.

"Where is he?"

A window stood open, as did the closet from which
Hans had taken the pistols.

"Is that why you kept me upstairs?" Vincent hissed.
"So he could escape?"

Lukas was ashen. "Why would I do that?" he improvised. "If I had a plan, surely I'd have been escaping with
him."

This seemed to make sense. Vincent didn't have time
to think and certainly didn't want to have to explain to Fabien why he had ended up on the second floor with Lukas
while Hans had been unsupervised on the first floor. They
needed to agree on a story: Hans had found a gun, threatened them, and escaped out a window at the back of the
château. They ran out together to raise the alarm.

Fabien immediately decided that Vincent and Lukas
should go to the right while he himself headed left, and
Georges stayed behind with the deminers.

The grounds behind the château led straight to open
countryside and woodland: Hans was safe. He'd made the
right decision in ditching Lukas. He felt so much more
powerful alone.

He didn't spot the cause of his undoing: a tree root
that tripped him. He heard the grizzly snap of ligaments
and bones in his ankle. He stood back up but his head-
long race to the safety of the forest was now compromised,
pathetic; it wouldn't save him. Vincent and Lukas spotted him first. Hans knew they would catch up with him
so he took out one of the guns and didn't even hesitate to
fire it haphazardly—the pain in his ankle precluding any
accuracy—to force them to back off.

He aimed for Vincent but, struck down in full flight,
it was Lukas who fell to the ground. Now the Frenchman produced a weapon, aimed at Hans's legs, hit him.
Hans slumped forward. Vincent reached him quickly,

immobilized him, and confiscated his weapons. He bran-dished the scallop-edged photo he'd found in the archives.

Vincent's dark eyes were now almost black and Hans was terrified by an expression he'd never seen on the Frenchman's face before, as if Vincent were revealing his true nature.

"What did you do to Ariane?" he asked, holding the barrel of his gun to Hans's head.

It took a moment for Hans to understand the words Vincent was barking at him.

"Look! You danced with her at your commandant's birthday. Late in the night, by the looks of it."

Hans gathered his wits.

"I didn't do anything wrong!"

"I don't believe you."

Vincent was still aiming his gun at Hans. With his free hand he tore the German's shirt and used it to tie his hands behind his back. It didn't matter to him that Hans was deathly pale, Vincent showed no mercy, just as none of the Germans had for Ariane. Now, Hans would have to talk. Vincent smacked him across the temple with the grip of his pistol. Then again. Blood sprang out.

Fabien stopped him when he was about to strike Hans a third time. He intervened and was aware of the risk he was taking: Vincent had lost control of himself. He was going to kill Hans. But when Vincent saw Fabien, something in him calmed. Fabien had this power. He put his hand on Vincent's shoulder, and Vincent handed him his pistol.

"What's going on?" asked Manu, who'd just joined them.

"None of your business."

Given that Manu was not to make this his business, he checked that Hans was tied securely while Fabien took Vincent aside.

"If you kill Hans, the whole team comes into question, starting with me."

Vincent was oddly absent, and this infuriated Fabien.

"Where's that gun from, Vincent? It's not German. Did you have it on you? What's your plan? For fuck's sake, wake up!"

They'd forgotten all about Lukas when Manu started yelling, "Hey! The other Boche, he's bleeding out!"

VINCENT'S BRAIN HAD CLICKED BACK ON AND, IN the heat of the emergency, Fabien had an insight into the energy that fed a wartime medic's work: the energy of despair.

The man who'd wanted to kill Hans was now busy trying to keep Lukas alive, and with the same determination. He had sworn an oath to save every life he could, and that ideal, that best part of Vincent, was still there, present in him.

"Will he make it to the hospital?"

"I hope so."

"The problem's gonna be the bullet. How do I explain that? Do I tell them we left a German prisoner unsupervised in their former HQ that's stuffed full of firearms?"

Vincent held Fabien's eye. Yes, of course, there would be an inquiry, they'd need to justify themselves: Why did Vincent have a gun, how had Hans gotten away from him, how could they explain this carnage? Fabien didn't need to extrapolate the consequences. And Vincent certainly didn't want anyone investigating him.

"Could you take care of him?"

Vincent was thinking. In a last-ditch bid to find a solution, he said, "There's a sickbay in the château. I could remove the bullet."

"Could you disguise the wound? Make it look like an injury from an explosive device?"

"I could."

With Manu's help, Fabien and Vincent improvised a stretcher and carefully carried Lukas to the château.

The sickbay, which had remained intact since the Germans left, had been equipped with obsessive precision. Vincent found what he needed in the cabinet. In similar but sometimes infinitely more precarious conditions he'd operated on prisoners in Germany. As he filled the syringe with anesthetic he remembered the German doctor who'd taught him how to use the drug, how he'd been surprised by its incredible effectiveness compared to the anesthetics delivered through a mask that he'd still been using in France. Once again he thought of the young Russian who'd been almost bound to die but whom he'd treated, directly contravening the Germans' orders. And today, the same extraordinarily brave doctor, the one who'd always refused to make a Nazi salute, who had treated and allowed him, Vincent, to treat all the prisoners regardless of their nationality, was here over Vincent's shoulder again, whispering that he could do this. Vincent delved resolutely into the wound to remove the bullet.

Outside, Georges was reveling in being in charge. Intoxicated by a degree of power he'd always dreamed of, he spontaneously adopted Max's mischievous tone.

"Come on, guys, are we gonna wait for these mines to dig themselves up? For them to jump up on their little mine legs, disarm themselves like grown-ups, and go line themselves up neatly on the roadside?"

Hans was tied to a piece of garden furniture on the château's terrace and had to endure disconsolate stares from the other prisoners. The improvised bandage on his leg was saturated with blood but he seemed to be coping with the pain. His face was puffy and his swollen brow made it difficult to keep his eyes open, so he closed them while he waited to find out what fate lay in store for him.

Having him shackled there cast a chill between the Germans and the French. The prisoners would surely have been envious of Hans had he succeeded in escaping. But equally they weren't pleased that the French had caught him again.

In the château's sickbay, Vincent had finally managed to extricate the bullet and falsify the wound. Working with feverish haste, he finished the bandaging, took Lukas's blood pressure, examined him again, and checked his vital signs. Lukas was having a lot of trouble breathing. There was something else. The priority that Vincent had tackled was a wound that stretched across his chest under his armpit. But there was another, more insidious one that he hadn't been able to assess because there was no X-ray equipment. A wound slightly lower down, between two ribs, that he'd thought was superficial because it was hardly bleeding. It must have been hiding a deeper problem. Vincent was concerned about hemothorax: He couldn't see the blood, but it was spreading inside the pleura like dangerously rising waters.

"He shouldn't be breathing like this. His lungs are compromised. We need to get him to the hospital. Urgently."

~

HE NEEDED TO BE QUICK. VINCENT USED THE time when Fabien was taking Lukas to the hospital to return to the château. He hid there and waited until nightfall before reemerging with the film and a projector. He loaded everything on his bicycle; it was a precarious balancing act, but he was so determined that he found a way to stop anything from falling.

Saskia was back at the studio, and he wasn't even surprised to find her there instead of in her own home. He should have told her that he'd passed her house and noticed that the grenadine was flowering, its blooms a heady bright orange color, but he couldn't spare a moment. If he'd taken the time, he would have noticed that Saskia had made a meal for him as a thank-you for his hospitality, and that she'd brought some things over from her house, some crockery and linen, and other less useful but still essential items: books, a vase, some flowers. Some wine too.

He saw none of it and went up and locked himself in his room, where he still failed to notice Saskia's thoughtfulness—the engraving on the wall and the alarm clock by his bed. He was agitated but managed to set up the 8-millimeter film in the projector. As if the whole process came naturally to him. His only concern was that he might damage the thin, fragile, sprocket-holed film that would bring Ariane back to life along with everything she'd had to endure, and he would be powerless to protect her.

He was immediately swept away by the tide of images that loomed before him, the more-than-life-size faces and bodies coming back to life. He knew how far the projector should be from the wall to get the sizing right, but he'd deliberately taken it farther back, so the past was writ large, filling the space.

Amid the smell of hot celluloid, the sound of a turtle-dove's wingbeats, and the wobbling light, the château's reception rooms that he'd demined were reanimated on the white wall of his room. During the war, the rooms had retained their former magnificence, nothing had been damaged other than the fact that the furniture, paintings, and chandeliers had to passively endure the presence of those Germans strapped into their uniforms, and their magisterial lack of guilt as they congratulated themselves and generously poured French champagne. Attending the commandant's birthday celebrations retrospectively was an unhoped-for opportunity and a form of torture. Everything about Ariane's future had been decided then. And if he wanted to understand what had happened, he must relive the evening until he was sick to his stomach, absorbing the atmosphere, working out who had played the key roles and who had changed the course of Ariane's life. Who had been guilty and who complicit. He'd tried to identify an officer who'd come to the farm for provisions, then he'd thought that it had been the commandant, and now he wondered whether it was Hans.

He didn't hear the front door close. Saskia had left.

Vincent tirelessly replayed the animated images of that party until he ended up feeling he'd attended it...because he could furtively watch Ariane as he had known her: alive.

The camera was captivated by her: Ariane arranging things on a tray, serving drinks, proposing toasts, weaving between the guests. But also, at the end of the evening, when the drunk and overfed Germans had deserted the dance floor to slump on Louis XV armchairs, Ariane was forced to dance with the only officers still standing. Hans as the photo had captured him. So huge in comparison to Ariane's slight frame that she almost disappeared when he put his arms around her. And another officer. This one dangerously fragile-looking with leering eyes. And yet another. A clodhopping type. And the commandant, whose party it was. Ariane as the ultimate birthday present, passed from one to the other: The sort of present you can even let your friends enjoy too. A French specialty, like champagne from Reims and petits fours, like Saint-Louis crystal glasses and Ercuis silverware. The Germans had still been doing it, taking advantage of everything, to the bitter end.

Vincent was hypnotized by this intolerable spectacle. The film stored in the château's archives allowed him to fine-tune his speculations. He was so close to reconstituting the fateful scene. He felt he was there. He had the setting, the characters, and even the dress Ariane had been wearing. The film was black-and-white, but he clearly remembered the slightly moiré azure blue color and more particularly the feel of the fabric because he'd held Ariane in his arms when she'd been wearing that dress. Cinched at the waist, a billowing whisper over the underskirt, he loved that silk for its softness, for the maddening little rustling sound it made when he pushed it up over Ariane's thighs to feel her skin beneath, skin that drove him to distraction.

He remembered what Ariane had said in her letter— *You mustn't believe what you hear, the Germans aren't all the same*—but he could see that these Germans, the ones at the château, had just allowed this to happen. They hadn't let Ariane escape the trap. How could she have believed she would be strong enough to poison an officer all by herself?

The commandant seemed to be obsessed with Ariane. He wouldn't let go of her, kept touching her, clutching her, clinging to her, while she tried to avoid him gracefully, as agile as a supple little fish. But the commandant also looked very drunk, he need only be encouraged to drink even more of that excellent champagne and, hey presto, *prost*, Ariane could have slipped out through a service entrance, and he wouldn't have noticed she'd gone until the next day—and then he wouldn't have mentioned the fact to avoid the humiliation. But here she was, twirling between all these brutes, unable to escape. Hans wasn't the only one to stay until the end of the evening to win her like a prize. They'd all tried.

Not one of the officers had protected her. Worse than that: They were laughing.

Silent laughter that rang loudly in his ears, laughter he knew so well. Coarse, unfettered, vulgar.

Vincent's demons were creeping up on him again. He hated everyone at that indecent party: Every laugh he witnessed in the silent film reminded him of the laughter he'd heard at parties in his prison camp and to which, as a medical officer, he'd been invited. The Germans there had slapped their thighs as they watched prisoners dressed as women. He would have found it hard to explain why, of all the injuries he'd suffered, it was having to endure this laughter that had wounded him most; but he'd never known anything as obscene as these men who were monsters by day and full of high spirits by night. Despite the prisoners' distress, they laughed. Despite the unthinkable chaos they were imposing on the world, they laughed. Despite what they were inflicting on the prisoners, be they civilian or military, on deportees, men, women, children, Resistance fighters, Jews, homosexuals, Romanis, all of them skeletal or reduced to nothing, still the Germans laughed heartily until they almost choked. Their loud laughter was an insult to the humiliated world, their laughter reverberated around the emptiness of a humanity stripped of all humanity, their laughter echoed all the way to hell, where their work was celebrated but where, although they didn't yet know this, their zeal was starting to be questioned.

∼

MAX HAD CONFIDED IN FABIEN THAT HE LOVED his wife madly, and he'd meant it. For her, he managed not only to sit up in bed but also to smile. His test results were inexplicably better. To Fabien, this was the only piece of good news at a difficult time. To the doctors, it was one of those miracles that reminded them that medicine can achieve nothing without the powerful and enigmatic forces of the human will and desire. For Gauthier, his friend from the early days, it hadn't worked: He'd slipped away quietly the day before. Matthias had been transferred to Germany. And there were four other badly injured men teetering between death and life as amputees. All that Fabien could now rely on to wrest them from their programmed oblivion was the example set by Max.

As for Lukas, whom he'd accompanied all the way to the operating theater, Fabien had exchanged only a few words with him, but those few words had been essential.

While he waited in the hospital's garden for the outcome of Lukas's operation, Fabien thought back over every aspect of Vincent's behavior and reactions. Having seemed so impenetrable at the time, they now seemed clear. The question was, what was Fabien to do?

As soon as Fabien met Vincent, he'd wanted to make a friend of him. That sort of luminous, spiritual intuition demands to be followed. Friendship, the kind that helps us live from one day to the next, even through the darkest times, is worth fighting for. It must overcome difficulties, laugh in the face of obstacles, and find itself strengthened by them. When Fabien had needed Vincent's help moving Hubert's body, Vincent hadn't asked any questions.

Except there it was: While he was in the Resistance, Fabien had promised himself that he would never accept lying again. He'd already broken this personal rule with Vincent. He'd already put his faith in him regardless. And yet he'd learned from experience that a man who sees lying as just another resource rarely sets limits on himself. The only way to stop him is for him to be found out.

And there was a difference between them, a significant one. During the course of his demining assignments, Fabien had learned to value the Germans who worked alongside them. With them, at least, he no longer had feelings of hate. And this intrigued him, captivated him. Only a few weeks earlier, this would have been beyond impossible, unthinkable. But it's a recognized fact that we know a person's value only from their trials. When the blockhouse had blown up, not one of the Germans had run away. They'd all automatically tried to help the wounded—so they still had generous instincts. And they'd done this regardless of nationality. Everyone had helped everyone else, French and Germans alike. Since then, Fabien had really enjoyed getting to know the prisoners better. Not just to cement the team. Finding the humanity in them fascinated him. Their different points of view and the things they had in common. Perhaps it was because of this genuine mood of reconciliation that Vincent hadn't been able to admit to his plans of revenge and murder. He hadn't wanted Fabien to try to dissuade him.

Wouldn't he, Fabien, have done the same?

If he'd been shown the German—or Germans?—who were guilty of Odette's disappearance, if he'd known who killed her and how, surely he would have been completely consumed with thoughts of revenge. Of course he would. To be sure he achieved his aim, he would have confided in no one, just like Vincent. Besides, why had he kept his cyanide capsule? Why had he never made up his mind to dispose of it?

Understanding Vincent didn't mean that Fabien had to keep him on the team, even if he did abandon his murderous plans. He was a danger to the rest of them. He couldn't control himself. And there would always be the question of his lies. Fabien must never forget them. During the war, lying had been synonymous with betrayal and death.

And what if Léna had been right? He understood the point she'd made, and so would anyone who remembered their own childhood lies: People sometimes lied out of fear rather than to manipulate, it was the ultimate weapon for those who thought all was lost, to protect themselves, save their skins, or to hold on to someone else's love. Who talks to tell the truth? No one. We talk to understand, to say what we like or loathe, but most important, most important of all, we talk in order to be loved.

Fabien needed to reach a decision. He took from his pocket the note he'd scribbled in the hospital, a note that divulged the truth Vincent had been searching for so desperately. With what Lukas had confided between feverish delirium and before succumbing to clinically induced sleep, Fabien held Vincent's fate in his hands.

THE NIGHT WAS DEEP AND DARK. THE IMAGES projected onto the studio wall were gaining in density, and Vincent was still hypnotized by that tragic party.

He had before him the last evidence of Ariane alive, possibly the last time she'd smiled, playing her role to perfection, happy, but her happiness was a forerunner to disaster. It was cruel; she hadn't been so alive in Audrey's photos. What if Ariane could now only ever smile in these films? What if she would always be a transparent figure in black-and-white, trapped on film like Mallarmé's swan trapped in ice on a lake, a "Phantom assigned to this place by his brilliance"?

Eventually the edges of some of the sprocket holes tore, threatening the balance of the animated images. The stuttering sound, the way the celluloid occasionally wobbled, like the flapping of a tiny distress flag…he must stop watching the films, must preserve them for fear of breaking them.

Except it was as good as impossible for him to tear his eyes away. He'd just spent several hours under hypnosis. The only way to break the spell was to walk away from that beam of light and leave the room.

When he went down to the kitchen, he finally saw the gifts that Saskia had brought for him on the table. He then realized that she'd been waiting for him when he'd returned home, probably to talk to him. He was so used to seeing her there in the evenings that he'd forgotten she would no longer be living with him.

He was annoyed with himself and paced around the studio. He opened one of the bottles, and the white wine, a sweet one, went straight to his head. It must be a muscat, from the Beaumes-de-Venise area. It was very drinkable, but he hadn't had anything to eat. Still, he downed a whole bottle, just like that, in no time, without feeling nauseous.

Then he decided to go and look in her bedroom. After all, he may not have heard her come upstairs. But the room was empty. She'd taken her few belongings and made the bed with fresh sheets. Everything was clean and tidy. There was nothing left of her. He caught himself looking out the window, as if he might see her on the roof again. Then he noticed something shining: a tiny piece of jewelry, a dove, which might belong to her—had he seen it around her neck? He decided to take it to her; this would use up some time without the temptation of starting the projector again. He felt slightly drunk, not something he was used to, but it wasn't so bad.

When he reached Saskia's house, all the lights were on. The garden gate was open. So was the front door. That wasn't like her; in the studio, she always locked the door, without fail. He stepped closer and despite his cautiousness, this felt like breaking and entering. He was struck by the silence.

And yet everything about the house was a reminder that a family had lived here: The quantities of hooks by the door for hanging coats, the two benches for removing shoes, the spaces where labels would have shown the names of the five members of the family; they'd been removed, but had left darker, oval patches on the slightly faded wallpaper. Five little clouds on the wall in the hallway. He felt bad being here, in this sanctuary, without Saskia.

He found her in the garden. Lying prostrate under the grenadine. As if there might be another treasure there to protect her.

He sat down beside her. He now knew what would keep bringing her back to this place, and what made her run away. He slipped the dove into her hand and suggested she come back to the studio until she felt she'd reappropriated her house.

He went inside with her to collect a few things. She walked through the house without breathing. Upstairs there were four bedrooms and she headed for the farthest one. She opened her wardrobe and hastily chose some clothes that the Bellanger children had screwed into a ball at the back of the lowest shelf. She didn't want to linger there.

Standing in the doorway, Vincent looked at the room, it couldn't have changed much since Saskia had left. He was immediately touched by its childish feel, wreathed in dreams, in promises that are accessible if you work hard enough, and in perfect love if you keep a pure heart. The colors, the soft light from lamps, the small bed, the

neatly stacked bookshelves—all of it spoke of uncomplicated happiness. When Saskia left this room, she'd been
a child. But hard work and a pure heart and perfect love
didn't mean anything anymore; Saskia would have to find
other reasons to live, and her serious, despondent mood,
her disenchanted expression felt out of place among these
vestiges of adolescence.

All of her mother's dresses had disappeared, but she
found a few that had belonged to her older sister. As
soon as she'd finished choosing them, they bundled the
clothes into a sheet, and she knotted it tightly. He took
her back to the studio on his bike, as he had on the day
they'd first met.

And like on the day they'd met, the cat was waiting for
them. He'd come back.

When Vincent opened the front door, he could tell
Saskia was breathing again.

He left her to settle in her bedroom and went back to
his own. He couldn't wait any longer to watch the films
again. Perhaps they hadn't had long enough to cool and
were still fragile. To give himself some Dutch courage, he
went to the kitchen for a bottle of muscat and brought it
upstairs. He inserted another reel and switched the projector back on.

With the elegance of a water droplet shimmying on
scalding metal, Ariane twirled around the dance floor
in Hans's arms. Vincent was hypnotized again. He went
from one reel to the next and it was time-consuming:
Some of them bore no relation to what he wanted to see.
He couldn't find the solution even though it was so close at

hand. He panicked and drank and started again, his hands shaking. Then he came across some boxes he'd missed. In four-minute bursts—that was the length of each reel—he was finally able to reconstitute the whole party. The party that Ariane had graced with her presence, and her smile.

By the end of the evening, she'd stopped smiling.

Hans was trying to kiss her. She stiffened, pushed him away, but the commandant cut in, replacing Hans and trying even more insistently. Then the frail pervert and the clodhopper. And it would start all over again. They were pursuing her. It was unendurable. Ariane seemed to be looking at Vincent, calling on him as a witness, her eyes huge. And he was looking at her too, it was like the old days, the two of them face-to-face, so close, looking into each other's eyes. But this was madness. The man she was looking at was the person filming, someone who was suffering along with her, and with Vincent.

The cameraman broke off at this point to tackle one of the dancers molesting Ariane.

And then, as he turned the camera away from Ariane, he himself appeared in a mirror, the man Ariane trusted, her friend, the person who stood up for her, who'd defended her to the very last when Vincent wasn't there: Matthias. Ariane hadn't lied in her letters. She'd had an ally. Audrey was right: It really was Matthias. And Matthias had been telling the truth when he said he'd been the one who knew her best. But now, projected onto the wall, Matthias was becoming the victim, picked on by these four men, just like Ariane. They beat him and forced him to start filming again.

Vincent was now sure that one of the men who'd forced Ariane to dance had committed the unthinkable. Perhaps all four of them had together. The commandant, the clodhopper, the frail pervert, and, of course, Hans. Hans whom he could have talked to alone when they were inside the château if only he'd known sooner, Hans who hadn't said anything when he'd battered him with his pistol.

It drove him crazy knowing that he'd had Ariane's rapist, perhaps her killer, within reach and he'd let him get away. Worse than that, he'd given him a chance of escape, handed it to him on a plate. He'd missed everything. Matthias was going to die in Germany, and Vincent would never have a chance to get near Hans again or to find out whom he must kill—Hans, the commandant, the clodhopper, or the pervert.

Then the thing he'd been dreading happened with a sharp cracking sound that reverberated like an ill omen: The film snapped and Ariane flew away.

It was a sign, he was sure. It was self-evident. She was dead. She'd come back to take her revenge and they'd killed her. Hans. Or one of the others. What did it matter which one. Only now did he understand that this was the truth he'd been looking for, and it had been obvious from the start: There wasn't just one guilty party. They were all guilty, the four dancing with her, the other people at the party—all of them complicit.

The solution presented itself quite naturally.

He thundered down the stairs to go out. Saskia had come back down to the kitchen, and he finished an opened bottle in front of her. She could see there was none left and he was getting drunk. He spoke quickly, rambling incoherently as he tried to reassure her but what he said was alarming: He said she must stay at the studio as long as she liked, even if he didn't return, he'd paid several months in advance. She wished she could calm him, convince him that she understood everything, but he didn't give her a chance. Saskia anticipated the worst, could almost see it: The catastrophe was right there, so precise and urgent, waiting for Vincent to go and join it outside, leading him to his demise with a steady, expert hand.

ONCE OUTSIDE, VINCENT COULD TELL THAT THE fresh air wouldn't sober him up straightaway. It felt good to be drunk. He wanted to prolong it as much as possible. The sweet euphoria allowed him to congratulate himself; he was magnificently in control of the situation and his thoughts were clearer than ever.

If he blew up the prison camp bunkhouse that housed all the officers who'd had their fun at the château, along with the one where Hans lived with all his accomplices, then Ariane would be avenged, he would be avenged, along with everyone whom the Germans had submerged into the darkness he'd experienced, the inky darkness in which not a single star shines, in which the damp rises through your feet into your bones, and there's no hope of ever finding hope again—he could at least make the criminals within his reach pay for that unforgivable damage.

He pedaled effortlessly over the kilometers that lay between him and the warehouse where he and Fabien had hidden the explosives. On downhill stretches, his bike flew above the asphalt. Drunkenness brought elation in its wake, but the speed and the wind were starting to sober him up. As his intoxication dwindled, the elation became something less pleasant but more furious, wilder, harsher.

He'd never killed anyone. The fretful darkness wasn't helping him gather his wits, which were jumping about like overexcited children.

Nothing made any sense now and it wasn't his fault. If he didn't avenge Ariane, he would never forgive himself. He mustn't back down. And even though the memory of those Germans laughing, revived by the grimacing images in the films, stoked a fierce energy in him, he couldn't be sure how he would react when the time came. So he summoned images of all the abuse he'd witnessed, and forgiveness seemed worse than weakness, a crime committed against other people and against yourself because what did he think? Yes, he must acknowledge the truth, forgiveness was an escape clause to have an easier life, there was no generosity in it. Could you forgive yourself for forgiving criminals? Forgiveness meant forgetting and forgetting was unforgivable.

He needed to get it done quickly. Not think about Lukas or anyone else. Remember his time in the prison camp when the Germans had still been a rigid, repulsive, faceless mass to him. Using explosives would mean he didn't have to see their faces. They would be pulverized, just as they'd pulverized millions of human beings. He was entirely wrapped up in this revenge and not once since the start of the war had he felt so completely in the right place.

Besides, he was coming close to his goal, he had no choice. He dismounted his bike and walked over to the warehouse. His legs carried him with no intervention from his will, as if he'd been programmed, each footstep automatically triggering the next so that his regular pace was dictated by the first step that had determined all the others, just as the idea that he must avenge Ariane had decided all his words, all his actions, all his months of existence since he'd escaped.

He had nearly reached the place where Fabien had hidden the key. Drowned between mist and clouds, the moon was almost smudged out and was shedding no light. He felt he was being guided: He found the key without even fumbling for it. Inside was everything he needed. More, even: a jeep that he could load up with the dynamite and would allow him to hurtle to the prison camp and get this done once and for all.

He didn't want to consider whether this was the best plan, so he forced himself to think about nothing but how to carry it out.

NOT A SOUND. EVERYONE IN THE PRISON CAMP was sleeping, or trying to sleep. Vincent had heard Fabien tell the authorities that the Germans were exhausted, they were working long hours and not eating enough, and their morale was at rock bottom. None of that softened Vincent's attitude. He'd been imprisoned by the Germans. Fabien hadn't.

He knew exactly which bunkhouse to target, having identified it the day he'd brought Lukas news of Matthias. But before handling the dynamite, he needed to clear his head completely. He took deep breaths and the drunken feeling that he'd been prolonging, like a deep-sea diver controlling his apnea, was now behind him. He sat down and thought through the three major questions.

Was he sure he wanted them dead?

Was he sure he wouldn't regret it?

Would it avenge Ariane?

He hated himself for asking this question last but put it down to tiredness and the remaining traces of alcohol. He wasn't thinking straight. The truth was he would ensure justice was served. This reasoning might be rejected later, but he could remind everyone what the Germans had done.

His mind was made up, he would do it.

When he stood up, a hand clamped onto his shoulder and held him back.

In the darkness of that moonless night, Vincent fought with all the strength he had, but he wasn't up to it: The man who'd attacked him and was now flattening him on the ground was a more experienced fighter. And he was helped by a weaker pair of arms, which made it difficult for Vincent to defend himself.

"Vincent, stop!"

It had all happened so quickly and his heart and brain had been flooded with an uninterrupted surge of adrenaline for so long that he was carried away and continued to struggle.

"What the hell are you doing? Vincent, it's Fabien!"

Now that Vincent had heard Fabien's voice, he could make out his face. He turned around to see who else's hand was holding him. It was Saskia's. And this upset him more than he would ever have guessed. He would think about that later.

∾

BACK AT THE STUDIO, VINCENT FACED FABIEN and waited for his verdict. Which didn't come. He didn't regret the act he'd wanted to commit but was disappointed with himself for lying to Fabien. He would understand if Fabien wanted to kick him off the team and report him to the police.

Saskia hung back near the piano, pained to see Vincent in this situation. It was her fault. When Fabien had come to see Vincent at the studio on his way home from the hospital, she'd told him what she was afraid might be happening. Fabien immediately feared the worst too. They'd gone to the prison camp, both convinced that that was where Vincent would be. Fabien was worried he might still have a gun but hadn't thought of the explosives.

Now Vincent would see that Saskia had guessed everything he thought he'd hidden from her, and she didn't want this to hurt him. She tactfully left them alone and went up to her room.

Meanwhile, Fabien still hadn't reached any sort of decision. In his pocket he fiddled with the piece of paper that could change everything for Vincent.

"You've been thinking about killing a German ever since you started demining."

Vincent lowered his head. "Not from the start."

"You changed your name so you could disappear and Vincent Devailly could take the blame for you. A double blow. You kill a German, sorry, a ton of Germans in his name, and you get him to take the rap. Talk about premeditated crime!"

"No, a crime of passion. I'm doing it for Ariane."

"If the judges go with passion, they'll exonerate you, but if they go with premeditation, you won't get out of this."

Fabien couldn't let Vincent continue with this madness. He took from his pocket a copy of the letter from the Resistance fighter he'd mentioned to Vincent, Honoré d'Estienne d'Orves.

"Do you know what he wrote to his sister just before he was shot? . . . 'Don't think about avenging me' . . . Do you understand? . . . No, you don't understand, but you will one day, I promise."

Fabien wasn't giving up on him: He believed in second chances, in reappraisals and new understanding. Not with everyone, but Vincent could do it, couldn't he?

He wanted to dissuade him from his plan but didn't insult him with sermonizing. He shifted away from criticism and moved toward more unexpected shores. He wasn't angry with Vincent, he needed him. Having a doctor on the team was an asset. Could Vincent continue with his three-month assignment and set up a mobile first-aid unit? Fabien would find a way to source the materials. He waited for Vincent's reply, which might be the determining factor.

Vincent wasn't expecting this suggestion and was so lost that he ended up accepting it. Fabien smiled. He knew that three months would be long enough for him to save Vincent.

He had the situation under control again.

"Did you think you'd get away with your false ID and commit the perfect crime?"

"I can't see anything perfect about it, the harm's been done, and no one will ever be avenged."

"Will you ever find peace?"

"Impossible."

"I'll make sure you do, believe me!"

It was stronger than he was; Fabien couldn't hold this against Vincent. He inevitably put himself in his shoes and that was his tragedy. Fabien understood it all, and when we understand something, we're already a long way toward accepting it, even if we don't want to. He handed Vincent the piece of paper on which he'd written the name of a village.

"Lukas talked to me. Not much. If Ariane's alive, she's in Italy. Probably in this village in the Aosta Valley."

"Did Matthias have time to tell him that?"

"I guess so. That's all I know. He didn't have the strength to talk."

Vincent looked at the note as if it had been written by Ariane herself. It made him tremble. Fabien couldn't help but be moved. Vincent's emotion blew everything else away. He put his hands on Vincent's shoulders, then hugged him.

"Go find her. And come back with her to help us."

Saskia had stayed on the landing to listen to their conversation. She now went to her room, surprised to find she was frightened. Frightened to be facing the world alone, again. And perhaps there was another fear too, a more secret and insidious one. She brushed it aside with all the fierce strength of her will. She would not let this hurt her. She had no right to. And, all things considered, she didn't want to. It wasn't that she wouldn't allow herself to suffer for love or friendship, just that it seemed beneath her. The only thing that could hurt her was the absence of the people she was grieving. She drew on her ability not to suffer for things that weren't worth it, finding renewed self-confidence and a strength that surprised her, reassured her.

The two men went out into the street. Vincent had waited so long for this moment that he couldn't wait any longer; he would leave that same night.

Parked in front of them was Max's Traction Avant. Fabien threw him the keys. Vincent didn't know how to thank him, but he didn't need to—one look was enough. That's the advantage of having risked your life with someone.

∼

VINCENT DROVE ALL NIGHT, PASSING A SEQUENCE of signposts: Marseille, Ventimiglia, San Remo, Savona, Turin...A storm, a beautiful spring storm, burst overhead, a harbinger of the summer storms to come, and it felt absurdly good to him that nature was in tune with his inner turmoil. The black sky, thunder, and lightning expressed his passion more surely than any words, sharing its intensity, its incandescence. It would take at least heavenly orchestrations like this to mark his reunion with Ariane.

He was driving so fast that eventually he had to stop, catch his breath, and perhaps use this time that was still his alone. What would he say to Ariane when he saw her? He'd tried to find out why she'd disappeared but hadn't found out anything about what had become of her or the ways in which the war had marked her. He didn't know what had happened at that party, how far the ignominy had gone.

How had Ariane coped with the trauma? Did she still want to live life to the fullest, as she always had? Or was she now hunted, cowed?

Nothing would be insurmountable for them. It didn't matter how long it took. Their reunion would be

unforgettable. They would pick up their love where they'd
left off, its blazing heat and its indolent languor, the softness of skin in the places where veins pulse, the inside of
an arm, of a thigh. Slipping naked into cool sheets. He
would take her to the beach at daybreak to see the sun that
appears for the chosen few and they would feel victorious,
forever.

His heart was beating wildly, and yet... despite the
images he kept conjuring of Ariane and himself throwing
themselves impatiently, ardently into each other's arms,
this wasn't the euphoria he'd so hoped for. He would love
Ariane with all her complications, all her changes, he
would be patient, he would love her all the more. But what
about her? Would she love him? He too had changed. He
couldn't help it.

Before the war he'd been lighthearted, his spirits gliding over problems, his smile defusing any difficulty. He
wasn't the same now. He was afraid of the seriousness
in himself. His bitterness, his disillusionment with the
human race, his furious vengeful impulses. Ariane was
bound to detect them; he couldn't hide anything from her.

The rain on his face washed away his doubts. He was
insane: The sleepless moonless night he'd just had was
scrambling his mind.

When, at dawn, he reached the village nestled in the
crook of the small valley, he knew that Ariane had found
a refuge that suited her. All he could see of the houses
below him was their beautiful roofs made of huge stone
tiles, a giant gray-and-beige jigsaw puzzle with every pock
and bump gleaming in the rain. A rugged, mineral world

perfectly integrated into the neighboring hills, as solid as rock. She must love this ancient assemblage of stones, the trees and plants that insinuated themselves into the walls wherever they could, exploiting a few square centimeters of earth between the slabs to delve their roots; and the cats that had somehow managed to survive and miraculously reproduce. Graceful young cats appeared on every street corner, bounding after the retreating rain. They were indisputable signs of a more powerful, easier life, and all its promise.

He parked the car on the edge of the village so as not to disturb this place that had remained unchanged for centuries. Then he walked down the street with its smooth, worn paving stones, glancing left and right in search of anything that might tell him where Ariane had taken refuge.

Women were coming out onto their doorsteps to enjoy the damp air after the downfall, to feel alive and breathe the fresh smell of freedom. Their close-fitting shirtdresses, the fine sandals on their bare feet, the combs in their long hair—everything looked beautiful on these cautious, unassuming women who didn't venture into the street before they'd looked all around, as if checking that the coast was clear. The fighting had been fierce until late April. It was now May, and the terror was still there.

Who could Vincent ask whether they'd seen Ariane? A lot of men had gone to work in France after the Great War—they would understand him and speak his language. But he could see only women everywhere, young ones, old ones with burnished skin, little girls, a population of women who must have pulled together to withstand the demands on every side. He imagined Ariane having no trouble blending into this women's world; after all, she could talk to anyone. But confronted with Vincent—a man, a foreigner—these women eyed him defiantly and stayed silent.

The sky between the houses had shifted from the gray of night to the blue of morning, and sweeping across it were a few sensuously sprawling clouds. In this pure air rinsed by a light wind, the women were hurrying to the washhouse, where they could resume their conversations sheltered within its three dry-stone walls and under its roof that skimmed the tops of their heads. Others had stayed at home to make the most of the bright spell and hang clothes out of windows to dry.

On laundry lines strung over the street between houses hung shirts, and dresses with flowers, polka dots, or stripes, all of them stretching and dancing. The wind was in a changeable mood, the sleeves weren't all blowing in the same direction and frolicked far from the buttoned bodies of their respective shirts, the dresses were half-crazed, quivering and twirling, then calming only to whip into a frenzy again.

One of them pranced at the head of this procession, wilder and lighter than the others, rolling itself up in the wind, rising, unwinding and waving cheerfully on the line...

The sight of this dress electrified Vincent: It was the one Ariane had shortened to make the scarf that he wore around his neck. He went over to the house onto which the laundry line bearing his beloved's clothes was attached, and he stood looking at the façade for a while. After all these months of longing to see her, he was afraid of disturbing her.

All his questions and self-examination would be spontaneously erased when he saw her. He would revert to his own name to reembark on his life with her. They would travel if she wanted to. They would be happy. Would Ariane sense that he was there, as she used to, anticipating the exact time when they would be together again in the small apartment in Marseille that had been the scene of their secret lovemaking? There had always been plenty of comings and goings in that nineteenth-century building, but every time he'd returned to it, he'd barely finished climbing the stairs to the top floor, and even though he tiptoed to avoid making any sound, she'd always preempted him, opened the door and thrown herself into his arms.

And just like before, on this warm May day, the door opened and Ariane was there in front of him. She didn't throw herself in his arms. She was already holding someone tightly to her—a very young child.

BLOND WITH BIG, PALE GREEN EYES: HE COULD have been Vincent's child but was only just over a year old. Vincent was frozen to the spot. He so often dreamed of taking Ariane in his arms, but this child now came between them more definitively than King Arthur's sword between Guinevere and Lancelot. What had happened? He didn't dare ask. It seemed so obvious. But he could see that Ariane wouldn't burden the baby with disapproval, not even with the weight of a shadow. She loved him unconditionally.

Ariane smiled at Vincent. She was happy to see him. But from the way she said his name—his real name, Hadrien—he knew she wasn't investing it with the same magic as before. She led him into a small multipurpose room. The bare stone walls, the simple basic furniture…He would have chosen the same home as Ariane, just as Ariane would surely have liked his studio. She put the baby into a highchair and tied him to the backrest with scarves to keep him from falling. Then she plucked some mint leaves from the windowsill and tossed them into a metal teapot. She put water on to boil, taking her time, probably wondering what she would tell Vincent, and how.

He wanted to break the awkward silence but was reluctant to raise the subject of the child first.

"I didn't tell your parents I was coming…"

"That's a good thing."

"Are they frightened that…"

"That I'm dead? Maybe it's better that way."

"You don't know what you're saying."

"Neither do you."

She looked at her child, her almost white-blond child, the sort of blond that comes from the north, not the sort with glints of red and gold warmed by the Mediterranean sun but the translucent blond of the pale German sun that makes eyelashes iridescent and frames heads with a metallic light. The boy was now making it clear that he was hungry, not by crying but with adorable little warning sounds. Ariane picked him up and walked away to nurse him, and Vincent could watch her from behind, her beautiful back, her Madonna-like back, the graceful way she held her baby with one arm, tilting her head toward him, that immemorial gesture of a mother with her child that he loved in the works of da Vinci and Raphael and was witnessing now as if he were part of the picture.

If Ariane returned to France, no one would be thrilled. She was right: It was better to be taken for dead, everything would be spoiled. It was easy to predict what people would say. This was a Boche child…an unforgivable sin.

Except that Ariane had done nothing wrong. She had been subjected to this crime that no one referred to as a crime, even less as a war crime, just another one of the rapes that are viewed as minor collateral damage, after all no man has died, there's just a woman who's fallen, she's foundered, and she'll pick herself back up very quickly because she has a dependent now.

Italy wouldn't ask any questions. France would.

He would fight for her. If Ariane didn't want to return to France, he would stay in Italy with her. Or they'd go somewhere else, anywhere. She had to agree to be happy. He waited until she'd finished nursing to tell her his plan.

"Ariane, I'll love your son. He doesn't change anything for me. I'm sure your parents will feel the same."

"I have to protect them. They don't need this."

"They need you."

"Not anymore."

"Everyone will understand. It's not your fault."

Ariane didn't hesitate and her reply poleaxed him.

"There was no fault…"

〜

VINCENT UNTIED THE SCARF AROUND HIS NECK and put it on the table, as if relieving himself of a tie that bound him, suffocated him.

The baby was asleep, and Ariane took him into the bedroom to put him down.

Vincent stood up. He needed to get some air, go out into the street. His thoughts were going wild. He should have been happy: Ariane hadn't suffered. She had chosen. She had loved. What had he expected? That she'd wait for years? Toward the end, the mail from Germany hadn't been getting through, she hadn't even known whether he was alive.

If he was honest, he looked at other women. The one he'd seen outside the recruiting office, with her daisy earrings, her floaty dress, and her Camus book. Léna at the café, whom all the men listened to, captivated. Until he realized that Fabien was watching her too, Vincent had been no exception to that rule. In the camp, they'd all become demented without women. It was impossible for a former prisoner to see a woman without thinking about her body and her skin. But none of that counted.

He gathered his thoughts. Yes, he'd looked at women, but he hadn't envisioned anything, ever. But then on the beach, in the sea, under the moon, the night he'd gone swimming with Saskia...But no. Saskia was different. He'd still been thinking about Ariane. He couldn't be sure now.

While he was a prisoner, he'd just clung to the idea that they'd be stronger, he and Ariane, and could start over again. That nothing and no one, particularly not the Nazis, could influence the course of their fate. Was he crazy to have thought that if you wanted to, you could do away with time?

He resented Ariane and he didn't resent her. Ariane was a free woman, and her freedom was also partly why he'd fallen in love with her.

Yes, but...a German? It seemed impossible. And yet he'd pictured her with Matthias. But he'd never really believed in it; his mind—having spent so long without answers—had simply wandered. And then when he and Lukas had been in that office at the château with the archives, Lukas had assured him that Matthias had been Ariane's friend, not her lover. But what did he know?

Ariane would obviously have an explanation; it couldn't end like this. She would put into words the things he didn't understand. That was it: She needed to explain. He was too tired, worn down by the rain and the storm, and the overnight journey to Italy.

He went back into the house, and she was waiting for him.

"I thought you knew. I asked Irène to tell you."

"I didn't see her..."

"I'm so sorry."

"Don't be."

Then he heard himself saying things he didn't believe: "Look, we can start again. Whatever happened in the past, it doesn't change anything."

"It does for me. That would be a lie."

What did she mean, a lie? Would being with him be a lie? Was the German still alive? Had he run away with her? For the first time since he'd met Ariane, he didn't intuitively understand what she was saying.

She sidestepped the subject, something he'd seen her do so many times, trying to lighten the conversation to avoid descending into nostalgia.

"Tell me about the Russian," she said.

"The Russian?"

"The one you treated. You mentioned him in your letters."

Of course, Vincent knew exactly which Russian Ariane meant, but he thought it a bad idea to discuss him.

"I can't tell you much more than what I wrote you."

"Of course you can! There's no censorship now."

"I don't even know the end of the story."

"And I don't know the beginning. I didn't get all your letters."

So Vincent told her that one day in the camp, the Nazis, as they often did, turned on one of the prisoners for no particular reason and beat him to a pulp. On that occasion it was a young Russian—the Russians were the most mistreated in the camp. The officers were savagely aggressive, hammering him with rifle butts, breaking his back and other bones. They left him for dead on the ground.

In an atmosphere dense with tension, the horde of prisoners and guards froze. When Vincent took a step forward, the German doctor held him back. With just one look, Vincent told him that he couldn't not go to the man's aid.

A guard roared at Vincent to return to his bunkhouse, but Vincent went and knelt next to the dying man. In the perfect German that he'd honed during his imprisonment, he stated the case for the oath he'd sworn to become a doctor and, surrounded by deathly silence, he asked to be allowed to treat the man.

The Nazis despised Vincent, who was so calmly opposing their crime. They spat on the ground when he knelt by the man, but some more senior officers told them to let Vincent go ahead. They were intrigued by the challenge he faced—repairing an irreparable body—not out of compassion on their part but curiosity.

There wasn't much Vincent could do, and yet he tried.

In the dispensary, he carefully cut away all of the Russian's clothes so that he could examine him. He very gently disinfected the wounds and realigned all the broken bones before bandaging and plastering them. It felt akin to remodeling the young soldier's body like a clay statue. He then spent a whole day and night building an articulated wooden structure whose separate parts were connected by a clever system of braided string. For several months he kept the Russian protected in this exoskeleton, which allowed him to slowly lift a hand or an arm, to raise his chest very slightly, and to have some small hope of survival.

As the days passed, Vincent's ingenuity became a remedy for boredom in the camp. Some of the men placed bets. They wanted to know whether Pinocchio—the nickname they'd given the Russian—would come back to life. There were a lot of jokes in those early days, but after several months, Vincent's tenacity had instilled respect. Prisoners had been sent to their deaths for less, but curiosity is a powerful motive.

The Russian spoke no French or English. Vincent spoke no Russian. But they had their own particular way of communicating. The expression in the injured man's eyes swept aside many of Vincent's doubts. But there was still one significant misgiving, and he admitted it to Ariane now.

"You see, I'll never know if he pulled through. I escaped before..." He didn't need to tell her that he'd escaped for her, she knew that.

"Maybe the doctor you liked took over his care."

"I hope so."

"I'm sure he did. And I think that, by saving that Russian, you saved yourself."

"I can't even be sure he'll walk again."

This feeling of unfinished business was still painful for Vincent, but Ariane had succeeded in taking his mind off another source of pain—the end of their relationship. She also fully understood what tormented Vincent, having read between the lines in his letters.

"I didn't manage to achieve what I set out to do either," she said. "I wanted to kill the top guy at the Kommandatura, can you believe it!"

"I can believe it, I heard about it. Poisoning him with digitalis."

"So you know I failed. And it all seemed so easy. You know as well as I do that digitalis can be drastic, but nothing went as planned." She would have preferred for him not to see this, but she had tears in her eyes. "I so desperately wanted to do something. I've hated myself every day for failing."

"At least you tried."

"I could have put everyone in danger with what I'd tried to do. It was better to disappear."

Her failure still nagged at her, but in the aftermath she'd had to find a way to live, and in more basic terms, to survive. She described her war to him, and he described his: His escape, his plan, joining the demining team, changing his name. She thought Vincent suited him better than Hadrien, the name of a Roman emperor who'd proved so cruel. She would try it out to see how it felt. Everyone was living different lives now, so why shouldn't he change his name?

He couldn't help thinking that this was how you recognized the end of a love affair: Avoiding talking about the deep, intense things, and not pronouncing the lover's name because it still came freighted with a magic spell of love. It was all over for Ariane and Hadrien.

Ariane was moving from one thing to the next with the vivacity he'd so loved in the past. Meanwhile Vincent needed to tell her about Matthias. But Ariane was working so hard not to make this reunion sad that he couldn't find the words to tell her that Matthias's days were numbered.

The baby started to cry and when Ariane stood, Vincent followed her. She picked up her son and walked around the room to soothe him.

"What's his name?"

"Louis, like his grandfather."

Vincent was transfixed by the way Ariane moved as she walked around the room with her son on her hip, her slender legs and the little elastic sound of her bare feet on the stone, the sound he'd thought of so often in the studio. He looked away so as not to embarrass her.

It was then that he noticed the drawings. Discreet drawings on a shelf alongside medical textbooks and novels. Drawings of her that so perfectly captured how she carried herself—the way she tilted her head to one side when she read, the way she sat in a chair with one knee bent up against her chest or both knees huddled close to her, or how she lay down and stretched, arching her back— and there were portraits too, elegant, spirited, adoring portraits, and Vincent was pained to recognize the style, having held so many portraits like this in his hands.

"Did Lukas draw you?"

Ariane turned around sharply. "Do you know him?"

And then he grasped what he could never have imagined.

"Is he…"

~

FROM THE LOOK ON HER FACE, THERE WAS NO need for a reply. He and Ariane were like twins—they always knew everything about each other in the end. They'd fallen in love because this twinhood had fascinated them. Why be surprised that they'd grown close to the same man? André Breton was now taunting Vincent, who'd never believed his story of objective chance, but here it was dancing before his eyes, vibrant and self-evident.

Lukas wasn't like the other soldiers: It was only natural that Ariane had noticed him, and only natural that he had noticed Ariane.

Lukas had drawn them to him and had played a decisive part in both of their lives, because he incarnated everything they were attracted to. Hadn't Vincent caught himself thinking that in another time, under different circumstances, he and Lukas could have been friends?

She asked him to understand, and he heard himself saying that he would understand and would accept what had happened. He hadn't survived the war only to add more tragedy to tragedy. The chaos they'd been through could at least serve this purpose: They could grow as a result of it and follow to the letter Rimbaud's instruction to reinvent love.

So he gave her longed-for news of Lukas, or what news
he had thanks to Fabien, but it would never be enough.
She needed to know more: How were the prisoners
treated? Was he injured when he was arrested? What risks
did he run in their demining work? Did Vincent think he
seemed despondent, confident, strong, wavering, lonely,
well-fed, healthy...? What had the doctors said? Would
he pull through?

Vincent noticed that, being tactful, Ariane made a
point of talking about him too, asking as many questions
about him as she did about Lukas. She was concerned that
Lukas wouldn't be well looked after in the hospital just as
she trembled to think of Vincent disarming mines. She
wished the prisoners weren't seconded to this sort of work
and also urged Vincent to return to medicine. He sensed
that she admired Lukas for his attempt to escape, just as
she admired him, Vincent, for escaping.

And then he stopped giving her opportunities to cut
in: He could talk about Lukas uninterrupted. He realized
that there was so much more to say than describing the
state of his health or the conditions of his imprisonment.
Lukas had become the key player in his plan to find Ariane or to avenge her. Vincent had watched him, appraised
him, gauged him. He understood why she'd grown close
to him, and he would return to the hospital to watch over
Lukas. He wouldn't abandon him.

They talked through the day and for part of the night.

In the morning, he promised to come back with news
of Lukas.

The mystery of the years Ariane had spent without him had made her all the more alluring. But as soon as the pain eased, he would find that there was more between them than their electric desire, the magnetic attraction that had propelled them unfailingly together and had woken them at all hours of every night they'd spent together. Just as a crystal alters subtly depending on how it is orientated to the light, his love remained intact but it was a different color.

SOME PEOPLE LOST THE WAR. VINCENT HAD LOST the postwar. He was frustrated with himself for spending this glorious period that was so laden with promise pursuing revenge and getting everything wrong. All the plans he'd put together and skillfully set in motion, the vast mental chess games constructed in minute detail in his prison camp, stealing a pistol, escaping, joining the demining team, hiding his identity, cautiously advancing his pawns, every expression he'd fine-tuned, every utterance he'd weighed up, every cigarette he'd handed out, the way he'd given it and lit it, every smile he'd granted... it had all been calculated so many times. Every day he'd spent with the Germans then analyzed that same evening, every night battling insomnia and calming himself to try to find sleep: His own personal Liberation had been subsumed by his obsession.

Despite everything he'd said to Ariane, despite the night he'd spent there and the day, despite what made sense and despite his best efforts, there was nothing for it: As Vincent drove back from Italy, he thought he would never be happy again.

The almond trees in blossom caught him off guard. When did the buds emerge into pale pink petals? He

hadn't even noticed. As he sat there in his car, the landscape unfurled through his windscreen like images in a
film in dazzlingly bright colors, and he was forced to watch
it. He opened the window and now he had the image *and*
the sound, the smells, the wind.

In Germany, he'd forgotten how quickly the seasons
pass in the South of France. And that there weren't just
winter months. It was only now that he was reawakened to
the fact that the natural world isn't always harsh, it's not all
mud clinging to your boots in heavy clods that shackled
you like leg cuffs, the cold chilling your bones, and the
starved skeletons of trees silhouetted against misted suns.
It can also be clear skies washed clean by azure winds and
the breeze flittering between trees in blossom. The sea
beckons you, the spring calls you, the birds watch you out
of the corners of their eyes, a cat weaves between your legs.

In Hyères, Ramatuelle, or Saint-Tropez he could have
spotted the discreet cyclamens flowering back in April;
he hadn't thought to look for them. But he should never
have missed the almond trees, which are always the first
to blossom.

He still had some of May. It was glorious. And then
there would be June, July, and August, the heady and sensual summer months when people fall in love, when their
lives turn upside down, and when they live as intensely by
night as by day. Yes, all that mattered now was the summer, which would soon be here. The first postwar summer.

Girls and women, who looked like girls themselves,
twirled in their light dresses, rewarding everyone with
their radiant smiles, and the very fact of being sad was

starting to feel arduous. Anachronistic. He didn't mind swimming against the current, but he still felt it would be wrong not to accept other people's happiness.

In Marseille, he stopped off at the apartment on Place Castellane, not wanting to stay long. He slipped his clothes into a small suitcase and thought about the studio he'd rented in Hyères, the way the sun spilled in through the windows, the life that had quietly worked its way into each of the rooms.

While he was looking through the bookcase to pick out any duplicate copies of books, he heard the soft rustle of mail being slipped under the door by the caretaker. This familiar, discreet little sound that he'd forgotten tugged at his heart. The caretaker must have seen him come in but not wanted to disturb him. He opened the door and said hello to her, and explained that he'd suggested Ariane could live here if she returned—the caretaker mustn't be surprised if she found her there.

Once he was alone again, he glanced at the letters. Two of them were from Cassel, where he'd been held prisoner. The first, which was from the German doctor, had been sent shortly after his escape. The doctor had asked for Vincent's address in the camp's administrative offices to give him news of the young Russian: He'd taken him out of the exoskeleton, removed his casts, and was starting to give him physical therapy. He had high hopes.

The second letter was from the Russian himself. He must have had it translated. The camp had been liberated by the Americans and the young man thanked him in distinctly Slavic high-blown terms. He would never forget

Vincent. If Vincent came to Moscow, he would always have a brother there.

These letters were a miracle and Vincent sat down to bask in the news they gave him.

Ariane was right: By saving the Russian, he'd saved himself. Or at least he was starting to remember who he was.

Then he went to the hospital to visit Lukas. He was able to talk to the doctors and was relieved to learn that Lukas was no longer in critical condition. Louis would meet his father. He was given permission to speak to Lukas, who was awake when Vincent came into his room. Lukas tried to sit up, embarrassed to be lying down while talking to Vincent, and Vincent helped him.

"Did you find her?"

"Yes and she's fine. So's your son. His name's Louis. But maybe you knew that?"

Lukas was so choked with emotion he couldn't speak. Happiness felt so straightforward . . . and so inaccessible. Vincent described his trip, then there was something he wanted to know.

"Why did you tell Fabien where she was?"

"I thought she'd be better off with you. How can she possibly live with a prisoner? I have nothing to offer her."

"Weren't you planning to escape so you could be with her?"

"Yes. But I won't make it now. Do you know what they do to prisoners who try to escape?"

Yes, Vincent knew.

"And what's going to happen now?" Lukas asked.

"I've spoken to the doctor, you're going to make it."

Lukas looked down and admitted, "To be honest, I didn't know what *she* wanted. We haven't had any mail in that camp for months, you know."

Vincent took from his pocket the letter Ariane had written for Lukas. "Here."

Lukas didn't dare read it in front of him.

"She's waiting for you."

"She shouldn't. They won't let us out for years," Lukas said, looking Vincent right in the eye. The intensity of his stare was painful for Vincent: All at once, he saw Lukas through Ariane's eyes.

Vincent promised he would visit again soon. He would go and take photos of Louis so Lukas could see how like both his parents he looked. He handed him the photos of Ariane that he had with him, and when Lukas looked at them, it was as if he was already healed. Vincent had overestimated his own strength and Lukas's smile hurt him more than he would have liked. He wasn't a saint, but he knew that time would remedy everything.

Back in the car, he took some paper and a pen from the glove compartment and started writing a letter. He was going to do something spontaneous, well, something he might regret, would be ashamed of regretting, but the bold move he was making right now might be his only salvation...

At the end of the day, he joined Fabien at the château. Raymond Aubrac was there to announce the news

personally: The deminers would be granted legal status. It
was fair compensation for their sacrifice and the recognition they'd all hoped to have. It was only a matter of days
before it would be announced in the government's official journal. And the graves of those who'd died—Enzo,
Thibault, Tom, Henri, Hubert, and all the others—would
bear the words: DIED IN THE SERVICE OF FRANCE.
TAKEN IN THE MINEFIELDS.

The war was over. Not for the deminers, even less so
for the prisoners.

It was still the case, more so than ever now, that the
German prisoners would continue to demine until everywhere was clear. And the projections hadn't changed: It
would take about ten years.

Vincent talked to Fabien privately to check that the
anticipated release, on application, of German prisoners
who'd shown dedication and courage still applied. Once
this was confirmed, he personally handed Aubrac the letter he'd written on his return from Italy. In it, he detailed
all of Lukas's fine qualities, the vital role he'd played in
making the château safe, and the information he'd fur-
nished on German mines.

Fabien had smiled when he'd read the letter. He
agreed wholeheartedly with Vincent, and the two of them
showed Aubrac the plans that Lukas had drawn up, the
same plans that were still displayed on large boards at the
entrance to the grounds. Thanks to Lukas, they'd been
able to enter the château and finally get hold of mining
maps of the region that were so valuable to their ongoing
work. If there was one prisoner to put forward for release,

it was Lukas. They felt strongly about it. Aubrac assured them that he himself would take care of it.

Vincent put his hand on Fabien's shoulder—as promised, he would continue to work alongside him. After all, he specialized in wartime medical care, and that was exactly what was needed. Fabien asked if he was okay. Vincent nodded.

When Vincent reached the studio, Saskia was playing the piano with the windows open. He stayed there a long while listening to her, sitting on the low wall opposite the house. He thought she hadn't seen him. She had, but pretended not to have noticed, staying calm and focused. She must have bravely opened the door for the tuner this time, because the piano was in tune.

The sun had positioned itself perfectly to stream in through the window, and it toyed with the upright piano and Saskia's face, flooding them with light through the combination of acacia leaves and wisteria. Vincent could have listened to her play for hours. The music filled the street. It gradually rinsed away his regrets and it was almost as if he could envision something. Perhaps even something very ambitious. And urgent. In Italy, Ariane had caused him excruciating pain. At the piano, Saskia allowed him to believe in a compelling happiness that would sweep aside all obstacles.

When she finished the piece, she turned to look out at him and smiled a dazzling smile that he hadn't yet seen from her, one that expressed how hard she too would fight for and against everything, how she would forget nothing and would still stand firm, invincible, free to embrace the new days ahead and the promise of the summer to come.

"So, did you like it?"

AFTERWORD

WHO WOULD HAVE PUT MONEY ON A RECONCILI-
ation between France and Germany in 1870, 1914, or
1939? Furthermore, who would have predicted that the
friendship between these two countries would be a force,
a bedrock?

Many stories have described major conflicts in our
history to explore powerful issues—How can war be
won? What do these stories tell us about war?—while the
postwar period has been relatively neglected. And yet the
stakes are just as crucial: How can peacetime be won?
How can lasting peace be established, shown to be self-
evident, genuine, and necessary? This paradoxical period
and its essential processes deserve to be examined, not
sidestepped.

Before the fighting even ended, it was in demining
groups that the French and the Germans worked together side by side for the first time. The idea was far from
straightforward: How to reunite men who despised one
another? Against all expectations, the miracle happened:
The historian Danièle Voldman, to whom we owe a debt of
gratitude for her remarkable work on deminers, deduced
that it was in these groups that French and Germans first
got to know and learned to appreciate one another as

they strove to rebuild France. When the demining was finished, they wrote each other, and this correspondence often continued until they died.

There were German prisoners in France and, before that, French prisoners in Germany. My grandfather, an army doctor, was among them, in an oflag in Cassel.

Internment changed him, as it did my great-uncle by marriage who escaped five times and was recaptured five times. These outstanding, generous men harbored a profound melancholy their whole lives and, at family gatherings, I noticed them take themselves off to smoke cigarettes, lost in their thoughts, unable to be wholly present.

When I read the letters my grandfather wrote while he was imprisoned, I was profoundly moved. But it was only by writing myself that I came to understand something I'd never grasped before and that now seems so obvious to me.

As a doctor back in civilian life, he had offered—as well as running his own office—to treat the inmates at his local prison. He would go there at all hours. On top of this, he had made a pledge: As soon as a prisoner was released, he could come and knock at his door, where he would be given a voucher for his first meal in a restaurant, with wine, and a packet of cigarettes (my grandfather had also been a smoker at one time). A first meal as a free man. A wonderful idea that, at the time, I longed for him to abandon. As a child of only modest courage, the thought of coming face-to-face with a prisoner terrified me...

Being deprived of freedom, suffering hunger, humiliation, and separation from loved ones can radically change a personality. But, occasionally, the noblest element persists. His overriding principle was the notion of preserving life at all costs, and I witnessed this many times. He was the sort of man to head out and treat someone in the middle of the night, even if they couldn't pay. Even if his own life might be in danger: The Russian treated by Vincent is the Russian whom my grandfather saved in his camp, despite the Nazis forbidding it. After the Liberation, the Russian sent him proof of his gratitude every year at Christmas.

This story is one among the many lived by my grandfather or other members of my family, stories that I have woven together in homage. I think it shines a light on what personal courage can be and on a doctor's vocation.

As for Saskia, she stepped onto the same bus as Vincent and I knew it was my turn to pass on what she had transmitted to me one evening, looking me calmly in the eye.

I didn't know her very well when she decided to open up to me one winter evening in a kitchen with some of her family members present. By chance, I ended up chatting with her alone for a while. I don't know what we talked about; in any event, nothing that prepared me for the description she suddenly gave me of her arrest and her time in a camp. I will never forget the intensity in her eyes, which she kept pinned on me, or the fury that built in her as she chronicled her past. Gradually, everyone gravitated toward us: She'd never spoken about this before. She was such a discreet woman, always kind and smiling, a tremendous lover of life, but there was also an air of amused detachment when she heard people complain about some trifle. She was sixteen when the militia came to her house to arrest her family. I don't know why but she was the only one to have a fake ID in the name Jacqueline Dulac, as far as I can remember. Her mother tried to save her by saying she wasn't her daughter, but she herself knew intuitively that, in order to save her mother, she must stay with her, so she flung her false ID to the ground. She'd been born in France, was now sixteen and not very tall—she never would be—but she displayed extraordinary courage. Unlike my heroine, she succeeded in protecting her mother for three years, hiding her during some of their chores and finding a coat for her for the winter. She carried her with her own frail frame and saved her life. Her father and three brothers were killed in another camp.

When they returned home, their apartment had been looted. And the local authorities in Paris asked them to pay their rent arrears.

While she told this story—why she decided to speak on that particular evening, I will never know—everyone fell silent in the fading light. Her account didn't end until we were in darkness, and no one had thought to get up to switch on a light. It would have been impossible, the mood was timeless, immutable. She was relieving herself of a weight, a rage, an indignation that had been held in check for so many years. At times she was weary too, tired, even though the words came easily, but she didn't describe all her experiences in the camp and this, we could tell, was out of a sense of propriety. And yet she'd forgotten nothing. Every part of it was vivid in her memory. And it has remained so in mine. When she told me that, at the Hôtel Lutetia, she'd been handed five francs and told, "Here. And don't make a fuss," time stood still. She wouldn't take her eyes off me, needing to share the outrage. She repeated those words several times. Like her prisoner number, which she never made any attempt to erase, those words were burned into her with a red-hot iron.

I've never forgotten her. I think about her often. And, although I hadn't predicted it, she came and found a place for herself in this story. It was my turn to pass it on.

ACKNOWLEDGMENTS

MY THANKS TO...

Patrice Hoffmann, the magician who allowed this book to travel abroad, first to the United States, almost before it was finished, and who allowed me to complete it despite my misgivings. I'm aware of how lucky and privileged I am to have worked with you.

Sylvie Banoun, a patient and demanding reader with boundless affection.

Isabelle Carrière for your unfailing support.

Céline Leray-Fribault for your energy and innate qualities, I know what I owe you...

Fanny Gilles for everything and more besides.

To Stéphane Jardin for believing in it.

To Cristina de Stefano whose comments were vital, meeting her was one of those magical things that give life its spice.

Muriel Beyer for welcoming me into her home.

Dana Burlac for being who she is, a passionate person with such pure emotions and enough energy to defy mountains; and Flandrine Raab who is so sensitive and necessary.

Manon Aubier at the Communications Department in Ramatuelle, and two impassioned archivists, Caroline

Martin in Ramatuelle and Hélène Riboty in Saint-Tropez, who were so kind in opening up their files for me, found a way to reconstitute a mood and a state of mind for me while also directing me toward the most useful documents. Archives were the most sensitive—and the most unexpected—part of my research. I'm indebted to them for the hand-grenade fishing trip enjoyed by the deminers and prisoners of war, and reported by a zealous informer...

Guillaume Müller-Labé. And Sophie Loria, who tenderly read through this text by the ocean and is always ready to debate about even the aptness of a comma—invaluable attention to detail.

SOURCES

THE MOST IMPORTANT BEING:

Où la mémoire s'attarde, Raymond Aubrac, Éditions Odile Jacob.

Le déminage de la France après 1945, Danièle Voldman, Éditions Odile Jacob. A key book about the deminers.

Les prisonniers de guerre allemands: France, 1944–1949, a thesis by Fabien Théofilakis, published by Fayard.

Mein Kampf, histoire d'un livre, an excellent investigation by Antoine Vitkine, Flammarion. I could also cite his documentaries, which are available online, including *Magda*, about Magda Goebbels.

La France libérée (1944–1947), Michel Winock, Éditions Perrin.

Important firsthand accounts by Charlotte Delbo, Primo Levi, Robert Antelme, Simone Veil, Marceline Loridan-Ivens, and Ginette Kolinka.

All of Pierre Assouline's books, for obvious reasons, because he makes no compromises and wants everything: historical precision and novelistic inspiration.

The war journals of Ernst Jünger, published by La Pléiade.

The World of Yesterday, Stefan Zweig, a visionary's firsthand account, read again and again.

Lettres à un ami allemand, Albert Camus (selected essays from the French version published in English in *Resistance, Rebellion, and Death: Essays*). They were with me all through the writing process.

ABOUT THE AUTHOR

CLAIRE DEYA is a French screenwriter and author. *Blast* is her first novel.

ABOUT THE TRANSLATOR

ADRIANA HUNTER studied French and Drama at the University of London. She has translated more than ninety books, including Marc Petitjean's *The Heart: Frida Kahlo in Paris* and Hervé Le Tellier's *The Anomaly* and *Eléctrico W*, winner of the French-American Foundation's 2013 Translation Prize in Fiction. She lives in Kent, England.